CLASH OF WILLS

"The shaft?" His fingers were rolling the blade over his thumb, keeping it flat to avoid slicing, and his voice had lowered.

Morgan felt herself blush but kept her gaze steady. "Are you finished playing with me?" she asked.

"Playing?"

"You turn everything into a discussion of lust, and it's nothing but play. You need to be serious if you wish to learn this."

"Not lust," he answered, and his voice got so soft, she could barely hear it, ". . . but love."

Morgan picked up the blade before he could gain another breath, spun around and threw both knives into the dead center of his target, where they quivered, making a clicking sound of blade against blade. She turned back to him. "I can put all twelve of my dirks any place I want them. I didn't learn that by playing at lust . . . or at love."

"You make it sound a filthy word."

"It is," she retorted.

His talk of love brought tears so close to the surface, she was caught up in the agony of stifling them. Tears were for women to cry; they certainly weren't for Morganna KilCreggar. They never had been. She'd lived her entire life, it seemed, just to kill the FitzHugh laird, and then she was ready to die. There wasn't a speck of room in that plan for anything feminine.

She walked stiffly over to pull the knives from the tree. "When you are ready to learn, I will teach you," she said.

BOOK YOUR PLACE ON OUR WEBSITE AND MAKE THE READING CONNECTION!

We've created a customized website just for our very special readers, where you can get the inside scoop on everything that's going on with Zebra, Pinnacle and Kensington books.

When you come online, you'll have the exciting opportunity to:

- View covers of upcoming books
- Read sample chapters
- Learn about our future publishing schedule (listed by publication month *and author*)
- Find out when your favorite authors will be visiting a city near you
- Search for and order backlist books from our online catalog
- Check out author bios and background information
- Send e-mail to your favorite authors
- Meet the Kensington staff online
- Join us in weekly chats with authors, readers and other guests
- Get writing guidelines
- AND MUCH MORE!

**Visit our website at
http://www.kensingtonbooks.com**

Lady of the Knight

Jackie Ivie

ZEBRA BOOKS
Kensington Publishing Corp.
http://www.kensingtonbooks.com

To Barbara,
who was with me for every chapter.

Chapter 1

The screams faded by midday, leaving the groans of the dying. Morgan waited, even then.

She knew the ragtag group of young men that followed her were impatient, and she knew why. That didn't make her give the signal. Not even when she watched other groups descend did she let her own lads go. There was no honor in stripping a dying man of his belongings. The vultures from other crofts could do so. Morgan wouldn't go until death took over.

She tossed her black braid over her shoulder, hunched down farther behind the rocks and waited for the *skelpies* and *poucahs* of legend to take the souls and leave nothing she'd worry over. The banshees she could deal with later, after the fog covered everyone's progress. Morgan swallowed her fear, looked at the others and gave the whistle.

Scots had no legal right to swords, belts, dirks, daggers known as skeans, or other embellishment, and a dead Scotsman had no need for either, although she drew the line at pulling the plaids from the bodies. She had to look away, as her lads had no such qualms. The bounty on the field in front of them would keep crofter homes warm and supplied with game, since few, if any, had done anything with a sword except sharpen it for its English owner.

The work was onerous, and several times her belly gave

every signal of emptying itself of its contents, but Morgan plugged on, lifting a hand here, a waistband there, checking for rings, bracelets, amulets, knives—anything of value—before moving on.

The moon came out, shedding light through the wispy fingers of mist, and Morgan shivered in her kilt and tartan. She lifted the *feile-breacan's* drape from where it slapped against the back of her ankles, to cover her head. That was dangerous and she knew it, for legs as hairless and shapely as hers couldn't belong to a boy, no matter how much she worked them. It couldn't be helped, though. Her ears were cold, and she didn't want anyone to see what the last remnant of the clan of KilCreggar had been reduced to.

There was an immense body lying facedown on what was once a clump of thistle weed. The warrior's body had flattened the bush, and it was easy to see why. Morgan narrowed her eyes on legs close to tree trunks in size, narrow buttocks, and such wide shoulders, she forgot all about anything except benign feminine appreciation.

He had a wealth of light brown hair, messily strewn about his head. She couldn't tell the length. She could barely tell the color of his sett. Her eyes sharpened in consideration. This had been a skirmish of battling clans, nothing more, nothing less. There weren't but fifty-odd men dead on the field, and none was wearing as finely worked a shirt, nor a kilt as richly made, as was the man in front of her.

Morgan pushed at him with her boot, and getting no response, knelt to shove him over.

She didn't have time to cry out as hands resembling iron bars seized her ankles and pulled, sending Morgan onto her rear in shock. Then the man was on all fours, straddling her and breathing as nothing dead could. Morgan hadn't caught her breath yet, and knew her eyes were wide and frightened. She only hoped the tartan covered her expression.

"You robbing the dead, lad? You dinna' know the penalty?"

What moonlight there was highlighted a fine-shaped nose

on a face handsome enough to make many a maiden swoon, and Morgan was no exception, for exactly four heartbeats. Then, she was kicking and shoving herself from him, in a lumbering backward crawl, to put as much field under her as she could before she dared swivel to her feet and run.

He was after her, of course, and there wasn't any part of his body that looked wounded to her as he easily kept pace on hands and feet. Clods of sod and pebbles marked their progress away from the battlefield and closer to the rocks she'd hidden behind. Morgan was moving like one possessed to reach them, and he was right with her the entire way.

The tartan was what tripped her up. Morgan's foot stepped onto the frayed end, stopping her with a jolt of her neck. She went down again, bruising what parts of her that hadn't been bruised the first time. He was atop her instantly, his weapon-hung belt digging into her belly, and thighs she'd known would be strong straddling her legs, immobilizing her. Morgan held him from her with arms that were hardened by work, but she knew she couldn't keep his weight that way forever. He was too solid.

Her arms started trembling with the weight. Then, they began shaking. Finally the support collapsed, dropping him onto her folded arms without his expending a hint of effort.

"You know the penalty, and this is the best you can do?"

Now she was going to die, and it wasn't even a warrior's death. Morgan closed her eyes and made herself ready to welcome it, since he was too heavy to allow her to breathe, anyway. Something about him changed, as his chuckling stopped. Morgan opened her eyes and met his, and the strangest thing happened. Almost as though she'd taken a swig of Mactarvat's finest whiskey on the coldest of mornings. She was never certain, even afterward, what it was.

"This is a woman's bane," he said finally. " 'Tis not fit for a youth such as yourself. Is this what we've been reduced to?"

Morgan thinned her lips. Her own father and four brothers had met their end on a battlefield just like this one. They

hadn't left one bit of security for Morgan, or her older sister
by twenty-one years, Elspeth, the village hag. Robbing the
dead wasn't what she wanted to do, but it brought in needed
funds for the crofters, and the lads needed someone to lead
them. The village elders needed someone they trusted, someone the lads would follow, someone who wasn't afraid of
poucahs, skelpies or banshees. They needed to have someone they could make do it, someone without anyone to take
care of, or to take care of her. The village elders needed
someone like her to do the deed. They needed someone they
could force. She hadn't been given the choice. She glared
at the man atop her.

"You're straw-thin, too. Food scarce? Game? Is that why
you rob the dead?"

"They've little use . . . for their riches," she panted in
what space he left her for breathing.

He laughed at that, a great barrel kind of laugh, and
even with her breasts bound, Morgan felt the reaction, like
lightning spears to the crests of her breasts. Her binding
wouldn't keep that hidden, and she was grateful her own
hands were smashed onto the offending parts. She spent
every bit of energy stopping the reaction, and missed the
beginning of his next words.

". . . take a squire where I can find one. You know anything about horses?"

She shook her head, more due to incomprehension than
an answer to his question, although it was the same one.
She knew next to nothing of any animal like a horse. Poor
crofters used their own legs.

"Well, you're about to learn. Get up. If I straddle a body,
I want to make certain it's a bonny lass with lush curves,
not a lad made of bones." He didn't wait for an assent, he
simply lifted from her, and before she could gulp in one
lung-expanding breath, he had a hand looped through her
belt and had her hauled to her feet.

The missing air was responsible for the way she weaved

right next to him, and Morgan sucked in great gulps as he appraised her. She was more than a little pleased that she reached his cheekbone, and he wasn't a short man. He stood over six feet, easily. She was just extremely tall for a lass. In fact, she was so tall, no one mistook her for a girl, ever. At least, they hadn't since she turned ten, lost everyone in a gore-filled skirmish with the most hated clan on the earth, and consequently changed her gender.

Not even the waist-length black hair, worn in a single braid, branded her the correct sex, especially to short men. Morgan caught the giggle before it sounded. This man was making her his squire? It was unheard of, and completely amazing. Surely there were youths available to him from his own clan?

"That's KilCreggar sett," he said, and there was a snide tone in his voice. "I'd recognize it anywhere, even if it's worn wrong, and in tatters. You aren't allowed to wear it. There isna' a KilCreggar walking the earth. My clan saw to it."

Morgan flushed, and her thoughts stopped. Her knees sagged, because she knew exactly who he was, and why she should have fought like demons from Hell were on her heels. He was from the most hated clan on earth: the Sassenach-lovers, the betrayers, the rapists, the Highland clan named FitzHugh. He was a FitzHugh. The realization had the strangest effect on her as her insides swam with a jelly-like sensation she recognized as fear.

Then her back stiffened, and her legs resumed holding her upright. She knew that every prayer she'd uttered from the age of ten was being answered. She, who'd had as much chance of avenging her family's demise as she had of flying, was being gifted with it. Nay, she was being forced to it. She was being drafted into service to a FitzHugh, and there was no one more despised.

Slivers of mist wrapped about their legs, making it look as though they rose legless from the fog. Morgan considered him, and told her blood to hush. She was no more female than the lads she led were. She'd killed off every bit of her that was womanly so many years ago, she rarely was even bothered by that most stupid of female ills, a monthly flux. Everything she'd killed off years ago was rising through her blood as she considered him, though. She had no doubt about what it was, either.

He was too handsome by far, with his sharp cheekbones, large lips, deep-cleft chin, shoulder-length hair, and lushly lashed, dark eyes of an indeterminate color. He was a healthy size, too . . . brawny and well-muscled.

He was also a FitzHugh. He might not look it, but he was bound to have weaknesses, and soft areas where a dirk could slip when he wasn't watching. He was showing the famous FitzHugh stupidity, too. He was asking his enemy . . . nay, he was forcing the one person who had vowed to harm him, into the closest echelon of his life. It was too heady for her mind to absorb, and Morgan watched him fold his arms while he waited.

She swallowed, then she shrugged. "It was warm and serviceable," she finally answered, lifting her chin to look him squarely in the eye.

"You probably took that from a body more than five, no, six years ago. You should have replaced it since. There's better on yonder field."

It was eight years, and I'll never replace it, you dolt, she thought. Her eyes narrowed. "I like the color," she answered with absolutely no inflection to her voice. She was very proud of it.

"Gray and dingy black? There's more color to the night sky. Come. I've FitzHugh sett in my tent."

He didn't see her reaction, and that was probably a good thing. He simply put an arm out and pushed her ahead of him back down the slope. He wasn't giving her any chance to say yea or nay, and the two times she stumbled, he shoved her harder. Morgan caught herself clumsily, bit any response and kept pace.

The battlefield was covered with mist, blanketing everything with a ghostly whiteness that was unnerving. Morgan crossed herself hurriedly, and saw that he'd seen, although he didn't say anything. She dipped her head and continued at his pace, jogging at his side.

If he recognized her stamina when they reached his horse, it didn't show. Morgan looked over the animal, saw that it was taller at the neck and shoulders than she was, and regarded it with what she recognized as the beginnings of awe.

She hung back when the man clicked his tongue, spoke softly and the horse whinnied in response. "You were na' here to fight," she remarked.

He looked up at her as he tossed a saddle over the animal. "Nay," was all he said.

"Then why did you?"

He ignored her, and lifted himself by the arms, above the horse, before swinging a leg over. Morgan watched him do it, watched the muscles in the backs of his arms, and then those in his legs, and swallowed the excess moisture in her mouth. She realized she hadn't seen a man so fine in her life.

She was as annoyed with her body's reaction as she was embarrassed by it. She wasn't interested in female things. She hadn't been in almost a decade. She was interested in besting everyone at sling-shot, archery and knife throwing. She was especially competent at hunting, and usually had an offering for the hag's pot. That was the only reason Elspeth tolerated her. Morgan hadn't said but fifty words to her sister since the family's demise. As far as she was concerned, Elspeth wasn't a KilCreggar. She was a slut, welcoming any man between her thighs, before stealing whatever she could from him.

Elspeth wasn't a very likable sort, but she was definitely feminine. Morgan was the opposite: proud, terse and hardened. Even Elspeth called her a lad, although of all the villagers, she knew the truth. She'd ceased teasing Morgan over it, years earlier. It didn't make them any closer, because there wasn't any part of Morgan that she claimed as female. She wasn't interested in a man.

She certainly wasn't interested in this man because he was a handsome man, and a sturdy, brawny one. She was interested in him because he was the man who was her sworn enemy.

"Give me your hand." He brought the horse over to her, and reached down.

"Why?"

"A good squire never questions his master."

"I've not said I'd be your squire," Morgan answered.

"I've not asked, either. Your hand? Or would you prefer it hacked off as a penalty for robbing the dead?"

She gave him her hand. She had to use her own muscles to straddle his horse's flank, since all the FitzHugh man did was lift her and fling her over his shoulder, and then command the animal to be on its way. Morgan didn't know how he did it, either. She was keeping her attention on finding a hold to prevent herself from slipping off.

She had to settle with latching onto the saddle at the sides of his hips. Morgan had never been this close to a man in her life, and never with a live animal between her legs. She concentrated on keeping the material at her loins from rubbing her in any fashion. She did it by tensing her thigh muscles and raising herself above the animal's flank. It wasn't as easy as it sounds. She realized it as the night darkened further, stars came out to litter the sky, and her leg muscles started complaining.

She was grateful for her size, as her legs were almost the length of his, and it wasn't as uncomfortable as it could have been to be splayed wide over a horse's backside.

"You might want to seek sleep while you can," the man said.

"Sleep? Where?"

"Lean against my back. It works."

"You'll not stop?"

"I've enemies. Why would I want to give them another chance at me?"

"Another one?"

"Yonder battle ground was na' a social call, and I did na' leave it unscathed."

"You've not a mark on you," Morgan replied.

He chuckled. "So . . . you've been looking, have you?"

"Nay, only remarking that you move too fast for an injured man," she replied.

"I took a bash to the noggin'. I've yet to clear my head. Traveling through the night is na' it, though. Take my word."

"Then, why are we?"

"Enemies abroad, lad. Everywhere."

Morgan raised her brows at that, and eased herself down to the horse's flank with as little ceremony as possible. Her thigh muscles were aching with what felt like warm coals inside them, and she realized the futility of it. The roll of the horse would just have to be tolerated.

She stiffened, told herself to ignore the movement, and then she yawned. It wasn't as difficult as she'd been thinking it would be. It was sort of nice actually, if one wasn't bothered by the masculinity of the man in front of her.

She yawned again.

"Name's Zander. Zander FitzHugh."

"Zander?" she asked.

"As in Alexander. Alexander the Great. Short version. My mother loves her history. She just has a problem spelling."

"Zander," Morgan repeated. *His name is Zander*. She nearly giggled before she could prevent it.

"You got a name?"

"Aye," she answered.

"What is it?"

"It is na' Zander," she replied with a hoot.

"You want me to make one up for you?"

"Go ahead," she replied.

"Morgan."

She started up in shock. "How did you—"

"Your name truly is Morgan?" he asked. "Fancy that. I've a vassal named the same as my horse. Morgan."

"I've na' said I'll be your squire."

"You will. You've na' got a choice. I've got many servants of my own. I have so many it's becoming something of a problem. There's few who obey, few who pay attention. I've been told I need structure. I don't know structure. My mum always tells me I need structure, though."

"Structure?" She was more than a little mystified.

"I've a house to myself, more of an old building no one else wanted. I've household serfs to clean, spread rushes and light fires. I've bonny serfs to take to my bed. I've serfs to fetch and carry, serfs to make my food, and serfs to play me music. I've no serf to see to my horse and my person. Well, I had one. Yonder battlefield took him. You robbed from the dead, you take his place."

"This is structure?"

"I probably need a wife. I dinna' want to be shackled to a wife. You know what that would do?"

"Nay," Morgan replied.

"End my play. Wives are na' tolerant of such."

"Things like bonny serfs to warm your bed, you mean?"

"You've a bonny face, for a lad. They'll take to yours, too. At least, I think they will. You ever have a woman?"

"Nay." Morgan didn't giggle, and she was absolutely amazed that she didn't. "But, my name is na' Zander, either."

"Structure is the death to play. I don't need structure." He was starting to slur his words a bit. Morgan lifted an eyebrow. It wasn't hard to find his weakness. He sounded like he had a household full of them. "Do you need structure, Morgan?"

"I don't need anything or anyone," Morgan replied.

He swiveled his head to look at her. "It's late, I've a lump on my head, and we're talking structure. You're a strange squire, Morgan. You got a last name?"

"Nay," she replied.

"Why not?"

"My parents lost interest," she replied.

He chuckled. "Lean on me, lad."

"I'll not need it," she replied, trying to find a comfortable spot for her chin against her collar.

"I'm not asking for your comfort."

"What?" Her mind must be as fogged as the landscape, because that made no sense. Morgan scrunched her face.

"It'll create a backrest for me, too. Try it, lad."

She leaned forward and touched her forehead into the space right below his shoulder blade. He immediately put so much pressure on her, she rocked backward with it. He snapped back forward.

"Try again. This time, put some strength into it. I know you've got your share, albeit your bony appearance. Lean into me."

This time Morgan hunched forward against his back, and made a brace for both of them. She didn't find his weight an issue this time as he leaned back. She simply closed her eyes and slept.

Chapter 2

Dawn cold evidenced itself as dew on every hair she had on her legs. Morgan shivered for a moment, and then opened her eyes. She was stiff from the top of her neck to the bottom of her spine, aching along both thighs clear to her knees, and she was staring at where her kilt had slid up, showing all and sundry that if she was a male, she wasn't a very well-endowed one. She blinked at the sight. Blinked again. Closed her eyes and rubbed them.

The view didn't change.

She pushed with her forehead at the same time she pulled the tartan into her lap, piling it between herself and the saddle. The large male body that had been blocking the dawn simply stirred forward, then rocked back, right into her abdomen.

His eyes are blue.

The thought took over as he focused on her with a frown. His eyes weren't just blue, they were a deep, dark blue, as deep as midnight, and as vast as Creggar's Loch.

"You a *skelpie*?" he asked, in a soft tone.

"Afraid not. I'm your new squire, my lord," she answered with a haughty tone.

His frown deepened. "Wha' happened to the old one?"

"Battle took him. He fought well," she answered.

She watched him scrunch his face further. "What battle?"

It would be easier to answer, if he wasn't leaning on her and pushing her closer to the horse's tail at the same time.

"As near as I could tell, it was reavers being punished."

"Reavers?"

"Thieves. Highlanders. Name of Killoren. They any relation?"

"Reavers?" he repeated again.

"I guess they was na' satisfied with stealing cattle. They had to avenge a taking."

"Taking?"

"Killoren had a lovely daughter. She is na' more."

His frown deepened. "They took her?"

"Took her and took her, if you ken my words."

"Who?"

"Mactarvat. Lowlanders. Large clan. Not much on riches and land, but clan a-plenty they do have."

"Why?"

"The Mactarvats brew whiskey. Best in the land. They don't take well to having their whiskey stolen. They did na' know it was the Killoren lass they took."

"That's the problem with this country. Too many clans fighting amongst themselves. What we really need is to—" He stopped his words and glared at her. "You a loyalist?"

Morgan blew the disgust through her upper lip. The horse replied with his own snort. "I look like a loyalist?"

"Yours is the boniest frame I've ever set myself against, and with not an ounce of spare, either."

"When you finish with your compliments, you mind setting away from me for a spell? You're numbing my legs."

His gaze sharpened on her. "Where are we?"

"Atop your horse," she answered.

"My horse," he repeated, stating it without question. "We near a tent?"

Morgan looked around. They were not only near a tent, they were stomping it into the ground. She looked down at the wreckage of poles, cloth, cooking utensils and smiled wryly. "Aye," she answered.

"Good. He's well trained." She watched as he pulled himself

up with the saddlehorn. "You lie, lad. We're ... not near ...."
His voice faded as he seemed to poise for a dive, before top-
pling full-out into the remnants of his own cook-fire.

Morgan nearly gave vent to the first dose of amusement
she'd felt in years, then stilled it. They were too close to
English soil at present, and she had a FitzHugh to torment.
It was enough for the moment that he was covering himself with soot at her feet.

Morgan slid clumsily off the back end of horse, told it not
to move, and slid into the trees to take care of her business.
When she returned, not only had the horse stayed, but Zander
FitzHugh was still lying atop the pile of ashes, a smile on his
handsome face, and a litany of snores coming from his
mouth. Morgan rolled her eyes, thought for half a moment of
leaving him, and then sighed. She wasn't going to toss this
gift aside. She'd lost count of how many times she'd prayed
to have the mighty FitzHugh in her power. She wasn't going
to waste any of it running from him.

She was going to enjoy making his life as short and
miserable as he'd made the KilCreggars'. She searched
for his bow, took one arrow, and left. Someone was going
to have to see them fed, and it wasn't going to be him.

She had another cook-fire going, a hare roasting and a
good dram of whiskey beneath her belt when Zander
FitzHugh next favored her with his midnight-blue gaze.
She didn't see it; she felt his attention on her by a shift of
the elements, a flare from the fire, or perhaps it was a
shake of the leaves above them. She looked across at him
from her perch on a log, where a small pile of shavings
showed what she'd been doing, and met his stare. She
didn't know it would feel as warming as the whiskey.

Morgan didn't say a word as he blinked, widened his eyes,
and then lifted his head from the ash-pile, snorting a nose
full of the stuff, before coughing like he had the ague. He
had to arch his back in order to wheeze it out. Morgan

watched him for a bit, before resuming the carving. She had to suck in on her cheeks to keep quiet, though.

"By all that's holy! What the hell happened to me?"

"You've been eating ash," she replied.

"Ash?"

"Ash," she replied, looking up. The amusement in her voice must have been what made his gaze sharpen on her. Morgan swallowed on the bubble of mirth in her throat. It took every bit of her composure not to react to the dark streaks of tears down his cheeks, though.

"How did I get here?"

"You fell."

"Fell?"

"From yonder great beast," she gestured with her carved icicle. "He's well-trained, you said. I don't know for what."

He swore, raised himself to his hands and knees, and then stumbled to his feet, wiping uselessly at the gray dust all over him.

"I fell into a fire-pit, and you left me lay there?"

"I could na' move you. You should've found yourself a stouter squire. Either that, or eat less."

He glared at her, his eyes blazing from that ash-white face, and Morgan controlled the shiver. She wasn't about to be frightened of him.

"Make yourself useful, and find me another tartan."

"I already made myself useful. I hunted a hare for your sup, started a completely new firepit to roast it in, and carved you a toy to bribe the next bonny lass into your bed."

He had his hands on his hips now. He didn't look amused. Morgan felt the rush of hair at her neckline warning her of it. She didn't care. She looked at him with complete indifference.

"I've a tartan for you, too."

"I like my own fine," she replied, "and I've not said I'll change just to please you."

"You'll change, and you'll assist me to do the same, and you're going to do it a sight faster than you are right now."

"You don't say," she answered, and had to ignore where he'd moved and the way he did. For a large man, he wasn't easy to spot when he shifted to another spot. Morgan narrowed her eyes and considered him. He was trained to move quickly and without attracting notice, like she had been. She hadn't seen him do it.

"Get fresh kilts. I'll not have KilCreggar plaid in my camp. My own clan will string me up by my thumbs."

"Why?"

"Are you going to get the kilts, or am I going to have to make you do it?"

"Now, how do you plan on doing that?" She lifted her icicle for inspection, spinning it this way and that before moving her gaze back to him. It wasn't pleasant when she couldn't find him.

"Brute force," he replied from behind her left ear, before gripping her about the belt and hurling her to the ground. She skidded along dirt and through the ash he'd been in, her knees taking the brunt of it, then she was rolling to her feet, pulling the nine hidden dirks from her socks. She had them by the blades when she faced him again, crouching slightly as she faced him.

"That's your response? Toothpicks?" He motioned to the knife blades protruding from between her fingers.

She sang one right to the center of his FitzHugh brooch, and he pulled back a fraction as it trembled on the dragon's eye it had speared.

"Lucky shot," he taunted, taking a step toward her.

She sent two more to the exact same spot, where he now had three, like a pin cushion sprouting from his chest. He had a bit more respect showing in him now as he lowered to a semi-crouch, although it was far shy of the one she was in.

"You have to have a bigger blade to stop a FitzHugh, boy. Your prior master should have learned you that much."

Her answer was three quick tosses, leaving all three knives embedded into the hilts of those at his belt. The next one went into his sporran, where a dark trickle started up.

"That's good whiskey you've hit, now," he replied. "The punishment is na' going to be as lenient as a bath and a change of clothing. I may have to take a strap to that scrawny body of yours."

"Back away, FitzHugh," she said, rotating the final two through her fingers, one in each hand.

"Why? You've not shown me one reason. A fool can toss a knife and miss even scratching their opponent. You've got but two left. You planning on barbering me next?"

"If I wanted to draw your blood, you'd be bleedin'," she answered.

"And sows will be flying," he answered.

The knife he got for that one sliced the inside tassel off his sock. Her next one took off the other one.

Zander looked down at himself, and when he looked up, she watched his eyes widen at the three dirks she'd pulled from the back of her belt. She twirled them, one in her right hand, two in her left. She watched him watch her hands.

She didn't want to hurt him. She didn't want to draw blood. Not yet. She knew as well as any that the dirks wouldn't stop a man his size, unless she hit something vital, or had some time for him to bleed to death. He'd strangle her before that happened.

She'd always received plenty of respect for her throwing aim before. It had never taken all nine of the dirks she kept in her socks. She'd never had to resort to using the last three from her belt. She and the FitzHugh started circling, the roasting hare between them. He wasn't as nonchalant as he was feigning, either, for a fine sheen of sweat was starting to make the ash coarse down his face.

"You ready to cease this, and get my kilt?" he asked.

The knife sliced through the hair beside his ear, taking off a lock. He didn't even flinch. Morgan was the one with sweaty palms.

"And yours?" he continued. "I've a hankerin' to see you clad decently, in my own green and blue. 'Tis a bold combination, not one you need hide yourself from. The lasses like it, too."

The hair beside his other ear received the same shaving. Morgan began sweating, herself. She knew she was down to the last one. She'd never been tested this far. The blade was slick with moisture from her palm and hard to hold. None of that showed, however.

He smiled, and amid the streaked ash, his face was horrible-looking. Morgan swallowed.

"I've been looking for a good barber, myself. If you'd told me your leanings, I'd have had a nice trim afore this."

"You have that much a-tween your legs, FitzHugh, that ye laugh at me?"

"Laugh at you? You're not worth the time it would take. You've one chance left, lad. I would na' miss again if I were you. I've a slew of ash to wash off, a fresh kilt to don, a nicely roasted rabbit to eat, and half, nay . . . ." He looked down at the sporran that was still leaking down his ash-covered clothing, leaving a dark trail. Then he looked back up at her. His eyes might as well have been black holes, for all the emotion they showed in that ash-white face. ". . . I'd better make that a third of a sporran left of me whiskey. Lay aside your blade and assist me. I'll give you that one bit of mercy. You won't like the alternative. Put down your toothpick."

Morgan held the blade. She wasn't going to let it go that easily. She had to pick her target. There was only one that would take him down without killing him. She was afraid to consider it. If he was smallish, or it didn't hit vitally, she was as good as dead. And, if it did hit vitally, she was as good as dead.

Zander lifted his eyebrows. "You having a little trouble

deciding? A sharp-eyed snipe like you? Come along, lad, put the blade down. We'll both shed our filthy garments and don fresh. 'Course I'll see that KilCreggar plaid shredded before I'd keep it, and—"

The final blade went slicing through the kilt between his thighs, ripping material and thudding as it hit the log behind him. She heard his roar, and it wasn't one of pain. She was already leaping obstacles and dancing around trees to escape him.

Damn him for being small, she thought.

Morgan was fast. She was light. She was able to move quickly and expertly, even though the sun was fast sinking, and he'd pitched his ruined tent near a lot of dead-fall from the trees. He'd also camped close enough to some source of water that the mist it would bring wasn't far off. If she could keep him at bay until then, she could hide easily.

She stopped, instantly attuned to the woods around her, and didn't hear a sound. She didn't feel the shove, either. All she knew was the tree he slammed her into front-first, before he had her shirt collar in one hand and actually had her dangling off the ground while he shook her. Morgan watched him with a stunned expression, not because he could heft her above him with one arm, but because her ears were still ringing from the blow she'd received.

Then, she was drowning as he shoved her under the water and held her against the creek bottom. Just before she lost consciousness and sucked in water, he lifted her, holding her up long enough to shake her until her head rattled, and then he shoved her back again. Morgan's belly was full of water, and she was coughing it up on the third dunking, and that wasn't enough for him.

The fifth time, Morgan forgot to suck in air, and just lay on the bottom of the creek, her face scraping pebbles, and being washed by moss. She was going to die, and all because she was too stupid to put a death-blow into her enemy when she had the chance.

She could actually see bright light behind her lids when he finally pulled her up and held her at arm's length in order to scowl at her. She wondered when it had gotten so bright, and had a chance to watch black dots swim through her vision before it settled back to semi-normal. There was nothing normal about the black hatred coming from his eyes and seeing into every secret crevice she'd ever hidden in, though.

He swore again, and heaved himself backward onto the bank, hauling her with him. He had her torso locked between his thighs, and that was stupid of him. She hadn't any fight left in her. None. She saw the glint of a knife and closed her eyes.

"Open your eyes and face your punishment, Morgan!"

He had one hand locked about her neck, lifting it from his chest, and the other holding a skean that made her blades look like the toothpicks he'd called them. Morgan felt the sting of tears, and hated every bit of herself for such a weakness, as they dripped out of eyes she didn't even dare blink with.

"Tears? You cry woman-tears, now?"

"Just kill me and get it over with," she snarled.

"As much as I'd like to, I'll not kill you. A good Scots squire is hard to come by. A fighting Scotsman even harder, especially one as talented with a dirk as you are. I'm just giving you a taste of your own barbering."

"Nay!" She screamed as his hand moved underneath her braid to raise it. She felt the cold of his steel against her skin.

"This hank of hair?"

He was slicing his blade through it, and Morgan started shuddering with the sobs. It was the only thing she had left of her childhood, and the only thing she had that marked her for what she was, a woman. Morgan hated herself anew for the realization. "Please?" she whispered.

He stopped sawing. Morgan held her breath.

"This means so much to you?"

She nodded.

"Why?"

"I don't know," she whispered.

"It's too long. It'll be in your way. It comes loose in a fight and you're useless."

"It does na' come loose," she answered.

"Mine does na' grow past the midst of my back."

"I'm na' you," she answered.

"I let you keep this braid, you obey me? You'll become my squire in every sense? Guard my back, and take care of my person with nary a complaint?"

Morgan swallowed with a throat that felt too sore, too tight, and too dry. "Hack it off, and have done," she answered, closing her eyes to all she'd hidden from herself and waited for him to do it. Her tears weren't subsiding, though, and the woman in her she'd tried to destroy was the one sobbing. She told herself it was only hair. It would grow back. It was stupid to keep something just because her mother, in another lifetime, had hair just like it. Nothing she tried to tell herself was working, though.

He shoved her away. "Get that KilCreggar sett off. I've a kilt for you. If you're not undressed, washed and awaiting it when I return, I'll hack more than your braid off you. You hear?"

She was already stripping the tartan off.

Chapter 3

Morgan didn't waste any time luxuriating in the water, but then again, she never did. She was quick enough to be brutal, but without her thigh-length jerkin, laced-on sleeves, or the yards of tartan folded about her body to form a kilt and cape affair called the *feile-breacan,* she looked exactly like what she was; a slender female. She raced from the water to hide behind a tree and await him.

She very nearly didn't make it, and his disgust at finding her out of the water was obvious.

"Morgan, lad! If you make me hunt you—"

His words stopped when he saw the pile of KilCreggar cloth on the bank. Morgan watched him kick it into the water with his boot, as though it was too filthy to touch. She shut her eyes on the desecration, before darting along the edge of the foliage to follow, watching the sodden black mass bob with what current there was.

"You wore it within an inch of its use, lad. You needn't mourn such a rag."

Morgan watched him call the words over his far shoulder and knew now was her moment. She was as good at shifting positions as Zander had looked to be. She was an excellent swimmer, too. Just about everything a lad could do, she could do better. She was beneath the water and sliding her body to where her KilCreggar plaid had gone under before he said another word.

". . . more use of my own colors. You've no need to shun them. You've more reason to welcome them."

Morgan heard him as she surfaced. She didn't know what else he'd said. She had a clear view of where Zander was still talking over his shoulder, as she propelled herself to a spot on the bank below him. She was going to be in plain view for a moment, but it couldn't be helped. She said a swift prayer for his continued ignorance of her position before she chanced it.

"Why, many's the lass who has fallen into a swoon at seeing FitzHugh plaid. It's a fine color, vibrant and alive. Not like that dark, ugly KilCreggar gray. Besides, the threads are softer, spun tighter, and the weave's done by skilled hands. You've not much to lose, you ken?"

Morgan slipped out of the water and back behind the curtain of bushes while he was still speaking. She knelt to wring the kilt out close to the ground, keeping the drops from making sound. She frowned as she realized the obvious. She wasn't going to be able to keep it with her. Not all of it, anyway.

For the first time in eight years, she wasn't going to be able to wear her clan colors. The certainty made her shake. She stifled it. She might be forced to wear the enemy's colors on the outside, but she'd keep a bit of KilCreggar plaid close to her heart. She would pretend to be one of them. She told herself she'd parade around in leopard skins and jewels if it got her the justice she was seeking. Then, she'd have another KilCreggar sett woven. Her ancestors would have to be content with that.

Morgan ran her fingers along an edge, searching for a particularly weak spot. She longed for one of her dirks. Water had made the fabric resilient against tearing. She found a frayed area and settled her teeth into it.

"Aside from that, such a sett labels you a KilCreggar supporter. Not a man alive wishes such a title. He'd be branded a coward."

Morgan bit hard on the cloth to prevent her cry of hatred and anger. She wished she had a dirk at her disposal now for a different reason. She'd not miss a vital spot. The tearing sound was slight, but she watched him move to cock his head in her direction. He looked to have excellent hearing. She'd have to remember that. She palmed the square she'd ripped and rose to a crouch. It wasn't much, but it would do. She used the foliage as she paralleled the bank, approaching where he stood.

"Come out of hiding, lad. This is stupid. You've a FitzHugh sett to don, and a master to serve."

Morgan stuck out her tongue at him.

"Why do you hide, anyway? I'll not punish ye further. There's no need."

"I'm na' hiding," she replied finally, from a spot directly behind him. She noted he didn't appear surprised to hear her from the new position.

"Yonder woods hold you bound, then?"

"I seek my privy, and he calls it hiding," she remarked to the air as if it were her audience. She knew it not only explained her absence, but her stealth. She watched him assimilate it.

He laughed. "You a shy type?"

"At times," she answered. "This being one of them."

"Well, if I was blessed with a thin, bony frame like the good Lord settled on you, I'd be lief to hide it away, too. The lasses must run at the sight of your white arse."

"I would na' know. I've na' tested it."

"Find yourself a lass who's heavy of foot, then. She'll be easier to catch."

He was laughing at his own joke as he sat to pull his boots off. Morgan turned away. She wasn't risking exposure again until he was in the water, and she still had a braid to undo and test for damage. She'd seen enough near-naked males anyway, that whatever he could show her wasn't going to be of any interest, other than sizing up her opponent.

She had the braid undone, had raked out a fistful of shorn hair from the back of her neck, and had it re-braided before she heard his splashing. She looked out. That quick check showed that he'd gone beneath the water. Morgan darted in, grabbed the smaller pile and retreated to the shelter of the trees to don them.

"Where did you learn to toss knives, boy?" he called over his shoulder.

"What learning?" she answered. "I missed." She was wringing out her binding cloth with the same twist her mouth made. She could hardly don it wet, so she tied it in a knot above her knee where it would dry better. She could put it back on in the morning. She secured the square of KilCreggar plaid beneath it. Then she stood, lifting the thin, linen under-tunic he'd brought. She pulled it over her head, lifted her braid out of the way, and relished the instant sensation of finely wrought, soft cloth against her bare skin for the very first time in her life. Morgan ran a finger along the hem, where it reached to mid-thigh. Even there, she could feel the perfectly wrought stitches. *He puts such clothing on a serf?* she wondered, her eyes wide.

"You've the best damn aim I've ever witnessed. Missed, he says. Missed. I've a dirk buried blade-deep in all my own hilts, and both tassels from my socks shorn off. Missed."

Morgan fought the smile before FitzHugh shoved his head beneath the water again, rinsing his hair, then she just did it. He hadn't shown the slightest inkling of respect before. She should have known it was an act. The man might be small, but he had no dearth of courage, she surmised. To stand and taunt someone to toss knives until they were depleted took more courage than she'd guessed he possessed. That was another bit of interest she committed to memory.

She tossed on the shirt he'd given her, buttoning the placket to her chin, and recognizing it was made from fine broadcloth as she did so. It fit well, too, curving down to cover her loins, while a corresponding length of material fell at the back to cloak her buttocks. Morgan ran her hands along the edges of the sleeves, creasing them.

"So, where did ye learn it?" he asked.

She glanced over at him. The water's warmth had brought an opaque mist to the air hovering directly above it, and she saw his head like a disembodied piece of him. Then she saw one arm, the other, then both as he washed himself.

"I may have taught myself, and I may not have," she answered the ghost-like figure she was watching.

"How are you with a bow?"

The kilt he'd given her was of the finest, tightest weave she'd ever felt, and Morgan ran it through her hands to feel it. It was made of such thinly spun wool strands, she could twist the width in her hands and it was thinner than her braid. "Why?" she asked.

"I like to know my own people. You've a talent. I want to know the extent of it. It may be of use to me in the future."

It was a good thing she couldn't see where he'd gone to as he said that. *Such arrogance!* she thought, then recalled. He was a FitzHugh. Their arrogance was legendary: the world existed to be trod upon and taken. She swallowed the quick retort. Until she got her dirks back, or any weapon for that matter, she was curbing her tongue. She didn't like his use of brute force.

"I've no talent with a bow," she replied.

"Pity," was his answer.

Morgan put on the belt he'd included. Although it was too dark to tell for certain, she could feel that it was worked from expensive leather from the thickness of it. She ran her fingers along the length, touching on the whipcord stitching. It had no weak spots, unlike her own worn, rawhide-braided one. She clasped it about her waist, shaking her head as it fell to her hips. That was probably a good thing. A waist like hers didn't belong to any boy.

"How about a hand-axe?" he asked.

"Rarely held one," she answered.

"That's not surprising. Weapons only recently being made legal, and that due to our new king. Where did you get your dirks?"

"I had them made, and then paid for them with barter I earned," she answered.

"Earned from stealin' from the dead?"

"I earned it with my skill. Not stealing."

You did na' take them from the dead?"

"What dead Scot would have a weapon? Dinna' you just tell me they've but recently become legal for us?"

"There's just so much of your tongue that I'll take, lad. Answer me square. That battlefield was probably littered with Scots' weapons, legal or no'. Why else would you be leading a group of lads through it like you were?"

Morgan sucked in on the surprise. He was brighter than she'd suspected, too, much brighter. She lifted the calf-high socks he was giving her and slid them on, sitting when she was done to pull on the boots he'd brought. To her surprise, they were nearly a perfect fit. She'd never had that happen before. Boots she could afford were usually full of holes from wear, and out of shape, and always too tight. His other squire must have been a large lad. She looked down at her feet, spread her toes wide, and somehow managed to keep the joy from showing. "You saw that much, did you?" she asked, finally.

"My head was hit. My eyes worked fine."

"Then you would have noted that I stole nothing. I don't steal from anyone, living or dead."

That stopped his questioning for a bit, and she listened for any response. All she heard was the liquid gurgle of the water from the burn he stood in.

"I suppose that much could be true," he said.

Morgan stiffened and had to bite her tongue. She was taking as much abuse as a KilCreggar was supposed to take without retaliation. The fact it was a FitzHugh parceling it out made it harder to swallow and set aside. "It is truth. What reason would I have to lie?"

"The same you use when lying to me about your other talents."

Morgan tried to pierce the fog he was hiding behind. Then, she shrugged. "I've not lied about them, either."

"My quiver is short an arrow, and yonder roasting hare didn't receive it. Beside which, it wouldn't settle your puny belly's hunger. You knew that, and you bagged bigger game. You took just one arrow to do it with because that's all you'd need. Tell me I'm wrong."

He wasn't just bright. He was very bright, she thought. She'd better take care to remember that, most of all. She cleared her throat and tossed out an insult to change the subject. "You thinking to stay in there until you shrivel to walnuts? Although as small as you must be, it wouldn't be far, would it?"

"You saying something with that statement?" he asked, his voice just a bit lower than it had been. She smiled.

"I am," she replied. "And not without cause. I aimed well and accurately with my last blade. I hit nothing. You must have nothing."

There was the sound of laughter, a splash and Morgan waited.

"Have it your way, lad. The lasses have no complaints."

She rolled her eyes. He was the FitzHugh. Of course they had no complaints about bedding such a rich prize! She was going to take back what she'd thought about his being bright at this rate. "Perhaps you should take more educated lasses to your bed, then. They'd not be so easy to please, I think."

"Why would I do such a stupid thing? When I take a lass to my bed, it's to learn them. I don't want some other man's incompetence spoiling my fun. Besides, I like educating my own women. Give me a maid any day, I'll return her a courtesan."

"You must have a problem finding, and keeping, servants

to warm your bed with such a requirement," she replied snidely.

"Nay. They find my bed warm and inviting. Nary a complaint have I heard. I keep them until they've outlived their usefulness. Or until they whelp a bastard."

"You've sired bastards?" she asked, the shock filling her voice.

"Not yet. I'm careful with my seed."

Morgan hadn't one reply she could voice. She didn't even know what he was talking about, although she had a very good guess.

"Never you worry, lad, there's lasses a-plenty in the world. There'll even be a share for you, although you'll not have first pick 'til your voice changes and you grow some hair on that bony chest of yours."

She was choking, but thanked God it didn't make sound.

"Enough of this. There's a response to such talk, and no woman handy to use it on. You'd best tell all, lad. I'm short on patience, lost most of my whiskey, have a head that wants to lift itself from my neck, and thistles that need pulled. You wish to keep your talents hidden? Fair enough. I'll find out sooner or later, although I wouldn't test me again, if I were you."

The apparition-like body didn't look like it had substance, let alone the threatening voice he was using. Morgan gulped.

"I was na' testing you," she replied in a stiff tone that didn't sound at all like her. She whipped the length of plaid cloth out, eyed a starting point and placed it against her waist. The cloth folded and draped as richly as she'd suspected it would. Morgan tucked it about her belt, double-folding the cloth at her front. Then, she bunched it into pleats all along the back, before bringing it forward again to pull the long end through her belt. She had enough to toss over her left shoulder, secure it through the back of the belt and make a short cape down her legs. She twisted her head to check the length, and noted with satisfaction that it brushed the backs of her calves, exactly where it should.

"You was na' just testing, you was showing off. Had to be. Otherwise, you would ha' killed me. Hand me a drying cloth."

She frowned at that, wondering first at the blunt truth of his words and secondly at the easy way he ordered her about. Then, she looked up. Her mouth dropped open. Shock was what held her immobile as he strode through the fog and foliage right toward her, and he didn't look like any male she'd ever seen in her life.

Zander FitzHugh was virile, healthy, toned, muscled and enormous. Everywhere. Even rising from a fresh-water stream into cold air he was impressive, and he wasn't small in the least. Morgan forgot to swallow around the instant increase of moisture in her mouth and felt it choking her before she shut her mouth and then her eyes.

"Well, look at you," he said, ". . . attired in FitzHugh sett and like to make any number of maidens' hearts a-twitter with such a fine spectacle. Your legs need a might bit more muscle, and your arms look like twigs, but your face is definitely a good feature. Boyish, yet manly at the same time. The lasses will go wild. They love an untried male."

He nudged her, and she moved back two steps with the force of it before opening her eyes on anything but him.

"You look ready to be my squire, and I see you've got your tartan on proper this time. A vast improvement."

"However did I miss?" she whispered, without thinking.

His laughter wasn't shrouded by mist now, and she felt such an unfamiliar heat that she knew she was blushing, and she never blushed. Never. Blushing was for young, virgin maidens, not for her, and definitely not in response to the man in front of her.

"I wear a loin-wrap," he replied. "I don it first . . . or I will, when I'm dried."

"A . . . what?" She couldn't keep speaking with him

when he was so casual about his own nakedness and she was feeling like every part of her own body was aware of it. The sun hadn't been down long enough to hide any of it.

"Fetch my drying cloth. Fetch my clothing, too. I'll show you a loin-wrap. A good squire has his master's needs already seen to, and wouldn't need prodding," he said softly.

"I've not agreed to be your squire," she repeated.

"Would you like another dunking?"

She shook her head.

"Then we're agreed you'll be my squire?"

"I'll not swear fealty to you," she replied, lifting her chin, although she wasn't meeting his eyes. It seemed safer to concentrate on the birch behind him.

"Not yet, perhaps, but in time, you will."

"Never." Morgan set her teeth and moved to focus on his face. It was one of the hardest things she'd ever done, and she didn't dare ask herself why. All she knew was that she was shaking with the effort of keeping his gaze.

He sighed. "We'll start your training with the basic things, then. Serve your lord. He has requested his drying towel, but since you've left him standing in the night air, he's no longer in need of it. Fetch his clothing instead. Now."

"If I refuse?"

"Why do you think I let you keep your hair?" he stepped closer to ask it, and Morgan whitened. She only hoped it was as easily missed as her blush must have been. "You still wish to own it tomorrow, don't ye?"

She turned and walked over to his pile of clothing. She didn't know what was the matter with her. She wanted to keep her braid, yes, but at what cost? Her own self-respect? She picked up the clothes with a vicious gesture. She wondered what his reaction would be if she hacked her own braid off while he slept, but she knew she wouldn't do it.

She was supposed to be tormenting him, threatening

him with her skills, and she was failing miserably. Not only was he unabashed by her knife-throwing accuracy, but he was using her own plea against her. To add insult, he thought her a manly boy! Tears of anger glittered in her eyes when she returned to him and dumped the clothes on the ground at his feet: anger at her own thoughts. She *wanted* him to think her a manly boy! What woodland sprite was stealing her wits?

"This is a loin-wrap."

He pulled a length of white linen material out and held one end of it to his right hip. Morgan tried to act interested in what he was showing her, rather than interested in what it looked like he was displaying for her. He had warmed, too, and that had an enlarging effect on . . . everything. She forced herself to watch his hands, and not any other part of him, and didn't hear a word of his lecture over her own pulse.

He took the material once around his waist, then in a loose fashion, he went down the front, between one leg and around the back. Then he was wrapping it around the left hip, down between the other leg and around the back. He ended at his right hip where he tied the ends together. He didn't leave anything she could have hit with her blade. Morgan stared at the finished product.

"That is na' very Scots," she finally replied.

"True. It's also not very manly, if you ask the right Scotsman."

"Do other lairds wear such?"

"I dinna' know. I dinna' care, either."

"Truly?"

He looked up at her, and Morgan's heart nose-dived into her belly. She very nearly put a hand to the spot to stop it. There was no sense to any of this. She had no use for men. She had no use for being female. She wasn't going to rest while this man lived. She had already vowed it. She was going to do her best to eliminate the laird of FitzHugh from the world, and gain herself every true Scotsman's thanks for so doing. She certainly wasn't going to stand rooted to the spot while he showed her an outlandish-looking swathing, much like a bairn might wear.

The thought made her giggle.

"Something amuses you?" he asked, putting both hands on his hips and leaning just enough that despite the loin-wrap, none would mistake him as unmanly or small. Morgan swallowed.

"I've seen bairns wearing much the same, FitzHugh."

"You address me as Zander, or I'll make you use my lord. You ken?"

"Certainly, my lord. As your forced vassal, let me tell you then that you've lent your manhood to the fairies to wear such a thing."

"Perhaps." He shrugged.

"Perhaps?"

"Let me put your mind to rest, Squire Morgan. I wear a loin-wrap only when I'm abroad near our borders, and trodding onto battlefields such as we left last eve. When I'm at my glen, I'm as Scots as any man."

"I dinna' understand," she replied.

"The English know our ways. They know the best place to weaken a man to save for torture, much like you did. They know."

Her brow knit with a frown. The FitzHughs were in league with the Sassenach. They always had been. Most clans that survived were paying fealty to the crown of England.

He cleared his throat. "Now you know why you dinna' hit anything vital. I had it protected. Assist me with the rest now. I've a burned rabbit to whet my appetite, and then venison to finish it."

She reeled at his words. "You knew?" Her eyes went wide. She'd skinned and hung it a goodly distance from his camp. Then, she'd set the hide out to begin drying. She didn't know he'd been gone long enough to find it.

"I knew."

"I dinna' lie when you asked. You asked my talent with a bow. My talent is na' with just the bow. 'Tis with the arrow."

He smiled at her. Morgan gulped in air at the sight.

"I'll try to be more accurate in what I ask. The hide has no mark I noted. Where did you take it down?"

"The eye," she replied.

His eyebrows rose to his hairline. "You that good?"

She nodded.

"From what distance?"

She lifted her shoulders. "I dinna' know for certain. I never had it paced off. I bring down what I aim at. The distance is na' a part of it. If it's too far off, I don't shoot."

He whistled, and she watched him pick up his own tunic, but he didn't put it on. "I begin to think you are a very good squire after all, Morgan, of no surname or clan. I'm also thinking you're handy enough to dig these thistles from my side, too, and I'm damn tired of pretending they don't exist."

He lifted an arm, and showed her at least a dozen reddish areas where a deeply imbedded spine still poked. Her eyes went wider at what had to be extremely aggravating and painful to him, and then she looked up at his face.

He winked, and coming from his handsome face, that was even worse.

Chapter 4

The sun was not yet up when Morgan was awakened. It wasn't a pleasant experience and she knew Zander FitzHugh didn't mean it to be. He'd grabbed hold of her braid and yanked, until she found wobbly legs beneath her, and stood blinking, without recognition.

"Don't test me with your laziness, Squire Morgan."

She lifted her hands to rub at her eyes, but was stopped by the cord about her right one. She narrowed her eyes at him, and looked to where he'd pulled on the other end, bringing it close to his shoulder. His stance said it for him. He wasn't allowing her one inch, and she knew why. She took a step closer to him in order to reach her own eye sockets.

When she was finished, she stepped back. He'd cursed and ranted at her over the pain she'd showered on him last eve, and looked none the worse for it, she decided.

"You look awful pleased with yourself, Squire."

"I dinna' ask to be your squire, nor will I stay as one. I said as much last eve, I recollect."

"You said much, and promised more. You'll stay now. You've no choice."

"No choice?" she spat. "I'd rather serve a *poucah*."

"You're wearing FitzHugh sett and you dinna' pay for it. I demand payment for such fine cloth. I will take payment by your service to me."

Her gritted teeth didn't stop the angry sound she made from deep in her throat. She knew it was frustration. It didn't help that he knew it, too. "I'll not stay and serve you for clothing I was forced to wear once my own were lost to me!"

"I saw no one forcing you to disrobe last night. What mean you by this force you accuse?"

He was enjoying her impotence. She could see it in every breath he was taking as he folded his arms, pulling her arm up with the motion as he regarded her. Morgan took a deep breath, held it, then eased it out. "Did you wake me to serve you, or bandy words with you?" she asked, from between her teeth.

"I woke you because we've some distance to travel, and not all morn to do it in. You were sleeping well past what I expect of my squire. I'll not be so lax with my punishments in future, either."

Morgan's eyes flared. She should have been quicker at escaping last night. She should have known when she started lancing the pus-pockets his thistles had been in, he'd not let her go. She should have had a plan before running from him. He'd been in pain, half of which she'd delivered purposely with each twist of her knife, and he was still fast enough to catch her. She wondered anew how he did it.

"I dinna' ask to be your squire, and I dinna' want it."

He ignored her outburst. "A good squire awakens before his master and sees that all is prepared for his day. We've a bit of learning to get under your belt, don't we?"

"I'll not stay and learn from you, or for you."

"You'll stay and pay for your clothing. If you agree to that much, I'll grant you leave once you've done so."

"But I dinna' ask for it," she repeated again.

"Then, divest yourself of it, and leave. I'll not stop you."

She glared at him. "But you kicked my own into the burn! No doubt it's joined the sea by now," she said.

"'Tis likely. You ready to grant me service?"

"I'll need my freedom to do so, won't I?" She snarled and made a fist out of the hand stretched between them.

"You have your freedom. I look about and I see freedom. What mean you about this freedom you lack?"

"I have three feet of room from you."

He chuckled. "'Tis as far as I can trust you."

"If I give my word that I'll stay, will you release me?"

"No," he replied, without hesitation.

Morgan clenched her teeth. "No?" she repeated, then again with more stupefaction, "No?"

"I canna' trust you, lad. Show me something to trust, and I'll reconsider your bondage."

She couldn't possibly be tied to him until that happened! Morgan's eyes probably showed her panic. She had yet to bind her breasts, and although she wasn't a buxom size, the pre-dawn cold was giving her trouble. He'd be certain to discover for himself why. It wouldn't be hard to ferret out her gender. Once he did that, she knew what would happen. He was too large a size to fight, and he'd already told her what he liked most was a woman who was a maid. She added to that thought that he'd already said she looked untried. She'd be ravished if he she stayed tied to him and allowed him the truth. She'd be raped when she fought. She didn't have to wonder over it either; she knew. He'd have every bit of the KilCreggar clan then. She swallowed. She couldn't stay tied to him!

"I dinna' kill you . . . last eve," she answered, grimacing slightly over the waver in her voice.

He considered her a moment. "Not for lack of trying."

"I could have put every one of my dirks into a vital part and you'd have bled to death," she pointed out.

"And since that failed, you decided to twist out every one of my thorns and cut me to make certain of it. I still bear the brunt of your handiwork."

He lifted his shirt and tunic, pulling the inner layer from the scabbing all along his side. Morgan looked with him, and had the insane thought that she hoped she hadn't scarred him. She kicked that stupidity aside. She had vowed to make him pay for the slaughter and defamation of the KilCreggar clan. What use would his dead body have for unblemished skin?

"You had poison to each thistle. If I had na' lanced them, you'd be suffering from the ague and moaning with the pain."

"And you'd be suffering my hand for leaving me lay in ash all day and allow them to fester."

"You near drowned me for that already."

"No. I dunked you for disobedience."

Morgan set her lips, stiffened her shoulders and looked across at him. The sun had lightened the sky while he stood, amusing himself with her words. The warmth was dissipating the remnants of mist, allowing her a better view. She had to swallow around her own response to the sight of his broad, hairy chest before he pushed his shirt back down and tucked it beneath his kilt.

She cleared her throat. "You woke me to serve you, Master? Very well, what is your bidding? What service do you require first?" she asked, in a sarcastic tone.

He grinned. "Aye, I need to be serviced. I'd have a need for a good draught from my sporran of whiskey to drink, if it hadn't taken a dirk and still held liquid; a bowl of gruel in my belly; and a moment to relieve myself. You can grant me all of that?"

She looked across the span of three feet as levelly as possible. "I've no talent for cooking," she replied finally, "and I'm not about to learn."

His answer was a hearty laugh. She wondered why. "You stubborn still? Dinna' say I haven't warned you."

"About what, now?" she replied.

"You want release from your bond, you'll learn what I tell you to learn."

She sucked in the breath again, held it, then let it out slowly. It still wasn't working. She couldn't best him with strength, and until she had her dirks back, she wasn't going to try. "Very well, Master Zander, I'll learn to make gruel. What is the stuff made of?"

That got her another laugh. "As it happens, we're camped not far from a MacPhee croft. The lasses there cook a fine pot of gruel. They'll not think it amiss if I need to purchase another breakfast. I'll barter for it with some of the venison you provided."

" 'Tis my own to barter with," she answered.

"You took it with my bow and arrow. You serve me now. I am your master. Everything you have is mine. Everything."

His words were making every part of her feel like it was jumping. Morgan frowned at such a sensation. "What have I done to deserve the likes of you? What?"

"I dinna' know, lad. Been poor long enough, I reckon."

"I've no wish to be a squire."

"You ever been one?" he asked.

"Nay," she answered.

"Then how do you ken you will na' like it?"

"If it's anywhere near you, I will na' like it," she answered.

He sighed hugely, his chest rising and falling with it. She watched it. "You were sorely in need of the employment, if your skinny hide, tattered sett, and hole-filled boots were any indication. You also have no family, or if you do, you dinna' claim them, and let's not forget that you forced me to do it."

"Forced?" She didn't have to pretend the confusion.

"You tried to rob my dead body. That calls for action."

"I dinna' rob anyone, dead or no."

"You lead robbers, therefore you are one."

She hung her head a moment, allowing him the victory. He'd earned it, for she'd thought much the same every time she had to do it. "There's bound to be dozens of young FitzHugh clansmen to choose from, for the honor of serving their laird. Why me?"

"Look about you, lad. We're leagues from FitzHugh

land. There's a shortage of my clansmen at present, and I'm not the laird. My brother is."

She was reeling, and it wasn't from the shock. It was from the despair that opened right in front of her eyes until she couldn't see him. She closed her eyes to keep it in. She'd vowed since the age of eleven to avenge the KilCreggars. She'd honed a skill at knives, swords, sling-shot, bow and arrow, any weapon at her disposal, just so she could accomplish that one thing. She was prepared and willing to die with the deed, too.

That meant taking their laird, The FitzHugh. Taking him and slitting his throat, and leaving him to bleed every drop in honor of the KilCreggar clan. She'd been trying to find her courage, and hating herself just last night for not having taken him when she had it gifted to her. She still didn't know why she hadn't, although she was beginning to suspect.

Morgan gulped, trying to suppress what it was before she had to face it. She wasn't used to being female, and Zander was more male than she'd ever been near. She was having to fight a response her body was woman enough to feel, and every prolonged moment in his company was making it intensify, and *now* she finds out he isn't even the laird?

He was speaking when she opened her eyes again. She watched him. He might not be the laird, but he was her means of getting to him. She'd use Zander to do it and force herself to stifle any reaction to being near him. All of which meant that she wouldn't fight herself free of him, after all. She wondered how to convince him of it.

". . . must have thought myself desirous of company, and you were the handiest one about. Now that I know your lack of nursing skill, I'd have lief just taken your hand for stealing from the dead and ridden away."

"I was na' stealing from the dead. I get tired of repeating it, and I have great skill with a knife, just not on your thick hide."

"I grow tired of your tongue, too, as tired as I am of your laziness. Relieve yourself. We've a gathering to attend."

And, so saying, he parted his kilt. Morgan averted her face, felt a huge blast of heat to her entire body, and cursed herself for that reaction as he finished. "I've no need," she replied stiffly.

He glanced sidelong at her, and waited until she looked. "You have the sickness?"

"I've no fever, if that's your worry."

"You've a flush to your skin and no need to do what every other man needs to. Both signs of the fever."

Morgan's eyes dropped. He'd noticed the blush she'd have given anything not to show? She was going to have to suppress that, too, and she didn't know enough about a blush to be able to stop one, or even if it was possible.

It was stupid, too. It wasn't as if she'd never been around lads before. She'd been working and living beside them for years. They just lost significance next to Zander FitzHugh, and for the first time in her life, she was afraid of why.

"If you've finished bandying words, come along." He didn't ask. He yanked on the cord and Morgan moved. "We've a deer to fetch, a breakfast to purchase and some ground to cover. There's a fair at Bannockburn. There'll be many clans represented. I've a hankering to be there."

"A fair? You woke this early to attend a fair?"

"'Tis as good a reason as any. Besides, who needs a reason to attend a fair? Hurry along." He walked at a pace that had her jogging, and kept the cord short to keep her near. "Yonder MacPhee lasses are fair of face, although a bit stodgy for my taste, but with the proper flirting, they'll cook you some eggs, and not burn them overmuch. They've a dearth of menfolk, too. Lost most of them to another useless clan skirmish. We've got to stop that. We've got to combine our energies to fight our real enemy."

"The FitzHughs?" she asked.

He stopped and turned, and she plowed into him. She already knew how solid he was. Her face now knew it, as she hit the side of his jaw. She rubbed her nose to keep it from bleeding while he looked at her with a look of surprise, and not one bit of pain.

"You follow too close."

She rolled her eyes. "You've the end of my bond," she replied.

"You behave yourself, and I'll take it off."

"Oh, I live to serve," she retorted too quickly.

"If I cut this bond, I do it for my own reason. You test me, you'll not enjoy it."

"Nothing about serving you is enjoyable," she replied.

He grinned. "You've a bit of learning to do, but you are quick. I'll give you that. Curb your tongue at the MacPhee croft. A squire does na' toss barbs at his master."

"Cut this bond, I'll curb it."

He pulled a dirk out and held it to the braided rawhide on her wrist. "I hope I don't regret this, Morgan, but I'd not like the MacPhee lasses to think us joined for a reason."

She shrugged. "Tell them I'm your prisoner. It's truth."

"A prisoner wearing my own sett? God, grant me patience!"

"I'll not test you." She waited until he raised his head and favored her with that midnight-blue gaze again. Her entire torso was afire with ache, from walking at too brisk a pace and not having the chance to relieve herself. She'd do whatever he required.

"Your word?"

"You have it," she replied.

He nodded, slit the cord on her wrist, and then his own. She was rubbing hers where it was red and angry-looking before he finished and looped the cord through his belt.

"Come along then, and watch yourself. The lass named Lacy likes to use her hands. Oft."

He set off at the same pace, and Morgan kept at his heels until he pulled down and halved her deer. He was concentrating on his task, although she knew he was listening for her. She didn't go far, but she knew he'd hear her taking nature's call. He wouldn't know how she used the time to put the swath of kilt against her heart and bind herself. She was surprised at how much confidence it gained her when the band was in place, and she no longer bounced and had to endure every rub of her tunic material. She didn't think she liked anything about being a woman. The restrictive feeling of her binding reassured her of it. She didn't want anything to do with Zander FitzHugh as a male, either. He was merely troubling her because she wasn't used to being around a handsome, virile, full-grown man. That was it.

She didn't care a fig for Zander FitzHugh, other than as a means to get to the laird. She didn't even care if he thought her shy, and she did her best to fuss with the front of her kilt as she rejoined him, although she had to ignore his smile. She had worse things to worry over. *This Lacy likes to use her hands? What does that mean?* she wondered.

The croft was not large, but everything about the MacPhee lasses was. Zander called them a bit stodgy? They looked capable of competing with the cows for girth. There were four of them, too. Four lasses that each outweighed Zander. They had favorable faces, though. On that, he hadn't lied. They looked like competing copies from the same mold, although the fat of their bodies detracted from the green slant of their eyes, the flaming red of their hair and the fact that they seemed to have all their teeth. She'd never consider them comely enough for a tumble, if she were really a lad and interested in such things.

Zander probably hadn't the same discrimination. She looked to him and caught his grin. "We're going to pay for our breakfast now, boy. Prepare yourself."

"Lasses!" Zander's voice was loud and full of admiration as he hailed them, and tossed the deer carcass outside their front stoop. "I've come to repay your hospitality, and beg for more of the same."

They twittered at that, sounding like a gaggle of giggling

geese. Morgan winced. She'd thought the way the hag acted was embarrassing.

One stepped forward, linking her arms through Zander's. "For you, Zander FitzHugh, I'll fry the best scrambled skillet you've ever tasted. Come along. I've just the spot to set you."

"Oh, Lace. I've barely recovered from the last you made for me. There's not a cook to compete for leagues."

She giggled at that, and Morgan felt a little of her trepidation leave her. Zander had Lacy, then?

"And who is this? Who have you brought to us, Zander?"

The other three ascended from the bowels of their croft to swarm about her. Morgan's eyes were wide as she sought Zander, but the great oaf had already disappeared inside.

"What's your name?" one asked.

"He's terribly young." One of them pinched her upper arm, and then immediately moved away, like it had been unintentional.

"But he's handsome. Very handsome. Or, he will be with some meat to him. What's your name, boy?"

Morgan stumbled forward as what had to be fingers fondled her backside. "Mor—gan," she stammered, and then had to endure a frontal assault as she was pulled into a very large bosom, and then let go before she could react.

"He's a bit thin. Come laddie, we've a hankering to see you well-fed and satisfied."

"Very satisfied," another whispered.

Morgan gasped, and then she was running, easily beating them to their croft. She stumbled down the three steps into it. Peat smoke blinded her for a moment, and then her mouth fell open at where the woman named Lacy had her hands. The woman had more breast than Morgan had ever seen, and Zander wasn't immune to holding to one. He was also enjoying Lacy's hands on the upward tilt of his kilt at his lap.

And I thought him large last eve, was her first thought. Then she was propelled forward by another of the girls, forcing her into Lacy, who side-stepped. Morgan slid right atop Zander's lap, taking the brunt of him in her belly. Stunned shock kept her immobile before she reacted, jumping to her feet like a reaver caught in the act. Then, she was backing into a wall, keeping her eyes anywhere but at him, or any of them. She knew her face was flaming.

"Behave yourself, Zander. My sisters are about," Lacy demurred.

"Aye, forgive me lassie. It's just the sight of your fair face, coupled with the delights of your frame, make me dizzy. I'm just a weak man, darlin'."

He was arranging his kilt, flattening the lump of him as he said it, and Lacy put her bodice back in place. Morgan didn't say a word as they rearranged their clothing. The room seemed to fill with twittering, giggling girls, all vying for attention. Then came the sounds of cooking, a bit of lard sizzling before a slice of black bread was toasting in it, a slew of feminine whispers. Morgan couldn't think beyond listening to each and every sound.

Her eyes moved to Zander. He was looking for it and gestured with his eyes toward the women. "Thank you," he mouthed.

Morgan curled her lip.

"He's young, but he'll grow," one of them whispered loudly.

"He's tall enough already, just needs some fattening. I think he's sweet."

"You should feel the strength in his . . . ."

Morgan's eyes were wide, her pulse was erratic. She had her own array of muscles in her belly, so Zander wouldn't have any clue of her gender from the contact they'd experienced, but every single nerve ending she had was aware and tingling. And the MacPhee lasses were discussing *her?*

"You like my new squire, ladies?" Zander spoke over his shoulder, his eyes never leaving hers.

"He's your new squire? Oh please, don't say you're going to take him with you, too!"

"His name's Morgan. You'll have to pardon the lad, he's a bit shy. You know," his voice lowered to a whisper, ". . . untouched."

"Untouched? Truly?"

Morgan panted with fright as they all looked at her. The smell of burning gruel on the fire's log was what stopped them. He was doing this on purpose, too! She knew by his smile.

"He's very handsome, Zander. Where did you find such a handsome lad to squire for you?"

He was still watching her, and she tried to control every reaction. They were calling her handsome? She'd never gone beyond an occasional glimpse in a creek. She had no idea what she looked like. *But handsome?* she wondered.

"The same place I find all my squires, ladies. A battle-field. Is na' that so, Morgan?"

"A battlefield? Truly? How exciting, and how brave."

Morgan's eyes were wide as they all looked to her. She knew she was hot with the flush and filled with hate at the man causing it. The MacPhee lasses really should have been paying attention to their cooking, though, as the croft filled with smoke.

Chapter 5

"Thank the lasses, Morgan, and assure your return. 'Tis the only way we'll be leaving."

Morgan stuffed another bite of milk-soaked toast into her mouth and nodded at all of them, without looking at any. She hadn't any idea food could taste so good, nor that she could eat so much.

"My squire is properly thankful, ladies, and I'm certain he'd tell it to you, if he could keep his mouth empty long enough. As I've said before, the greatest cooks in leagues. Morgan?"

"Aye," she said, after swallowing, "my thanks."

"Come along then, lad. We've a fair piece to walk."

Morgan beat him out of the croft. She wasn't going to be left alone with those women. It was some moments before Zander joined her, and he had a girl linked through each arm when he did. She kept backing and waving until Zander could catch up.

"That was uncalled for, lad."

She had already told herself she wasn't ever speaking to him again, and then he had to go and remonstrate her. *Her!* Her back stiffened. She reached with a fingernail and pulled a wheat piece from her front teeth and spat it out. "Do you have another of those loin-things?" she asked.

His eyebrows raised. "Aye."

"I'll be needin' it."

"You will?"

"I'll not have lasses poking and prodding where they've no business."

He hooted at that. She wrinkled her nose at him.

"You could sit back and enjoy it, too, you ken."

"You were na' enjoying Lacy. Otherwise, why would you thank me for stopping her?"

"We've got a ways to go, and I've a bit of posturing and speaking to do. I canna' do it with legs that tremble."

Morgan glanced at him, and wished she hadn't. *Legs that tremble?* she wondered. *What does that mean?* He had legs stouter than the tree he'd rammed her into the previous eve.

He laughed at her confusion. She didn't like it. She didn't like it one bit. "Lacy is a lot of woman. It takes as much energy to mount her as it does to run a league's distance. Maybe more."

She was gasping. "Do you think of nothing else?"

She had his confusion now. "Of course I think of other things. Blood. War. Drink. Food. But love is at the forefront, lad. It was for me when I was your age, and it still is. Don't tell me you don't hanker, too?"

"Of course I hanker. I just have better taste in women."

That got him hooting again. They were almost back at his camp, Morgan noted, hoping the conversation wouldn't last beyond their reaching it. It was a forlorn hope. She realized it as he dug through a sack and tossed her a length of white cotton.

"Lacy may not be the most desirous of lasses, but she makes up for it with gumption. You need help tying that?"

Morgan turned her back on him, lifted her kilt and started winding the material about herself. "If I need it, I'll ask."

"You are shy," he said. "Either that, or you're woefully under-size."

Her face was flaming again. "I'm shy," she answered.

That got her another burst of amusement. She was rapidly tiring of being his entertainment. "Why dinna' we ride the horse, my lord?" she asked, hoping to divert the subject.

"Because we're going to look like all other Scots.

Down-trodden by the English, with little more than the clothing on our backs and the humility of our bowed heads."

"I thought the FitzHughs were in bed with the Sassenach."

"My brother is. He's the idea the clan will be safe that way. He will na' listen to anyone. He lays the dignity of FitzHugh at the feet of the English trash, and wonders why he's na' looked in the eye, anymore."

"And you dinna' believe the same?"

"I detest everything about the English. Especially their laws. But we Scotsmen curse ourselves rather than our true enemy. We spill our own blood, instead of theirs. You carry any weapon beside that sling?"

Morgan lifted her left arm, surprised he'd figured out what the leather straps about her lower arm were, and disgusted at herself for letting her sleeves ride up as she finished with her loin-wrap. "You have my dirks," she replied.

"Aye. Until I'm assured of your loyalty, they'll be safer with me."

"Nay, you'll be safer with them there."

"Change of words, same meaning. You ready?"

Morgan adjusted the front of her kilt over the loin-thing. It actually made her look like she had a bit more substance where she needed it, too.

"Aye, she replied.

"Good. Follow me."

He was already taking his large strides from her. Morgan broke into a jog behind him. He was but five inches taller, but had the walk of a much larger man. Either that, or she'd no inkling of how a grown man could walk.

"So tell me, Morgan lad," he turned his head sideways to ask as they left the trees and started across a knee-high field of grass, "just what sort of lass are you looking for to make a man out of you?"

She closed her eyes for a moment, took a deep breath and looked at his back. "One with a bit of shape to her."

"The MacPhee lasses have shape. They have handfuls of the stuff."

"They're like sows, with teats to match."

"You canna' lie, Morgan. I saw where you were looking."

He did? she wondered. *He saw, and he had it wrong?*

"And that Lacy has a strong pair. Ripe-feeling. Just the kind—"

"I like a lass with some leanness to her. I would na' want to fall off her," Morgan interrupted him, before she had to hear more of Lacy's charms.

He chuckled and turned his head back again. "Describe your lass," he said.

Morgan rolled her eyes. He truly didn't think of anything else. The lads she'd been leading hadn't been so one-minded, or if they were, it was a well-kept secret. Then again, she rarely was forced to keep company with them for as long as she had been Zander, without a break of some kind.

"Well?" he prompted.

"Hair like this tunic-weave you've thrust on me, so she can pull a curtain of it about us. Sweet lips, fair of face. I think I'd like lean hips, long lengthy legs, a slender waist. It will na' matter if she's buxom, or no, I've no hankerin' for that sort of thing."

He shook his head. "Trust the young."

"You ask my idea of a woman, and then you mock it? Dinna' ask again."

"I'm not mocking you, lad. I'm simply wondering at why you save yourself for a nymph that does na' exist."

"This is the woman I'll have. When I meet her, I'll know."

"Have? Jesu', lad! Women are for taking, not having. I can see your learning will have to include women. There's women a-plenty out there for the taking. Taking, lad."

"I'll na' take a woman by force," she answered, grimly watching the muscles of his back through the one shoulder his plaid wasn't covering.

"I dinna' mean that. A woman needing forcing is a chore, not a feast. Remember that. Woman can be made ripe for the tasting, or they can be bitter to the core and stiff. If a woman is that, let her be. That's my advice."

"Where is this fair we're attending?" Morgan was starting to feel the stitch in her side from the huge breakfast she'd consumed, and her steady jogging was making it bothersome.

He laughed again. "Alongside that vale. Keep your eyes on it, lad, you'll see a burn, and then the entire field will be awash with tents."

"I dinna' see . . . ."

Her voice faded as what she'd assumed to be boulders became the rounded tops of tents constructed from sack-cloth.

"What is it, lad?" He stopped and she joined him.

"Tents. Scores of them." She pointed.

He was squinting and then turned to her. "You can see them?"

"Aye," she answered.

His brows raised. "That could be part of your secret with knives and taking down game. Your sight."

She turned and stared at him. "You canna' see it?" Then, it was her turn to chuckle. "You? The great Zander FitzHugh . . . a poor-sighted man? No wonder you think the vast wench, Lacy, worth tumbling."

"I've na' said I was great, nor did I say I found her worth more than my breakfast."

"But, you were . . . I mean, you had . . . ." Her face was flaming again, and the look on his face made it worse.

"If I had na' had that response, it would ha' been an insult. I thanked you for a reason, lad. Rescue."

"I dinna' understand." She was mystified and sounded it.

"Grow a mite, and I'll find a wench to show you. Come. Pull that sling from your arm, and warm it. A cold leather does na' have the right feel to it, and I want you showing off."

Morgan was surprised again. "You know that?"

"A Scotsman was na' allowed weapons a-fore Robert the Bruce championed us and crowned himself king. We can still be imprisoned if caught using them. You know the Sassenach laws."

"You can sling a stone?"

"I'm capable," he answered, starting his pace again.

"And, what . . . do you mean? Showing off?" She was jogging again, so the question came in the span of three breaths.

"There's bound to be contest, lad. I've a wish to put my squire up against their best stoner."

"I'll not sling stones for you."

"You any good with that, or do you wear it to entice the ladies to look at your scrawny arms?"

Scrawny arms? Morgan wondered, trying to keep the insult from showing on her. She had well-developed and tanned arms. She could do a hundred push-ups, and take down any of her lads in an arm-wrestle. And Zander FitzHugh called them scrawny? "I'm as good with it as I am with my dirks. Maybe better."

"Just as I suspicioned. On your toes, lad. We've been sighted."

Morgan looked up at the thirty-some-odd men cresting the hill and coming head-on at them. Unconsciously she stopped her pace and stepped a bit to the back of Zander. They were approaching a Scottish gathering, and wearing FitzHugh colors? They were going to be surrounded and captured, maybe even stoned themselves.

"FitzHugh?" One of the leaders bellowed

"Zander." He bowed deeply. "Of the Highland FitzHughs. Dinna' mistake me for my elder brother."

"We've heard of you, Zander. You may approach. You can bring your frightened boy with you, too."

Zander's glance said enough of his disgust that Morgan didn't have to guess what he thought. She set her lips and stepped out from behind him. She'd never done anything so insane before. She'd been the only one in her village brave enough to challenge the ghosts of the dead! Yet now she had acted so completely against her own character, she didn't know what to think.

She hung her head a bit, then raised it. She had acted like a frightened rabbit for a moment or two, when she hadn't done anything like that in more years than she could count. It was all Zander's fault, too. He had her dirks.

"Smart lad," Zander whispered. "They'll na' suspect your expertise if they expect fear."

Morgan's face split with a grin, then she stopped in her tracks. She was smiling because the kin of her mortal enemy praised her? She was going insane! She pulled the sling-shot from her wrist and started stretching it as she jogged to catch up with them.

There were more people in that gathering than in her village, and more than she'd seen, alive at one place, in her life. Morgan hung back behind Zander, catching the interested eyes of lasses as they eyed first Zander, and then her. She had to look away from more than one who would lower her lashes a bit and then boldly stare back at her. Morgan knew her cheeks were rosy. She just didn't know how to stop it.

"Look about, lad. There's lasses a-plenty here. There might even be one fitting your ideal maid."

"Perhaps. There's also sow-size ones for you, I notice."

His lips twisting was the only sign he'd heard. "I've seen their stoner. He's of a slender size, like yourself. Very accurate. If you best him, I'll give you one of your dirks."

"Two," she returned, beneath her breath.

He glanced sidelong at her. "Very well. Two," he agreed.

There were two stuffed dummies placed on poles, already showing the results of earlier contests. Morgan eyed them. From the marked-off distance, she could take out any piece of straw on either dummy's head.

" 'Tis too easy," she complained.

Zander held up his arm and started speaking, in such a loud booming voice, Morgan wasn't the only one staring at him with her mouth open. "My friends! I've a gamble to make today! I've a newly acquired squire you see before you. Not much, you think? Well, this lad will take out your target's eye at this range, much less any hit. I suggest we double the distance! Are there any takers?"

Three. Morgan eyed them as they did her. Three young men, not one as tall as her, but none with what Zander would describe as scrawny arms.

"He's got no strength to toss with, and you've not shown us the color of your silver."

"A Scotsman with silver? The fairies have stolen your wits. I've more than silver, though. I've this squire. He'll make any a fine servant, and well-trained he is, too. I'll personally guarantee his service for three years."

"Zander!" Morgan gasped, lifting her eyes to his. She had a perfect aim, but had never had it tested with her own freedom at stake.

"The lad begs to differ!" Zander shouted. "His aim is so true, he'll give five years, and mark off another ten paces!"

He wanted to be rid of her that much? Morgan felt what had to be her heart hitting the region of her well-filled belly, and then she was angry. So angry in fact, that her entire body shook with it. She controlled it viciously, until only her hands felt it, and then it stilled. Zander FitzHugh was going to rue the day he put her on the bargaining block. She was going to enjoy making him, too, and he was going to give her two dirks back for the pleasure.

She narrowed her eyes and glared at him.

"What is the contest?"

"One of your stoners hits the dummy. If my squire hits the same spot, I gain another servant for a term of a year, either the stoner or a member of his family. If he loses, the stoner gains my servant for a period of five years. Who takes the challenge?"

The three young men all stepped forward again. Morgan eyed them again and her lips tightened. *What was Zander going to do with three more squires?* she wondered.

The distance was doubled, by taking both dummies and marching them a significant piece away from the tents. Then ten paces were added. Morgan ignored what they were doing as she went looking for stones. That's when the nymph she'd described earlier to Zander tapped her on the shoulder and held out seven perfectly rounded stones.

Morgan looked up into the most beautiful green eyes she'd ever seen, set in the most beautiful face, surrounded by a wealth of reddish-brown hair, and atop the most perfect form a bliant could wrap. Morgan wasn't male, and she knew she wasn't male, but everything in her that was female was instantly alerted.

Her eyes widened at the instant emotion, and her nostrils flared with it. She had her teeth so tightly gritted that her jaw twinged. The girl smiled.

"For luck," she whispered, picking up Morgan's hand and dropping the stones into it. Then, she blew her a kiss. Morgan's knees jerked and she searched for Zander. The last thing she needed was a lass like this making love-struck eyes at her. Zander would be unstoppable with his teasing.

"Who wishes to be humiliated first?" Zander called loudly. "My squire grows impatient, and I've three servants to gain! Come, my friends! Put your champion forward!"

The largest stepped up, fit a stone into his sling and started swinging. He spun it too fast, Morgan noticed, intent more on speed than accuracy. She wasn't surprised when he hit one of the dummy's arms, although a great cheer went up in the crowd.

"Your turn, Morgan," Zander said.

Morgan fit one of the stones into her sling, and started looping it cross-wise at her side, barely missing her own body with it. Then, she let it fly. The arm fell off with her shot, and the gasp that ran the crowd was more gratifying than anything she'd ever experienced. Morgan lifted her eyebrows and met Zander's gaze.

"Check it, Ian."

"Aye! See it checked! It must be a trick," one of those gathered about said.

A young lad ran to the arm and brought it back, and there was some consternation as they tried to find where Morgan's stone had hit it. Zander explained it to them before he dug out her stone. She'd put it in the exact same hole.

That gasp of reaction was even more stimulating than the first had been, and she smiled before ducking her head.

"Is there another taker?"

"Best two of three!" The stoner yelled. "Lucky shot!"

"Morgan?" Zander asked. She shrugged. "My squire accedes to my wishes, and I'll grant it. Best two of three. You! Take your shot."

This time, he was sweating, and tried harder. His shot was faster than the previous one, but did as little damage, as it winged where the hip would be, leaving a half-hole.

"Can you hit the same spot now, squire?" he taunted Morgan.

"How will I prove it?" she asked quietly.

"What the lad says is truth. There is na' way to prove it unless we fill the hole with something," Zander's booming voice replied.

"Hit the other side," someone suggested.

"I have a better idea," Zander spoke. "Take a bit of this biscuit and plug the hole. Ian?" He motioned for the young lad again. "Go out and stuff this into the hole." He held out one-half of a MacPhee irresistible biscuit to the young man and everyone waited until it was set into the gap.

Morgan stepped up to the line, selected another of the stones and set it. Then, she began spinning her sling, letting it fly when the arch was perfect. The biscuit didn't move.

"He missed!" the stoner yelled.

"Did I?" she asked quietly.

Zander met her gaze. "Send Ian out for the biscuit. Go lad."

They all waited until he returned. Morgan knew what they'd find and enjoyed every bit of the surprise, awe and then applause at the hole that went right through the center of it.

"The lad is good, FitzHugh. He's very good. My boy will be honored to accompany you as your newest squire."

Zander bowed his head, accepting the lad. Then, he motioned to the remaining two men. "Who takes the challenge next? Well? Speak up lads! I've a hankering for a new tent and servants to assist with it. Who is next?"

"I'll na' take the challenge," one of them said and backed from the line.

"That leaves Jaime," someone said. "Jaime canna' take the challenge, either."

"Hush, Ma," he said.

"But you're my only lad, son. I canna' do without you. The crops, the babes, you know with your father gone . . . ."

"Hush, Ma," he said again.

"Does the lad have siblings?" Zander yelled. "I'll not ask more than a year of fealty from them. Then, I'll return the child to you, Mistress."

"I've seven daughters, m'lord," she replied.

"Daughters? What say you, Morgan? Can we take a servant girl with us?"

" 'Tis unseemly," she answered. "Who would be there to see to her modesty?"

"Have you two daughters you'd send with us, Mistress?"

"Two? Jaime?"

"You already have me losing, Ma," he protested.

"True, but you saw the lad. We all saw the boy."

"It will mean two less mouths for you to feed, Mistress Hobbs. Two less. And Zander FitzHugh is a man of his word. If he does na' return them next year we'll all search out the why." The old man talking had the respect of the group all about them. Morgan watched the nodding of heads at his words.

The murmurs seemed to surround them. Morgan listened to the hum of sound without hearing it. She wondered why Zander was so insistent that he have new servants. According to him, he already had too many. She shook her head at it.

"I take the challenge," the lad named Jaime said and stepped up the line.

Chapter 6

Morgan followed at the rear of Zander FitzHugh's new band of servants, trying to ignore the lasses. She should have known that Jaime's sisters included the chestnut-haired nymph, and worse, that Zander would spot her and start his teasing. Morgan tried to keep from catching the girl's eye but every time the girl turned around, she was looking for FitzHugh's first squire, and eye contact was made.

Morgan blushed the last time, and hoped it would get dark soon. She had yet to relieve herself, and it was going to be even more difficult to do so with as many servants as Zander FitzHugh seemed intent on gathering. That was coupled with the distinct displeasure of not having him to herself, too.

She could hardly wreak any amount of vengeance on him with another squire serving his every need. Worse still, this new squire knew about horses. Zander kept a companionable arm about the boy's shoulder and talked horses and battles and manly talk, while Morgan brought up the rear, doing her best to avoid catching the beautiful lass's eye.

She probably should have missed the dummy, she thought.

"Morgan!"

"Aye?" She lifted her head and met Zander's eye.

"Show the lasses the cook-fire. Not the one I bedded in, the other one, and then go get us another meal. I've a hankering for partridge. Can you hunt me a partridge?"

"I'll need an arrow," she answered.

"You hear that, Martin? He needs but one arrow. He's that cocky and self-assured. You're a fair shot, too, though. That's why I wanted you. Can you imagine squires as good as you two are at stoning? There won't be an enemy allowed near me."

Morgan snorted her disgust. *As good as what two?* she almost asked.

"Hello," the girl said.

Morgan's eyes widened and she mumbled something the girl took as a greeting as she matched her steps to Morgan's. Morgan walked a bit faster with each one, forcing the girl to increase her stride. The girl was even more beautiful up close. She was small, too. She barely reached Morgan's shoulder. Morgan already detested her.

"You're called Morgan? 'Tis a manly name, to be sure. You've a very good aim, too. I've never seen such a shot. I had shivers!"

"Thanks," Morgan answered. She looked away from where the girl was hugging herself, easily forcing a bit of cleavage to the top of her shift. She wondered what the girl would say if she was told that Morgan's real name was Morganna. She decided against asking it.

"Her name is Sheila, Morgan." That voice Zander had used on the crowd was just as loud in the forest near his camp, she decided. She cringed from it. "You'll have to give him a bit of time, Sheila. He's shy. So shy he can't even ask your name when it's what any lusty lad would be for asking."

"I was going to ask it," Morgan replied loudly. Then, she turned to the girl. "Your name is Sheila, then?"

"Aye."

She met Morgan's glance, dropped her eyes and blushed. Morgan nearly choked.

"And my sister's name is Amelia."

"Sheila . . . and Amelia?" Morgan asked, looking to the

younger, even more petite one. That one met her gaze and blushed, too.

At least my gender isn't in question, Morgan thought, although everything was getting plenty mixed up and confusing. It was all due to trying to turn Zander FitzHugh over on that battlefield, too. She should have listened to her instincts and stayed at Elspeth's hut, eaten another unpalatable sup, bedded down on the earthen floor, and left that field unpicked.

Morgan nearly cheered their arrival at Zander's camp, and she didn't waste any time showing the lasses where the cook-fire was. She also wasn't wasting time when she pulled his bow and an arrow out, looked at Zander and took another. Then, she was off, loping through the forest in such a hurry, she was scaring off game.

She didn't stop until she'd gone far enough away that her lungs were on fire. She didn't like the heavy pressure on her chest, either. She didn't know what to make of any of it.

She only had to use one arrow to bring down his partridge. Without waiting, she drew aim and took a second bird. Now that they were five, it would take more to feed them. She still wondered why he wanted it this way.

Morgan had everything back in perspective when she got back to camp, finding it easily from all the noise. Martin was hacking away at logs, the girl named Amelia was sighing over his use of strength, Sheila was trying to make some semblance of order out of the sacks all about the ground and Zander was erecting another tent, although there was already a red-striped one tucked between two trees. Morgan stood at the edge of the clearing, the birds hanging by their claws from her hands, and took it all in.

It looked like more of a permanent settlement than a camp. She wondered what that meant.

"There you are! Gone ages and avoiding all the work, as usual. It's a good thing you're a good provider. Give those to the lasses to pluck and skewer and come assist me."

Morgan tossed them to the ground beside Sheila, avoided her smile and hurried over to him.

"Stand in the center and brace it until I get it tied down. I couldn't use anyone else. They're too short."

Morgan tried not to feel pleased about being needed, but she did. She stood until her arms were numbing, while he drove in some stakes, pulled on ropes and kept up a tune-less whistle, in between flirting outrageously with his new servant-girls. All of which hit Morgan in her belly while she stood there impotently holding a tent up.

He had new servant-girls, and they were probably maiden girls . . . and he liked them that way best of all . . . .

And Morgan had procured them for him! She had to swallow the bitter taste in her mouth. She couldn't be ill. She was never ill. Her eyes stung with unfamiliar moisture as she looked over at him nonchalantly leaning on one hip, his hand planted on it, and showing a clear silhouette of that manly physique to Sheila and her sister.

Morgan glared at him, giving every bit of her hatred to it. Zander looked up then, caught her gaze and grinned. Then he pointed down at the girl, before pointing back to himself.

Morgan sneered. If she had to pretend jealousy to keep the girl safe, she would. It was the least she could do for the girl's mother and her brother, Jaime.

Zander pulled back in surprise. Then, he was pointing down at Sheila and over at Morgan.

She narrowed her eyes and nodded.

He stepped back, lifted both hands in surrender before walking back over to her. "About time you found some of it, lad," he said when he got there.

"Get back to purgatory where you belong," Morgan hissed.

He chuckled. "I'll bet Sheila's hair falls just like a curtain when it's loose."

Morgan clenched her teeth until her lower jaw hurt.

"It probably feels as fine as that tunic you wear beneath your shirt, too. What say you to that?"

"You owe me two dirks," she replied finally.

"Well, I'm not so sure I should give them to you."

"You a liar as well as a lecher, Master Zander?" she asked, snidely.

"You're jealous."

"Perhaps," she replied with as little inflection as possible.

"I would be stupid to put knives in the hands of a rival, no?"

"You touch her, and I'll be carving my initials in your heart," she said.

"You *are* jealous. The girl's in luck. As are you."

"Luck had nothing to do with any of it. 'Twas skill. My skill."

He shrugged, and folded his arms across his chest to consider her. Since she was still stuck holding up the tent, there wasn't any place she could go, or any escape she could make, but for once, she controlled every bit of a blush.

" 'Twas a good day, Morgan. Celebrate, rather than stew over it. I've earned fealty from more villagers, for who among them would fight the man in possession of his children? And the wench of your dreams has been delivered to you. Just think of it. You describe a nymph to me, and before the day is out, you've won her. From the looks of things, she'll be easy to coax into bed, too."

"You touch her, and I'll—"

His laughter rang out, interrupting Morgan's words, and everyone stopped what they were doing and looked over. Morgan still had control over her flush. She was very proud of that.

Zander lifted his hands in surrender. "She's all yours. Tame her gently." Then, he walked away. "You can let go of the roof, too. It's finished. Has been for some time."

Morgan lowered her arms, flexing every finger and then her arms, to get the feeling back. Then she swung them back and forth, to loosen her shoulders. It felt good. She hadn't done any exercising since coming upon Zander, and her muscles were stinging her at the lack. She didn't realize she was being watched until Zander coughed. She looked up, right into the adoring gaze of the lass, Sheila. That time, Morgan couldn't control anything, and she knew she was flaming before she averted her gaze.

Martin had a good stack of wood, the second tent was decreed Zander's, and the ladies were given the red-striped one. Martin and Morgan were welcome to the floor of Zander's tent, or they could sleep on the ground outside.

Morgan chose the ground. She lay, comfortably full of partridge and some sort of dumpling-enhanced gravy they'd made, and covered herself with the drape of her kilt. The fire flickered every so often, illuminating both tents and the place where she lay. And she didn't remember sleeping.

Morgan was awakened this time by having two dirks thrust into the dirt beside her nose. Her eyes flew open a moment before she was on her feet, both dirks in her hands and ready. Zander had already leapt back, expecting it. Her eyes narrowed as she took in the pre-dawn clearing, where fingers of mist were still hanging in the air.

"We've some work to do today. I wanted you awake before the others," he whispered.

"Why?" she whispered back.

He pulled in a breath, filling the chest in front of her. Then, he shrugged. "You're different," he said, finally.

She didn't reply and waited for him to explain.

He didn't. He just blew out his inhaled breath and gestured with his head. "Come with me. I want you to show me how you toss your knives."

He already had a target etched on a tree, although she could barely see it. Morgan looked at it in surprise. She hadn't heard him move. Some guardian of virtue she had turned out to be, she thought.

"I've seen knives tossed, and I've seen some hit a spot, but I've never seen anyone place them so perfectly, nor from any finger. Show me how you do such."

"My knives are perfectly balanced. That's the first trick."

"Balanced?" he asked.

"Pull your own out."

He did.

"Lay it flat in your hand. Can you feel a difference in weight, one side to the other? Top to bottom?"

"The hilt is heavier."

"Not in the hilt. In the blade. Can you feel it?"

He shook his head.

She snorted in frustration. "Hold out your other hand."

He did, putting it parallel to the one he had out already.

"Now, close your eyes."

"What?"

"Trust me. Use something beside your poor vision. Feel the weight. Close your eyes."

He did. Morgan lowered one of her prize dirks onto his palm. The instant spark when her fingers touched the pad of his palm frightened and appalled her as she snapped her hand back. So did the frown line across his forehead.

"What did you do?" he asked. "Make lightning with your blade?"

He felt it, too? Morgan swallowed the increased moisture in her mouth. It always happened when she was close to him, and it wasn't pleasant. Well, maybe it was, but it was dangerous.

"I did naught. It was the blade," she whispered.

"Your blade has the touch of a blacksmith's hammer to it, then. How did you do that?"

"Will you hush, and feel, as I've asked?"

"What am I feeling for now?"

Morgan rolled her eyes. "The weight! Feel the difference?

My blade is of an exact weight all along the shaft. No end is heavier, no end lighter. Do you feel it?"

"The shaft?" His fingers were rolling the blade over his thumb, keeping it flat to avoid slicing, and his voice had lowered.

Morgan felt herself blush but kept her gaze steady. "Are you finished playing with me?" she asked.

"Playing?"

"You turn everything into a discussion of lust, and it's nothing but play. You need to be serious if you wish to learn this."

"Not lust," he answered, and his voice got so soft, she could barely hear it, ". . . but love."

Morgan picked up the blade before he could gain another breath, spun around and threw both knives into the dead-center of his target, where they quivered, making a clicking sound of blade against blade. She turned back to him. "I can put all twelve of my dirks any place I want them. I didn't learn that by playing at lust . . . or at love."

"You make it sound a filthy word."

"It is," she retorted.

"Who could have hurt you so, Morgan lad?"

The most horrible thing in the world was happening, and Morgan turned before Zander spotted it. His talk of love brought tears so close to the surface, she was caught up in an agony of stifling them so severe she could hear the blood pumping through her body. Tears were for women to cry; they certainly weren't for Morganna KilCreggar. They never had been. She'd lived her entire life, it seemed, just to kill the FitzHugh laird, and then she was ready to die. There wasn't a speck of room in that plan for anything feminine.

She walked stiffly over to pull the knives from the tree. "When you're ready to learn, I'll teach you," she replied.

"Fair enough. I may even gift you with another of your precious, balanced dirks, too. You show the same concentration when you learned stoning?"

"I taught myself stoning. I found out it was easier to tilt the sling to the side rather than arc it. It probably looks strange, but it's more accurate."

"Do you never take time to play, Morgan? Never?"

"I'm so deadly with an arrow, no one will challenge me. I can place it in an animal's eye from almost any distance, any season."

"I suppose that's my answer?" he asked.

"You asked me once how I was with a hand-axe. I wasn't truthful. Well, I was truthful, but I wasn't accurate."

"Play, Morgan?" he tried again.

"I said I rarely held them. That is true. I haven't much use for them. They're a difficult tool for hunting. Makes a blood-spill second only to a claymore."

"Morgan," he said, in what he probably thought was a threatening tone.

"I'm deadly with a hand-axe. I'm capable of dueling the English way. They call it fencing, although my swordsmanship is geared more for ending a battle, rather than dancing about and prolonging it, as they seem to wish. Spectacle. That's all they want. That, and blood."

He sighed, and this time it was loud. "I get the message, Morgan. You don't know how to play. You've spent your entire life turning yourself into a killing machine, and that doesn't leave much room for teasing, taunting or playing. I begin to see why I chose you to be my squire."

"You choose many to be your squire, it sounds. I was just the first on this journey. Martin the second. I assume we'll have more before we return to your structureless home, too."

"Didn't you figure it out, yet?" he asked.

She snorted. "Of course I did. You earn, take or force the poor crofter's children to come with you, serve you, become a part of your household and your life, and in so doing, you are gaining supporters throughout the countryside."

"Very good," he replied.

"Do you ever return them like you promise?"

"Most of the time they won't go. I swear."

"They won't?" she asked.

"Don't act so surprised, Morgan. I'm not an ogre. I'm a very lenient master. I've a large, warm house with no dearth of foodstuffs and other amenities, like tapestries and furniture. Most of those who serve me find it a comfortable lifestyle, unlike the one they had at their village. I can't get them to leave. I send messages to their folk to retrieve them, and when they come, they stay too, giving me more servants."

"No wonder your mother thinks you need structure. You do."

"I think I was needing someone like you, Morgan."

Her heart stopped. If the sun had been shedding any amount of light, everything she was forcing herself not to think about was probably written all over her face. She couldn't even speak.

"I mean, it just occurred to me. I don't know why. You're different, and I can't fathom it. I know I want you near me, Morgan. I forced you to be with me because I somehow knew I needed you. I felt it the moment you touched me on that battlefield, and I feel it now. Stranger still, I'm not alone. You need me, too, if only to show you a little play."

The moisture in her mouth choked her when she tried to swallow. Then, she was coughing it out. He smacked her on the back and almost sent her to her knees with the force of his blows.

All of which brought the rest of his entourage into the clearing. Morgan responded to Sheila's barely-clad form with the most male reaction she could manage. She ran from it.

Chapter 7

Less than two weeks later, Zander's band had grown by six lasses and nine lads, and Morgan had to use more arrows and, consequently, more time to pull down enough meat to feed them and have leftover to barter with. She took four arrows this time, nodded to the grouping of young, sullen-looking men and started out. It gave her pause when one gestured toward her and turned to the others.

"You're going to have trouble with that one," she told Zander, since he'd accompanied her, treading loudly enough to alert any game.

"You see into the future, too?" he asked.

Morgan slid an eye sideways at him. He was wearing a kilt today, no shawl, and no *feile-breacan*. His upper body was clothed in thin, woven flax, and with the mounting rain, it was plastered to every bit of his physique. She looked up and caught his eye.

"He angers at my expertise and the fact that Sheila turned him down last eve," she replied.

"She turns everyone down, Morgan. She only has eyes for you. When are you going to do something about it?"

Morgan stopped and held up her hand. "You gaming or talking? We can't do both."

Zander dropped to a whisper. "Sheila offered herself to me not two nights ago, you ken?"

Morgan's eyes flared before she could hide them, and

she felt, rather than saw, his amusement. "You dinna' take her?" she asked.

"I told her I'd been warned away by you."

Morgan frowned. "That explains my sweetcakes," she said finally.

"She's trying an age-old recipe, lad."

"Sweetcakes?"

"Nay, food. No lad your age can resist good cooking. I'm not the only one to notice. You've put on a stone since we met. It's improved you, although you fill out in the face much farther, and I'll not be able to keep the wench, Bonnie, away from you."

He was referring to his latest maiden, who had been named in a fit of optimism. Her face resembled a flat pancake with a berry for a nose. Morgan smirked. "Bonnie?" she asked.

"Aye, Bonnie. All the lasses would welcome you to their beds, and how do you repay their yearnings? Ignore them. Nothing whets the appetite more. Should you unbend your morals enough to take one to your bed, you'll have a right wild romp, if I dinna' miss my guess."

Morgan decided to ignore him. It was easier than bantering about what he called love play. She also perked her ears. There was a sow with two of her yearlings within sighting distance, although if Zander continued his teasing, they'd not root about so calmly, awaiting death.

She held up her hand.

"You wish boar or elk today?" she asked quietly.

He looked at her. "Serious?" he whispered

"Pick," Morgan returned.

"Both." He grinned.

Morgan had four arrows. There was a huge elk behind them and atop the ridge. She'd sensed it more than seen it, by the behavior of the sow. She fitted an arrow, and pointed to the pigs. Zander followed her line of sight, squinting his eyes at it.

Morgan spun and had the elk before another breath. She had another arrow in place and pulled it on the sow with her return spin. The reaction was immediate, as the pig went down, grunting and squealing, and her yearlings took off in opposite directions. Morgan drew bead and had the farthest first. Beside her Zander was stiffening, and she'd meant him to. She'd left the boar that was intent on charging them for last. And she didn't use her arrow. She held the six dirks he'd given back to her in her hands. Methodically, she put them into his snout and eyes, until he came to an abrasively loud, squealing stop less than a body length from Zander.

Morgan was astride him, pulling her dirks and slitting his throat before his hooves ceased thrashing. Then, she was after the sow. Death throes had already finished in this one and Morgan slit its throat, too, to bleed it. Then, she was on the farthest one.

Her tongue clicked as she saw the broken arrow shaft. She wasn't that careless, usually. She generally brought all his arrows back to him. She reached to break it off. Zander stopped her and did it himself. Then he was rotating it with his fingers.

"You broke a shaft," he said, shaking his head at it.

"Sloppy aim," she replied with a shrug.

"I was beginning to think you perfect, Morgan."

He gave her a lopsided grin and she gulped. The slice on this pig's throat went deeper than she wanted, and she received a spurt of blood to her chest as a result, and more of it pumping onto her boots.

" 'Tis a good thing it's raining," Zander commented. "I'd hate to have to force you to bathe again."

"Only a fool thinks a burn is wetter than a good Scots day," she replied. "The rain washes me fine. Besides, I bathed last eve."

"I know."

"You . . . know?" Her voice caught and she only hoped he wouldn't notice it, or if he did, not comment on it.

She'd been lax with everything, but it had been a moonless, rain-filled eve, and she could bathe naked, let her hair fall about her, and pretend to be the nymph he claimed Sheila was. She could also leisurely paddle about the surface, experiencing the change in her breasts as they bobbed in the water, and wonder at why they sensitized with the change in size.

She could also stiffen with dread when he claimed that he knew about it. Her breathing was so shallow, it was painful.

"Everyone knows when you leave, Morgan, although none of us are brave enough to seek you out. I knew why, when you returned with a wet braid."

"No one knows anything about me," she answered, feeling the fear slide out of her spine and leave her trembling.

He shrugged. "True enough. Tell me something to change that. Tell me your surname, your clan, your lineage, why you're so damned good at everything. Anything."

"I've no hand for cooking," she replied.

He laughed. "True enough, but we've lasses a-plenty competing at that skill."

"They want you to notice them," Morgan said. She knew very well why. All the new girls mooned at Zander, to the point it was embarrassing. He knew also, if his wearing less and less clothing and making all the lads participate in sports like wrestling was any indication.

"Nay, lad, they want you to notice them."

"Me?" she asked.

"You bested me at push-ups last eve. I dinna' think a man existed that could do two-hundred-fifty of them, and you probably had more in you. And I called you scrawny."

Morgan beamed before she could help it.

"I'll not live that one down soon. If my brothers find out, I'll ne'er hear the end of it, either."

"Brothers?" She asked, careful to keep any emotion from her voice. *He has more than one brother?*

"Aye, my brothers. A heartier band you'll be hard-pressed to find, too."

"You've many of them, do you?"

"Aye. Five."

He has five brothers? Morgan closed her eyes. It was a good thing she hadn't vowed to kill all the FitzHughs, she decided.

"Tell me something, lad. How can you have such strength in such slender limbs that you best me?" For demonstration purposes, he rolled up his sleeve, giving her a very good look at well-hardened muscle and sinew. He had strength evident all over him. She looked away. He had acquitted himself well. Her arms had trembled for hours afterward when he hadn't ceased until they reached two-hundred, twenty push-ups.

"Appearances can be deceptive," she answered in a whisper.

"I agree there. Take that Sophie lass we picked up not two days ago."

"We picked up nothing. I won her. You touch her, and . . . ." She let the threat lie unfinished as she wiped her dirk on the wet grass and stood beside the pig to glare the intent.

Zander was unrolling his sleeve back into place. His hair was plastered to his head, and his midnight-blue eyes were sparkling like the surface of a starlit loch. Morgan had to look away.

"And you wonder at the havoc you create," he remarked.

She snorted the disbelief. "I create nothing of the sort."

"You warn me from every lass, and then leave them be, yourself? You don't call that havoc?"

"I call it ravishment."

Zander was trying to keep the smile from his lips, but wasn't succeeding well. "Lasses have lusts, too," he said, laying an arm across her shoulder like he had Martin's.

Morgan side-stepped from it. She knew her face was

flaming. "I've not said they don't. And I've not stopped any of them."

He considered her. She knew that he was, for the smile left his face and he had the frown lines across his forehead again. "'Tis true enough. You haven't threatened any of the lads. You'd probably allow any of my new servants to bed with any lass, except perhaps Sheila. 'Tis only me you warn off. Why is that?"

"I'd warn all. The others have na' pushed it, though."

"And you sleep too soundly," was his answer.

Morgan stared at him. She'd taken a spot in the midst of each camp, lying beside the fire so she could defend virtue should it be warranted, and now he was telling her it was for naught?

Then, he laughed and gave her a shove. "You're always so serious, Morgan lad. My horse has more humor."

Morgan glared across at him.

"And we'd best not be gone too long. The camp needs its leader."

"Leader? You?"

"I bested you last eve, didn't I?"

"At arm-wrestle only, and that because I'd just taken down Martin. I can take you at every other contest," she declared.

"What if I declare the contest one of love?"

Morgan gasped. "I'll not take that contest," she replied finally.

"No courage?" he asked.

"Nay," she replied, stepping back as he walked toward her. "No experience. I would na' know the first thing about it."

"You know more than the first thing, Morgan. I would venture a guess you'd be expert at it, too."

She gasped. "You jest, and I dinna' like it."

"I am serious, Morgan lad, and if you wish to take me up on it, I'll be ready."

"I'll not accept a challenge like that!"

"Why not? Faint of heart?"

"Nay. Only thinking it stupid. And you forget too easily. You already have a win. I canna' take you at arm-wrestle. You proved that last eve."

"Only because, as you already pointed out, you'd already wrestled Martin, and before that Seth and Dugan and even big Ira. You forced the issue."

"Forced it?" she gasped again.

"I had to best you, lad. You took down all the other lads. You were gaining a swelled head and creating havoc in my camp."

"If there's any havoc in your camp, 'tis not of my doing, but your own." The havoc he kept referring to was merely leaving lusty young men and women together with no structure. No wonder his mother moaned about it to him. They needed a leader, and he left them to their own devices. That was his havoc. "I've nothing to do with it."

"You best every other male there and then refuse to toss a wench who lays it in your lap. That is havoc of the worst kind. It's lust-borne havoc. I've suffered it myself."

Morgan blushed as pink as the rain-diluted blood on her blouse and band of plaid across her chest. She hadn't asked Sophie to plant herself on her lap and plaster a wet kiss to her face, nor had she desired the feel of the girl's breasts rubbing along her shoulder. That was the last thing she'd asked for. In fact, Morgan still felt complete mortification at the recollection. Sophie was a brazen lass. She was also experienced, and had hands that wanted to go too many places. Morgan had just finished besting Zander at push-ups and had to find the strength to hold the girl off her and it hadn't been the least bit amusing. None of the others looked like they thought so, either. Now, Zander was claiming that Morgan created lust-borne havoc, and he suffered it, too? It was ridiculous. The entire conversation was beginning to be so.

"I've done nothing," she replied finally.

"The girls won't even look at the others. They barely tolerate me. They all want the handsome, young, great 'god of the hunt' named Morgan, to look their way. And when he does na', they are left to wonder at the why, and try to out-pretty each other. And that's just the lasses."

"The great god of the *what*?" she choked out.

"Have you no idea what you are, and how you are perceived?"

"I'm nothing and no one," she answered.

He rolled his eyes. "You're amazing at anything you try. If you ever take up cooking, there won't be a palate or belly that's safe for leagues. It's not easy to compete against you."

"I don't compete because I want to. You make me do it to get my dirks back."

"I'm not talking about the fairs. I'm talking camp. Zander FitzHugh's camp, and the havoc Morgan, of no-clan and no-name, creates within it."

She wasn't blushing anymore. She was pale. She'd never been around peers her age, and what he was describing seemed to fit how the girls had been acting.

"And the lads?" she asked, finally.

"They'll most likely lay a trap for you. One can't take you, but together they can."

"They'll gang together against me? Why?"

"Because nobody likes perfection that can't be besmirched. You shouldn't strive so for it."

Morgan looked down at her blood-covered boots and FitzHugh plaid. "I'll leave, then," she finally said.

He snorted at that answer. "I'll be sending them all away to my home ahead of me, a-fore that happens. You owe me for the plaid, remember?"

"How much do you want for it? How many deer? How many boar? How many game birds?"

"If I give you a figure, you'll fill it?"

She nodded.

"What if I need a constant supply, not all at once?"

"How many per season? I'll get them for you."

"You show so little emotion, Morgan. It's interesting, and a bit daunting, I must admit. I should na' puzzle the reason, but I do."

"All about you is emotion, FitzHugh. Your camp reeks of it. And you wish me to show more?"

"Nay, I wish you to show *some*. Just a hint would do. It might make you more human."

"I show emotion," she countered. "I flush. You've seen it."

He folded his arms and looked across at her like they had nothing else to do all day except debate her state. She noticed when he lifted one foot to the pig's back, lifting his kilt enough to show his knees. Morgan glanced there and frowned more.

"You just took down three pigs, slit their throats while one was still in the death throes, and you showed nothing. Not even exhilaration at the hunt, or the kill. That is worrisome."

"I took down three pigs *and* a bull elk," she replied stiffly.

"Death means little to you. Does life have the same value?"

"Everything that lives dies. You wish me to lament that?"

"You don't fear death, then?"

She shrugged. "When it comes, I'll welcome it," she replied.

"You don't worry over the pain involved?"

"Pain means nothing to me."

"You've not had it then. Blades, for one. You ever suffer one?"

Morgan rolled up a sleeve, displaying a jagged scar. "I suffered."

"Did you get that learning your skill?"

"Nay. I got it from a challenger."

"That what it takes to make you lose?"

"What loss?" Morgan replied. "I have two arms."

"There is no amount of meat that you can provide that I

will accept to release you, Morgan of no-clan and no-name. None."

"Why?" she asked.

"You're inhuman and I'm going to change that. I don't know how, I don't even question the why, but I know I'm going to."

"I'll na' change for you," she answered.

"You're also a braggart."

"A braggart? Me? I've said nothing I canna' do."

"You said I had a choice of the pigs or an elk. I see no elk."

Morgan looked across at him and tossed her head. "You were na' looking, then, and you move too slowly. Follow me."

He whistled at the size of it when they came on it. The death hadn't come easily, although Morgan had pegged it through the eye as was her usual way. The beast had kicked clods of sod all about and rearranged the hillside with his hooves. Morgan looked at it dispassionately for a moment, then knelt to slit its throat. She felt Zander's eyes on her the entire time.

And she was flushing.

Chapter 8

Zander helped her dress out and quarter the elk before he left to get his horse. Morgan watched him walk off, a yearling pig draped across his shoulder and a jaunty flip to his kilt. He had a well-muscled backside, if the sway of his kilt was any indication, and she already knew the extent of his masculinity on the front of him.

Morgan's face flamed. He was an attractive, virile man, and he'd not found a woman to release himself on, or with, since she'd met him. That couldn't be normal, and for some reason, it was bothersome, too. She didn't dare wonder at the why.

She lay on her belly amidst the gore of her kill and waited for him to return. The smell of the animal's blood hung heavy in the rain-filled air, but it didn't occupy enough of her senses to think on it. It was the same as any clansman-strewn battlefield. Things lived . . . then they died. If this great bull wasn't put on earth to grow to maturity, rut, procreate and then die to fill a man's stomach, what was he put there for?

She looked over at the sightless eye, where Zander had already pulled the arrow out. The elk's rack was the largest she'd ever taken. Heavily pointed and bowl-shaped, with a size to match. There was enough meat to feed them through most of a month. It was a great beast. Now, it was a great, dead beast.

She rolled over and looked up, through the tunnel the rain-drops created, at the gray-filled sky, blinking whenever a drop landed near her eye. She'd never wanted attention. If she'd known, she'd have fought it. She didn't want lasses panting for her, nor lads plotting against her. She wanted to fulfill her destiny, lay on the ground, close her eyes and wait for the oblivion of a good death. That's what she wanted, what she'd always wanted.

So, why was it bothersome what Zander had said? Why did the man say so much, anyway? What was it to him if Morgan, of no-clan and no-name, cared about death, or life? The man made no sense. He was also taking up too many of her thoughts. More frightening, he was taking up more of her dreams. She wondered what that meant.

He had strong hands. Hands that had gripped hers last eve and left her no doubt who would be the victor of their arm-wrestle. He had very handsome features, too. She'd thought so when they first met, and nothing was changing that impression. He kept using his dirk to scrape the stubble from his chin, showing off the cleft, the strong jaw, the high cheekbones. Why, if she were a lass who cared for such things, she'd think him the most handsome man birthed.

She sighed.

"Day-dreaming atop blood? That is how I envisioned you, too. Oh Morgan, what am I to do with you, lad?"

She was up before he finished, letting the rain soak away the elk's leavings and watching him carefully. She hadn't heard him approach, and he had his horse with him. Morgan eyed the animal, and wondered at its newly acquired stealth.

"Or, perchance you were asleep?" he asked, jovially.

"I was neither. Your steed tip-toes through heather, and you made little sound yourself."

He shook his head. "We startled every bird for yards. Face it, Morgan lad. You're making up for lost sleep."

"Why would I be losing sleep?"

"Trying to protect the lasses' virtue, is my best guess. Secondly, I'd have to say that you're afraid."

Her eyes widened. "Afraid of what?" she asked.

"Dreaming," he replied.

She had to look away, then she looked down, and then she sucked in the fear at the sight of every woman's curse. Morgan went to her knees on the blood-soaked sod and put her head in her hands. She was having her woman-time? *Now?*

"Find a burn and cleanse yourself. I'll load Morgan. He's used to the smell, but he won't like it all over you, too."

Morgan fled. She was shaking before she plunged into the burn, soaking herself further than any rain could have. She had to hack away part of her under-tunic to use, and the loin-wrap Zander had devised was heaven-sent, too. She hadn't been cursed for almost a year, and now it had to come? She wondered why. She'd done nothing different, except eat, and lay about more.

She wondered if that were the cause, but had none to ask it of. If any of Zander's other lasses suffered their time, it had been in secret. It should be in secret. It was another secret for her to keep, and she couldn't even remember how long it was supposed to curse her for. It shouldn't happen. The last thing she wanted was a reminder of her gender. She wasn't going to allow herself to be a woman. She didn't have the time or the inclination. She was exactly what Zander called her, a killing machine.

There was a set look to her shoulders and a sneer on her mouth when she rejoined him.

"Well, you look none the worse for your bath. Slightly wetter, less blood-covered. What is it?"

"Nothing," she replied viciously.

He lifted his eyebrows but said nothing. He had all the meat loaded and the reins in his hand. As he always taunted, she had missed the work and returned for the benefit.

She followed him back, attempting to keep her eyes anywhere but on the width of his shoulders, or on the muscles of his back where the shirt was plastered to him, or on his legs, or where the back of his kilt seemed to caress each step, and especially from the back of his head, where damp, curling brown hair started before it fell over the width of his shoulders . . . reaching the middle of his back . . . .

Morgan swallowed the instant excess moisture and rolled her eyes, stopping her mental listing of his attributes. As if he knew of her skittishness, he started the tuneless whistle he was always making. Then, she had to try to ignore the great hulk of him, and the noise he was making, too.

Killing his brother, the laird, had better be worth all the trouble, she told herself.

The camp was up, well up, and too quiet. Zander halted and Morgan ran into the back of him before she could help it. His hand came around his side to stop her, but she'd already moved away and was taking in the scene. Two of the new lads he'd acquired were facing off, a dirk in each hand and squatting low as they sliced toward each other.

Sophie's disheveled shift and the gratified look on her face told the story. It was obvious they were fighting over her, although if they'd think with their heads instead of their man organs, they'd know Sophie was available for any of them, or all of them. Morgan took it in with a glance, and had her six dirks in her hands before another move was made.

"Drop them," Zander said quietly.

One of them looked up, the other snarled and used the opportunity to slash at his opponent's lower arm. Morgan let her own knives fly and knocked all four dirks from their hands to the ground before anyone could catch their breath. There was a collective gasp. Morgan stepped in front of Zander, her final two dirks held between her thumb and forefingers, blades out. The lad named Collin started rubbing at one hand, while the bleeding one stared open-mouthed at her.

"The next two go where you least want them," she said.

Her announcement got her four hands raised and more admiring glances from the females Zander had peopled his

encampment with. Morgan stepped aside, allowing Zander
to pronounce the judgment, and wondering at her stupidity.
If his lads wanted to gang up on her, as Zander predicted,
then she'd just signed her own assault notice.

She looked askance at Zanier. He looked at her, then at
the two combatants. Morgan returned her gaze to Collin
and the other.

"We've leagues to go before we reach FitzHugh land,"
Zander spoke up. "Martin?"

"Aye?" The lad from their first fair spoke up.

"I want you to lead the menfolk to my house. I've told
you the direction?"

"Aye," Martin replied again.

Morgan stepped closer to Zander and got his glance
when she did so. She motioned with her eyes.

"You've a better plan?" he asked softly.

"You have enough servants already. True?"

He nodded.

"I'd gift them to the MacPhee lasses, then. They'll gain
strong backs and strong . . . uh, men, and you'll gain peace
from some properly grateful lads who won't have any time
left over for such nonsense as killing each other."

She watched his lips quirk. Then, he grinned. Next, he
was roaring with laughter. Morgan stepped away from him
and tried to join the trees beside them. The lads were
glaring hatred. She didn't have to ask what was in their
eyes. She knew.

"Can you write?" Zander was looking at her.

"Only with a blade, My Lord," she answered evenly.

Zander looked disbelieving for a moment, then turned
to his other followers. "Can any among you write, then?"

"Aye." Martin was the one answering. "I can write if
you've ink and parchment."

"I've both. Martin? Scribe me a note to sign. I've decided
your punishment, lads."

"What is it to be?" Collin asked.

"Yea, what is it the lad Morgan would have of us?"

Zander frowned. " 'Tis the lad Morgan who thought of it, but you'll not find it onerous. Unless, of course, you've nothing a-tween your legs. Don't write that, Martin."

"What does that mean?"

Morgan recognized the male bravado behind Collin's tone, and she flushed as he glared at her.

"Only that Morgan has remembered where four lusty lasses reside. They happen to cook as well as, if not better than, my own lasses here. The MacPhee ladies have a dearth of menfolk to till their soil, provide their game and warm their beds. I've decided to gift them with your indenture for the year. Write that last down, Martin."

Both young men looked stunned for a moment. Then, they started grinning, too.

"Don't think it isn't punishment, lads. I sincerely doubt, once you meet the MacPhee lasses and begin your service, that you'll be walking anytime soon. In fact, I guarantee it. Martin?"

"Aye?"

"You know the MacPhees?"

"Everyone knows the lasses." He was grinning, too.

"See that our friends, Collin and Seth here, reach them safely, and then return to me. I'll be near Chidester's Quarry. You know the spot?"

"Aye," he replied again.

"Get walking, then. 'Tis a three day walk, maybe four. Morgan? Come with me."

He strode through the center of the group, picked up the entwined dirks and kept walking, Morgan at his heels. When they were at his tent, he opened the flap and gestured with his head for her to enter.

As soon as the flap settled, the camp started making sound again. Morgan heard it through the weave of his tent material.

"Have you no idea of your foolishness?" He was pulling

her dirks from the handles of the other ones and handing them to her, and he wasn't being gentle. His arms were rippling with every movement, as were his shoulders and his chest, and . . . .

Morgan very nearly groaned at her own thoughts as she watched, unconsciously receiving the dirks he held out to her. She didn't even blink.

"Now, there's no stopping them. Dinna' you ever think of missing?"

"Missing?" she echoed, taking the last dirk and holding it. "Missing?"

"Aye, missing. Is it such a foreign idea?"

"What should I aim for, then?"

He rolled his head upward, then back. "You should na' aim for anything. You should miss."

"But I've never thrown without an aim! I may send a knife flying into a vital part if I'm not aiming."

"Pick a stone behind, then. Pick a blade of grass, pick a spot of sunlight on the damned dirt!"

Morgan was still looking at him, unblinking. "My talent is given to me from God," she whispered. "I dinna' ask for it, I dinna' deserve it, I certainly dinna' enjoy it, but it's a God-given thing. I canna' turn away from that."

"God does na' give gifts of death."

"I've na' killed anyone . . . yet," she replied.

"That's just it. Yet. You're a killing machine, without a bit of remorse. It's inhuman, and it's frightening. It's also turning you into a demigod everywhere we go. The lads hate you for it. The lasses swoon over you. I don't even know what to make of you."

His voice was calling to every bit of her that was female, and Morgan fought it before she realized she was losing. She should have known she'd lose. "I feel remorse," she whispered.

He looked up at that. Morgan's eyes were awash with tears and she watched him stare. She didn't dare blink.

Something was passing between them, too, and her eyes widened when she felt it.

"You'll make your bed in here. With me. It's not up for argument, either."

He was angrier than before, if the clipped tone of his words was any indication.

"I refuse," she answered.

"It's not open for refusal. I canna' keep you safe, and I will na' wake to find your throat slit."

"I can protect myself," she answered, blinking the tears into existence down her cheeks.

"No, you canna'. You sleep too deeply. And with too many dreams, if your tossing is any indication."

She raised her hands up and slashed them across her face, to wipe the moisture away. "I dinna'," she finally answered. Then, she lowered her arms.

"You do. I've watched you."

He watched me? she wondered, catching a breath and holding it so tightly, that it burned.

"When I canna' sleep, I like to stare into a fire. You sleep close enough to it, you should be burned. But you're not, are you, Morgan, of no-clan and no-name? You're never burned. Only those about you are."

"No one is ever about me," she replied.

"That's probably true. You would na' let them. They're burned, nonetheless. Trust me."

Morgan frowned. He wasn't making sense. "I canna' sleep here, even if you order it so."

"You'll not argue further, or I'll tie you to my bed. Will your swooning group of followers appreciate that, d'you think?"

"I have no followers," Morgan protested.

"You give the word, there's not a lass out there that wouldn't follow you. Anywhere. Anytime. Most of my lads, too. No followers, he says, like it's not a God-given fact." He wasn't looking at her, he was studying his fingernails.

Morgan watched him. "Were I as gifted with an aim as you are, I'd have legions of followers, and all aiming for the heart of every Sassenach bastard on the face of the earth. But, since I am na' . . . ." He stopped and sighed, "I must make do with the use of yours."

"I still will na' bed in here with you."

"Why do you argue, when I've said it's not open for such? I'll brook no argument, and I'll use brute strength to make it so. Don't force it. Neither of us will enjoy it."

"But I sleep on the ground. I am used to that. A tent is too fine for the likes of me."

"There's ground beneath the rugs. You can have the floor. I'd as lief give you your freedom as gift you with my cot. What do you take me for, a fool?"

"Nay," she replied. "You are my master, but a fool? Nay."

"You're mistaken, lad, now that I think on it." He had ceased staring at his hands and put the focus of that midnight-blue gaze on her. Morgan wasn't prepared for it, and probably showed it. "I'm the basest fool. I only hope I don't get worse burned. There's a hell for what I desire and need right now. You ken?"

Morgan squinted her eyes before lifting her shoulders. She hadn't the smallest notion what he was talking of. It probably showed. "May I leave now? I've a hide to scrape, and a boar to prepare for your next fair."

"Aye. Prepare it nice and sweet, and then weaken it to the point of no return. That's what I like about you, Morgan lad. You truss up your victims and get them ready for slaughter, and they don't even know it's happening."

"I don't think I ken to you," she said.

"Thank God," he replied. "I've been thinking, too. About what you said."

Morgan waited. She'd said so much, it could be anything.

"I do have too many servants already, and no taste for correcting them and making them obey. We'll ask for something different this time."

"You canna'," she replied.

"Why not?"

"There is nothing that will guarantee you fealty like taking their offspring. You said it yourself, and it's true. I've watched. Everything you said is true."

"What should I do, then?"

Morgan shrugged. "You've brothers and parents? Gift some servants to them. You'll need to make certain of their loyalty a-fore that, though."

"My brothers are all loyal!"

Morgan shoved out the amusement on one huff of air. "Make certain of the servant's loyalty, na' your brothers'."

"We could use more cloth, though. And more flour."

"Flowers? Whatever for?" Morgan asked, totally mystified.

"Not flowers, flour. Wheat flour. What do you ken the bread we eat is made from? Air?"

"Trade the boar for it, like last time."

"You've an answer to everything, don't you, Morgan lad?"

"Your problems are small, and therefore easily solved," she answered.

He took a step toward her and let those midnight-blue eyes bore into her. Morgan was afraid to breathe.

"If only that were true," he whispered, and took another step toward her.

Morgan began backing up. Then, she was unconsciously holding the dirks out. He didn't so much as glance that way. He didn't move his gaze from hers.

"You've a taste of the forbidden about you, and not one inkling of it." He was whispering the words so softly, Morgan didn't think she'd heard them right. She didn't think she was supposed to hear them, either.

Her eyes were wide, her breath stolen, and her back against a tent pole. She was terrified. He snarled, and spun from her. He reached the other side of his tent in two steps.

"You may go," he said.

Morgan gulped, then began inching her way to the door flap. The man wasn't making any sense. He was making every bit of her body sing with something akin to the anticipation she felt whenever a challenge was made, and starting a tremor not unlike the flush of victory when she hit her mark. He was too immense for her.

"You know something else, Morgan lad?"

She stopped at the tent flap.

"You have horrible dreams."

Chapter 9

What followed were four of the worst days of Morgan's life, and even worse nights. It was the same for anyone in Zander FitzHugh's proximity and it began the morning after she started staying in his tent.

Before the sun had thought of appearing that day, Zander was awakening her, and not by any previous method, either. He simply put the bulk of his foot beneath her ribcage and kicked her right out the door flap. Morgan rolled to her feet, dusting herself off and choking with the surprise and the temperature. Her *feile-breacan* was askew, too, and he snarled at her over it, before pointing down his arm at her.

"I'll not listen to your snoring another moment. I'll find the method for tiring you out! Now, move!"

So saying, he'd shoved her to an open field, and put her through such a rigorous series of exercises and movements that sweat was literally pouring off both of them. He matched her push-up for push-up and when they reached two-hundred, he had her on her feet doing squats and thrusts with either leg from a crouch position. When that didn't suit him fully, he had them go from knees to feet, back to knees. Then, to feet again, jumping, falling, jumping, falling. Then he had her working with stones. Not small stones, either, large boulders that she was required to lift over her head, hold and then swing. The first one he chose was so heavy, when Morgan went to swing it, she went with it, making Zander more furious.

He didn't slacken when she begged a moment to clear her innards. He simply glared at her, waved his hand and gave her exactly to the count of ten to do what needed doing in the bushes.

Then, he was tossing her in the small loch, since she refused to disrobe for him, and while she was swimming with the burden of wet wool and full boots, he was taking off every stitch before diving in himself. Morgan was out of the water before he broke the surface, and was wringing out her plaid, then her shirts, and then her braid.

"You have a problem serving me, squire?" he'd snarled, when she ignored him.

Morgan was on her feet and handing him his clothing, piece by piece, and she was doing her absolute best to see none of him when the sky was lightening yellowish-red and he had a body made for running her eyes over.

He got angered over that, too, and told her to find a wench to stare at, and Morgan flushed. Then, he was off at a fierce, bone-jarring pace back to camp. His temperament didn't improve, though. He simply turned it on anyone in his way. He told Sheila to cease putting good oats through the torment of her gruel, he flung one of Amelia's biscuits to the ground, told her if they were going to be the consistency of stones, they might as well be one, and called his lads together for what turned into a marathon race.

Morgan had more than one cramp to her belly before they reached camp, but she was only one of two to stay with him. The others had long ago lost the ability to keep pace, and were left to wander in as they might.

Zander put his midnight-blue gaze about camp, told the wenches their laziness wouldn't be tolerated much longer, grabbed a huge slice of roasting boar meat and yelled for the lass, Heather, to service him in his tent.

Morgan's eyes were as wide as anyone's as Heather jumped to her feet and followed him into the tent. She was out moments later, however, and she wasn't happy about it.

No one said a word. Then Zander tossed open the flap and yelled for Morgan. He hadn't lost a bit of stridency in his orator's voice, either. The entire forest jumped at the sound of her name, not just Morgan.

He sneered at her, told her to cease being an irritant and get her backside to sleep. Otherwise, she'd pay for it with the next day's exercise. Morgan had just closed her eyes when he had her suspended by her belt and was hauling her out of the tent to dump her on a log in front of everyone.

"Eat something first," he growled, and stomped back into his enclosure.

He gave her exactly what time it took to put a dirk into the meat and start carving before he was bellowing her name again. Morgan ripped off what she could, and was shoving it into her mouth as she went back into the tent.

The second and third and fourth day had the same pattern to them, although as far as she could tell, he wasn't even sleeping. He was cursing her, cursing the tent, cursing every lazy Sassenach on the face of Scotland, and drinking heavily. She tried putting her hands over her ears beneath her kilt, but that just seemed to make him more angry when he pulled her awake the second morn and saw her position.

She paid for it with another series of exercise, another brutal run, and then she had to practice swordplay with him until it felt as though her arms might fall off, and all that was before the fourth night.

She'd barely been kicked out of his tent for the second time and was rubbing the sore spot on her left buttock, where she'd landed, when he was out again, bellowing for her to cease her lazing about and follow him. Morgan was on his heels and that made him angry, too. He turned, barked at her for being his shadow, and then cursing her for being so slow to answer his demands.

He wanted Morgan, the horse, saddled, and he was going into the village. He gave Martin less than the count of ten to get it finished, despite Morgan's assertion that it couldn't be done.

"When I need your words, I'll ask for them, Morgan. Time is up, Martin."

Morgan met Martin's eye, and his look of empathy, and then she was tossed up onto Morgan, the horse, by a less-than-gentle hand. She bent forward over the saddle with the momentum, and had barely lifted her head back up when Zander planted himself into the saddle in front of her.

"Hold to the saddle or fall off, Morgan lad. We're late as it is."

Late for what? she wondered, and then she ceased thinking, as the horse broke into a gallop, rapidly enough to fling her off. She wasn't holding to the saddle, either; she had both arms wrapped about Zander, and linked together at his belly. He had more muscles in his stomach that any other she'd ever seen, and they felt even more rigid and strong beneath the skin of her forearms and wrists. Morgan put her cheek against his back and tried to ignore how it felt.

He pried her arms off of him as they approached the torch-bedecked village, and he flung them from him as if they were filthy. Morgan hung her head, but knew enough to cling to his saddle. He walked his horse behind the crofts and looped back to the end of a street. Then he took them down an offal-filled alleyway to a dark, unwelcoming croft.

He was off the horse and pulling her with him by her collar, and marching around to the door before Morgan had a chance to find the ground. She ran alongside him in a tip-toe sort of fashion until they reached the stoop and he let her down a fraction. Then, he lifted his fist, and she saw that it was white-knuckled and shaking. He sucked in a breath before he knocked with a quiet, soft touch.

"Who is it?"

The melodious voice belonged to a woman so closely resembling Morgan's kin, the whore, that she gasped. The woman had breasts that were ripe and falling over the top of her dress to the point the pink part surrounding her nipples was showing. She'd tied her belt high on her ribcage to get the effect, too. She had black lines encircling her eyes, her straggly-looking hair brushed into a cloud about her and the reddest lips Morgan had ever seen.

Morgan's mouth fell open and she stared.

"I only serve one gent at a time, lover man," she said, motioning to Morgan.

Zander let go of her collar, and Morgan swayed at the shove he gave her at the same time. She knew what he was doing there, now. He wasn't going to take a woman from his camp. He was going to take a woman that gave to any man. He was going to service a harlot, or she was going to service him. Morgan didn't know anything about it, except that the place where her shirt's button placket ended on her breast was one huge, ceaseless, pumping ball of hurt.

"You move, and I'll hunt you down and cut every hair off your head," Zander leaned to whisper. "You ken me, lad?"

She nodded and sat.

The door closed beside her, releasing a heavy, perfumy sort of odor into the air, and Morgan had to shut her eyes to staunch the instant film of tears. If Zander had a woman, what was it to her? He was a man, and he'd told her women were for the taking. She definitely wasn't interested enough to care. She didn't want anything to do with him. He was her ticket to the FitzHugh laird. That's all he was. That's all he would ever be.

The sound of laughter was followed by the woman's murmur of awe. Morgan put her hands to her temples and held them there. The ball of ache in her breast wasn't easing, either. It was growing into a fire-like agony. She heard the swish of what was probably clothing falling.

The whore should have built her croft better. That way Morgan wouldn't have to sit on the front stoop and hear everything that was happening. She should have made her walls of mud-brick, rather than straw and peat.

"Oooh, lover-man. That's a sight many a woman would give her fortune to see, let alone feel. I know just where . . . ."

Morgan sucked in breath, shoved it out, sucked it back in, shoved it back out, pounded her fists at her temples, and nothing was stopping the sobs. They were tearing through her, climbing her spine to come over her head, and her eyes were filling with the stupid tears, and all because the man she'd sworn to hate was having relations with another woman?

What sort of insanity was that?

"Try again, wench, and this time use your hands!"

Morgan's hands moved from her temples to her mouth, and she sucked both hands full of fingers into her mouth to make certain no sound escaped. If she was sobbing her heart out on a whore's front stoop, the least she could do was keep it to herself.

" 'Tis hard to pump life into a lifeless thing like that, dearie."

The whore's laughter followed her words and Morgan would have given anything not to have to listen. She was nearly ready to run as far and as fast away from this as she could, and to blazes with her hair, when Zander's voice came again, this time surlier and angrier than she'd heard it all week.

"Perhaps I like my wenches with a little less flesh and a little less experience. Try again. This time use your mouth."

Everything stopped for Morgan, and she knew shock was what was happening to her. She heard the sounds of slurping, gasping and then a kissing-type of noise, and she didn't even know what a kiss was supposed to sound like. Then she heard nothing for so long, she had to let the held-in breath out. She was afraid to put meaning to anything. She was afraid of her emotions, and she had every right to be. So far, she was exhibiting every bit of a jealous woman's reaction. She couldn't believe it. Zander FitzHugh was a rutting, lusty male, a man who ordered a woman to do something so horrid he had to pay her to do it for him. He wasn't worth the time for Morganna KilCreggar to cry over him, and she told herself she wasn't crying.

She never cried, leastways over a bit of dung like a FitzHugh. She certainly wasn't bemoaning Zander's pleasure. He was free to get it anywhere and with anyone he wished, just as long as it wasn't with her.

She pulled her hands out of her mouth and wiped at the drool and tear-mixture that had started to slide down her arms. She mopped at her face with the end of her kilt, and then she tried to act like nothing out of the ordinary had occurred.

"Blast you, woman! Save your efforts. I have better things to do than await you."

"Await me, he says," the whore-woman remarked, sounding a little insulted. "I've ridden men for days, my fine, perfectly-sized gent. I just wish you'd come to me a-fore your lass stole your desire and turned it against you."

"'Twas no lass," Morgan heard Zander grumble. "Heave off and take payment. I feel worse than when I arrived, no thanks to you."

The woman laughed again. Morgan heard more sounds that could be clothing, and then light was streaming out the door and over her. She averted her face. She had no idea what the results of weeping were, but she certainly didn't want Zander seeing any of it.

"What, by all the saints, do you think you are doing sitting there?"

"You ordered me to—"

"Cease!"

He stopped her explanation with the order, accompanied with a bellow of rage, and he followed that up by coiling a fist about her upper arm so strongly, she knew she was bruising. Then he marched her back to Morgan, the horse, and this time he threw her so viciously, she almost went over the horse's head before gaining her seat.

"And cease acting so fragile and lost. Hold to the saddle

this time. You touch me, and I may not be able to stop what I do."

Morgan held to the saddle with every bit of strength she had. She also had to cling to the horse's flank with every muscle at her disposal, and she would rot in Hell before she touched Zander. He could save his threats for those who cared. She didn't. She sniffed, smelled the fresh, rain-soaked scent of heather, and tried to stop every emotion. She'd rather be a killing machine.

No one was about when they returned, and that was strange. It hadn't felt like they'd been gone so long. She saw the banked fire, the sleeping shapes of two lads next to it, and knew the truth. They were well into the night, and if Zander was intent on her exercise in the morning, she'd better get as much rest as she could, and she'd better get it as quickly as possible.

Zander hadn't said a word. He walked the horse around the tents and into the roped-off affair that held him.

"Get off," he said.

She slid off the right side, weaving a bit once she landed.

"Unsaddle and curry my horse," he said next as he dismounted on the opposite side and glared at her over the horse's back.

She nodded, uncinched the saddle strap and pulled it off.

"Faster," he demanded.

Morgan flung it atop a tree stump, and pulled the curry comb from its hook. She started at the horse's neck, and then got to his foam-flecked sides. She hadn't realized they had ridden him this hard. Steam was rising from the animal as she wiped, and she shivered in the same chill.

"I've not got all night," Zander spoke again, his voice as disembodied and harsh as the night.

Morgan renewed her efforts, covering Morgan, the horse's, other side as quickly as possible. Then, she re-hung the comb and awaited her next instructions.

"You sleep with me. You ken?"

She looked toward where he was standing, although all she could see was a bit of skin and black holes where his eyes were. She nodded.

"Then cease delaying, and get to the tent. Turn down my cot and assist me from my kilt. Be a good squire, for a change. That's why I keep you."

Assist him? she wondered, in growing panic. *Now?*

He reached out to grip her shoulder and Morgan winced at the pressure he put on her collarbone. He pulled her a step toward him, then another, until she was standing close enough to feel his breath on her nose.

"Are you my squire, Morgan?" he asked softly.

She nodded.

"Do you like men?"

Morgan stiffened to her toes, then she snarled. "Of all the disgusting questions! I detest men! All men. Every man."

"Do you detest me?"

"You're a man, are na' you? Now, unhand me, and allow me to serve you, My Lord. We've na' got much left of the night to rest if you are intent on the exercises on the morrow. I canna' seek my own rest until I've seen you a-bed, now can I?"

He groaned and lifted his hand.

"Thank you, Morgan," he whispered, and turned her about to face the tent. He wasn't following her when she got there, either, and after waiting what seemed hours for him, she lay on the floor and slept.

Chapter 10

He woke her differently this time. Morgan saw him sitting on the floor watching her when she started awake, her face covered with tears and her heart hammering. She blinked at him, watched him smile, and then she collapsed back onto the dirt. The second time, she opened her eyes, and he was still sitting there, cross-legged and massive, as though he'd been there all night.

"Are you ready to exercise?" he asked, when all she did was blink, rub both fists into her eyes and blink again.

"Exercise?" she asked.

He shrugged. "Of a sort. Bring your knives. I stopped you from showing me how you use them. I could use another lesson, I think."

Morgan didn't know what to think of this new mood, so she thought nothing, and told herself to respond the same way. She simply rose, shook her *feile-breacan* out, put her braid down the back of her shirt, donned her boots and followed him.

The sun wasn't out yet, but that wasn't strange for Zander FitzHugh. The man was a slave-master with his regimen. It was surprising that he only made Morgan and himself follow it, though. She would have wondered why, but she was telling herself not to think, and her mind felt too clogged with wool to puzzle it through, anyway.

They'd been out late, and while it was making every muscle in her body angry at her, he seemed not to notice.

He had lines she'd never seen before etched onto his cheeks and his forehead, though. She wondered if he'd slept in a position that created them, and told herself not to think about it. She wasn't going to think of anything. She was simply going to endure whatever she had to, until she got her revenge. Then, she was going to cease existing. Thinking of Zander FitzHugh was a waste of time.

Unfortunately, he was too immense and vibrant and vital to ignore. Her hands told her as much when he stopped at a stand of trees and pointed at a target he'd carved. Morgan looked at it. It wasn't but ten, maybe twelve paces away. It was child's play.

"Can you hit that?" he asked.

"In my sleep," she replied, reaching for a dirk. She stood and, without taking any time, pegged the center.

"How do you do that, with that accuracy, and that lack of emotion? I would give anything for that."

"You throw?" she asked, instead.

He shrugged. "I managed to gain myself several servants before I met you. I'm fair at it."

"Toss your knife," she replied.

He stood, took two pumping motions over his shoulder and let fly his own dirk. It landed beside Morgan's.

Her eyebrows rose before he turned to her, and his smile was devastating before it faded.

"Can you do that every time?" she asked, in the uncomfortable silence that followed.

"More times than not," he replied.

"Do you know why you fail?"

He shook his head.

"Balance," she whispered. "Get another knife and do this with it." She stooped to pull another dirk, turned and flung it, from a position on one knee. It landed right between the two previous ones where it shuddered, kissing both blades with the quiver of it.

"Glory," Zander breathed the word, awe staining his voice.

"Aim, and try it."

"Not from my knee," he responded.

"Oh that," she smiled up at him. "I was fairly young when I started tossing. My vantage point wasn't much higher than this. It makes for good tosses at any level."

"You started tossing knives at what age?"

"Childhood," she replied, evasively. "Toss your knife. Let me see how you do."

He did the same two pumps over his shoulder before letting it fly. He wasn't bad. She could tell that as his knife landed a finger-width below the other three. She had her eyebrows up again.

"Damn!" he said.

"It isn't bad. Truly."

He turned a look of complete disgust down at her. "But you're a master. Why? What makes you so different?"

Morgan pulled two more dirks from her sock. "When will you let me have all my knives back?" she asked.

"When I have another hold on you," he answered.

She met his eyes, and had to ignore the feel of a sudden drop, as if her innards rolled over onto themselves. "You have my hair," she said finally, rising to her feet.

"True," he remarked. "And you've got six of your knives. Finish the lesson."

"Watch this." She started walking backwards, keeping a straight shot to the target in sight, until she could see it as a spot smaller than the tip of her finger. Zander was standing where she'd left him and he was squinting at her. "Watch the target," she called.

She knew exhilaration as the knife sank into the wood amidst the other four, and her sixth joined it. She knew why she was showing off, too. She just didn't want to think of why it was so important to her.

Zander walked to the target and pulled the knives back

out. Then he walked toward her, a look on his face that was everything she wanted to see. He was in awe of her ability, and it was as gratifying as it was stimulating, and other feelings she wasn't going to put a thought to. Zander stood in front of her and held the knives out.

"Tell me about balance," he said.

"You don't learn well, though. Balance is in the feel. The perfect coordination of blade to hand, and from there to the target, like an extension of the body."

He had too intense a blue to his eyes, and much too handsome a face to stand as close to her as he was, for her not to expect the gasp she experienced. Morgan stepped back, putting some necessary space between them. Zander didn't say anything, although he raised his brows and waited.

"Hand me the knives," she said, extending her cupped hands.

He deposited them one at a time, as if she could be hurt somehow and, surprisingly, it felt like she was getting cut, or worse, each time a blade left the warmth of his skin to caress hers. Morgan watched his face until she had all the knives. He wasn't watching her; he was watching himself put each blade into her hand, and then another. Then he looked up and locked gazes with her.

The earth opened up, tossing her to the heavens before letting her fall back, carefully placing her back in the exact same space. It may have felt the same to him, since his eyes were telling of it. Morgan's own eyes went wide and her lips parted of their own accord.

She watched his eyes drop to her mouth and come back. Then, he did it again. Then, he licked his lips. Morgan had to shut her eyes on the spasm, and knew it was audible as the knife blades clicked together in her palms. When she opened them back up, he hadn't moved. Not an inch.

"Now, close your eyes and put out your most sensitive hand," she whispered.

"You certain that's a good idea?" he asked.

"We're finding out about balance. It's the only way."

"It may be too late for that, Morgan," he answered, but he shut his eyes and put out both hands.

"For what?"

"Finding balance," he replied.

"Whose dirk is this?" she asked in a soft voice, laying one of hers atop his left palm.

She watched him tip his hand one way, then the other, a frown on his face. Then he brightened. "It's yours," he crowed.

Morgan picked it back up.

"Whose is this one, then?" She put the same one on his right palm. His frown came and stayed as he tilted his hand back and forth, back and forth, without a clear answer.

"I canna' tell."

"Do you ken why?" she asked.

He shook his head.

"'You're left-handed. 'Tis the left that has the sensitivity, not the right."

His eyes opened and he stared at her. Morgan forgot for a moment who she was, who he was, and everything, except how dark a blue his eyes were and how they were tying her belly in knots *again,* the longer she held his gaze.

"This is true?"

She cleared her throat, in order to find a voice. "Try and toss one left-handed next time."

"You believe it will help?"

"Close your eyes again."

Zander rolled his eyes, but he did it. Morgan reached down and plucked a bit of fuzz from the top of a dandelion. She placed it atop his left hand, which immediately closed on it.

"What foolishness is this?" he asked, opening his eyes to glare at his hand. He opened his fingers, turned his hand over and they both watched as the fuzzy seed-pods floated away.

"No foolishness. I'm only showing you how sensitive your left is in comparison to your right."

"What difference does that make? A warrior attacks from the right, a claymore comes from the right, a sword comes from the right. The left always holds the shield. Always."

She nodded. "All true," she replied.

"Then, why are you making me stand and hold weeds?"

She laughed aloud and missed the surprise on his face at the sound. "Sometimes the most unexpected is the best," she finally answered.

"You do laugh," he said. "I would na' have guessed it of you."

Morgan pulled her lower lip in. "Are you ready to return to balance, now?"

He looked at her, closed his eyes and held out his hands again.

"Why do you waste my time with your right?" she demanded.

"We already know it hasn't the sensitivity to feel the difference. Put it down."

He moved his head about like he would argue, but he lowered the hand.

"Now, whose blade is this?"

She put one of his on his hand and watched him tilt it to one side. "Mine," he replied.

She lifted it and put it back on. "And this?"

"Mine," he returned quickly.

She did it again, lifting it from his skin for a moment and then putting it back. "Mine, he replied unerringly.

"And this?"

She lifted his, and put two of hers down. She watched him tilt his hand just a bit before grinning. "Yours. Both of them."

"Very good," she responded. "Very, *very* good. You are an excellent pupil."

His eyes opened again at that and Morgan darted her

glance away before she could be swallowed by them, and lose all sense of time and reality. This was Zander FitzHugh standing in front of her, grinning like a boy. He was a FitzHugh. He was a man.

Nothing was working.

Morgan moved her gaze to his. The grin died on his face. She cleared her throat. "Now, let's return to your target, and try again."

"With your blades?" he asked.

"And with your left hand," she replied.

He looked over at her. "Left?"

"Where is it written that knives must be tossed from the right hand, anyway?" she asked.

He considered that for a moment, then smiled at her. "I dinna' know," he answered, "for I canna' read."

Morgan laughed again, then stopped. They were back in his glade, and the morning sun was making it magical. Dew drops sparkled on every surface and light danced off the very air, as the mist clung for a few moments in its silent retreat.

"The center?" Zander was asking, holding his blade above his right shoulder as he did just before his pumping action was due to begin.

Morgan's fantasy environment dissipated and she looked over at where he stood. She gave him an 'I'm-severely-disappointed-in-you' look.

"What?" he said, lowering his arm.

"Left-handed?" she reminded.

He moved the blade into his other hand. "This is ridiculous," he complained.

"Toss it. Don't pump your arm, like this," she mimicked what he did. "Just look at your target, envision planting a knife in it and then do it. Now."

He tossed the blade. Not only did it completely miss the target, it didn't even reach it. Morgan laughed delightedly. Zander swore.

"You put too much strength into it."

"If you ruin my throwing aim, lad, I'll have your hand."

"Then, I'd best not ruin it. Watch. I'm going to do it very slowly. Watch."

Her hand was shaking because he was watching, but she forced herself to ignore it as she placed three dirks between the fingers of her left hand, blades out. Then, she held the hilt of one between her thumb and forefinger.

"I use an under-handed motion. Against everything you've been taught. It's more effective, and more accurate. You aren't coming down, guessing on things like winds, rain and battle conditions, you're coming upward, where there's less to interfere. Watch."

She turned to the target, and flung a blade. Before it hit, she already had another loaded between her forefinger and thumb. "Don't watch the target! 'Tis too late to change that blade. Watch the hand!"

She showed him how she had another blade in place before she turned and flung it. He was watching as she maneuvered the third into place and set it flying. When she looked up, all three were trembling from the dead center of his target.

She walked over to pull her knives back out, ignoring the fact that he might be watching, and then she blushed because when she turned around, he was definitely watching.

She walked toward where he stood, trying to keep every bit of sway out of any part of her walk, and held the knives out to him. "Now you try," she said.

"What?"

He pulled his eyes from where they'd been, on her bare legs that showed beneath her kilt, and looked at her with a befuddled expression. Morgan sucked her tongue up over her upper teeth and ran it over them, making her upper lip jut out. Then, she finished, with a snapping, sucking type of sound, and lifted the knives to a point below his chin.

"Take the knives and put them in the target," she repeated,

and watched a flush go over him, turning those eyes even more intensely blue when he looked over her hand at her.

"I'm na' good enough," he replied.

Morgan rolled her eyes. "I'll do it again, then, but this time, hold to my hand and feel the release. Here." She turned and backed up until she reached his chest, and put out her arm. "Hold onto the outside of my arm. Zander?"

She waited until he did as she asked, although his shuddering was making a connection difficult. Morgan didn't dare turn around to see the cause. She was afraid of what made the pressure against her buttocks. Zander FitzHugh was every inch a man, and he had a woman in his arms, and he didn't even guess it? It was amusing if she thought of it.

She didn't.

"Hold to the back of my hand, Zander. Mold your fingers around mine."

"Oh, sweet Jesu'," he murmured into her hair, but he did as she asked, his palm easily covering the back of her hand, and then he was weaving his fingers through hers.

Morgan's knees were knocking and her breath was coming too shallowly and quick. She swallowed the increased moisture in her mouth and concentrated. "Now, feel how we're holding the blade in our fingers."

His answer was too garbled to decipher, and Morgan ignored it and went right on talking. It was the only thing she could think to do.

"We're going to fling it now. It takes about a one-to-two finger-length of movement. Ready?"

She didn't wait to hear his answer, she simply moved her hand as she'd done for years, and his was right there with her. The knife struck dead-center. She moved another into place, and felt his fingers moving with hers. Her insides were turning to liquid, and her throat was closing off so she could not swallow.

"We're tossing the other one."

She flung it, and heard it thump against the wood. She

was concentrating on putting the final blade into place and attempting to ignore every nerve-ending in her body that was in contact with his.

It was an impossible chore.

"Are you ready, Zander?" she whispered.

The answer was groaned into the back of her neck. Morgan didn't have any recourse but to fling the final blade, and she listened to it clang against the others, before her entire world was upended and completely and irrevocably changed. Forever.

Zander pivoted her body in the enclosure of his arms, grabbed both sides of her head with his hands, and launched his mouth into hers. Morgan didn't have time to gasp a denial, or even one of acceptance, before he was marauding about in her mouth, seeking nourishment from her tongue where he sucked on it, and enticement from all her tissues, as he brought her to the brink of heaven and held her there. Morgan's hands grabbed onto his belt to keep her from falling as he took every bit of sod beneath her and turned it into bog. Her knees no longer worked, her ankles were too far away to matter, and her thigh muscles were trembling with a fire-and-ice combination she knew no name for.

His breath filled her nostrils, his taste filled her senses, and his tongue was a driving force not to be denied. Morgan's mind ceased functioning, her heart ceased beating and her lungs forgot to breathe. All she could hear was the harshness of his breathing.

Then he raised his head and met her gaze. Wonder glimmered momentarily in those midnight-blue eyes and then such horror that his eyes widened to complete circles.

"Nay!"

The cry came from the depths of his gut, and it was just as brutal-sounding. He flung Morgan from him and spat, wiping his hand across his mouth like he'd rather it was a dirk slicing it off. She landed hard, taking the brunt of the force on her elbows and knees. She felt the jolt all the way up her spine to the back of her head. She would have twisted to look up at him, but the moment she tried, a twinge in her neck stabbed at her, taking her breath.

He came around to face her, and then yanked her to her feet. Morgan couldn't prevent the cry of pain as her neck crunched again.

"Damn you! Damn you, and your soul, to Hell!"

"Yes," she whispered. The agony in her neck was throbbing to the middle of her back, and painful enough to make her physically ill. It could also have something to do with how he held to her, his fists wrapped about her upper arms, and her toes barely touching ground, just as he had done the previous evening, while he shook her. All things considered, she wished she was back at the whore's croft and had another chance at the morning, she decided.

"I'm leaving, Morgan of no-clan, and no-name," he spat, and waited until she looked at him. "I go to seek a priest for absolution. Tell no one of this while I am gone."

"I won't be here when you return," she whispered.

"Oh yes, you will. You leave, and I'll hunt you down and kill you, and I will very much enjoy it. You ken?"

He flung her down again, and she didn't have the ability to halt the cry as her neck snapped a third time.

Chapter 11

Zander was gone six days, and in that time, Morgan managed to conceal her injury, continue her hunting and keep the others from each other's throats. She couldn't do anything about the blow to her self-confidence, however. She, who had hated the FitzHughs beyond all reason, beyond even seeking a normal life for herself, she had betrayed everything, and for what?

A stolen kiss from one of them.

She still slept on the ground in his tent, because there wasn't any other place for her. She only toyed with the idea of running away. There wasn't anywhere she could go. She didn't know the direction home; she was clad in FitzHugh colors; and she was seriously injured.

Not one of the others knew it, though. Morgan settled onto her floor by going first to her knees, easing to her buttocks, and then falling in one swoop onto her side, gasping at the pain as she did so. No one else noticed if she made any noise. They didn't note that she never sat. They didn't notice anything about her, although they brought her the choicest pieces of meat and the most cylindrical of their open-fire biscuits.

Zander had been mistaken, too. Amelia made passable biscuits. Morgan often told her of it, and received the girl's dimpled smile in reply.

On the sixth day, there was more than one horse arriving; there were at least eight. The noise alone told of the number, and Morgan caught the tears of self-pity before she rolled onto her hands and knees, preparing to rise. Once she made it to her feet, she had a chance of appearing normal and well. *If* she made it to her feet.

"FitzHugh!"

It sounded like Martin calling out the greeting, and the others joined in with greetings, so it wasn't an uninvited and armed group. That was a good thing, since she hadn't made it to her feet yet, and until she did, her mobility was questionable.

"Break camp!" Zander's voice was loud and clear, and not a bit weak.

"This late?" someone asked.

"We've ten leagues to go to reach Argylle Castle, and I'm bound by troth to my future. Where is my squire, Morgan?"

Morgan was on her knees, and making every effort to get to her feet, when the flap opened. She hung her head in defeat, and welcomed the agony of fire that settled into the center of her back.

"Get up," he ordered.

Morgan tried. She shoved herself from a kneeling position and used every bit of strength in her thighs. She managed to reach a crouch before collapsing back onto all fours, where she retched from the core of pain, in front of all of them standing there.

"What did you do to him?"

Someone was beside her, and it wasn't Zander, but it was a close relative. Morgan closed her eyes to mask the pain, bit her cheek and tried to move her head, scrunching her face at the effort.

"He's hurt," the man at her side said. "Back? Neck?"

"Aye," Morgan whispered.

"How long has he been hurt?" Zander wanted to know, in that orator-tone of his. "Who among you did the deed?"

There was an annoying and confusing number of answers from the group outside, and then Zander was in the tent again. She knew it although he was accompanied by too many of his clansmen to count, since her view was what she could see of their lower legs.

"Who hurt you?"

Zander was on one knee, and lifting her head to look at him. His action made the absolute and complete agony worse, and Morgan cried out with it, before she could stop it.

"You can't move his head, Zander. Someone injured his back, and you're making it worse."

"Oh."

He rolled into a reclining position to look up at her. Morgan closed her eyes, but when she opened them, he was there still. Even through the blur of tears he was heart-rending and handsome still, she decided.

"Who hurt you?" he asked.

"You," she replied.

His brows fell, shadowing his eyes, and he frowned. "Last week?" he continued.

She would have nodded, but it hurt too much. She settled for a whistled "Aye," through her teeth.

"You've lived with it this long?"

"Aye," she replied again.

"Then get off the floor and get moving. We're breaking camp. Cease this and get your dirks. I've told my brothers of your talent, and that as long as you have it, I'll let you live. He's a robber of the dead, decked out in KilCreggar plaid, as bold as you please, and I took him on as my squire. I'm truly amazed at my generosity, sometimes."

He was rolling from her and moving away, and Morgan closed her eyes to keep the emotion in.

The other FitzHugh was at her side again, and Morgan slanted her eyes to look at him. He was older than Zander, and even more sturdily built, but he wasn't as handsome, and he was alive, as her own brothers were not. She snarled at him, but lost it in a cough that made her back spasm with pain.

Tears obliterated him for a moment. She had to wait for

them to recede. When they did, he was looking at her with compassion and no small amount of pity. If her back wasn't as stiff and straight as possible, she'd have been in that position by the look on his face. No KilCreggar accepted pity from a FitzHugh. She'd rather die.

"Zander says you're a lad," he said softly. "Is he blind?"

Morgan shut her eyes again and caught the sob of defeat. She knew what it was, too.

"Come along, I'll try to get you on your feet without hurting you further. Take a deep breath." He was above her, and linking his hands under her belly.

"Get your hands off me," she snarled.

The hands disappeared. "Pride at the cost of pain. Good. I like that in a squire. I begin to see why Zander kept you. Come along. Rise by yourself, then."

Morgan took two breaths, sucked in the third and pushed herself back into a crouch. Her thighs wobbled with it for a moment and then she locked them. It was easier without an audience, but it was done. She stood, meeting the other FitzHugh's gaze from an exact level. She watched his eyebrows raise once she reached her height.

"I can see the mistake," he offered. "Perhaps Zander isna' the blind one, but myself."

"Appearances . . . are deceiving," she replied, and turned stiffly to exit the tent.

He was at her heels.

"There you are!" Zander called. "Thank goodness. Here. Take your dirks and pepper my brother, Phineas, with them."

He has a brother named Phineas? she wondered, as pain stabbed at her with just the thought of giggling about it. She sucked in a breath. "I canna' reach my dirks," she replied finally.

"Here. Take the rest, then." He opened his bag and gave her the other six. Morgan placed three in each hand. "Now, watch this," Zander said.

Morgan narrowed her eyes. There were more than two FitzHughs about the enclosure, if their cloth was any indication. "Which one is Phineas?" she asked finally.

Zander walked over to another version of himself who was seated on a horse, disdaining the camp about him. This FitzHugh hadn't the cleft in his chin, nor a full head of hair, nor when he looked down at her, did he have midnight-blue eyes. His were ice-water-blue and cold.

Morgan let fly, plugging his falcon band, where he held the reins, the brooch on his shield, the handle of his *skean dhu*, and the heavy leather wrist band on his other arm, twice.

The camp noise turned to applause.

"My, my." The one called Phineas said, reaching to pluck out her dirks without the slightest bit of interest showing. "He is good. He is very good. How is he with a bow?"

"Terrible," Zander replied. "He's perfect with the arrows, though."

Morgan closed her eyes and caught the sway. She hoped Phineas was the laird. If he was, her life work was almost over, and she'd be able to collapse into her own grave, where pain such as she was enduring didn't survive.

"Come along, Morgan, get your knives. You have them all back now. Am I not the most lenient of masters to my squires? Even the disobedient ones?"

She looked up at him. "Aye," she answered with no inflection whatsoever. "That, you are."

His grin slipped and she ignored him to go get her dirks back from Phineas. As she reached for them, he lifted them from her reach and smiled. He was missing two of his front teeth, and that wasn't adding to any attractiveness. Quite the opposite, she decided.

"Favor me with a kiss first," he replied.

She looked down, grit her teeth and backed from him. She had no idea what Zander had told them, and didn't want to know, but at least the other brother had gotten her gender right. For a moment, anyway.

This one might prefer that she was a lad, she surmised.

"Give them to Zander, then," she said and started walking toward her master. One of her dirks landed on the ground at her right, the other five, in a row, on her left. She looked down at them, then swiveled with her entire body to look over at Phineas.

"We'll have some wonderful times together, I think," he said.

Morgan didn't pretend the snarl as she locked her jaw and made ready to go to her knees. It was every bit as painful as she'd known it would be, too. The jolt as her knees hit slammed the shoulder pain into her neck and even made the skin holding her hair to her head hurt. She sucked in the agony and moved to pluck her knives up. It wasn't any worse than she'd experienced while bringing down the deer three days earlier for their consumption. She just hadn't had an audience for it.

"Come along, Morgan. You tarry and we've a long walk ahead of us."

"Walk?" she asked dully, wondering how she was going to get back to her feet without bursting into sobs.

"You dinna' think I'd take you up on my horse, did you?" Zander asked quietly.

Morgan kept her attention on the hilts of her dirks, then on the motion of putting them into the back of her belt, and finally into her socks. She felt better just knowing she had her weapons back. Then she sucked in breath, gathering the courage to get to her feet. The only one still watching her was the unknown FitzHugh.

She ignored him.

Zander, his brothers, and the rest of the clansmen he'd brought, made them march through the night and into the next day, intent on distance, rather than subterfuge. Morgan noticed that the lasses hadn't gone but twenty steps before they were offered rides in front of the men. Morgan wished them well of it. She much preferred walking, to being anywhere in the vicinity of Zander FitzHugh.

"You interested in a ride, young Morgan?" It was the unknown FitzHugh at her side, looking down at her as he asked it. Morgan kept her eyes steadfastly ahead, and on the backside of her master's horse, Morgan, ignoring him. It was easier than she'd suspected to give this attitude, since her head wouldn't move enough to look up at him, anyway.

"Give yonder squire, Martin, a ride first. He's na' angered my master as I have."

"How did you do that?"

Morgan would have lifted her shoulders and shrugged, but that would only invite more pain to each step. "He dinna' like my method of tossing my dirks. I tried to show him, and he detested it."

"Zander is a world unto himself. You are the strangest of creatures, Morgan. Do you know that?"

"I am nothing," she replied.

"I would na' say that. I think you're either a very pretty lad, or a very pretty lass. The fact that you look either is confusing and unsettling. What do you look like in a dress?"

Morgan tried ignoring him for a span, but he didn't do anything except keep his horse in pace with her and wait. "I've never worn such, My Lord. I hardly know what I look like now. How would I know what I'd look like in women's clothing? Besides, where would I hide my dirks?"

"I'm beginning to think I was correct the first time. You are a lass. I think my brother is blind, after all."

"No law against thinking, is there?" she replied.

"Zander is very anxious to get his future decided. He says he longs for his house. I don't know why. The place is a disaster. Not one of his servants obey. It's not comfortable."

"I've been told," she replied.

"Why did you pledge yourself to him?"

"I have na' pledged anything to anyone. I'm bound by

debt to him. He threatened to strip my clothing off me if I dinna' take it off, then when I did, he tossed it into the burn. I had no choice but to wear FitzHugh sett. I owe him for that."

"He's making you pay for your clothing, after a trick like that? I'll speak to him."

"You're na' to do any such thing."

"Well, someone has to. The woman he just betrothed himself to isna' going to. She's the biggest mouse I've ever met."

Morgan stumbled and fell, taking the jolt once again with her knees. The agony wasn't as easy to staunch this time. She sat, ramrod straight, with her hands on her thighs and gasped with it. Not one of the horses seemed to have turned about or stopped.

Then she noticed the horse at her side, and the man at her elbow. "You tripped. Here. I'll help you."

"Get your hands off me!" she hissed.

"I know, you'll probably stick a dozen knives into my gizzard if I don't. Fair enough. Flay me. I've finished with this farce, anyway. You're riding with me. Here. Ugh. You weigh more than you look."

He had her in his arms and then settled into the front of his saddle and Morgan wasn't capable of saying anything to stop him. Her mouth was clenched tight with stopping the scream from his rough handling. Then he was in the saddle behind her, pulling her against his chest and murmuring words that brought tears to her eyes again.

"Zander is a fool," he said. "The fool went and got himself betrothed not two days hence, regardless of whom he hurt or whom he stepped on. I don't know why. Used to be he would have died before accepting a wife. No matter now. I can't change it. You probably can't, either. If you lean that direction, think it through. He's lost to you. I'm not. I'm available, still. My name is Plato. Plato FitzHugh. At your service, Morgan lass."

She laughed and caught the agony before it made much sound. Another FitzHugh with a ridiculous name. Their mother must be a sow to force the issue, and their sire a rabbit. Plato. She was still smiling over it when Zander turned his head to check on her.

The smile died and then turned to consternation as he motioned for a halt and then rode back to where Morgan was ensconced in Plato's arms. She watched the brothers look each other over.

"You've got my squire there, Plato. I'll not take kindly to this treatment of my serfs."

"Allow me to pay off his debt. How much cloth did he get? At what price?"

"How much?" Zander exploded. "Get down off that horse, Morgan, and keep your claws from my brothers. I command it."

"I'll buy his freedom, Zander. Only quote the price and I'll send it over. I'll even send my serf, Roberta, over to sweeten the deal."

Zander looked at Morgan, and his midnight-blue eyes were as cold and hard as Phineas' were. "No amount of silver is going to set him free. Ever. I guarantee it. Now get down off that horse, Morgan. Now."

She pulled away from Plato, and was shaking as she swiveled her entire body to make the lunge for the ground easier to take. Plato helped her, putting his hands on her upper arms and lowering her. When he did, he brushed the sides of her breasts. Morgan sucked in the intake of breath, while Plato's expression didn't change. He didn't give indication that he'd felt it, at all. He was glaring straight at his brother.

"You treat Morgan harshly, and you'll deal with me."

"What?" Zander looked from his brother, down to where Morgan attempted to remain standing, with both hands about his brother's saddle horn in order to do so, and then back to Plato. If there was any gentleness to him, it was impossible to spot.

"Walk beside me, Morgan. I'll not come to blows over a piece of spittle such as yourself. Plato? Keep your tongue and your influence from my household."

Morgan held to the horse, Morgan's, mane, and nearly screamed with every step forced on her as they looped back to the front of Zander's column. She was dying, and wished God would just take her and put her out of her misery. It would be more merciful of Him. Morganna KilCreggar deserved a small bit of mercy, didn't she? She deserved the blessed unconsciousness of the dead, the silent sleep of eternity. That was what she deserved. She surely didn't deserve another moment of this.

Chapter 12

Zander called a halt near midafternoon. Morgan's existence resembled Hell, to the point that she wouldn't have known if it was midafternoon, midnight or midsummer. All she knew was that the horse stopped, and two steps later, so did she.

Since it was impossible to turn her head, she swiveled slowly and looked back at the group behind her. All the servants Zander had been intent on gathering were now riding with his clansmen. All, except Morgan. She turned back, to face forward. How perfectly Zander FitzHugh carried out his creed, and he didn't even know it was a KilCreggar he was torturing. Morgan's back stiffened. He never would know it, either.

"You'll call a rest, finally? Your servant looks like he's taken a touch of the whip."

The man speaking was probably Plato, although she didn't know their voices all that well, but she doubted the brother named Phineas would care.

"Morgan lad? Surely you're mistaken. There's not a more prideful, stubborn lad born. He's simply hungry. We'll all partake. Sheila and Amelia! Gather foodstuffs!"

He was using his orator's voice, and Morgan stepped away from the horse so Zander could heave himself off and see to everything. She wasn't capable of moving fast or well. She turned slowly to watch as men, lads and lasses headed for the bushes on either side of the dirt path.

"You dinna' need to relieve yourself, Morgan?" Zander asked at her ear.

She gasped inwardly, although nothing showed, and held onto the stab of pain the movement caused by keeping her teeth clamped shut.

"I've no need," she answered, finally.

"Well, I've not your vanity, nor your shyness. I very much need to see to emptying myself. I'll not be long. You move from this spot, and I'll have your braid," he answered. "You ken?"

"I ken," she replied.

It was starting to rain, although only bits and spurts of moisture touched her nose, cheeks and hands, but it felt good. Morgan closed her eyes and settled her head back the tiniest bit, in order to lick a drop from the skin above her upper lip.

"Dinna' do that again."

She was already stiff, but Zander's quiet command made every part that wasn't locked in place, tighten. Morgan lowered her chin slowly and looked across at him. She didn't say a word.

He nodded and left her then, and she breathed normally the moment he did, so. *What is the matter with me?* she lamented to herself, but there wasn't an answer. There never was.

She heard the sounds of a feast, smelled a bit of bread and pig, even caught the odor of mustard seed. She kept her eyes on Morgan, the horse, and forced her belly to calm. She couldn't eat, because if she did, she'd have to take nature's call, and if she did that, she didn't know if she could get to her feet again. She swayed slightly and reached out for Morgan's mane.

"You don't eat, Morgan?"

She looked at her hand on the horse, touched the rough hairs of his mane, and told her heart to hush. "Nay," she answered.

"Why not?"

She didn't have to look to see it, she knew how he'd be standing, resting one hand on his hip, with a hank of bread or meat in the other. She only wished the pain of her body overrode that in her breast. "I dinna' have to answer to you," she said, finally.

There was silence for a moment as he probably swallowed his bite. "You don't rest, either."

"That is na' true. I am resting."

"Come then, sit."

"I do not wish to sit."

He didn't say anything, nor was there any sound of eating. Morgan examined the horse's mane in her hands.

"You sicken, and I'll flog you," he warned.

"I'll not sicken."

"I'll fetch you a carrot, and a bit of boar meat. 'Tis only fitting, since you brought it down."

"A master does na' serve his squire, I think," she replied.

"If I could perhaps interrupt?"

"Go away, Plato," Zander growled.

"Methinks it's you that should disappear, Zander. Yon lad's face is etched with pain, and he is na' sitting for a reason. Probably the same reason he is na' eating."

"He's na' doing either because he wants me to look bad before my brothers. I already know how my squire thinks."

Morgan, the horse, had small braided portions to his mane. Morgan, the squire, found one of them, ran it through her fingers, then found another one. Zander had been braiding pieces of hair while they journeyed? That was interesting, she told herself.

"Canna' you see? Your squire's incapable, at present."

"Incapable? This lad has more capability in his foot than any other man. I've seen it. And, he will na' take a rest. I asked, and he refused."

"Did you ask him up onto your horse?"

"Dinna' overstep, Plato," Zander said.

"He asked me," Morgan spoke up. "I refused."

"And he also offered food and rest?"

"Aye."

"You lie well, Squire Morgan. Face me when you do it."

Face him? It was all she could do to remain standing. Morgan took a deep breath and swiveled with her entire body, carefully blanking out the sharp stab between her shoulders.

"You see, Zander, it's written all over the lad. He's a back injury, in agony, terrified of having to stand again, and you've marched him all night and most of the day. At least give the order to encamp here. We can reach Argylle tomorrow, dawn."

If Plato was hoping for gratitude from Morgan, he was sadly mistaken as she glared at him. A FitzHugh pitying a KilCreggar? And worse, asking for leniency? All her life was spent for a moment such as this, and she lifted her chin, ignoring the minute gasp she couldn't prevent. "I was na' resting because I dinna' need it. I dinna wish to eat, because I'm replete, and my injury is just that, FitzHugh, *my* injury. Dinna' trouble yourself over me and I'll na' stick a dirk in you when you least expect it."

Zander chuckled. "Well, I did try to warn you, Plato. He wishes me to look bad before my brothers. Nothing more."

Plato looked unconvinced, but he left them. Morgan took another slight breath, before she could pivot back. Zander was still there. She heard him take a bite of his carrot. She watched the splash of a drop on her hand, then another. She hoped it wouldn't rain in earnest. The mud might be more than she could walk through.

"The Earl of Argylle has an English lord staying with him," he said.

"So?" she replied.

He took another bite of his carrot, noisily chewed it, and just as loudly swallowed. "This English lord has a champion. A fencing master. An English fencing master."

Morgan watched more raindrops fall onto her hands, then felt them on her head, thumping with the weight of water each carried. She sighed. God was as merciless as a FitzHugh, obviously. "So?" she finally replied again.

"We'll speak more of this when we get to the castle. Have you ever seen a real castle, Morgan?"

"Nay," she whispered.

"I receive rooms in the keep. My squire stays at my side."

She probably should have joined them in the bushes, Morgan realized, as the sickness fell to the pit of her belly. He was punishing her for his own lack of control. She hardly dared be put in that position again. She wasn't strong enough to withstand him—not to withstand his punishment.

To withstand the paradise he'd given her a glimpse of.

"Squire Martin will enjoy that," she answered.

"Squire Morgan will, too."

"Squire . . . Morgan?"

"Phineas wishes you for his squire. Would you like that?"

She sucked in breath, tinged with rain. It felt cool in her mouth and down her throat. It felt good. "Phineas?" she asked. *Phineas,* she asked again to herself. *Too?*

"Phineas. I've told him the same as I told Plato before him. There is no amount of silver that will release you from me. Besides, Phineas abuses his servants."

Morgan almost laughed. "Abuses?" she asked.

"He uses the whip. Branding irons. I've heard. I've seen his handiwork. I'll not stay at his home."

"Branding irons?" Morgan repeated.

"Aye. And chains. He also claims more bastards than there are days to the week. All delivered to him by the women he takes. I don't believe they enjoy it."

"Why are you telling me all this?"

"I don't know. Because I could always talk to you, maybe."

Rain was slicking Morgan, the horse's, hide and darkening it to a brown shade, that resembled Zander's hair, for some reason. Morgan, the squire, looked at it and then turned to face him, ignoring every ache at the movement. She could swear they were getting easier to bear, too. *In comparison to her failure, anything would be,* she thought. She knew what failure felt like, now, and it wasn't a pleasant experience. She, who had always tasted success, was now a failure. She'd been broken. A KilCreggar had been broken by a FitzHugh! She realized she was, too. She was broken in everything that mattered; her spirit, her body . . . her heart. How her ancestors must be writhing with disgust.

She sighed. "You dinna' wish to talk to me, Zander FitzHugh. You wish to punish me. You know why. I know why. No one else does, nor will they ever. Very well. I accept your punishment. Now go, and find someone else to converse with. I've tired of it."

His face was as shuttered as her own felt. He was still a very handsome man, with rain molding everything he wore to him. He lowered his jaw and blazed every bit of his midnight-blue scorn onto her.

"I wish to warn you of what your lot could be should I take Phineas up on his offer."

"Is that supposed to be worse?" she asked.

He pulled back. "I dinna' mean to harm you," he whispered. "I dinna' know my own strength sometimes."

Oh God, that was *worse*! she thought. She sucked in on the newest agony, and realized that it hurt more than anything her back had been giving her. She didn't want a FitzHugh's pity! Especially this FitzHugh!

Morgan slitted her eyes and regarded him. She'd rather have his hatred. It matched her own, if she found it again. She sneered a bit at him. "You forget yourself, FitzHugh," she said coldly.

"Forget?"

"There are others all about you."

"True. We're surrounded by others. What of it?"

"If you tarry much longer at my side, they may suspicion why, you know," she whispered.

His face turned to a stone-like mask, and she watched it happen. It felt like every piece of her was crying, but the

rain covered any such motion, and her eyes remained dry
and hard.

"Our rest is over. We make Castle Argylle by dark."

Morgan blinked her acknowledgment and turned back
around as the word was given. She decided, after another
thousand steps, that the ache in her back, sending shooting
pains down each leg, was the easier to bear.

Zander had been right. Morgan had never seen a castle.
She hadn't much will to look at this one as they walked up
a hill toward it. All she could tell was it was immense, and
torches from the walls shed light all around the surrounding acreage. The column halted, and then she was walking
across wood, listening to the echo of horses' hooves and
her own boots.

Since she wasn't capable of turning her head, she took it
all in with unblinking eyes from a position beside Zander's
leg. There were more torches sputtering and spewing light at
every curve of the steps, and Zander walked his horse right
into a building and up a flight of steps. Morgan tripped only
once, and when she did, the immediate pressure of Zander's
hand was on hers, holding her up, and keeping her up until
she steadied.

Then, he let her go. Morgan didn't say a word.

The wide flight of steps ended in another courtyard, and
then they were at the stables. Morgan took in the vast
amount of horseflesh all about her. The Lord of Argylle
appeared to maintain his own legion of servants just to
care for the horses. The noise and confusion was evident
as Zander's group came to a halt in the middle of the yard.

Morgan stepped back on legs which seemed to be
kneeless, in a jerking fashion, as Zander dismounted.
Her legs were still holding her up, although they weren't
working properly. He glanced down at her, then away.
He had a nerve twitching in that chiseled jaw. He had

also freshly scraped his beard. She knew, because she'd heard the sounds of him doing it as they approached.

Morgan had to command herself not to reach out to touch him, and hated herself anew for the weakness.

"You are to stay at my heels, Morgan. Dinna' lose yourself."

"Aye," she answered.

"Martin!" Zander barked loudly, startling her into four faltering steps backward before she caught herself and actually managed to remain upright. "There you are. See to Morgan. Not him! My horse!"

This last, as Martin had reached for her elbow. Morgan nearly gave it the amusement it deserved, and then she had to force away the silly tears that started up, just because another human was about to help her, without pitying her. She was weak. That was it. She was weak from lack of sustenance, walking a day and night, and she was weak from having to keep her back rigid to prevent further trauma.

She convinced herself that she was weak from everything except the real reason, and she looked at the straw-strewn ground beneath her feet with a kind of wonder. They had made a terrace of steps to reach the stables. Amazing. She wondered if the straw-littered ground was earthen, or if there was more stone beneath the straw. It looked like dirt, but she could hardly bend down and check at the moment. They'd taken a space the size of a large village, and walled it in with stone. This was a castle, then?

"Morgan!"

She raised her head, ignoring the dull throb of ache at the movement, and saw Zander gesturing at her from across the span of servants and horses. *How did he get clear over there?* she wondered, and started a shuffling walk to reach him. As she did, she knew the ground was just that, ground, and they'd leveled off the hill to make a courtyard within the walls.

"I told you to keep at my heels!"

Morgan tried to focus on him, but he had a torch right

behind his head. He sounded angry, but then again, he always sounded angry, anymore. She twisted up her nose, squinted against the light and regarded him.

"Well?" he asked.

"Turn about and keep walking, then," she answered.

She received his exclamation of frustration, and then the punishment of trying to keep up as he took steps two at a time. Morgan gave up after the second one. She couldn't lift her leg that high and her knees weren't cooperating much. About the only good thing was the walls were uneven and rough. The rock made excellent hand-holds for what appeared to be a recalcitrant squire, who didn't have the strength left to serve his master.

Zander was gone when she reached the next level. It was probably quarters for the laird's army. That was her first guess, and was borne out when she was shoved aside by a burly sort with no patience.

"Out of the way, lad!"

The uneven wall was just as hard as it felt. Morgan had that much decided as she hit against it, opening a cut in her cheek. Then she was walking forward, taking a guess at where the Earl of Argylle would place a guest.

Smoke stung her eyes, making them water yet again, and she rubbed a sleeve across them, with an ugly gesture. She couldn't cry *now*! She was deep in the bowels of an English-loving Scottish laird's castle, surrounded by fighting men, and disobeying her master again. Tears would be the final humiliation.

The corridor grew narrower as she walked along it. The doors on either side grew more ornate at the same time, all oak with brass fittings, and then there were tapestries. Morgan halted for a moment and looked. She couldn't crane her neck up, but she could see far down the corridor that there were immense rugs, worked with needlework of all descriptions, blanketing the walls. It was too dark in the torchlight to make them out, but it was rich. Richer than she'd ever seen or believed existed.

Morgan kept pushing herself, stumbling along with one hand on the wall to keep herself upright. She was probably approaching living quarters of some kind. She wished she hadn't annoyed Zander, and she hoped he wouldn't be more angered when she finally located him.

"Who are you?"

Morgan halted, her eyes wide as a young girl came toward her, black hair flowing all about her, and wearing a bliant and over-dress of sunniest yellow that was so exquisite, Morgan's mouth dropped open.

"Well?"

She stood in front of her and waited. Morgan moved her hand from the tapestry-covered wall and stood. The girl reached exactly to her nose. Then the girl giggled, sounding like a small bird.

"You can close your mouth, now. I'm properly gratified at your response to my presence. I think I like it, but you must hasten away from here now. My maid will na' allow me out long. She'll suspect."

"Suspect?" Morgan asked finally.

"That I've stolen away to a love-tryst."

Morgan's mouth fell open again. The girl trilled another giggle.

"I don't have them, of course. I only threaten to have them. 'Tis the only way I can escape my betrothal."

"Your . . . betrothal?"

"To that great, hulking beast, Zander FitzHugh, of the Highland FitzHughs. You don't know him, do you?"

Morgan's eyes closed on an agony severe enough to make the pain in her back disappear. It was centered in her chest and pumping into every piece of her with every beat of her heart. She sucked in breath to counteract it, and when that didn't work, she silently cursed everything and everyone. Soundly.

There was a purgatory on earth, and Zander had brought her right into it. As a KilCreggar who had failed to avenge her family, and as a woman who had failed to kill what he made her feel, she was devastated, completely and totally. She opened her eyes and hoped it didn't show.

"I am his squire," she finally answered, with a harsh whisper of sound.

"Oh dear! This is worse. If Letty finds me talking to you, she'll think the worst! She'll think you're here for a reason!" She stopped, narrowed her eyes and looked Morgan over. "You aren't here for a reason, are you?"

"I'm lost," Morgan replied.

"Quick. Over here. Take this passage, and the second door on the left leads to where they've put him. Quickly, I say!"

For a wench who supposedly was a mouse, she wasn't immune to grabbing a lad's upper arm and pulling him along. Plato hadn't taken a good enough look at her, either. This girl was beautiful, she probably had a large dowry, and she was no mouse. Zander had done well for himself in the span of six days, since he'd kissed his squire and turned her completely inside-out.

Morgan stumbled along behind Zander's betrothed, feeling like a great, awkward bull next to the petite fraility of her future mistress. The girl opened a door.

"You see?"

"Aye."

Morgan didn't even look. She just wanted the torment ended. She wanted a hard cold floor to stretch out on, and she wanted oblivion. She could not care less about killing anyone or anything, not even the FitzHugh laird.

Chapter 13

Zander was standing in front of his fireplace, staring into the flames. He whirled when she got the door opened, and he watched her slide inside to hold herself up on the door as it closed.

"Where have you been?" He demanded it, and when she didn't speak right away, he was across the room, and glaring at her from an arm's length away.

Morgan couldn't meet his gaze. She had too much emotion just beneath the surface. "I got lost," she replied.

"What happened to your face?"

He was reaching for her cheek and she pulled back, ignoring what she used to think was pain, when her neck twinged at the movement. His hand stopped shy of her cheek.

"I dinna' move quickly enough," she whispered.

"Who hit you?"

" 'Twas no hit. I'm clumsy."

"Clumsy? You?" He stepped back and looked her over. "What's happened? Something has happened, hasn't it? What?"

Useless, stupid, female tears flooded her eyes at the gentle tone he used. She looked down at the same moment they trickled onto her cheeks before dripping off her chin. She watched them darken her blouse and the kilt band across her chest.

"Oh, Morgan, pray cease this. I canna' stand for it."

His breath was at her forehead and she made fists of her

hands. *He couldn't stand for it?* she wondered. She blinked until she could see again. Then she raised her head to glare at him.

"Back away, FitzHugh," she spat, "and let me see what a great Highland lord is given for rooms."

He raised his eyebrows and both arms, and stepped back and to one side of her. Then, he gestured to the luxury all about. Morgan's mouth dropped open in awe.

There was a large bedstead along the wall: the headboard, footboard, and connecting mattress-support along the floor made from what appeared to be the same log. There was a mattress on it, and more than two blankets, if the differing colors were any indication. There were tapestries covering the walls, another one across the floor and more needlework on his linens, although it looked more like moths had been at work, since there were symmetrical holes and gaps throughout.

There was a large chair across the room, with a footstool in front that looked large enough to bed down on. They had given him another blanket across that, and a fur covering of some kind draped across the back of his chair. There was a huge fireplace covering the length of the opposite wall, although only a small blaze was kindled in it. There was a shield of some coat of arms above the fireplace and several torch brackets were on the walls, although none of them were lit at present.

The ceiling was beyond her scope of vision at the moment, but it looked to be very high, if the shadow was any indication. There was also a sturdy-looking table beside the chair, although the ornate carving underneath seemed more to damage the sturdiness than accent it. They had given him a silvered tray, covered with fruits ripe enough for the vine, and what appeared to be an entire loaf of bread sat next to his flagon, which probably held mead. Morgan took it all in and then looked back at Zander.

"Well?" he asked.

"It'll be too hot," she answered.

He smiled and walked over to the table, lifting a bunch of grapes for her inspection. "You hungry?"

Her belly answered for her with a loud rumble. Morgan flushed as they both heard it. He laughed softly.

"Come along, Morgan, and taste of my feast. I canna' have my own champion wasting away on me."

"Your own—?" Her voice didn't finish it.

"I've accepted a challenge from the Earl of Cantor. He's a Sassenach bastard of the worst kind. He has a fencing master he's brought with him. I told you of him already."

She tried to think. "I dinna' recall," she finally answered.

"Come along. There's more than I can eat, although if I needed more, I can simply open the door and get Martin to go for it."

"Martin?" she asked.

"Of course Martin. I've lent his services to Plato, for the time being, but he still squires for me, if I have need of him, anyway."

"What of me?" she asked.

"Plato asked for you first, if that's your question." He wasn't hiding the anger very well, she noticed.

"I have na' reason to wish to squire Plato, Master Zander. I was assuring myself of my position in your household. If you've need of foodstuffs, I will go for them."

"As slowly as you obey? I would na' trust you to return before it spoiled on me. Come along, Morgan lad, enough taunts. Join me. 'Tis a rich room they've given me. A very rich welcome."

"You're the future son-by-law. What else did you ken they'd give?"

He looked across at her. "You know about that?" he asked.

"I met your betrothed," she replied.

"Gwynneth? Truly?"

"She dinna' tell me her name. I assume it to be Gwynneth if you say 'tis." Morgan gathered her courage and moved away from the support of the door. The table was as far away as it looked. It was also waist-high, which was a good thing. She could hardly bend down to pick up anything.

"What do you think of her?"

She gathered some grapes without looking and popped one in her mouth, as if considering. "She's beauteous and young. Very young. You like them young, though, I recollect."

"She remind you of anyone?" Zander asked.

Morgan popped another grape into her mouth and sucked on it before she broke the skin and ravished the sweetness from it. "No," she replied.

"No? Think, lad. Black hair. Young. Beauteous. Fit. Active with the mind. Untouched. That jog your memory?"

Morgan shrugged, cursing herself the moment she did so as she failed to hide the reaction of pain. She choked on the grape before swallowing it whole.

"You still suffering?"

She had it under control before he finished asking, and looked at him with her eyes half-lidded. "I've finished my meal, I think. I would seek my rest now."

"Two grapes?"

She couldn't afford to shrug, so she didn't. She didn't answer, either. She simply put the rest of her grapes down, and backed a step, then another.

"You canna' move, can you?"

Morgan twisted her lips. "I moved to here. I moved from the camp. I move."

"I mean, you canna' move to feint and parry, can you?"

"If you're asking of a weakness, let me set your mind at rest. I'm na' weak. I'm never weak. You set up a contest. I'm your squire. I will do what you require."

"I dinna' think you're weak, Morgan. I think you're the strongest, bravest lad I've ever met. That is what I think."

Oh God! Morgan sucked in the onslaught of sobs as viciously as she'd ever done in her life, and for once was rewarded as her eyes only thought about weeping before they cleared. If a FitzHugh thought that of her, perhaps the KilCreggar dead wouldn't walk the earth and search her out for punishment, after all. A FitzHugh praising a KilCreggar?

She smiled slowly. "It's very hot in your chamber, Master Zander," she said.

"And . . . that means?"

Something had changed, and she didn't know what it was. It wasn't good, though. A log fell on his fire, sending a burst of light out onto the floor. Morgan backed another step.

"Does na' your chamber come with a window?"

"Aye," he replied.

She turned by moving her feet as he walked past her, went to the end of his bed and pulled a tapestry aside. The fresh air was rewarding of itself, even without the smell of the continuing rain.

"Now, answer my question. Straight, this time. Can you move enough to fence?"

"I'm no slackard at fencing. I'm no slacker at anything I set my mind to," she answered.

"But, can you move?"

"What is the prize this time?" she asked.

"Self-respect. Twenty pounds sterling. Another squire." He grinned. "An English squire."

Morgan considered him. "And what is the penalty for losing?"

"What do you want it to be?" he asked.

"Death," she answered.

His eyes widened, and then he took the flooring between them in three strides to grip her upper arms and yank her toward him. "Death?" he asked with a shocked tone, then he said it again, only this time he was angry. "Death? You want a man's blood that badly? Why?"

"Dinna' touch me again, FitzHugh," she whispered, through teeth clenched against his assault.

He let her go, ignoring how she stumbled jerkily backward into the table before finding her balance against it. The flagon he'd been drinking from rattled at her collision with its support, then settled back onto the silvered tray alongside the grapes, peaches and pears. Morgan watched Zander glare at her.

"For God's sake, why?"

She had to look away then, and her eyes roved about the room before settling on the open window. *Because death is the only mercy God is willing to give me*, she thought. "I have my reasons," she whispered.

"I'll refuse the challenge. Martin!"

He strode over to the chamber door and hauled it open, hollering loudly enough to wake everyone on the same level, and probably the ones above and below, too.

"Zander," Morgan said softly.

He turned back to her. Morgan filled her eyes with how beloved he was, and let herself feel every bit of it, held it to her breast, allowed it to fill her until she swore she glowed, and then she shoved it away. The paradise he'd allowed her a glimpse of was just the pinnacle for a hellish descent into agony. She wanted him to know of it, too.

"Shut the door," she finished.

He did.

"I will fight this English champion. I will na' lose. If you dinna' wish his death, then I will na' give it to you. Besides . . . ." *The only way I'll lose is if I continue living*, she finished in her mind.

"Besides . . . what?" he asked.

The door was knocked on and then both Martin and Plato were in the chamber, finally making it appear normal-sized.

"You called for my squire?" Plato asked, his glance flicking from where Morgan held herself up by the table, to Zander.

"Morgan has a back injury."

"You woke everyone in the castle to tell us of that?" Plato looked from one to the other of them again. Then, he smacked a hand to his forehead. "You're either dense, or a very slow learner, Zander FitzHugh. Mother always did say she saved beauty for her final-born, but to the rest she gave wits. You should have held out for wits, I think."

Zander shook his head. "Nay. Only to tell you of the rest. This back injury, 'twas I that gave it. I dinna' mean to. I guess I'm a brute when it comes to him."

"I could have told you of that," Plato remarked.

"And I need to ask your help," Zander continued.

"You want help now? With your squire? Good heavens, Morgan, what are you doing to him, now?"

Zander was grinding his teeth. She could tell by his voice when he answered. "He canna' fence if we do not get him mobile enough. Have either of you a suggestion? Something to try?"

"Call off the duel," Plato said.

"Morgan will na' let me."

Plato looked over at her then, and she watched his features soften. She only hoped it wasn't as noticeable for the others. Then, she asked herself why she cared. Zander couldn't possibly punish her any further than he already was.

"Find the heat stone," Plato said, finally.

"The what?" Zander asked.

Martin was already rooting about in the basket at the foot of Zander's bedstead.

"Heat stone, for warming beds."

"They use such?"

"These English-bred lairds like their comforts. I have to admit that 'tis very welcome on a cold Highland night, too. You'll see when, and if, we ever get you home again. You have it, Martin?"

"Aye."

Morgan looked at the strange, flat boulder, and watched as Plato took it from the lad and walked over to the fire. He set it down and with two long-handled tongs, picked up the stone and set it in the midst of the blaze.

"Now, Morgan. Your turn." Plato winked at her. "Take your clothing off."

"I will na!" she burst out.

He was grinning across at her, now. "Well, since your squire is so shy, Zander, I suppose we'll have to see if this will work through the stout FitzHugh sett he wears. Lie down."

Morgan looked at the three men in the room and felt panicked. She wasn't going to a prone position with them watching. She'd already shown too much of her weakness.

"You heard him, lad. Now." Zander was motioning to the center of the room.

"Back away, then," she snapped.

She waited until Martin and Zander were at the walls. Plato was still at the fire. She ignored him. She was rosy with the reaction of having an audience to her weakness, and that was transferring to a sheen of sweat all over her body, and Plato was warming a stone for her? She was going to expire of the heat.

Morgan forced her legs to move, hating the jerking motions she had to use, since she'd been upright and in one position for too long. She looked toward Zander only once, and watched his lips thin and his face stiffen.

Then she was at the center of the rug, looking across at the window as she prepared to take the jolt on her knees.

"Morgan?" Zander's whisper touched her ear.

"Dinna' move!" She snarled the command in his direction and slammed her knees into the tapestry on the floor. Then she was shuddering with the blast of heat from the fire while she waited, panting through the throbbing until it became bearable.

"Plato, assist him," Zander said, "since my touch is so abhorrent."

"Dinna' touch me! Either of you. Any of you."

She scrunched her eyes shut and took the landing onto her buttocks with only a gasp this time. She didn't hesitate before falling the final distance to her side, either. She didn't dare. She lay for a few moments while the pain eased away.

Then, she grit her teeth and rolled onto her back, opened her eyes on the amazing height that was the ceiling and smiled. "There. 'Tis done. I'm down. What next would you have of me?"

Zander was at her shoulder, and his eyes had never looked so big, nor so blue, as they did with a sheen of moisture coating them. Morgan shifted her gaze away before his emotion transferred to her. She should be feeling the mortification more than anything, but instead, all she knew was relief.

"Now, we ease the stone under his neck. Zander, you lift his head. Watch when I place it. 'Tis hot."

Zander didn't move. Morgan forced herself to meet his gaze.

"Go ahead, lift my head. Move my neck," she told him. "You already have. One more time won't do more damage, now will it?"

"I dinna' know," he said. "Dear God, I dinna'—"

"You still dinna'! None of you. I'll stick a blade in the first of you that says he does know, and I will na' miss. You ken?"

Zander smiled, although it wasn't a very strong smile like his usual. In fact, he looked a bit white around the lips. Morgan narrowed her eyes as she considered that. A little weakness and he turns sick? Good thing he wasn't the one forced to raid battlefields.

"Lift my head, FitzHugh, or I will. And if I have to expend my strength to do it, I'll take every bit of it out of your hide."

"Is that a promise?" he whispered, sliding an arm under her, while his other slid beneath the small of her back where it arched above the floor.

Morgan closed her eyes then, and let herself feel his touch. She felt it so keenly that she wasn't aware when he lifted her, although she felt the heat when he put her back down. She smiled again.

"That's awful nice, Master Zander. Very nice of you. All of you. My thanks."

Sweat was breaking out all along her hairline at the heat, just like she'd guessed it would, but the blessed warmth was saturating every bit of her spine, making it limber, protected, relaxed and comfortable-feeling for the first time since Zander had assaulted her mouth with his.

She used to think it a kiss; now she didn't know. It didn't resemble what Sophie had tried to plant on her, it didn't resemble what she'd seen the hag doing. It didn't resemble any of that. It must not have been a kiss, and that meant it wasn't given as one.

"When the stone cools, we have to replace it, Zander," Plato spoke from what seemed leagues away.

"Get the one from your room, too. We'll not waste time heating one when it could be on his neck."

"You want him well enough to fence, that badly?"

Morgan kept her eyes closed and listened to the voices floating about in the almost obscene height of this Argylle castle room.

"I dinna' ken what I want anymore, Plato. All I know is this is my fault. I wish it undone. I feel all hurt inside watching him. I wish it atoned for, and I wish my squire healed. I'll heat stones all night."

"So he can fight for you?"

"Nay. I want him well. I dinna' care if he ever fights again after tomorrow."

It's all right, Zander, she longed to say, *I will na' be fighting after tomorrow. It will be nigh impossible to do anything after tomorrow. I guarantee it.*

Chapter 14

In her dream, it was Zander smoothing over her hair, caressing it, leaving it to cascade about them. It was Zander's perfect, muscled body lying alongside hers, his lips touching hers, searching, reaching, accepting nothing less than she give to him absolutely everything she had, and everything she ever would be. If she did, his lips promised her the same.

Then, Morgan woke.

The Argylle castle floor was hard, the stone at her neck was cold, and the man sitting cross-legged beside her was all strength and rugged masculinity. He wasn't paying much attention to tending to her, either. He was sliding his fingers through her loosed hair and combing every strand between his fingers, before putting several little braids in.

"Zander?" Morgan whispered it, and he dropped the miniature braid he'd been weaving. " 'Tis morn?"

He smiled, and he looked more worn and haggard than she possibly could. "Some hours ago, it was," he replied.

"Truly?"

"How do you feel?" He brushed the strands from his lap and reached under her hair to touch the stone beneath her neck. "I let it go cold. Forgive me. 'Twas my chore."

"Your chore?" she asked.

"The others had things to see to. Actually, Plato had to see to things. Martin had to see to Plato. I think that's what I was told."

"Have you been awake all night?" she asked.

He tipped his head in a slight nod. "Most of," he replied. "Don't move. I'll get the other stone."

Morgan turned her head and watched him, and then it occurred to her. *She'd turned her head.*

She was smiling so widely when he turned, that he stopped in place and the stone in the tongs trembled.

"I can move, Zander," she said, and to prove it, swiveled her head about. "It does na' pain, either."

"Plato said it would be so. He said you had to work the injured part back into place with heat. Once that was done, you'd be as right as before. You'll have ache where you held the injured part stable, though. He wanted you warned of it."

She went to rise, and groaned. "He was right," she answered, falling back.

"If you do that again, I can place the stone."

"How did you do it before?"

"Lifted you. You're not very heavy, although you've gained two stone since we met. You're still light as a thistle, and about as strong, I might add."

"I am na!" she protested, and caught the hint of his teasing smile.

"I was thinking while you slept, that you should trim that hank of hair you own," he said.

Morgan considered him for a moment. She supposed it wouldn't matter actually, if that's what he wanted. Then again, after the duel, it wouldn't matter, anyway. "I will, if that is your wish," she replied, softly.

He knelt at her shoulders, his hands busy with the stone. She watched as they shook, banging the tongs together.

"Morgan," he said, her name like a plea.

"What is it?" she asked.

Blazing, blue eyes bored into hers at the question, and she gasped at the answer. Then, the stone hit the floor and she was in his arms. Morgan didn't even know how she got there. All she knew was complete and utter joy. Zander's hands filled with her hair, wrapping it about his fists, and he plundered her mouth, much as he had before.

Morgan wasn't letting him have all the motion, though. She was using everything he'd taught her, and she sucked on his tongue until it squirmed out of her grasp. Then, his lips were on her jaw, her throat, tracing to the button placket of her shirt, and sending nerve signals throughout her body in anticipation of a pleasure so vast, she'd have no comparison. It was exactly what she needed before she sacrificed herself to the English champion.

She wondered how Zander knew.

Then, she knew she couldn't let it continue. If he found her true gender, he'd finish this, *they'd* finish this, and she wouldn't be able to meet her destiny. She'd get nothing other than a lifetime as his play-time wench, while the beauteous, perfect, Gwynneth Argylle got the position of wife.

Not that a KilCreggar would even consider the position of a FitzHugh wife, but his whore? She pushed at his chest, and received tighter arms about her for the effort.

"Dinna' stop me, Morgan . . . please?"

Breath caressed where he'd just moistened with his tongue, and if she hadn't a binding holding everything in place, the pin-pricks of her nipples would be trying to bore into his chest. Morgan gasped at the sensation and pushed harder against him. She was preparing to die, rather than contemplate him being matched to the Lady Gwynneth.

"Nay, Zander. Nay!"

He lifted his head, stared at her, and then shut his eyes. His groan wasn't as raw or tormented as it had been on the target field, but it meant the same thing. Morgan knew it the instant he pulled away, sliding from beneath her without looking her in the eye.

He was on his feet and adjusting his kilt about himself and looking anywhere but at her.

"Zander?" she whispered, trying to get her body to follow

his; Plato hadn't exaggerated the ache she'd feel. "I've got something that needs saying."

"Don't." He put a hand, palm outward, toward her and placed his other over his eyes. "Please, don't . . . say another word. Not one. I beg it of you."

Morgan lay flat, her hands making fists at her side, and her lips tightening so they could force her not to spew the truth. She was stiff, and it had nothing to do with her back. It had to do with keeping him from the truth until they prepared her body for burial.

"Sweet Jesu', but I hate myself, Morgan. I dinna' wish this. I dinna' like the feeling."

"Zander—"

"Dinna' stop me, and dinna' interrupt again! I've words that need spoken, and then we speak no more of this, you ken?"

"I ken," she whispered.

He moved to sit on his bed, put his elbows on his knees and rested his head in his hands. Morgan had a very good view of him, from her vantage point, and he wasn't wearing his loin-wrap. Her face was hotter than any heat stone could make it. She was lucky that he didn't look up.

"I've no taste for boys. At least, I dinna' afore you. I dinna' know why, either. I have no leanings towards other lads, just you. You, Morgan, and I dinna' know why. Oh, God."

She watched as he tensed, and then he was shaking with what could only be sobs. Morgan bit her tongue until it bled a pool of the liquid into her mouth. She was not going to tell him! She was not going to be his whore! She was not! She was not!

She repeated it over and over again to herself as he shook with emotion. He could find out when they buried her, and not before. As the last true KilCreggar, she demanded nothing less. She rolled her head back to look up at the ceiling far above her and the beams that crossed it to hold up another floor above it.

"I went to confession. I told a priest about you . . . about us. I asked him for absolution. I want you to know this."

He was sniffing away any evidence of his lack of control and sounded like the little boy he must have once been.

"What happened?" she asked the ceiling.

"All I received was a proposition to go to his chambers. The lecherous bastard! A man of the cloth, and he—! They—! Blast and damn their souls to Hell, too! Along with mine!"

He didn't sound like a little boy anymore. Morgan didn't look to see why. She could imagine, and she wasn't telling him anything. No matter what he said, she wasn't telling him anything. She wasn't going to spend her life as a FitzHugh whore. She wasn't.

"I begged Plato not to leave me alone with you, too. Damn him. Damn me, and damn him again. I surrounded myself with clansmen so I would na' be left alone with you, and what happens? They abandon me."

"I recollect that they tried to purchase me from you," she remarked.

"No one purchases you from me. No one!"

"You canna' be with me, Zander, and yet you won't save yourself from this? Why?"

"I dinna' know. Just as I dinna' know why I feel this way. I dinna' ask for it. God forbid! I had no place in my life for a love such as I feel for you."

She was not telling him a word! Not one! Morgan moaned with the vow, and choked on the horrid-tasting blood in her mouth as she swallowed it. She was not telling him a word! "Zander?" she whispered, despite every restraint she was putting on herself.

"Dinna' say a word, Morgan. 'Tis I who must face this. I who must try to learn to live with it."

"Live . . . with it?" she repeated, in a broken whisper.

"I canna' have you, but I will na' give you up. I will na', although Plato asks oft' enough. I will na' give you to any man, for any amount of silver. I dinna' ask why, anymore. It's enough that I know it as fact."

"I will na' serve another anyway, Zander. I am too stubborn."

"That much is true. I hope that is one trait my betrothed does na' have of yours."

"Your—?" She couldn't finish it. She was afraid of what it meant. In the next words, she knew, too.

"Why do you ken I picked a bride who matches you?"

Tears filled both eyes and she didn't know how she managed to still be breathing. He'd gone and selected a bride because he wanted Morgan? *Oh, dearest God!*

He sighed, loudly enough for her to hear over her silent grief, and then he was speaking again. Morgan knew that if she'd told him when she'd shown him knife-throwing, he'd have wanted her. He'd have wed her instead. She, rather than the petite Lady Gwynneth, could have been his wife, the woman to bear him little, black-haired bairns. *Oh God!*

Morgan moaned, feeling the rivulets of emotion wash over her in wave after wave of belly-churning sickness.

". . . something I need to give you. You are na' to tell a soul the significance. You ken?"

He was waiting for an answer and she had to get control over herself in order to give it. She focused on the ceiling above her, and begged God to numb her heart until it ceased beating. If He would do that, she'd be content. She didn't think she could manage to take this long enough to make it to the evening duel. Any more, and she'd be putting a dirk into her own heart to numb it.

"What?" she finally managed to say.

"I've got something for you."

"I'll na' take another thing from you Zander FitzHugh." Her shoulders were shaking on the floor with the repressed feeling. "I . . . I will na' . . . I canna' repay it."

"I do na' give it as a debt!"

Tears were blinding her when he knelt beside her again, and she didn't do anything other than let them slide into her ears, and stare at the ceiling. She didn't dare look at him. She was being stupid, too, she tried telling herself. What, but knowing he'd sent the woman he loved to her death, would be better payment for anything the FitzHughs had done to the KilCreggars? The only thing better would be if he were their laird. Perhaps the laird would hear of it, and know. It was actually a perfect revenge, if she thought of it, but it was torturing her worse than it ever could him.

At least her torment would be short, however. His was going to be life-long. She hoped the Lady Gwynneth had the tongue of a serpent, and aged poorly.

Morgan blinked the tears from existence, rubbed at her eyes and turned her head to meet his eyes. Zander looked like he'd been through a torturer's embrace, by the dead look in his eyes. He was holding something out to her, too. Morgan forced herself to sit cross-legged, face him, and look at what it was.

" 'Tis a *skean dhu* known as the dragon blade. 'Tis said it possesses magical powers. I dinna' know of any of that. It's very old. Very valuable. It bears my family crest, the dragon."

The blade was stiletto-length, and polished to a slick-water shine. There were two dragons molded into a hilt, their mouths open and appearing to spew forth the blade, while their tails intertwined to form a mysterious, beautiful, and wicked-looking handle. At the crest of the hilt was a heart-shaped, blood-red ruby. Morgan's eyes were as wide as her mouth as she looked at it.

"Take it," he said, holding it out.

"I canna'," she replied.

"I understand." He placed the knife on the floor between them. "I canna' touch you either. Things happen. 'Tis a curse. 'Tis also wondrous, if you ken what I mean."

She nodded slightly. "I ken," she whispered.

"I give you this with one condition, Morgan."

She looked across at him and waited. The dragon knife's ruby was winking at her from the floor, drawing what light it could in order to tempt her to touch it, embrace it, caress it, and own it.

"Yes?" she asked.

"You are to use it on me the very next time I canna' control myself. You are not to miss. You miss, and I will be forced to kill you with my bare hands. You ken?"

Morgan gasped. He smiled sadly at her. "Put your mind to rest, for I dinna' expect you ever to use it."

"You dinna'?" she asked.

"I dinna' ask for this, Morgan, my love, but I will na' give you up. I canna'! I will wed my black-haired lass, and I will slake my lust on her. That should give me enough control of whatever we have between us, that I can be with you. I will give her my lust, but I will never give her my love. I canna'. It belongs to you."

Morgan closed her eyes. She couldn't take the sight of Zander FitzHugh baring his heart for another blood-spilling moment.

"Such a love is not sanctioned by God. I canna' change that. Neither can you. That is where the dragon blade comes in. I will na' give up my hope of heaven. Nor yours."

Her innards twisted and she opened her mouth to tell him. She no longer cared about anything like revenge, or honor, or the little black-haired lass he was going to give himself to. She only wanted the torment over with. The door flying open was what stopped her. Morgan had the blade, that was supposed to be hidden in a sock, tucked into her belt behind the kilt band, in the same motion she used to rise, and she stood beside Zander to glare across at Plato and Martin.

"He moves!" Martin expelled, with a whoosh of air, probably brought about by the shock.

"I was fairly certain he would be, by now. What have you two been up to, anyway?" He looked from Zander to

Morgan and back, and he had a frown etched into place
when he finished.

"Nothing of interest," Zander replied.

"The Earl requests the duel to start immediately. He has
tripe scheduled for sup. He wishes the blood-letting over
with by then, and expects a swift end. Come along. We
were sent to fetch you."

"Have the conditions been met?" Zander asked.

Plato looked right at Morgan. "Aye," he answered.

"Good. Go along now. We'll be at your heels. At least I
will be. I've got some words of encouragement for my
champion."

The door shut behind them. Zander waited, without
saying a word. He didn't have to. Morgan knew what he
was saying.

It was time. They both knew it.

She turned her head and nodded at the same moment that
he did at her. She'd never seen anything so beautiful in her
life as the look in those midnight-blue eyes. She hoped
she would recall it when she was given her death-blow.
She'd like it to be her last recollection of this life.

He strode to the door, opened it and went out first.
"Come along then, Squire. We've a Sassenach to best, and
tripe to eat. Damn the man and his taste for that delicacy.
I prefer haggis."

He was still bemoaning the Earl's menu as he led her
through the corridors and down one flight of steps after
another, Morgan keeping pace with only a slight limp. Then,
they were out on a parade ground, surrounded by gray, stone
walls, and filled with humanity. Morgan kept her eyes on the
light-blue, satin-jacketed man she was supposed to fence
against. He was wearing a strange-looking outfit, completely
showing his legs, and leaving not one muscle hidden beneath
the dark blue-colored tights he had on.

He was also standing in front of a platform that held a
petite, black-haired lass with a heart-shaped face and a

bow mouth. She recognized Morgan, and her face broke into a smile. Morgan didn't return it. She couldn't. She turned away.

"You can still halt this," Zander said at her shoulder.

"You already know it's too late. Dinna' speak of it again."

Her words sounded strange and slurred and Zander narrowed his eye at her. That's what came from a bitten tongue, swelled with the cuts. Morgan's lips twitched at the thought. She sounded more like she'd been drinking.

"As the challenger, you have first pick of blades, My Lord FitzHugh!"

"Go on, Morgan. Find the balanced one."

Morgan stepped to the velvet-lined case, holding two swords. Both were made by a master smithy. That much was apparent instantly. They were used often, if the wear along the inner part of one's hilt was any indication. They had also been sharpened recently. Morgan picked up the heavily-used one, and tested it.

It had perfect balance. Smooth. Easily moved. Light. She made a few motions with it, and watched the English champion's reaction to it. He was a conceited prig, but his worry wasn't hidden well enough. She put that sword back in and picked up the second. The difference was slight, and only one attuned to blades, like she was, could have noted it. The arc was not nearly as perfect, nor did the weight move as smoothly. In fact, the blade seemed to be a hairs-breadth of time behind the slicing motion she made with it. Morgan smiled.

"I will take this one," she said.

As duels go, it was a stunning sight, lasting past the perfect serving temperature for the Earl's tripe supper, and well into the night. Torches were brought and lit to make it more easily observed and enjoyed. Morgan had told Zander what she liked least about fencing was all the dancing around, and here she was faced with a master of it.

She just wished he was good enough that she could put her neck in his path without it looking that way. He wasn't. He was good, though, and she spent hour after hour trying to get him to take his stab. Time after time their blades clanged against each other; sometimes he gained ground, backing Morgan into a corner from whence it looked she'd falter for certain, and then she'd be sending his next lunged blow to the ground, where his blade kicked up grass and straw while she leaped to the side to torment him from another vantage. Other times, Morgan clearly had him, although all she'd do, when she had him cornered, was more fancy dancing with the blade while he recuperated enough to attack again.

Sweat poured off both of them, and it trickled from beneath his wig, until he took the stupid thing off, and then it gleamed off his shaved head. Morgan, on the other hand, hadn't thought to re-braid her hair, and it was flying about her, from the opening parry to every move after that.

She was constantly having to toss it out of her way, and more than once had her attention caught for a moment by Zander's frown over it. He'd warned her what would happen if her hair got in her way during a battle.

The English champion wasn't good enough to take her, and she wasn't humiliated enough to let him. She finally accepted the inevitable. No Scotsman would allow himself to be taken by such a pitiful specimen.

She started attacking with a vengeance, serving him blow after blow, until one flick of her blade had his sword flying through the air, and right into her left hand. Morgan stalked him with both, then, slipping a button here, and a stitch there, until his waistcoat popped open. He was on his knees, begging her. Morgan raised both swords above her head.

"Morgan, nay! The bargain was changed! Morgan!"

It was Zander yelling with that orator's voice of his. She

ignored him and flung both swords through the material making up the open flaps of this English braggart's doublet, the force of the blows and her accuracy putting him on his back in a knee-cracking arch, and pinning him to the turf, where the hilts swayed on either side of his frightened torso. The crowd was making noise, but it had been throughout the fight. She hadn't heard it then, and she didn't hear it now.

Morgan lifted her head to the heavens and yelled her frustration, hatred, and pain as loudly as she could. It wasn't directed at anyone except herself.

Chapter 15

"Name your sum, friend FitzHugh! I will pay it. The lad is worth anything. I offer half my horses and all my land for the lad."

The Earl hiccoughed halfway through his offer. Morgan drained her flagon of ale and set it on the table beside her. She giggled as it fell off, right into Zander's lap below her. She watched him immediately put his hands on his manhood to protect it. That was even more funny, she decided.

"I thought you offered *all* your horses and *half* your land." Plato guffawed from further down the table as he said it.

"Slight difference, FitzHugh, only slight. Very well. I will give all my horses, all my land, and my wife, too."

"Cease threatening me with your wife!" Zander complained, sitting up long enough to groan, before falling back to the floor.

Morgan thought it was as hilarious as trying to get her tongue to work, right after the cuts were numbed by mead, and caressed by creamed beef. She laughed so hard the tears slid from her eyes. She wiped at them with her sleeve, before motioning the serving wench to refill her tankard.

"I will give everything for a lad with his talent. Where is that FitzHugh? He has yet to bargain. I will give him my in-laws, too."

Phineas was looking everyone over with a cold, light-blue gaze. Drink wasn't improving his temperament, Morgan noticed, and she wrinkled her nose at him. She decided it would have felt better to stick her tongue out at him, then she just did it, although the moment it was out of her mouth, she had to tuck it back in with her fingers. That was even funnier than having it large and plump-feeling, and it was in the way no matter what she tried to eat or drink.

"Is he still here?" The Earl was eyeing the vacant spot next to Morgan. She thought that was just as hilarious, especially since his wig was awry and hanging from one ear.

"I'm here." Zander was attempting to get himself off the floor and looking like it was the hardest thing he'd ever done. He made it to his stool where he teetered for a moment and fell back down. "And the lad is not for sale. Ever. Cease this topic."

"But he handles a blade better than anyone!"

"You should see him with a bow . . . as long as the arrows are included!" Zander choked on the laughter and Morgan put her foot on his belly to make him pay. She shouldn't have. The next moment she was flat on her back, and Zander was atop her, pinning her easily. He had a lobe of her ear in his teeth, too and was nibbling.

Morgan literally cooed at the sensation.

"Now stop that, young Zander. That's na' a woman! If 'tis a woman you're wanting, take my Sally Bess to your chamber. She's lass enough for you." The Earl offered it amid a spate of belching.

"I'll not take a lass, unless you give one to my champion! 'Tis he that deserves one. What say you, Morgan? You ready for your first tumble?"

Morgan shoved at him, but he wasn't moving, and she was too dizzy to get out from under him without his cooperation. She started doing push-ups with him, and after about thirty, he started getting the idea. Then, he had his hands on her shoulders and was doing his own push-ups.

Their eyes locked. *This is terrible,* Morgan thought. Then she giggled. It wasn't remotely terrible.

"If we can do two-hundred separately, we should be able to do four hundred this way, no?"

" 'Tisn't fair. You're heavier than me," she complained.

"So . . . I actually do best you at push-ups?" He was grinning and lowering his mouth toward hers and Morgan barely missed the contact as he collapsed onto her.

"Get him off me!" She complained, trying to roll away.

"My brother's tastes appear to be wider than I thought," Phineas remarked, lifting Zander by the belt long enough for Morgan to crawl out from beneath him.

She would have thanked him, then she saw who it was. She slapped his helping hand away and stood on her own, although everything was bobbing and weaving about once she got to her feet.

"Sally Bess! Take the young champion to a chamber. Make a man of him!"

A huge woman came striding over, taking up her entire view, and Morgan's eyes widened. She turned to run, but wasn't a wobbly step into it before she was pulled atop this woman's shoulder and carried away like a prize of war.

She thought that was the most hilarious thing that could happen.

Morgan opened her eyes as slowly as possible and still the light was screaming into her head, making her retch with the throb. She was on her belly and heaving before another moment passed. Then, she was held in a motherly embrace against a wealth of bosom.

"You poor, wee lass. Have you no idea what the mead does to you?"

Lass? Morgan wondered, falling back into the softness of the bed and holding to both sides of her head to keep it from exploding.

"Where . . . am I?" she whispered, wondering why her

teeth didn't just fly out of her mouth and save her the trouble of checking for them.

"In my bed. Sally Bess at your side. World's champion bedder. Pleased to meet with you, I am, Morgan. Or is it Morganna?"

"Oh God." Morgan was on her belly, retching again, and the woman was there, holding her over a pot, the entire time.

"There, lass, it's all right. I would na' tell a body your secret. I think it's rather a grand thing, actually. A woman . . . besting that Lord Cantor's swordsman! And doing it in such a grand fashion, too. As I live and breathe, makes me proud just to be one. It does."

"Where . . . are my clothes?" Morgan asked.

"The FitzHugh is having another kilt delivered. I told him to make it sturdier than the last, since it tore."

"It . . . tore?"

"Oh, my yes. As did my blouse. You're an impatient devil when you want to be."

"Where . . . are my clothes?" Morgan tried again, clenching her teeth. It wasn't for emphasis, although it sounded it, but to keep them from chattering on each other and making more trauma for her.

"Well, let me see now. Most of them are scattered about the hall, although I left a bit of your under-tunic on the steps. It was all ragged and only half a garment, anyhow. And, you had the strangest bit of gray plaid stuck to your chest."

Morgan came off the bed, and was shoved right back down by Sally Bess. "Dinna' fash yourself. It's safe. I figured you needed it. As a charm, or some-such. It's right here."

Morgan tipped an eye to the fraying square of KilCreggar plaid the woman was holding. She watched her own hand tremble as she reached for it, and wished she could blame it all on the mead. She'd almost lost it! She didn't care that Sally Bess was watching as she brought it to her lips.

"I knew it was a talisman. I knew it!" The woman's glee carried too much thumping with it. Morgan put both hands to her temples to stay it.

"Forgive me, lass. It's the excitement."

"What excitement?"

"Why . . . knowing what I do of the FitzHugh champion, and having said champion in my very own bed, and best yet, having everyone else know of it!"

"Where . . . did you say my clothing was, again?" Morgan was choking, and it wasn't on any bile.

"Well . . . your boots are in the hall. There's a sock on the stairs. Your belt's at the door, along with your knives, and I'm wearing this."

"In . . . the hall? The stairs?"

"You had a very wild night, you did."

"I . . . did?" Morgan whispered the question.

"Oh, my yes. And quite an animal you are. Had me shaking and shivering and screaming until dawn arrived. You should have heard the noises I made."

Morgan opened her eyes again. The light was just as hellish, the woman just as broad, but the amusement on her face was a thing of beauty. Morgan's grin was wide enough to split her cheeks.

"You've got the whole day off to rest, too. I've told them you'll need it. You're young, but I managed to wear you out. You're completely exhausted and sleeping with the broadest smile on your face. The last is no lie, by-the-by. You were. The greatest smile. Of course I let that Zander fellow see it, too."

"He . . . what?" Morgan tried to put all her aggravation into it, but the combination of her aching head and her enlarged tongue made it sound like a small child talking.

"He had to make certain where you were, and that you weren't harmed. I showed him you were na' coming to any harm in Sally Bess's bed, and I was properly angered, too, at him thinking you might be."

"He was in here?"

"Aye. First thing this morn. Probably when he sobered up enough to notice you was missing. That's a fine man you've got for your master. You should na' have let him betroth the lass, Gwynneth, though. She's na' woman enough for him. You are."

Morgan's entire body was blushing beneath the sheets. "What did he see?"

"Who?"

"My master, Zander FitzHugh," she replied.

"Well . . . I had it so you'd look a bit . . . you know."

"Sally Bess," Morgan began, using a threatening tone good enough to attribute to Zander.

"Oh, very well. I had you on your front, hair all about, and you've shoulders more befitting a lad than a lass, any-way. You had one foot off this side of the bed, and another down the end. Then, I made certain I was na' wearing much. In fact," she lowered her voice to a whisper, "I had nothing save your kilt wrapped about me."

Morgan started laughing and had to halt it as her teeth complained about the effort. Then, her head joined in. She clenched her mouth shut and held to her head at the same time to get the ache in the same rhythm.

"It was perfect! You were even snoring!"

"I do na' snore! Ouch!" Morgan held her head tighter.

"You do. Well, not loudly, but you had that great grin on your face, and a bit of a rumble to your breath, and it was perfect! You should have seen the look on his face! It was priceless!"

The bed was shaking with Sally Bess's amusement. Morgan lay in the midst of it and tried to keep her eyeballs from aching as much as her tongue.

Zander FitzHugh was as good as his word, and not only was a fresh outfit delivered, but the Earl of Argylle had food delivered four times that day, instead of three, and a warmed bath sent up, too. He was also offering a pick of his stallions to Morgan, should she stay and favor them with an exhibition of skean-throwing. Morgan sat in her hipbath and considered it.

She'd never had luxury of any kind, and Sally Bess had washed and pinned her hair atop her head and even scrubbed her back. The woman had also had the audacity to stage more graphic rounds of physical lust. Morgan had to put her hands over her ears to shut it out as the woman hollered and moaned and jumped on the mattress to make the proper sounds for what seemed like hours that evening, and thrice more through the night.

Now, it was morning again, and time to face everyone. Morgan waited until Sally Bess finished her braid, tucked it along her back and gave her nod of approval to Morgan's entire outfit. Then she opened her chamber door and proceeded to announce to the world that she needed some time off.

There was an audience all down the hall, and more on the steps, and Morgan swaggered as much as possible through all the whistles and applause. She even managed to keep her face from flaming.

Zander had a look of murder about him when she saw him, and he wasn't even looking for her. Actually she knew he was looking for her, but doing his best to act like he wasn't. Morgan sauntered across the parade ground to join him.

"You are a worthless squire, Morgan," he began.

She stepped back and didn't need to act confused. Her entire body was in that state.

"Do you still have your dirks?"

"Of course," she replied.

"And the dragon blade? You let that harlot get her fingers on that?"

"I—" She stopped for a moment. How was she supposed to answer that? Either answer was bad.

"You lost it?"

"Of course not! I have it, just like I have all my dirks. I would na' lose them."

"You were stewed in ale and falling-down drunk. How do you know what you lost and what you didn't?"

"I dinna' lose a thing."

"You lost your innocence, dinna' you?"

Morgan wasn't about to lie. She had to resort to a shrug. "What of it?" she asked.

"What of it? This innocence? You can only give it once, and I recall hearing all about the woman you were going to have. Not take, mind you. Well, blast it all, Morgan! You didn't have, or take. The fat harlot did the having and the taking. You were like butter to her and probably as satisfying."

"Now, that's not true," Morgan responded.

Zander favored her with a side-long glance. The midnight-blue of his eyes was vivid and intense with the redness to his face. *He was so angered, he was flushing?* she wondered.

"It's true." He ran fingers through his hair, shuffling it again on his shoulders and then faced her. "I thought you were different, but you're not. You're like everyone else, aren't you?"

"I'm human," she answered.

"Yes. Yes, you are. Congratulations. Welcome to Hell."

Morgan would rather he just hit her and be done. "Hell?" she whispered.

"I was actually beginning to think you might be an angel, Morgan. An angel on earth. A vengeful, killing angel, but an angel, nonetheless. I'm a little disappointed to find out I was wrong."

"No one is an angel, Zander."

"No doubt about that, is there? I've the proof standing right in front of me," he replied.

"I never said I was anything other than what I appeared." It was true, she told herself.

"True enough. And appearances can be deceiving. You also said that. Angelic face, human needs."

"I'm sorry I disappointed you," she mumbled. She was, too. She should have stayed at his side and hidden in his chamber, and since they had both been so drunk they were almost caressing each other on the floor in front of witnesses, they most certainly wouldn't have stopped once they got to his chamber. She was smart enough to know that. She and Zander would have been intimate. They would have been very intimate. She wondered if that was why he was angry. He wanted her . . . or he wanted the Morgan he knew.

"You did more than disappoint me, lad, you've put soil all over my ideal. I had you up on a pedestal, and right now I'm swallowing a very vinegary potion of my own making about it."

"I've never claimed to be perfect."

"Well, you're are na', either. You lost perfection when you let that harlot cart you off."

"I could na' stop her. Why dinna' you stop her if it meant so much?"

He sighed. "I dinna' know what I felt then. I know now. I knew when I looked down at your angelic face in the filth of her bed."

"I've na' lost my innocence, Zander," Morgan whispered, finally.

"You lost more than that, lad. You lost all your clothing, too. That constitutes quite a loss to me. Now, you owe me for another sett. Your time of servitude has been doubled."

"Oh," Morgan replied. It was all she could think of.

"And after all your words about how you'd save yourself for the bonniest of lasses, a nymphet that looks like our Sheila, and what was all that? Posturing?"

"It was—"

"It was the idealism of youth, and I thought it true. Stupid me."

"I dinna' understand this," Morgan whispered.

"What's to understand? I fell in love with an ideal. A youth above all that's earthy and wicked and lustful, and what happens? It gets tossed in my face by a fat harlot."

"Sally Bess is more than that."

"Of course you'd defend her now. I'm not even surprised."

"But . . . you told them to find a lass for me. I heard you."

"I dinna' mean it. I would never have sent you off to find release in a whore's body. You're so much more special than that. I'd have found the perfect receptacle for you."

Morgan felt his complete and total censure, and was so close to tears she hoped he wouldn't hear it in her voice. She didn't know what was wrong with him. "There is no perfect receptacle for me, Zander," she whispered, and it was almost inaudible. She knew he heard he as his jaw tightened.

"This little talk is getting us nowhere, and I've work to do."

"What is it? I'll assist."

"My squire, Martin, tends me well enough. I could hardly wait for you, now could I? While all else is falling down about my ears, you're locked in with a wench, fulfilling your fantasies. Not once, mind you, but four, or was it five times? You're insatiable. What do you have to say for yourself?"

"It was five," Morgan finally said.

He glared at her. "And I thought you were different. Stupid me."

He turned his back on her and stalked away. Morgan looked down at the grass where he'd been standing, and watched as it sprang back from his footprint. She didn't know whether to follow him or not. Martin was squiring him? Did that mean she was supposed to be squiring Plato, then? She supposed she should have asked it when she had the chance.

"Your presence is requested at the earl's private rooms, Squire Morgan."

Morgan looked over at the small lad who stood there, an

arm out with a towel draped over it, for some silly reason. She frowned. "Now?" she asked.

He nodded.

She looked after Zander's retreating back and sighed. She obviously wasn't needed by him. She followed the earl's servant, her fingers flying to the three dirks at her back and the dragon blade at her stomach.

If the earl wanted a knife-tossing exhibition, she'd give him one, but only if her master approved it. Morgan took the steps easily, only the slightest ache in her back, and then found herself in such stuffy luxury, she couldn't breathe.

The earl hadn't dressed yet, and his close-cropped head looked strange without a wig. He looked her over from his position lounging on his bed, then be beckoned her closer.

"I have heard of your prowess, lad," he said.

She colored uneasily, wondering which prowess he was referring to.

"And I wish to purchase your talents for myself. Name your price. I will pay it."

"I belong to Zander FitzHugh," she replied.

"FitzHugh can be dealt with later. Name a price, so I know how much. Together, we'll make a fortune in London. They'll pay so much to watch you, it will be like robbery."

"I belong to Zander FitzHugh, and my talents are his to sell."

He sighed, and waved his hand at another lad holding a cloth over his arm. "Send for FitzHugh." He waved the boy out. Then he turned back to Morgan. "I don't like arguing." he said.

She swallowed nervously and waited. *Please, Zander? Please don't sell me to this great buffoon. Please?* The litany of her plea went on and on, gaining in cadence with her fretting. Zander arrived within moments. Morgan wondered how they'd found him so fast. Although he had a shuttered look about him, Morgan could tell he was worried. She could only guess about what.

"The lad will not toss a knife unless you approve it, FitzHugh, nor will he come into my service. I do not know where you find such loyal servants, but I wish to purchase the lad's services for my own. Order it."

Zander looked at Morgan. She had her eyes wide and was shaking her head with a quick, hummingbird-type motion, so it wouldn't be as easy to spot.

"Morgan will toss for you on my terms. You've offered a stallion from your stables. I accept. Otherwise, I dinna'. The lad's talents are not for sale, not for any amount of silver and not at any time. Morgan? Go to my chamber. Prepare yourself for the exhibition. You'll have a chance to use all your weapons. Put out the word, Argylle. Invite your Sassenach friends. I would like to show what a real Scotsman can do. Morgan? Why are you still standing there? I gave you an order. And another thing, My Lord. About the fencing duel the other eve. I believe . . . ."

Morgan didn't hear another word. She was racing to his chamber.

Chapter 16

Castle Argylle was filled to the crenellations with humanity, and more seemed to keep arriving, and no one had asked, or would let her exhibit anything, and it had been four days. Days when Zander wouldn't let her out of his sight. Days when she'd had to caress the dragon blade's hilt whenever she caught his eyes on her. Days when he'd be laughing and charming, and then sullen and moody. Those were the days he was drinking.

Those days were the worst.

Morgan felt pulled taut, much like the string of a bow, and on the fifth day, she knew she had to get out. The castle's walls were thick, solid, and stifling, and the bowstring she felt she was becoming was at the peak of flex and due to snap.

She walked out of Zander's chamber with the remainders of the previous night's feast, and tripped over one of the bodies in the hall. Dishes went flying, lads of all ages and description started up to stare at her, and several of them grabbed for her dirtied flagons and the tray, before begging her to allow them to serve her.

Begging? she wondered. Morgan backed into Zander's chamber and slammed the door.

"What is it lad? Enemy inside the walls?"

He probably thought he was being amusing. Morgan glared at his reclining figure beneath the off-white, cut-work linens. "'Tis a village full of lads in the hall."

"The entire castle is crawling with lads, Morgan. And lasses. Let's not forget the bloom of them."

Morgan stiffened. "I care not about that. Why? When is the exhibition, and when can we be gone from here?"

"Be gone? Why? The Earl has excellent mead, his kitchen is more than capable, and his entertainment . . . well, they leave nothing wanting, now do they, lad? Or was Sally Bess taken?"

"We've been prisoners for almost a sennight, FitzHugh. I dinna' ken why."

"The earl wants to make certain his Sassenach friends arrive. I heard it. They're setting up quite a contest. Takes time."

"I have changed my mind. I dinna' wish to compete," Morgan complained.

"You have no choice now, lad. I spoke for you. Calm yourself and get me another mead."

"I canna' step from the chamber without running over bodies. 'Tis denser than the worst battle-field. What fairy has stolen Argylle's wits? Surely there are encampments for these lads."

"There are camps all over outside the walls, Morgan, but everyone wants to be here."

"Why?"

He raised onto an elbow to study her. She should have been in the kitchens by now and then she wouldn't have to see that great, haired chest, naked and immense, and contrasting nicely with the off-white color of his sheets. Morgan turned her face aside and hoped he wouldn't spot the blush. It was a forlorn hope.

"You rosy up pretty well for a broke-in lad, Squire Morgan. I would na' have believed it. Nor, I might add, would all your followers."

"What followers?"

She looked back to ask it. She shouldn't have. He was sitting now, his arms on his knees and not another stitch on. As many times as she'd seen him thus, it was still bothersome, and she backed away before she could help it.

"The lads camped at your stoop. You dinna' think they stay for me, do you?"

"I have no followers. 'Tis stupid of you to think so. There must be no other room for them."

"Morgan, if I dinna' think you serious, I'd accuse you of vanity for wanting me to notice. They are your followers. They wait for a glimpse of the young squire that bested Lord Cantor's best swordsman. Worse, the rest of my servants have been regaling them with tales of your hunting skills."

"I dinna' wish to be talked of that way."

"Worse still," he continued as if she hadn't spoken, "are the lasses. They've been listening to that Sally Bess. You show the same prowess between a lass' legs as you do on the field of battle. You're becoming quite a legend. Why, you've only to look a maiden's way, and you'll have your pick. I would na' take that Sally Bess again, though. She has na' kept to herself. Why, just last eve—"

"Will you cease this? I will na' be talked of! I will na' be discussed this way!"

"You will na' that, you will na' this. Fame is uncaring of your desires, lad. Someone should have forewarned you."

"Zander, I need to get outside."

"Open the drape. 'Tis airless in here, anyway."

"You dinna' ken! I have to get outside! I have to! I am being held hostage, and I dinna' do anything!" She knew her voice was rising, but couldn't stay it. She was barely holding in the tears.

"You bested an English champion. You sliced open his clothing, and then pinned him uselessly to the ground by it. You didn't harm a hair on his head, and yet humiliated him, so he will na' show his face. Now you say you dinna' do anything? The clans have awaited a champion like you for years. Mayhap longer than that."

"I dinna' wish this," she whispered.

He waited for her to look over at him before he answered. "What is it you do wish, then?"

"I wish to go hunting."

His eyebrows rose. "Hunting?"

"Surely the earl needs meat to feed all these guests. Surely there is game in yonder forest, or I'll go further afield."

"All true, but why? You need to take life that badly?"

Morgan's eyes moistened, but she didn't blink. She was hoping he wouldn't notice. "I need to feel alive," she answered finally.

"Fetch me my clothing. You wish to hunt? We'll hunt."

He stood. Morgan backed to the wall.

"I canna'," she whispered.

"Canna' . . . or will na'?" he asked.

It wasn't a blush any longer, it was full-out fire licking at her cheeks when he stood up. She looked above him. She looked at the floor. She looked to both sides of him. She looked at the door. She closed her eyes for a moment, and started all over again. Above him, the floor . . . and all she saw was the immensity of Zander FitzHugh. "Canna'," she answered finally.

"Morgan?"

His voice lowered and then he was walking toward her. Morgan had a hand to the dragon blade at the same time she slid to the chamber door. Her movements stopped him in his tracks.

"I'll await you outside," she whispered and slid out before he could stop her.

She was surrounded by more lads than she could count, and all clamoring to be near, touch, and possibly serve her. One actually asked if she needed a squire. *A squire to a squire?* she wondered.

She was back in the chamber before Zander had his under tunic pulled down. The door slammed behind her and he looked over. Then he laughed. Morgan knew her eyes were huge. "I have decided to await you in here, FitzHugh," she said.

"You having a bit of trouble with your popularity?"

"I dinna' ask for it and I will na' accept it. I will na'! I want them to go. Make them go."

"I canna'."

"You are my master. You must protect me. I dinna' wish followers. I will na' accept this fame. I will na'!"

Zander yanked on his shirt, hooked his belt, had his *feile breacan* on, and was sitting to pull on his boots before he spoke to her again. Morgan watched every movement, every time the sinew beneath the skin twinged in his forearms, every time he drew breath with that great chest, and she wondered what it would feel like to be in those arms, and against that chest, and protected by someone else for the first time in her life. She shook her head to clear it.

"I don't see much choice for you, Morgan. I canna' send your followers away."

"You have to keep them away from me, though. You have to!"

"Having others awaiting you frightens you, does na' it?"

"Nothing frightens me," she answered.

"Very well. I'll stay here, while you hunt alone." He lifted his foot to take the boot back off. Morgan rushed him.

"Nay, Zander! You have to get me out of here! You have to get me through all of them."

"I do, do I? Seems to me, I only have to go back to sleep. I dinna' have an urge to go hunting. I dinna' need to escape my Lord Argylle's hospitality. I dinna' have leagues of followers awaiting my every movement and word. I dinna' seem to have half your problems."

"Please?" Morgan whispered.

He rolled his eyes and stood. "Very well, Morgan lad. We'll gird ourselves to deal with your followers together. I only wish it was me they were waiting to see. I could use every one of them to sway their clans."

"Take them," Morgan said.

"You canna' take followers, Morgan. Followers go where they wish. That's the beauty of swaying them to a cause. They follow, and they are na' easily dismissed. The English are finally learning that, thanks to our king, Robert."

"Then, use your big orator's voice and speak with them. Sway them. Tell them I am nothing, save your squire. Tell them I am what I am, thanks to you. Go on, tell them."

"My big orator's voice?" The smile was in his voice. Morgan grabbed his arm.

"You must use it! I need deep, gulping breaths of air, and I canna' get them in this stuffy castle. I need space! I need the exercise. The little you have me do in here is not enough! I have to get out! Zander?"

He was looking down at where her fingers were still wrapped about his bicep. "You should na' do that, Morgan," he said, and his voice was lower and deeper then before.

Morgan lifted her eyes to his and sucked in breath. "But I need to get out. You should understand, of all men."

"Lift your hand from me," he whispered.

Morgan gulped, lifted her hand, and pulled the dragon blade half out with the other, as she backed away.

"Now, let's see to getting you through all your followers," he said and walked out.

It was a frustrating and very long day. Those who Zander called her followers were everywhere, in the bushes ahead, the trees behind, practically falling over themselves to see Morgan take an animal in its eye, and they were scaring off any kind of game. And that was just the lads. She was angry when Zander called it a waste of a day even though they'd walked a league and a half, and soaked up enough rain water to fill one of Argylle's wells. Then she had to get through the sea of lasses awaiting her.

Morgan colored and stayed at Zander's heels as women of all ages, sizes and shapes called for her, and what they were offering made her face flame.

"Your Sally Bess does have a large mouth, does she na'?" Zander remarked. "At least, for talking. I've no idea what she does with it while she beds, although I can guess."

Morgan glared at him.

"You dinna' hanker for another lass, Morgan? You are the strangest lad. Any other that had the breaking-in that you did, would na' just leave it. Yet you have done naught but keep me company and hide. Look about you, lad. You can have any lass here."

"Pray, cease this and get me to your room," she replied.

"I recollect you wanted out of the room. You certain you would na' wish a pint of ale? Another joint of good Scots beef? Yonder wench seems ready to serve. In whatever service you need."

"If you dinna' get me to your chamber, I—"

"You'll what?"

He stopped and she did, too, and all that happened is they were surrounded. Morgan groaned as she was hemmed in against him.

"You wish another bout like you had with Sally Bess?"

"I wish to be back in your room," she replied.

"Sally Bess has a good set of lungs on her, does she na'? You must not be small, after all."

"Please, don't say it again. 'Twas not what you think, 'twas—"

"'Twas almost more than I could bear, Morgan," he whispered, "and damn me for admitting to it. If you only knew how hard it was not to beat that door in and stop you. I nearly died with each bit of pleasure you gave the wench, and I canna' stand myself for it!"

"Zander?" Morgan began, but then she was jostled against him and almost pulled from him, and only by clinging to his back was she still with him.

"You should na' stay this close to me, Morgan."

Her eyes were wide, as the crowd grew larger and more boisterous.

"I have na' choice! I'll be pulled limb from limb!"

Another jostle, and then hands were pulling at her arms, her kilt, then Morgan felt her neck pull back as someone got hold of her braid and yanked.

"Zander! Save me!"

She didn't think he'd heard her, then he was leaping atop a stack of baled hay, Morgan stuck at his side, until he reached the top and turned.

"Friends and countrymen!" Zander shouted, earning the attention due his oral delivery. He looked aside at where Morgan was clinging to him. "Methinks it time for a contest. Fetch his Lordship! Fetch a challenger! Don't just stand there! Fetch them! My squire is due to show his skill at dirks. You there! Set up a target."

"Already there! See?" Someone shouted it.

"Zander?" Morgan whispered.

"I already told you not to touch me, Morgan. I will na' say it again. I will pry you off and you will na' like it."

She moved her hands from where she'd been wrapped about him and moved her eyes before he'd spot the flash of tears. The bales he'd climbed gave a very good view of the playing field that was set up. There appeared to be four targets, one at each compass point in the inner bailey.

"This is most hasty and most unprepared, FitzHugh."

The earl joined them, walking amidst a large grouping of over-dressed and frilled gentlemen, obviously English, and Morgan had to dip her head to stop the smile. They looked more feminine than she ever had! They had obviously been at a feast, for some carried platters of food, some had flagons, and some still had bibbed fronts.

" 'Tis a riot we will have, if we dinna'!" Zander returned. "Isna' that right, lads?" There was a din of noise, then Zander was yelling again. "And let's not forget all the lusty lasses! They too wish Morgan to throw?"

The chorus of girlish voices was almost as loud as the other.

"His champion is stewed, and mine isna' capable either."
One of the elegantly dressed gentlemen complained.

"Fair enough," Zander replied. "Morgan will toss by
himself. Watch close, my fine lords, and see what you've
come to be bested by. Give room around the target! Not
that one! The farthest one!"

The crowd started moving. Morgan squinted. He was
referring to the target set up clear across the yard. As the
sun was in its setting phase, torches weren't needed, but it
was far enough away to make her nervous. She wondered
if Zander knew.

"Can you peg that?"

" 'Tis a silly time to ask," she replied, and bent to take
the nine dirks from her socks.

"Is there any among you desirous of a little wager?"

Zander was speaking to the noblemen who had separated
themselves to the row of galleries along one side. They
wouldn't wish to mingle shoulder-to-shoulder with com-
mon folk. Morgan's lips thinned.

Hands went up.

"Argylle? You have someone to keep tallies?" The earl
nodded once. "Then take them. Morgan throws eight dirks.
He hits all into the target. Then, he is done. No more tossing.
No more wagering. No more exhibition until the morrow. We
agreed?"

There was a huge uproar. Morgan didn't know what it
meant, but it sounded like neither agreement or disagreement
to her.

"What if he misses?" someone yelled.

Zander held out his hand and the crowd quieted. Morgan
watched it happen with her eyes wide. "Then, he misses!"
he replied. " 'Twill make the official games interesting, no?
Now, back away from the target. Give him room to peg it
without pegging a countryman. If you must stand in my
squire's way, plant a Sassenach in front of you!"

There was a loud reaction to that. Morgan looked over at him, met his look and tried to keep the smile off her lips.

"We ready?"

The sound resembled an 'aye', or something close. Morgan planted her feet on a bale of hay and tossed all eight, one after the other, and knew they were landing, by the reaction about the target. What noise there was quieted before she had the sixth in, and by the final two, there was absolute silence.

"Good God, Argylle," one of the noblemen was heard to say, and then cheers drowned out everything.

"My dirks?" Morgan leaned over to whisper.

"Martin has them. See? I would na' have anything happen to your perfectly balanced dirks. Now, follow close while we make good our escape. We dinna' have much time."

"But, they agreed! One toss. I dinna' ken, Zander."

Zander shook his head. "Do you wish to stand about and watch, or are you one with me?"

She couldn't get her voice to work, so all she did was nod.

Chapter 17

Morgan bested every opponent, and then bested herself. There turned out to be over twenty champions the nobles were sponsoring, and each lord got to pick a contest, whatever it be. Once Morgan won the contest, however, she designed the challenge. Then, when no one could achieve it, she would, and more.

It began with knives. The original challenge was to put two dirks in the same spot. Once Morgan showed that two was child's play, she showed her skill at encircling an opponent's two with ten of her own. At archery, she not only showed how to put an arrow into the center of one target, but how to put arrows into the dead center of all four targets before the applause had a chance to start up for her first direct hit. At hand-ax, she planted four of them in a straight line across, and then four down. With the English mace, she flung straight and sure, and had the chain wrapping itself about the implanted, spiked ball, and then uncoiling, pulling the mace out with it. At sling, her aim was so accurate, the next morn saw almost all of her swelling group of followers practicing a sideways spin on their slings, rather than vertical. But it was dirks that were her specialty. Everyone seemed to know of it, too, and when she took a dummy and placed it in front of a target, and then put a dirk into the threads of the outer sack, all about the outline of it, pinning it to the target, without spilling one bit of the seed innards, the crowd was absolutely quiet, before the deafening applause.

It was as exhilarating as she'd suspected it would be, while it was happening, and it turned out to be just as disenchanting at almost every other moment. She became a prisoner of her own fame. Her swell of followers grew and expanded until Zander had to send for more FitzHugh clansmen to group about her and protect her whenever she left his room, and that just restricted her more. Toward the end of the exhibition, she was going from elation to fear, celebration to despondency, and joy to despair, with equal measure given to each emotion.

The nights were filled with such debauchery that contests were being set up for drinking, wrenching, and wrestling. Those, Morgan stayed far from, although she could hear the revelry from Zander's room, until late at night when he would stumble in, his eyes bloodshot, his step uneven, his mood surly and abrupt, and more than once amorous enough to make her threaten with the dragon blade.

On the tenth day of the competition, there was only the young Squire Morgan of the FitzHugh clan left. All takers had been not just eliminated, but annihilated, and the earl was requesting one more showing. He wanted the finale of his games to be a one-man exhibition of Morgan's skills before the tournament could be called complete, all the side bets finished, and his hosting considered ended.

For the occasion, Zander had a ceremonial outfit delivered, along with a silver-dragon brooch, pure hammered-silver wrist bands, and silver embossed belt. The richness made Morgan gape, while Zander's smile was wider than she'd ever seen. Then a tub was brought into what had become her cell, and everything she'd been experiencing for the entire ten days became merely a foretaste of what was to come.

Morgan's eyes grew wide and she gulped the immediate moisture from her mouth. She watched as the tub, looking like an oversized bucket, with curved oaken sides kept together by large metal bands, was put into the middle of Zander's room, displacing the footstool. She watched as the stream of water was delivered and poured in, making the air moist with steam, and she watched Zander watch her. The dragon blade's ruby-topped hilt was in her fingertips the entire time.

Then, Zander sent everyone out.

"They'll take it amiss if I dinna' wait upon my champion for this moment," he finally said when all she did was stand beside the tub and stare across at him.

"I canna' allow this," Morgan whispered.

His face looked gray in the morning light, and his smile was no longer wide, but slight, then it faded. "You dinna' accept your master's admiration and appreciation of the honor you have brought my clan?"

"I can accept all of that. I will accept this raiment that I will wear and return, in honor of a Scot winning this tourney, but I will na' allow you to stay while I prepare myself and don it." If she'd had less moisture in her mouth, the words would have made more sense. As it was, Zander listened through all of it and then smiled.

"There will be no return of this sett. There will be no payment required, nor will there be an argument. 'Twas made with care, just for you. 'Tis what a clan champion should wear . . . will wear. Even if I have to take the kilt you now wear and hide it." His eyebrows raised, then lowered. "I will na' be shamed by miserly dealings with one such as you. The earl's offer for your service doubles with each of your wins, and I will not have it said the FitzHugh clan needs even listen to such offers, for lack of our own silver."

"With the amount of it to this one outfit, that will na' happen," she teased. "but I have na' been a champion long enough for the making of such a garment, Zander."

"At times, I wish you were na' so bright, lad." He sighed. "But you are. 'Tis true enough. I had it ordered when I first left you and went for my brothers. I knew then what you would mean to me, and I wanted you to know what station you hold in my household. You are na' just a squire, Morgan. You are, forever, my friend."

"I will na' add to my service time with such a sett," she said, lifting her chin.

Zander smiled shakily. "There is no servitude I can add to the lifetime of it you have already cursed me with. Cease this argument. We've still to prepare you for this exhibition. Give me your kilt."

Morgan paled. "I'll not disrobe for you, FitzHugh."

"You must have some assistance. 'Tis Plato insisting it must be me."

Plato? Morgan wondered. She should have known. "I dinna', and will na', accept assistance from you, Zander, whether Plato decrees it or no."

Zander's smiled faded. "I am na' fond of the duty, myself. Now, hand me your raiment and get beneath the water."

"Nay," she whispered.

"Plato says I must."

"Plato is a fool. No squire is attended by his master. 'Tis always the other way around. Always."

"Except in times of honor. That's what Plato says."

"Plato is na' right all the time!" Morgan argued.

"It will also earn me high marks with your followers. It will show my respect and high regard for you. Now, give me the kilt. We dinna' have all day."

Morgan was getting desperate, and Zander was seeing that. She stepped back to the fireplace and pulled the dragon blade out. "Does Plato know about the blade?" she asked.

"Nay."

"Tell him, then. Tell him he canna' insist on something like this. Tell him there are consequences."

"I did. He knows. He says he is hopeful of that. He dinna' explain."

"He *what*?" Morgan lost the second word in a high-pitched cry.

"Morgan, I know this is as abhorrent for you as it is for me, but it makes sense. I am showing my respect. I am showing my willingness to serve you in this matter, for your service to me. Now, cease this arguing and get in yonder tub, before I take the garments from you and force you into it." Then, he was taking the chamber in floor-eating strides.

Morgan twisted the blade in her hands, the ruby catching the light. She hated Plato, she decided. "If you touch me, I will na' stay with you, FitzHugh. You will lose me. Forever. Do you ken?"

The blade was no longer pointing toward him. Morgan had it against her own stomach. That stopped Zander's approach. He narrowed his eyes. Then, he turned and put his back to her. "I canna' do this, either, but you must be served. Shall I send Squire Martin? Perhaps Plato should assist you, since it is his plan."

"I dinna' need to be served. I am a lowly squire, a base-born lad of no name and no clan. I raided the dead for their riches. I am nothing."

"You are none of these things. You are the FitzHugh champion. I will find you an assist. I will send Phineas."

"Nay!"

"You dislike him, too? Whom do you wish me to send then, Morgan. Whom? I will na' leave you unattended."

"Send me Sally Bess, then," Morgan replied, quickly. It was the best she could think of.

"The whore?" His back was as stiff as the answer. Morgan watched him.

"The wench. I request Sally Bess."

"You wish her . . . you wish *that*?" He sounded like he was choking. Morgan watched him.

"Plato wants me served. He is forcing you to serve. I will na' accept such service. I will accept Sally Bess to assist. I dinna' wish more of her than that. I swear. Have her fetched, Zander. Do it for me."

She didn't know if he'd do as she asked, for once the door slammed, she couldn't hear what was happening, but she wasn't taking one shred of clothing off with Zander anywhere in the vicinity. The consequences were too immense, and too life-altering, and Plato was too smug with his certainty that she was a lass. Morgan decided that she really did hate him.

"You sent for me?" Sally Bess's eyes were twinkling and her smile was broader than her face seemed capable of containing.

Morgan's knees sagged. She hadn't realized how taut and nervous she'd been. "Thank God. I've got to get dressed and prepared for my exhibition. I canna' allow the FitzHugh to see me."

"He will na' then. Sally Bess will make certain of it." She turned and shoved the bolt into place. "Now, divest that kilt. We've a champion to dress, and I've a debt to repay."

"A debt?" Morgan asked, tossing off clothing.

"You have raised my value a thousand-fold, Squire Morgan. You dinna' understand the ways of men and women, or maybe you do, but I am nothing save an old, used, servant wench, and then I get called to serve the FitzHugh's squire with the donning of his raiment. Have you no idea of the honor you have just bestowed on me? Mercy! In the middle of the morning, too. I swear, the others about me were seething with jealousy. Get yourself beneath that water. I'll handle the hair."

The water had cooled while Morgan argued with Zander, but it was still warm and luxurious-feeling. Sally Bess's hands at her temples, and the relief from Zander's presence, were combining to make her slouch pleasantly in the tub and soak in the water, and make her mind a complete blank. The exhibition she had yet to put on seemed a hundred leagues away, her vow even farther—and then

Sally Bess started jumping up and down on Zander's bed and making her lusty words and sounds of mating.

"Cease that!" Morgan commanded. "Cease it now!"

The woman only got louder, her movements more boisterous, and she even sent the silver belt dropping to the floor, where it made a heavy thud.

"Sally Bess! If you dinna' cease that, I'll tell all and sundry—"

"That you're a lass?" She had stopped her bouncing, and pinned a sly look on Morgan to ask it; then she started up again.

"Morgan, I will kill you with my bare hands!"

Zander's shoulder was hitting the door, stopping Sally Bess for a moment as the bolt held. Then, she started up again. Morgan slouched down into the water, and wondered why she had been so stupid. She could have sent Martin to a corner while she bathed. She could have tossed a cloth about herself. She didn't have to be naked in a tub, greased soap-scum lapping at her chin and shoulders, and feeling the water's chill against her blush, while a woman she barely knew pantomimed intimacy with her. It was all her fault.

"Morgan! Open this door! Mor! Gan!" He actually yelled her name in two distinct breaths. Morgan's eyes widened. She could imagine what he probably looked like, she didn't have to see him. And it was frightening to imagine. "Begone all of you! Now!"

There was another heave on the wood; Sally got louder. Zander called her name again. He cursed again. Another heave came against the door.

"I said begone!"

Morgan didn't know who he was using that orator's voice on. She could hear every word. Then he was hitting the door again.

"Morgan, as God is my witness, I'll have every hair on your head. Every damned hair!"

Sally screamed. The door bolt splintered, and Morgan actually watched it break apart with what looked like slow motion. There was no one with him, and no one in the hall, either. Then she met Zander's incredulous look as he took in the scene, followed by the most genuine amusement she'd ever heard.

His bow was mocking, and his order for her to carry on, just as much so, and his laughter as he put the door back in place was worse. All in all, it had to be the most embarrassing morning of her life.

The crowds were as thick as before, although this time Morgan bowed to all, starting with the galleries of nobles, and ending with the serfs, Zander at her side. The garments he'd had made for her were making her glow in the afternoon sun, and whenever she lifted an arm, shifted stance, or swiveled, silver glinted in pinpricks of light. She caught them every so often.

She was doing her best to ignore Sally Bess's smug face and all the other lasses who were twittering every time she looked their way. She also ignored Zander's betrothed, sitting on the stand beside her father, and with newly crowned King of Scotland, Robert the Bruce, on her other side. He wasn't as prepossessing as she'd envisioned, but he was regal. That much couldn't be mistaken.

And she was having trouble with Zander's eyes on her every move, and those midnight-blue eyes were alight with more glow than the silver could possibly have.

It made her hand shake for a moment before she stopped it.

"Step forward, Squire Morgan of the FitzHugh clan. Greet your sovereign."

Morgan bowed low, Zander at her side.

"I hear there is no one as good as you are, Squire Morgan. I look forward to seeing this, in fact. It is a good thing that in the Scotland I now rule, weapons are again allowed. Isna' that right, my lords?"

The king turned to those about him for assent.

"You have to watch closely, Sire," Zander informed him from Morgan's side, "for Morgan has the gift of lightning to his hands, and the speed of wind to his blades. This is the exhibition."

They had discussed it the prior evening, and she listened to him describe what she was going to show. Her lips twisted and she glanced away the moment her eyes touched Plato's, sitting behind Zander's betrothed. She colored.

It was a good thing she and Zander had discussed what series she would follow since she was still not talking to him since the bath. She may never talk to him again, she decided.

The king nodded, and Morgan raised from her bow.

"You may begin, Morgan. Dinna' look at me like that. You have lightened my heart from a cartload of heaviness. I think this is the best day of my life."

He was whispering it to her, but that only made it worse. The embarrassment, at least, she could handle.

Morgan's weaponry were arrayed in a semi-circle in the midst of all four targets, and she stopped for a moment, to pick her starting point. The crowd ceased to exist, the king ceased to be of import, and all she could see was Zander's perfect, midnight-blue eyes. She picked up the claymore and began.

She had arranged four of every weapon, one for each target, and she went in a seemingly faultless motion through each, pivoting back and forth, first to the first target, pick up a weapon, plant it into the third target. Then, the second, finally the fourth. If she placed the claymore in the center, the next weapon went right below it. The arrows went to the right, the hand-axes to the left, the *skean dhu* to the top, and finally, three dirks to each target in the seemingly nonexistent space between the already-planted weapons. The entire exhibition took less time than one previous contest had, and when she placed the last dirk, she went to her knees with her arms wide.

The roar of the crowd was what reached her first, and then Zander was at her side, waiting for her to rise and join him. She only met his eyes once, and the glow was warmer, more personal, more frightening. He said something, but she didn't hear it. The crowd's roar made it impossible. Then, he was escorting her back to where the king sat beside the earl and the lovely Gwynneth.

Morgan touched glances with the girl, and saw the same hero-worship gaze every other lass was looking at her with. It was unnerving. There was something else in the girl's gaze, too. It wasn't easy to decipher what it was, and then she knew. She'd seen it often enough in the hag's eyes. Gwynneth was unhappy, desperately so. *Unhappy?* Morgan wondered.

She didn't have time to puzzle it, for Plato's gaze on her was completely unnerving. Morgan told herself she didn't care. Plato was an annoying, inquisitive, bothersome man. She didn't care what he thought of her, or what he thought he was doing.

"Your betrothed seems a bit . . . quieter, Zander," she told his shoulders as he led her back to his chamber, leaving clansmen and her followers behind. No one wanted to miss the feasting and revelry. No one except the Squire Morgan.

"I have moved the wedding up," Zander swung his head to inform her. "I have said I will na' wait. I will take her to wife in three days. She is properly quieted by it, I would say."

"You moved the wedding up?"

"Aye. 'Twas no effort, with the earl. He is still trying to sweeten me enough to part with your servitude to him."

"I will na' serve him."

"I know that. You know that. He does na'. He thinks silver buys everything. He has been around the Sassenach too much. 'Tis the way they think."

"But . . . three days, Zander? Only three?"

"Three days, Morgan. 'Tis all the sooner he would move it."

"You wanted it sooner? Why?"

"You canna' guess?"

He opened the door and waited for her to enter. Morgan felt rooted to the spot with pulse-pounding ache. FitzHugh would be lost to her in three days. She couldn't stay with him once the wedding was over. She didn't dare. She was afraid of the heart-wrenching loss. She knew it was going to be there, too. It already was.

"Come along, Morgan. I go to accept your purse. They've entertainment arranged for the eve. Some sort of English nonsense called theater. I've never seen theater. You wish to attend this time? If so, I will have you protected. None of your followers will be allowed near. You have my word."

"Nay," she whispered. She was surprised her voice actually made sound.

She was afraid to stay another moment with him, as it was. She'd be on her knees begging him to take her as his woman . . . and make her his whore. Her body and heart wanted to force him to take her and make it reality. Her pride, and the years of hatred, training, and sacrifice, were demanding otherwise. She was shaking. Zander may have noticed, since he was looking at her so closely. She didn't dare meet his gaze.

She walked past him. The door closed. He didn't follow her.

The tub was gone. Morgan stood in the center of the room, and realized how deathly quiet everything already was.

Chapter 18

"Morgan, you must do it. There is no one else. The production will fail, if you dinna' assist them."

"Get out of the chamber, Plato." Morgan spoke the words more to the top of Zander's footstool than to the FitzHugh who was disturbing her from the door. The smooth wood of Zander's furniture had hid her sorrow well enough, once she put a blanket on it. Morgan put her nose back into the cloth, more to dry the offending tears from her face than anything else. She hoped the interloper at the door wouldn't notice.

"But Morgan, we need you. Zander needs you, too."

"Zander does na' need me. He has yon beauteous wench, Gwynneth, at his side. I am not needed. I will be in the way. I am useless at anything save killing great, wooden targets. Play is no time for weaponry. Now, get from this chamber!"

Her voice sounded neither as authoritative nor as strong as her words. It sounded wounded and lost, exactly as she had been since Zander left her.

He chuckled. "They need another for their theater."

"Then get another!" Oh, why didn't he just leave? Morgan put her hands against her eye sockets and wished she were outside and near a fresh burn, to soothe the tissue she'd sobbed into a wretchedly hot, swollen state.

"From where?"

"Take one of my followers! They're everywhere. Look about you. Now go!"

"There's na' another in sight, Morgan, save Eagan, here. Isna' that true, Eagan?"

The large clansman Zander had left at the doorstep answered on cue. Morgan ignored him.

"Although Eagan is probably wishing he could attend the fest, too."

"Does na' anything get into your thick skull, Plato FitzHugh? I dinna' wish to be part of this play! I dinna' wish to be anywhere! I dinna' wish to be entertainment, for anyone, any longer!"

Her shout died away.

"What is it you do wish?" he asked.

Her heart surged, and Morgan gulped. "To be . . . free," she whispered. "To be outside. To be back in my old life. To finish what I set out to do, and cease the doing and the living. That is what I wish."

Plato sighed. "And sobbing in this room is going to get you all of that?" he asked, in a quiet voice.

Morgan lifted her head, and watched the torches flare and spit. She wasn't sobbing. Only a FitzHugh would accuse a KilCreggar of a weakness like that. Her back stiffened.

"This play needs another. The lad they had is taken ill. The play canna' go on without this part played."

"I canna' play a part," Morgan told the fire.

"Only you would say that as if it were true. You have played a part all your life, Squire Morgan. Tell me I'm wrong. Go ahead. Tell me. Make me believe it."

"Go away."

"He's wedding her in two days, Morgan! Two days! You know you can stop it, and you will na'?"

"Three," she replied.

"Did he forget to tell you today was one? My little brother, Zander. Always the light-hearted, playful one. Always the tease."

Fresh tears threatened her eyes at that, and she held the blanket to them. Behind her, Plato blew his disgust.

Then, more brightly, he said, "I have someone who wishes to speak with you, Morgan. 'Tis the Lady Gwynneth. Gwynneth? The squire, Morgan. Perhaps you two can comfort each other with your tears."

"I dinna' cry!"

Morgan swiveled and glared, defying any to state otherwise. Plato had the Lady Gwynneth with him, although she had a widow's veiling on her face and a shudder to her frame before she lifted her covering.

Morgan's heart sank. The girl's sadness was apparent.

"Why do you weep?" Morgan asked softly.

The girl tried to smile. Morgan couldn't believe how much she had changed in the fortnight since they'd met.

"They need another for the part, and there is na' lad left who will suit. I beg it of you," she whispered.

Morgan frowned. "This is the cause of your sadness?" she asked, finally.

The girl looked up at Plato, then back at Morgan. Then, she nodded, although her lower lip trembled.

"If I play this part, you will cease weeping?" Morgan asked.

"I . . . I will do my best."

The Lady Gwynneth's lower lip trembled worse, and huge tears spilled from her eyes. Morgan's heart went out to her. She knew exactly what Gwynneth felt like, although it was stupid to cry over something so slight as a canceled performance.

She sighed. "I canna' be so unchivalrous. Show me this part you need played."

"Come then."

What Plato said must be true, for the moment Morgan agreed, the girl brightened, and held out her hand. Morgan looked at it. "I will follow you," she said simply. She couldn't touch Zander's betrothed in the guise of a lad and still function. It wasn't possible.

They were approaching the Great Hall, which had been set aside for this production, and then Plato pulled Morgan aside, by gripping her upper arm. He motioned the Lady Gwynneth into an antechamber.

"I need to warn you," he said.

"Of what?" she whispered, feeling every hair whisper along her neck.

"This part is for a woman."

Shock hit her first, and then she had a fist aimed at his jaw. He caught it with one hand and squeezed. Morgan took the pain without wincing. Zander had delivered far worse and with far more lasting effect. Plato held her fist and tightened until her knuckles cracked.

"You canna' win this. A real man has na' the light easy motion of a blade, dearest Morgan," he whispered. "Nor is he so easily played with. I was hopeful you and my brother would find this out for yourselves, without my help. But you leave me no choice."

"I dinna' ken," she answered.

"Oh yes, you do. Now, hurry along. Lady Gwynneth awaits to help you costume yourself. I will await your arrival in the Hall."

"I will na' do it. I refuse."

"You refuse and I will force you."

"You canna' force me. I have the dragon blade." Morgan slipped it from her kilt.

Plato's eyebrows rose. "'Tis fitting, I suppose. The blade goes to the strongest of the FitzHughs. It is won. I'm not surprised he gave it to you today."

"He gave it to me afore the exhibition."

His grip eased. "Why?" he asked.

"To use on any FitzHugh who accosts me. Any FitzHugh."

"The man is mad. Gwynneth?" He dropped Morgan's hand. The petite Lady Gwynneth stepped back outside. "'Tis

almost time, Morgan. Hurry. I still have to paint your
face!"

"Paint my face? As what, a . . . harlot?" Her voice was
bitter on the word.

"Nay. 'Tis but a bit of greasepaint. All actors wear it,
especially those portraying a woman. Takes the ugliness
from their faces and creates illusion. You understand
illusion?"

"Morgan understands that best of all," Plato answered
for her.

"You are a lady welcoming her brave lads back from the
sea. You have but three lines. 'Well and good, lads.' 'Thanks
be to God', and ''tis done.' You can remember these?"

"I have to speak? I canna' speak women's words, nor in
a woman's voice," Morgan protested.

"But, Plato says you are the only one who can!"

Gwynneth picked up Morgan's hands and held them in
hers. Fresh tears appeared in her eyes and then on her
cheeks at she looked up at Morgan. Morgan glared her
complete hatred at Plato. He responded with a grin.

"Who can resist such an entreaty? Any other lad would
be on his knees, begging for a favor, but not you, eh,
Morgan?"

"I have no teats. What am I to use for them?" She spat
the words.

Gwynneth looked at Plato for an explanation and when
he gave it, her lips twitched a bit, but her tears stopped.
Up close, she was actually more beautiful than Morgan
remembered.

"They have sacks for such a problem. I will fetch them
while you change. Get in there now. Get the dress on. Plato
will help. We have little time as it is! I'll be right back to
paint you."

"Morgan?" Plato was gesturing into the chamber of her
transformation. Morgan found her feet wouldn't move.
"You can always use your own teats," he finished.

***

She had her back to the crowd when the third act opened.

They had torches lit all about the Hall, sending smoke-filled light about, but the stage had a stranger lighting system yet. Someone had filled a big caldron with oil, put wicks in it, and then lit them. The combination of lights swelled into a clearer, brighter whole, and it shined on the rippled length of Morgan's hair as she sat, posed on what was supposed to be a balcony but was, in fact, two logs cross-hatched into two other logs, with a stone-colored tapestry draped over them.

The dress she'd been forced to wear was of burgundy-colored velvet. It was too short, it was too big, and it was old. It had sweat-stains where the sleeves were laced on, and the white linen collar cascading from the low-cut, squared neckline had more than one stain on it. Plato had immediately decreed that the dress was too loose, as if that was its lone fault. Morgan had stood helplessly while he took a length of black cording and crisscrossed it about her ribcage and down to the flare of her hips, leaving the slender waist she'd always hidden completely outlined. She only hoped her hair hid it.

The Lady Gwynneth had told her she was entrancing, whatever that was, and proceeded to put so much greased color on her face, it itched. Morgan had never felt so different. She had never felt the swish of skirts about her ankles, the feel of air on skin above her bodice, nor the rub of velvet against her own, unbound breasts.

The last was her own fault!

Morgan didn't ponder the why of her actions, she only knew she was experiencing what it felt like to be female for the one and only time in her life, and when Gwynneth brought the foul-smelling bags that draped from a cord behind her neck, Morgan had known she wouldn't wear them. She had stepped behind her screen, and tossed them into the corner with the moldy rushes, and she had untied her own binding, replacing it on her knee, where the dragon blade and KilCreggar plaid, even now, rested.

She hadn't questioned them about unbinding her braid. It would work well as a curtain, she hoped. She hadn't counted on the ripple once it was brushed, since Sally Bess had braided a tight, inter-twined affair just that morning. There was no mirror to see the transformation, but Morgan knew there was one. She knew it by the look of satisfaction in Plato's eye, and the looks of the others when she took her place behind the curtain.

There was complete and utter silence when the curtain parted for Act Three. Morgan waited for her cue. She had never been so frightened in her life.

"What is my daughter doing on that stage? Stop this immediately! No woman walks the boards!"

Morgan recognized the earl's voice. Then Plato answered, "'Tis the FitzHugh squire, Morgan, My Lord. Calm yourself. Your daughter sits at your side. That isna' a woman. That is the champion, himself. I swear. See the silver wrist bands? I dressed him myself."

Then, there was a loud commotion and someone told Zander to sit back down, and cease blocking the view. The four lads in the play came in from the back of the stage, and Morgan waited for her first line. When it was time, she swiveled to face the audience, and said in the highest tone and with the most mockery she could use, "Well and good, lads."

There was laughter at her delivery. She could sense that much, and then Zander FitzHugh was ordered to sit back down again. This time by his brother. Morgan narrowed her eyes to see him through the tint of black smoke rising from their caldron.

She wished she hadn't, for she didn't need paint for how pale she went the moment his eyes touched hers. Nor was he in the back in the audience. He was in the front row, and rising again.

Plato had to pull him back down that time, and use strength and words to reach him. The play was continuing about her, but Morgan had no sense of space or time. It was lucky she had no further lines. All she had was the all-consuming gaze of the man fifteen-odd feet from her, and displaying such masculine desire and passion, every person in the room had to be aware of it. Morgan certainly was.

Her eyes did not move from his until the curtain closed with the same stuttering movement it used to open. She was not needed until Act Five, so she went back to her antechamber to await. Phineas was the FitzHugh waiting for her there. Morgan looked at him from the doorway, and watched him smile. Her mind went absolutely black.

"Can I get that kiss now?" he asked.

Then, she was running. She didn't care where, or how far. She was brought up short by Plato, and his restraining arms about her middle did nothing except gain him a struggle.

"Hold, Morgan! Hold! You canna' go out into the masses like this! You canna'! Stop! They will na' know the illusion. They will na' know the part you play! There are too many. They will discover the truth, and then they will take what belongs to my brother! Cease!"

His brother? At the recollection of a horror so vast, the struggling began anew. Plato tightened his arms, squeezing off her breath, and making his own labored and harsh.

"Morgan, cease this! I will hurt you if you dinna' cease this! Cease this, I say! Cease this! Damn you! I will na' let you do this to my brother. I will na'! Now, cease this and get back into the play. Zander will be expecting you. He is close to seeing the truth for himself. Do you ken, Morgan? He is seeing it for himself. You canna' run from that."

"The FitzHugh . . . ." she whispered.

"Aye. Zander FitzHugh. He loves you, lass."

"Lass?" she repeated, whispering the word.

"You dinna' look much like a lad in this. You dinna' feel

like one, either. If the crowds outside see this, you will na' remain innocent long. They will tear you apart. You ken?"

"Zander?" she whispered again.

"You've quieted. Thank the heavens. I would na' like to hurt you, but if Zander sees me, with you, like this, he will be for hurting me. You ken?"

Rivulets of emotion cascaded over her, and Morgan grew stock-still. Zander FitzHugh was the FitzHugh she loved. Zander. It was his brother Phineas whom she would kill.

"Zander?" she whispered again.

"He is a devil to keep hold on, and he'll be storming the stage next. I would na' wander far next time."

"Next time?" she questioned.

"The play isna' finished."

"I will na' finish it," Morgan replied. She knew now what she was going to do. And acting like a woman in a silly production wasn't it.

"You will finish it. You will finish all of it."

"You canna' force me, Plato FitzHugh. Now unhand me."

He had her gripped with both arms and held against his chest, and off the ground, and his arms were every bit as hard and muscled as Zander's were. He probably had just as thick a chest, too. "I can more than force you, lass. I can take you. Any man you come across, dressed like this, can. You ken?"

"Where is my *feile-breacan*? My shirt? My boots, then?"

"In my possession. You be a good girl and finish this, and I'll see them given back. You have my word."

Morgan closed her eyes. The experience of being held in Plato's arms wasn't pleasant, she decided, and it wasn't unpleasant. It just wasn't anything. She opened her eyes.

"You're every inch a lass, too," he whispered when her eyes met his. "You are very desirable, too. I see my brother's attraction, but I dinna' see his blindness. You ken that much, too?"

"Put me down," she responded. "Or I'll tell of this."

"It might be worth having my throat slit by Zander if you tell. You've teats, too. I can feel them, just as I can feel how your heartbeat quickens when I speak like this."

Morgan's eyes narrowed further and she pulled her lips back. She was rapidly deciding that she didn't like anything about being a woman. "Dinna' think me stupid, FitzHugh. I will na' tell my master, Zander. He may not believe me, and if he does, I'll have brothers split asunder. I will tell your lass, Gwynneth, of this."

His eyebrows rose. Then, he had her on her feet, one hand on her elbow. "You guessed?"

"Aye. It is your rotten luck she is spoken for, though. And wedding your own brother in two days hence."

His features stiffened. "You can stop the wedding, Morgan."

"Me? What power do I have?"

"You have every power. You dinna' speak, but you change everything. Release her. Release Gwynneth from her betrothal."

"I canna'. I had naught to do with it."

"You did, and you must. Only you can do it. You know this."

"Why should I help a FitzHugh?" she asked. "Especially one who tricks me, steals my proper clothing, and dresses me thus?"

"I'm begging you, Morgan. I love her." Plato had blue eyes, too. He had light brown hair, not unlike Zander's. He didn't have the cleft to his chin, nor the full lips, nor was he any taller than herself, but he had every bit of the same sincerity Zander possessed. Morgan swallowed.

"You love her?" she repeated in wonder. "And does she return this love?"

"Aye," he answered.

"Then, how can she give herself to Zander?"

"She has no choice. The earl made the betrothal. By rights, I would be first choice, but I was too slow. Where do you think Zander found Phineas and me? Right here. I was leading up to asking for my love's hand, and then my brother comes riding up to search us out and receives her hand in marriage from her father. I dinna' know what he was up to, or I would have stopped him."

"I am sorrowed for you all," Morgan replied, "but I repeat. I had naught to do with it, and I canna' stop it."

"Show him what you are, Morgan. Give him what he needs. He does na' need Gwynneth. He does na' even see her when she is right beside him. You canna' do this! Have you no heart?"

"If I ever had one, it was taken from me, and it was a FitzHugh that did the taking."

"Make it whole again, then! Give Zander what he needs, what you both need. Please? I beg it of you."

"A FitzHugh begging me?" she questioned. "A squire of no-name and no-clan?"

"I would beg the devil himself for my lovely Gwynneth. You dinna' understand the power of love, or you would know!"

He was shaking with emotion. Morgan looked across at him, and smiled sadly. " 'Tis not what you think, Plato," she whispered.

"Zander loves you. You love him. I am not blind. Go to him after the play. Show him, Morgan!"

"I canna'," she replied.

Plato dropped her arm and cursed her. Then he glared at her. Then, he spit at her feet. Morgan watched him do it with a strange sort of detachment.

"Gwynneth has vowed to take her life before she lets him touch her."

Morgan paled. She was actually grateful for the paint

that hid it. "Everything that lives dies, Plato," she responded automatically.

"But it does na' have to happen! You can stop it! Please?" He had ceased reviling her and his eyes filled with tears. "Please?"

Morgan turned away. "I canna' stop the lass from what she feels she must do," she said softly.

"Damn your soul to Hell, Morgan."

"'Tis already done, FitzHugh. You canna' make it worse," she whispered. "You can only repeat what already will be."

"Then I curse you. I curse you, Morgan of no-name and no-clan. I curse you to abide in Hell for eternity, one far worse than the one you have created on earth!"

Morgan swallowed. Her shoulders slumped. It didn't change anything. Nothing did. "I have created nothing, Plato. I have simply been. I was nothing before. I will return to nothing. You, Zander, Gwynneth, all have your own lives to finish out, no matter how long or short they turn out to be. I will na' be here to witness it."

"Oh, you're wrong there. I'm going to make certain of it. If he weds her, and she takes her life, I'm going to make certain you endure every moment of how it will feel. Every single damned one. I vow it."

If he said another word or made another plea, her eyes weren't going to be able to hold back the moisture. She was going to ruin the dried black soot outlining her eyes, and make it run all down the grease paint Gwynneth had painted on her face. She was going to do all of that, and every KilCreggar killed by a FitzHugh would still be dead.

She waited, forcing her heart to calm, and her vision to clear. The time was almost at hand. If she took her vengeance before the wedding, the lady Gwynneth wouldn't take her life. Plato FitzHugh might still have a chance at gaining the lovely lady's hand. Phineas was going to be rotting in Hell, though. Morgan was going there too, to assure it.

She straightened, blinked the moisture away and did her best to achieve complete detachment before turning back to him.

"Come, Plato, you have wasted too much time. I will miss my lines, and ruin this part you have forced on me. I must return now. I must continue living until I complete my own vow."

"Does nothing I've said sway you?"

"When the final curtain falls, you are to get me my garments back. I will na' be caught again dressed like a weak woman and prey for any man. I want my kilt and tartan back, and all my dirks. I want an escort back to Zander's rooms. I will na' leave Zander's rooms until the deed is done. You ken?"

"You will na' reconsider?"

"Nay," she answered.

"But, why? Why?"

Morgan wasn't going to answer that. She wasn't going to look back into the farthest reaches of her memory until she had to. Now that she knew exactly what was there, she no longer hid from it in dreams. But now wasn't the time.

Chapter 19

Finishing the play was the exact form of torture she'd been telling herself it would be. Plato was back beside Zander, although where one of the FitzHughs looked to her with a combination of pain, panic and lust, the other glared only hate. And the one she was going to kill showed nothing in those light blue eyes, just as he always did.

The play continued, even without her participation. It was a good thing, too, for she missed her line, and the lads simply acted around it. She did nothing except sit on her perch, look out on the crowd and watch everything blur and clear with the moisture that kept rising in her eyes.

The final act was worse, for Plato had moved over to his beloved, and must have appraised her of what had occurred, for the silent tears on the Lady Gwynneth's face reflected more than the light. It reflected every bit of heartache right back up at Morgan, who could do naught but embrace it and add it to her own silent cloak of agony. Once everything was ended, what did it matter how many she hurt, or how much it hurt her? The KilCreggar clan was going to be avenged. That was what mattered. That was all that could matter.

Morgan didn't recall what her line was, but said 'it's finished,' when it felt like the others were awaiting her. It must have been what was required, or close, because the theater went on. Then, the curtain closed for the final time. Morgan didn't move until someone forced her to bow, and then she received cheers, whistles and suggestions on what a fine lass she could look. She hated the attention. She hated the burgundy dress. She hated her body. She hated herself.

The lying bastard, Plato, didn't return her clothing, her dirks, or her dignity, either. When she got to the antechamber she'd left them in, there was nothing. Morgan sat behind the screen and used the bottom of the burgundy dress to wipe at the grease and filth. Then, she took the dragon blade and hacked off a goodly portion of the front of her skirt to fashion a veiling of her own. She knew she was leaving her legs bare from mid-thigh down, more bare than ever in her kilt, but she had no choice.

That was what she always received from any of the FitzHughs: no choice. She got no choice in granting them her service, no choice in her attire, no choice in her own destiny.

Morgan slid along the walls to Zander's chamber, keeping to the dark as much as possible. She was in luck that the earl had hired himself a minstrel, and the man had taken his lyre and begun his own entertaining. The singer had a goodly voice, and his words were enjoyable enough to keep most revelers seated, although the FitzHugh squire's exhibition was being featured when she slid out. It wasn't only her skill with weaponry being sung about, either, it was the haunting beauty of the FitzHugh champion when clad in woman's form.

Morgan's face was hot before she reached Zander's chamber. She nodded to the hulk of Eagan on the stoop, although he was up and opening the door for her like she was a requested wench of the evening. Morgan fled inside to don her original garments. She could seek out Plato when she was properly attired. She was going to retrieve the sett and her dirks, or she was going to find out why not.

She had everything in its proper place, down to her braid and her breast binding, and was just sitting next to the fire to contemplate its secrets when Zander entered. She watched the fire stir at the sudden air without turning around. She didn't move. She didn't breathe.

"Morgan?" he whispered. "I dinna' know what to say."

She breathed then. She sucked in on the emotion, and let it out. *Soon, Zander,* she thought. *Soon you will be free of me, and free to return to your unstructured, teasing, play-filled life. Soon.*

She lifted a tong beside the flame and poked the log, rolling it over and showering sparks about the hearth. Zander didn't move, or if he did, she couldn't sense it.

"My brother tells me to trust my senses. Trust the illusion."

Morgan's eyes widened on the fire. *Damn Plato!* she thought. "Your brothers . . . lie," she whispered. "Both of them."

"Both?"

"Aye, both. Plato lies to confuse, whereas Phineas? He has . . . he is . . . ." Her throat closed off with it.

"Yes?"

She shook her head. She couldn't say it.

"Phineas and I were never close, Morgan. He is much older than I, and much too serious. Almost as bad as you are, yourself."

"Phineas is a FitzHugh. You are a FitzHugh," she whispered.

"True enough. 'Tis a fine name. A fine clan. You, yourself have been adopted into it. The cloth looks good on you. Almost as good as yon burgundy dress did."

"Zander—"

"Plato tells me to force you to wear it. Force the illusion into reality. Is that what would happen, Morgan?"

"Plato has his own reasons for such a story, Zander."

"He does? What?"

"It is his secret, not mine," she replied.

"And what secrets does my next older brother keep from me?"

"He is in love."

"With you? I'll kill him!"

"Zander," Morgan said, turning on the hearth to face him. "No man can be in love with me. You ask if there is an illusion, and I say 'aye', there is. Love is it."

"Love is no illusion, Morgan. 'Tis very real. I think if you put your hand out, you can touch it. It's within your grasp now. With me."

"Nay Zander," she began and she rose to her feet, since he had taken a step from the door and every part of her was alert to it.

"I am in love with you, Morgan."

"I know," she answered.

"And you feel it for me."

"Nay," she whispered, but she couldn't face him and say it.

"Nay?" he chuckled. "I know who the liar is now, Morgan, and 'tis not my brothers. 'Tis you."

"I dinna' lie. I have never lied!"

"You love me. It is in every look you give and every word you say, and in the way you do both. It is in the illusion you created for me tonight. It's in the image I canna' get from my head. Get out the blade, Morgan."

He took another step toward her. Then another. Morgan pulled the blade. "Stop, Zander," she said.

"Stop? When everything I want was shown to me not an hour past? Stop, when all that my blood sings for and has been denied, was just put on show for me? Stop, when the woman I wish you to be, was put into form in front of my eyes? Stop, when I've been unable to perform with another wench since I was cursed with you, and I just saw curves blessed by fantasy? Stop? Aim the blade, Morgan!"

"Zander, you must stop. You must!" She was stepping up on the hearth, and backing to the point the fire was singeing the backs of her legs.

"Stop? When your wide eyes and slender form could be hiding everything? Stop? When my hands itch to taste your innocence, claim you and make you mine? Fling the blade, Morgan! Fling it now, damn you!"

Damn the curse of women's tears! Morgan heard it as clearly as if she'd said it aloud, then he blurred, becoming one with the room around him. She knew the knife in her hand shook as he kept coming, his booted feet barely heard on the tapestry-covered stone.

"Now!"

She took aim, and threw. The knife slid perfectly into a slit in the stone across the room, and Zander stopped, closing his eyes. With her instincts, she saw how clearly the pain and panic were showing on those perfect features.

"Damn you, Morgan lad," he said, opening those midnight-blue eyes and locking them on hers. "Damn you."

"You'll have to do it, Zander. I canna'." Tears were obliterating everything and she watched him stand beneath her, his entire frame shuddering, both fists knotted at his side. "You'll have to do the killing. Do it quickly, though. Make it fast. Don't give pain. I beg that much of you."

The tears slid from her eyes, blinding her, and then she heard his roar. The chamber door flew open, sending fire into the backs of her legs. Morgan didn't even feel it.

Zander was yelling for Plato. He was using every bit of his orator's voice, and it was filled with self-hate. Plato finally answered, his voice just as loud and angered, and then both voices faded down the hall. Eagan was in front of her then, helping her down from the hearth, and beating at the spots of cinders glowing on her socks.

"You've burned yourself, lad," he said.

"Where are they going?"

"Yon master has gone to fight Plato. I was told this might happen, although Master Plato laughed about it."

"What might happen?"

"Master Zander seeks release from the demons in his head."

"What demons?" she whispered.

"I dinna' know. I only know what I heard. Plato may know."

Morgan was afraid that she did, too. "How is Master Zander going to get this release?" she questioned.

"They will fight. Physical exhaustion is what the youngest master is looking for. That is the release he hopes for. They will use claymores and shields. I've seen it before. You don't watch six FitzHugh men grow without witnessing battles such as these. Come. I'll assist you with these. If you need a poultice to stop the pain, you let Eagan know. I'll see it fetched."

"Pain?" she repeated. *What did this kindly faced clansman know of pain?* she wondered.

"You may've burned yourself, lad."

"Burned?"

He frowned. "You take a burn badly? I would na' have thought it from what I was told about you."

"Where did they just go?" she asked.

"The FitzHugh lads? I've just told you. To do battle. The master asked Plato to help him exorcise the demons should it need doing. I heard it. I dinna' think it would take place, but I dinna' ken these two. Dinna' worry yourself, though. They be evenly matched. It will na' go either way for some time."

"Battle?" Some of it was sinking into her mind, and she stared over at him. "Plato is fighting Zander?"

"Aye. With claymores and shields."

"Claymores?" She gasped on the word, for the large, heavy sword was capable of taking a man's limb off. "We've got to stop them!"

"You canna' stop a FitzHugh set on battle, lad. They be hard in the head over something like that. Master Zander was clear. They will na' return until one wins, or there is no strength left in him. I heard him."

"Get out of my way, then!"

Morgan raced down the corridor, leaping over bodies and

sleeping forms to reach the parade ground. The minstrel was still whining his ballads of strength and unrequited love and other ills, and was missing the drama of it right in front of his nose. Morgan flew out the door, jumped the four large steps to the earthen ground and lifted from her crouch to get her bearings.

She heard the clang of steel against steel before she could see the brothers. The night was filled with rain and mud and lust and pain. She could feel it, sense it, almost absorb it. She crossed the same ground on which she'd taken her victory bow that afternoon, and approached where torches were being lit and cheers being given. She forced her way to the front of the group, and went to her knees as the FitzHughs raged against each other.

She knew what it was they felt. She also knew it wasn't directed at each other, but at her. She knew it and received absolutely nothing from it, except complete and utter dread. The claymores kept swinging, covered in mud and grass, and more than once a grunt of pain came from either of them. Shields, that had started without a dent, were now pocked with them, and steam rose from their bodies as the contest continued.

The minstrel must have lost his audience to the parade grounds, for the crowds about Zander and Plato swelled. Morgan had to get to her feet to maintain her view. She didn't want to watch, but was unable to take her eyes off the battle even to blink. Rain slid off her hair into her eyes, into her mouth, into her ears, and she ignored it. Every time either of them stumbled, she was catching her breath on a silent prayer, and then winging thanks as the FitzHugh who had been down, rose and continued.

Then, it was finished, as harshly as it began. She watched Plato stumble to his knees once too often, and bow his head in defeat. It didn't stop Zander. He hit his claymore into one of Morgan's exhibition targets until the wood splintered and came off the support. Then, he turned in a semi-circle and hollered with that great orator's voice at everyone.

Morgan had to stop him. She was the only one who could. She knew it. She approached from his right, but he turned on her. "Stay away from me!" he ordered, the claymore pointed directly at her belly. "Never come near me again! Never!"

"Aye," she replied. "I will na'. 'Tis finished, Zander."

He slammed the claymore into the ground, and even though it was wet, everyone gaped as he sank the sword to its hilt.

"Nay!" He turned on her, wiping the wet strands of hair from his forehead. "'Tis not finished yet. I go now to finish it! Check my brother. He does na' deserve what I gave. You know who does."

Morgan watched him go back to the castle, flinging anyone brave enough to block him out of his path, and she waited until he disappeared behind the door. Rain made the ground slick and the air hard to breathe. It also chased every weak English observer back into the warmth and dryness of the castle.

Morgan approached the mud-covered lump that was Plato. He had yet to stand, and was clasping his claymore with shaking hands.

"You all right?" she asked when he just sat there, heaving for breath.

"You have created a monster, Morgan."

"I have done nothing," she replied.

"Of course you would say that. He is impossible to beat when he is angered. That's why he had the dragon blade. He can beat all of us, if we get him angered. He won me because he had the emotion to do so, and I did na'. He was angered."

"He did not beat you because he was angered," she said.

"You wish me to take more offense by such words?"

"Nay, only to set your mind at ease."

"He has the strength of ten when he is angered, and he

is still so. I did na' tire him enough. Maybe if Ari were here, too, we could have done it. But by myself? I dinna' stand a chance."

"He would have won you without anger, Plato FitzHugh, and I dinna' say this lightly," Morgan replied.

"Now, you have offended me. For punishment, I sentence you to return to that chamber of horrors you have created with him and deal with this anger you say he does na' possess."

"I dinna' say he was na' angered. I said he beat you without the anger, and I still say it. He was using his left hand." Her voice held the awe, too. She had seen how perfect he was with it. She wondered if he realized he'd done so, yet.

"His left? Blast and damn him! He tricked me!"

"Nay, he only used the one with the most power. I told him of it some days past. I dinna' think he listened, though."

"Go to him, Morgan," he said, trying to rise, by putting the claymore's tip in the sod and leaning on it. He fell back down.

Morgan watched him dispassionately for a moment. "Where are my clothes, Plato FitzHugh, and my dirks?"

"Is that what all this is about? Tartan and knives?" he asked.

"Nay, not only that. 'Tis more than that."

"He tried to claim you, and you used the dragon blade? Was that it?"

"I dinna' use the dragon blade," she whispered in reply.

"Then what angered him so?"

"That I dinna' use it," she replied.

The muddy lump sighed. "Go to him, Morgan. Show him what you are. Let him claim you. Heal this."

"No man claims me! Ever! Especially not a FitzHugh."

He shook his head. "You still dinna' understand, do you?"

"Understand what?" she asked.

"How much do you require?" Plato asked, startling her.

"I dinna ken your meaning," she replied.

"How much do you require, to bring my little brother back?"

"You wish him back, after he just trounced you? You canna' even lift your sword."

"I was na' meaning that," he spat, and blood came with it. Then, he tested his jaw with a hand. "I mean, how much do you require? How much more do you need?"

She pulled back, absolutely stung. "I will na' whore for any man! Not even for Zander FitzHugh."

Plato shook his head wearily. "I dinna' mean that. I meant how much more do you ken he can stand? How much more of his anguish do you need to satisfy yourself? How much more of this, when it is within your power to fix it?"

"I dinna' have that much power. I'm a lowly squire of no-name and no-clan. I have no power."

Plato stretched out his arm and gestured. "Look about you, Morgan, what do you see?"

She looked. There were groups of men huddled about under overhanging porches, some talking, some pointing. There was mud, a splintered target, great gray stone walls, pouring rain. She said all of that as she observed it.

He shook his head. "Do you know what I see?"

"You see more than that?"

"Aye. I see lads taking to a different form of sling-shot because a lad named Morgan showed them how. I see knives getting tossed differently, and with greater accuracy, because of a lad named Morgan. I see Scotsmen glowing with pride and jostling each other every time a Sassenach was sent away from the field, his dignity in tatters, all because of a lad named Morgan. I see young clansmen all clamoring for the chance to be a squire, so they can be like a lad named Morgan. I see a warrior like my brother, a score and eight in years, hardened by exercise, and faultless in battle, changing his attacking arm, all because of a lad named Morgan. You see any of that?"

Morgan squinted her eyes against the rain and considered

him. Her legs felt a little wobbly, and it wasn't the rain doing it. It was what he was saying.

"I did all that?" she asked.

Plato grinned, his teeth white in his mud-splattered face, although the rain was washing off some of the muck. "That and more, Morgan. There is a dark part of this power you wield, too. Dinna' think there isna'. Dinna' ken Zander is the only one suffering with it, either, for he isna'."

'I'm suffering, too," Morgan replied, "And none among you knows my reasons!"

"I dinna' care what your reasons are, anymore!"

"I'll not stay and listen to another—" Morgan turned her back on him, but he interrupted her.

"Do you know where the lass, Sheila, is?"

She stopped. "Sheila is not my concern."

"Oh, that is where you're wrong. I happen to know where the lass is, and it will na' be what she expects."

Morgan turned back around. "Where is she?" she asked.

"In my bed."

Morgan gasped. "But, I thought you loved Gwynneth," she protested.

"Love and lust are two different things, Morgan. That is where you have confused them. My brother is also confused. He thinks he can place his lust on the woman I love, and keep his love for the woman I am starting to detest."

"Now, wait. I had nothing to do with—"

"Do you not even wish to know why Sheila is in my bed?"

"You will tell me, even if I dinna' wish to hear it. Go on then, Plato, tell me."

"She is learning how to be a whore."

"What?" Morgan's knees were definitely wobbly. She rocked in place. "But, why? There is na' need for such a life. She has my protection! Everyone know it."

"That's just it, lass. She has the great Scot's champion, Squire Morgan's protection, but he does na' want her for himself. Oh nay. He wants to slake his lust on a fat, old whore named Sally Bess with a big mouth and ceaseless tormenting words about it."

"I dinna' know," Morgan whispered.

"So, if her protector wants a fat, used whore, then Sheila will do her best, because she wants what Sally Bess has."

"Sally Bess does na' have anything of the kind!"

"You go tell them of it," Plato said.

"I dinna' know. You say I am responsible, then help me! How can I change it? How? I dinna' know it was happening. I dinna' mean it to happen. I dinna' mean any of this to happen."

"It gets worse," Plato said softly.

"It . . . does?" Her voice wasn't even audible, but he heard it.

"Aye," he answered.

Morgan's knees gave and she went to them on the wet grass beside him. "How?" she whispered.

"You want Sheila?" He asked, glancing sideways at where she sat. "You want to take her to your bed?"

"That's disgusting!" she blurted out. "And you know it is!"

"Do I?" he asked.

"I dinna' want anything of the sort!"

"You dinna know how it feels to roll a teat around in your teeth, then? You dinna' ken how they tighten into a knot just made for sucking on?"

"Stop!" Morgan screamed it, slamming a hand to her mouth to stay the sickness.

"How about her moist womanness? You wish to feel that about yourself? Have you considered that? Her moistness pressed to yours? Well?"

"Stop! Stop! Stop!" Morgan screamed it until her voice cracked, and sobs filled the gap. She slammed her hands to her ears and still seemed to hear him, see the images, feel the bile churn warningly. "Stop! I canna' take it! I canna' listen! I canna' think! I hate the images you give to me! Stop! I beg you, stop!"

He didn't say anything while Morgan moved her hands to her belly, clasped them about herself and rocked with the feeling of revulsion.

"Why are you doing this to me? Why? Why, Plato, why? I dinna' want to know. I dinna' want to hear. I would rather die than think this through. Do you hear me? I would rather die! Why do you do it?" She lifted her head and looked at him, and all she could still see was the horror he'd described.

"So you will see what you've done to my brother," he said finally.

Morgan's eyes widened and her mouth fell open. "Oh my God," she whimpered, and then she was running back the way Zander had gone.

Chapter 20

Morgan stood outside Zander's chamber, put her forehead to the door and tried to convince herself not to interfere. She had the length of her flight to reach here and realize that Plato was getting her to do his bidding, not the KilCreggars'. He was making her forget that everything the KilCreggars had vowed for was within her ability to grant, right here and right now. She could not only wreak blood-vengeance from the FitzHugh clan, by taking one of theirs from them, but she was actually doing it without her having to spill a drop of blood.

Every KilCreggar that had gone before was with her, their blood singing through her veins with her own blood, their pain adding to hers, until her heart was one large ache. She told herself to wait. All she needed was to wait, and hold it to her, and not interfere, and it would come to pass. If she stopped Zander, she would be admitting to the one thing she didn't dare believe.

She'd have to admit that there was love in the world, and it was stronger than vows, it was stronger even than death. If she opened this door, there would be no going back. She knew that. She knew that Plato expected it of her. He expected her to whore for him, to get him what he wanted, what Zander wanted . . . what she wanted.

Morgan sighed and pushed away from the door. She wasn't going to whore for anyone, but she couldn't deny her heart, either. Love was too strong. She was going to have to stop Zander some other way, and there was only one way she could think of . . . by telling him the truth.

She opened the door.

Zander was lying on his bed, the dragon blade in his fingers, and he was turning it this way and that, just watching it. Morgan shut the door behind her softly, and lowered the newly constructed bolt into place.

"Have you come to say good-bye?" he asked.

"Nay," she said. "I have come for my blade."

"Why?"

"Give me the blade, Zander. We'll talk."

Zander looked over at her. He hadn't wiped one bit of mud from himself before gaining his bed. She knew it was because he didn't care. She knew what he had planned. The same thing she would be doing in his stead.

"You may take the blade from my dead hand, Morgan, and not before. You ken?"

He raised it. Morgan opened her mouth and started talking.

"I am not Morgan, of no-name and no-clan, Zander. I come from a family of four sons and two daughters. My father was the laird. It was na' a large clan, nor was it a rich clan. I had uncles, cousins . . . all older. We did na' have a castle like this one, nor were we poor crofters. We had a stone house, very sturdy, with a loft. I knew love, too. I was surrounded by it. I remember it perfectly, although it was lost to us when I was very small."

Nothing. The blade was still hovering over his chest. Morgan choked and kept stumbling over the words.

"My oldest sister is named Elspeth. She is a score-and-one older than me. She looked like me once. Same long, black hair, same eyes, same face. We took after our mother. My sister had a man of her own, too, one bairn, with another on the way. I had that, Zander. I knew love. I knew life. Then, it was taken. I was four years old."

The blade glinted. She didn't know what that meant. She didn't dare stop long enough to ask.

"The reavers came in the earliest of morn. All the men-folk were gone. There was just my sister, my ma, and the bairn home with me. I still remember the colors they wore. I have never forgotten it. I never will." She looked down at the identical colors and shivered before she could stop it.

"My ma was taken first, and I did na' know what they did to her, over and over while she screamed and bled all over the table. I watched from the loft, and then Elspeth was with me. She gave me her plan. She was going to drop me from the loft. It was a long drop, Zander, especially to a four-year-old in the earliest of dawn.

"I remember Elspeth calling to me, making certain I was all right. Then, she asked me to catch her bairn. His name was Samuel. He was a bright boy, although only a year in age. He was healthy. He was beautiful. He was perfect. I held up my arms."

The blade wasn't hovering above him anymore, but Morgan didn't see it, anyway. She was seeing that morning again.

"The house was starting to catch fire, but I knew none of that. I was concentrating. I was ready. I planted my feet to catch him, and the explosion knocked me flat. I dinna' know houses could do such a thing. I still canna' explain it. I only know I was na' there to catch my nephew because of it. He was already on the ground. He looked up at me with his big, trusting eyes and then was still. I was trying to awaken him, when Elspeth landed beside me, clutching her swollen belly and screaming about my clumsiness. Her screams brought the rest of the reavers."

"What did you do then?" Zander asked quietly.

"I hid. I did na' know what else to do. The house was burning, smoke was everywhere and Elspeth screamed and kept screaming. I dinna' know then, why."

"Do you know who did the deed?" he asked.

Morgan swallowed on the enormous lump in her throat to answer. "I do now," she answered with a rasp in her voice. "Back then, I only knew the clan. I told my father when he got there, too. He, and my brothers, and my uncles and cousins, and Elspeth's man, although I dinna' even recollect his name. I thought Elspeth was dying. She was covered with blood, and screaming about how I'd killed her bairn, and then she delivered a still-birthed one there on the grass."

"Oh my God." Zander's voice was exhibiting the same horror she was seeing. Morgan shut her eyes.

"Elspeth went mad. She still is, I think. I call her the hag, when I call her anything. She still calls me the bairn killer. Always has. Always will."

"But you were four at the time!"

She opened her eyes and met his. "Four is not too young to learn life, nor death, Zander. I can attest to it. I must have learned it well, too. You have remarked how I am about it."

"I dinna' know."

"No one does. 'Tis no matter, anyway. 'Tis past. It canna' be changed."

"Your clan swore vengeance?"

"Aye. And spent six years trying to get it. I spent those years learning about it, too. Learning killing. Seeing killing. Burying our dead. Sneering at theirs. I became my father's shadow. Wherever he was, I was in the shadows. If anyone chanced across the homeless clan we had become, they would have seen a waif, in the shadows behind them. My father was very learned with weapons, although not as quick and accurate as I am. I learned knives first. You probably guessed that much."

"Go on," he said.

Morgan swallowed around the dryness. "Every season we lost clan, but we made them pay, too. My clan had sworn to gain blood-vengeance. The killing went on and on. We could na' stop until it was done. Then came the end."

"The end?"

Morgan couldn't see anything except that night. She didn't hear Zander's question, either. All she could hear was the screams, then the groans, then the silence. "I was ten at the time, and I was na' allowed to join the battle, so I was in the shadows watching. I watched as my clan was wiped out. All of them. There were thirty-seven men killed that night, and a score of them were mine. All I had. Every cousin, every uncle, everyone."

"What did you do, then?"

"What do you think I did? I buried them. It took me eight days and I had to hide when they came for their dead. I was na' very adept at digging, and who was I going to ask for help, the hag? She could na' stand the sight of me. No one could. I took the sett from some of the smaller bodies to keep for myself, and then when I got too weak from lack of food, I went back. I dug up and purloined every weapon they had from their graves. They are walking the earth still, looking for their sett and their dirks, to this day. I know it. I feel them, sometimes."

"They would na' do that, Morgan. They would have understood. They would ha' wanted nothing less," he said softly.

"What do you know of it?" she spat. "Safe and secure in your clan, and surrounded by all your brothers, and with all your kin? Well? You dinna' know what it's like to have no one, save yourself. You dinna' know what it's like to watch your mother raped and burned. You dinna' ken the torment of knowing you killed your sister's bairn. You dinna' know what it's like to have ancestors walking the earth looking for you because you robbed from their graves! You know nothing of that, Zander, nothing."

"You're right, Morgan. I don't. I'm beginning to understand a little, though."

"I vowed I would finish it. I was na' afraid to die once it was done. I expected it. I needed it. I would gain vengeance and then I would die. Then, maybe the corpses of my clan would rest in peace and leave me be."

"Your dreams?" Zander whispered.

Morgan nodded, and brought her gaze back to his chamber. He was dangling the dragon blade by two fingers about the handle, but he still had it.

"Then, I met you, Zander FitzHugh. Or rather, I was taken by you. Is there a worse fate for me? Taken by a FitzHugh? One of the most arrogant, filthy-rich, Sassenach-loving, Highland FitzHughs? Worse yet, I was taken by the youngest, prettiest, play-loving, strongest, most manly FitzHugh. You have no idea how much I have tried to hate you."

"I can guess," he said.

"You set about learning me, though, and I did na' wish to learn! I knew what my purpose in life was. To seek vengeance and die. That was my sole purpose. That's the reason behind everything I do, everything I've done, and then you had to go and force me to squire for you."

"Which leads you to what? Are you going to claim a new joy of living, a new reason for love? What, Morgan? Say something to make this ungodly day make sense."

"I canna' deny anymore that there is such a thing as love. I did na' think it existed anymore, but you made me face it. Aye, there is still love in the world. There is still joy. There is still a reason to all of it. There is still a God who cares. There will still be bairns born and raised to become old men and old women. There will still be death. There will still be brutality. There will also be life. There is still love in the world."

He sighed. "I understand now, Morgan. I'm sorry. You dinna' have to tell me this, but I understand. God help me, anyway. I understand what you're saying and I understand why. With as much killing and death as this earth already holds, why would I add to it? That is what you're saying, isna' it?"

"I could na' bear to dig your grave, Zander. It pains me deeply to know I might have to. You must give me my blade now."

"Will you promise not to miss me next time I risk our hope of heaven by trying to claim you?"

"I have no hope of heaven, Zander. Have na' you been listening to me?"

"Everything you have said to me was done when you were a child! Little more than a bairn yourself! No God would be so unmerciful."

"I have just started believing in God again, Zander FitzHugh. Pray don't take my belief too far, too fast. I knew what I was doing. I knew why. I have to finish this vow and I have to die. I know my clan will rest when I have satisfied both, and not before. You dinna' understand!"

"I understand the vengeance, Morgan, but none have to die except this devil! He must die. Only tell me the name of the clan and I will help you. They deserve all you can do."

Morgan felt like she'd been tossed over a waterfall and into the deepest loch, and was just breaking the surface for air. She sucked the breath in and it burned. "I canna' ask your help, Zander. 'Tis my own curse, and my own vow. I am speaking now because I have made another vow. This is what I wanted you to know, and for it, I need your help."

"What is it?"

"I am going to correct the wrongs I have done. Though they were na' intentioned, they were still done. I will na' be able to rest in my own grave if I dinna' correct it. I will need you alive to do so. After I have finished, you may seek death if you wish. I will join you. Now give me the blade, Zander."

"You must not miss again."

"I dinna' miss before. I did what you said to do. I was aiming for a crack in the rock. I hit it."

He sat up and flung it toward her. Morgan was as astounded as he was when she moved in that direction and caught it. She held it up to the light and watched the ruby in the firelight.

"Do you believe in magic, Zander?" she asked.

"I believe in illusion," he replied, with a ghost of a smile.

She shrugged. "I will think on that instead. Seek sleep now. You are going to need it. I will be back in this room before the sun sets tomorrow."

"Where are you going? To whom? If you seek out that harlot, Sally—"

Morgan put her hands on her hips and lowered her eyebrows, and gave him another I-am-so-disappointed-in-you look. "Zander FitzHugh, I have just told you more than any other soul on earth knows. Dinna' press me now."

"You will come to no harm?"

"I am the FitzHugh champion of weapons. Harm? What fool would attempt it?"

"Where will you be? How will I find you?"

"I will not leave the castle. You have my word. Rest. Bathe yourself. Ask Plato for any assist. Find a *feile breacan* befitting the most handsome of the FitzHughs, and dare to dream, Zander. I promise you magic. Not illusion. Magic. Until tomorrow."

She opened the door and slid out. Then, she went looking for Sheila and the Lady Gwynneth to make a woman out of her.

The bath they filled for her was a pleasant experience, once she got over three women all assisting her. Sally Bess wasn't going to be left out of the creation of Morganna, the mysterious one.

Lady Gwynneth had been surprised and pleased at Morgan's request, and Sheila had been open-mouthed and astounded, and giggling non-stop at what Morgan had done, and the lads she had bested. Sheila no longer wanted to be a fat, lazy whore, either. She wanted to be of service to Morganna, wherever that would be.

They exclaimed their dismay over the amazing wealth of muscle in Morgan's abdomen, her back and her shoulders. Not to mention the thick cording of sinew at the backs of her thighs and her buttocks. While Lady Gwynneth clucked her tongue over muscles no woman should have, she discovered that Morgan's legs weren't any larger than her own, and her waist was much smaller.

The last was a surprise to the Lady Gwynneth, who had a length of heavy, black satin that was being formed into a dress for her. It hadn't been hemmed yet, and it was pronounced just the thing Morgan should wear for her seduction of Zander FitzHugh. Then they set about oiling Morgan's hair and skin, and making her drink a concoction of herbs and spices guaranteed to calm her enough to sleep the afternoon away.

When she was awakened, she strapped the dragon blade and kilt square to her thigh despite any arguments, was dressed in a frail, almost see-through shift they called a chemise, had woven stockings rolled into place up her legs, where they kept slipping, and was wrapped in the black satin. Sleeves were laced on. Black cording was criss-crossed about her ribs and the slimness of her stomach, and ribbons were woven through her hair. Then, she was finally pronounced ready, and escorted under heavy veiling to the chamber.

That's when her courage very nearly failed her. The ladies must have known, for they simply ripped the veil from her, opened the door and pushed her in, amid a great deal of giggling. Then there was complete and absolute silence.

Zander was off his chair and across the floor and in front of her before Morgan could take a breath. The one she managed when he stopped right in front of her, was more a gasp. Those midnight-blue eyes were large and shocked and stunned, and very, very pleased. She could tell.

"Oh . . . dearest God," he said, going to his knee before

her. She watched him pick up her hem and hold it. She watched the hand shake. Then, his shoulders. "Tell me I am not dreaming. Please, God?"

Morgan dropped her hand to the top of his head, running her fingers through it, until she had strands of hair where she usually kept dirks. "You are na' dreaming, my lord FitzHugh. My father had two daughters. Elspeth, whom I told you of . . . and Morganna," she whispered.

"Oh Morgan, you wretch. You complete and total wretch. When I think of the nights, the images I've had, the—"

"Would you waste time telling the floor of past frustrations, my lord?"

"Oh Morgan, I canna' believe you're real."

Morgan pulled her hands from his hair and held them out, palms up. "Zander, if you dinna' come off the floor, I'm going to search out Plato and ask him what else I'm supposed to do to make you believe! I am as female as any other. I always have been."

He stood, sucked in air and looked very carefully from the top of her head down the slight shadow between her breasts that he could see, down to the tips of her stocking feet, since Lady Gwynneth's closets hadn't any slippers of a sufficient size, and then he brought his gaze the same way back up. He was close enough to touch, but refraining from it. It didn't matter. It had the same effect, she decided.

"You will na' get that far from me. And you will na' search for Plato, or any other man again. Ever. I dinna' want another soul in this room. Not tonight," he reached behind her to drop the bolt, and came back around. "Mayhap not even tomorrow."

"You are being wed tomorrow, Zander."

He frowned and looked her over. "Only if the bride is you," he finally answered.

"You canna' break a betrothal, Zander."

"You come into my chamber, promising everything I've

been afraid to envision and tell me to wed another? Jesu'
Morgan, make up your mind! I will na' take you except
upon promise to be my wife. I swear it."

Morgan's eyes filled with tears. He was asking the impossible, but he didn't know it. Only she did.

"Besides, Plato told me the truth about them. He loves
Lady Gwynneth, and she him. He will take my place. He
told me I would na' regret it. He was right. I dinna'. I may
even miss his wedding. Oh, Morgan, have you eaten?"

He still wasn't touching her, and Morgan kept the same
distance he seemed to wish as he turned to show her the
table. There were grapes, cheeses, wine, and a blood pudding on his table. There was also a fresh linen on his bed,
and it was in deepest red. Her eyes widened. He watched
where she was looking and smiled.

"Plato was in on your surprise. He designed my chamber. There may even be musicians later to serenade us. Will
you mind?"

"I dinna' understand, Zander."

She watched him walk over to the table, pick up a goblet
and fill it for her. Then he brought it back. Her eyes were
brimming with tears, but she wasn't about to weep. Zander
FitzHugh was wearing his family kilt, a black doublet and
wide-sleeved blouse. He was absolutely amazing, but he
was acting differently than she'd expected. He had the complete right to touch her, and he wasn't?

He held out the goblet for her. Morgan reached for it,
and he shied away from the minute contact of her fingers,
flushing strangely as she watched. She was shaking so
badly she had to hold it with two hands.

"What dinna' you understand, my sweet?"

"You dinna' touch me," she replied, then it was her turn
to blush as he stared at her.

"I dinna' dare," he finally answered.

"I am still Morgan, the squire," she whispered.

"Aye, and I will be like an unleashed beast if I touch you.

I have been too long denied, Morganna. I know myself. I am not touching you for a reason. A very good reason. Now, sip your wine, and cease looking at me with those big, gray eyes, while I kick myself for not seeing what was right in front of my own."

She choked on the first sip of wine, and he chuckled, leaving her to pour his own. Morgan walked across the chamber, allowing every bit of swing the ladies had instructed her on, while she did so. Zander's reaction was like a balm as he pulled his head back and opened wide, shocked, midnight-blue eyes to her antics. Morgan decided there were a few things about being female that she could come to like.

"I would like to try some of your pudding, I think," she said when she reached the table.

He was serving it on a platter to her before she was seated, and then he watched as she broke a piece off with her fingers and raised it to her mouth. Then, she half-lidded her eyes and licked at her fingers before she chewed. Zander closed his eyes and gulped. Morgan nearly giggled.

"You are na' eating?" she asked when he opened his eyes again.

"I dinna' think I'll be able to swallow," he replied. Then he proceeded to show that for a falsehood by draining his goblet of wine and putting it back on the table. "Jesu' Morganna, you are the loveliest lass I've ever seen. I canna' believe I've had you with me night and day for almost five sennights and never guessed it. I canna' believe I was so blind. I canna' think! I can only close my eyes and welcome the shivers. Jesu'!" He finished the impassioned speech, and Morganna picked up a bite of her pudding.

"Open your mouth, Zander," she whispered.

Chapter 21

Zander opened both his mouth and his eyes, and she watched his stunned expression as she placed the morsel on his tongue. Then, she put a finger on his upper lip and commanded him to close it and eat. He was trembling beneath her fingers. Morgan felt and saw him do it, and decided it was very satisfying to be female, actually. Then, she drank from her own goblet, allowing a few drops of the red liquid to sit on her lips before licking them off. Zander was choking at that. She sucked in on her cheeks and smiled.

She picked up a grape next, and rolled it between her fingers. "Zander?" she whispered. "Open your mouth again."

He flinched and pulled back a fraction. Then, he was shaking his head in almost the same humming-bird fashion she'd done in the earl's chambers not a fortnight since. Morgan did giggle then. She couldn't help it.

Zander reacted by picking up her goblet and draining it, too. Morgan watched him do it. "Are you thinking to avoid me by getting yourself drunk?" she asked.

He put the goblet down and lowered his head. Her ears filled with a roaring so loud, he should be able to hear it, too.

"Oh, there will be no avoidance tonight, Morganna. I love your name, Morganna. Morganna . . . beloved of Zander FitzHugh. Morganna, mother to FitzHugh bairns. Morganna, uniter of the clans, champion of weapons. How many things you are, and will be, Morganna, my love, and I've just touched on the tip of them."

She had to shut her eyes or he would spot the way his words assaulted her, wounding her to the bottom of her soul. She was none of those things, nor would she ever be. She wasn't going to speak of it, though. She was taking care of her vow. That was all she was doing. All the things Zander said she was, and wanted for her, they were for a Morganna that didn't exist.

She sucked in on her pain. She wasn't here for love and she knew it. She was here to whore herself. It was what she had to do to right her wrongs. She was saving Sheila from herself, Plato from a loveless, hate-filled existence, Gwynneth from a self-inflicted death; and she was clearing the demons from her beloved Zander's head, because he was too silly to see the truth for himself. None of it was real. It couldn't be real. It wasn't illusion, either. It was magic, purely and simply magic.

She opened her eyes. Zander responded by tipping his head and slurping the grape from between her fingers. Morgan snapped them away the instant his lips started sucking, for the contact burned hotter than had the pinpricks of blisters on the backs of her legs.

"Zander?"

"I would like another grape, I think," he replied, tipping his head, and opening his mouth.

Morgan plucked one and held it gingerly above his open, grasping mouth. Lips again burned, only this time he nipped a bit at the underside of her forefinger. Her eyes widened as he brought his head back up, to catch and hold her gaze.

"Another," he commanded.

Morgan was clumsy, and lost the first one she plucked off. She was forced to grasp another and was shaking long before she had it hovering above his mouth. This time he had her wrist in his hand and she couldn't move as he sucked the fruit from her fingers, and then kept sucking until he had the tip of her finger in his mouth. Morgan's eyelids drooped half-way of their own accord, her knees started quivering and her lips opened to pant for breath before he let go of her hand and released her.

"Another one," he commanded.

Morgan's fingertips weren't just burning, they were tingling with sensation, and felt scorched raw with every contact from his mouth, then cooled with the shape and texture of the grape. She dropped two grapes before she managed to hold onto one this time, and her hand was hesitant when she held it out.

Zander's hand had her wrist, he had the grape, and then he had his tongue on the sensitive part of her palm making miniature circles in the midst of it before she could gasp. Then he released her.

"Another one," he commanded.

"I think . . . I need . . . to sit down," she whispered.

He grinned, and went to his knees to make it easier for her. Morgan looked down at him, and swayed before catching herself against the table. Zander had his eyebrows up and a sparkle to those dark eyes before she fell into the chair, put one hand to her breast and caught the tremor.

"What is happening to me?" she whispered.

"Oh . . . that. 'Tis what you've fought against for years. 'Tis all that horrid love stuff. That is what's happening to you. All that you denied yourself. All that is life. All that is play. Come along, Morganna, play with me. I have hunger for another grape, and I want you to feed it to me."

He put his head on her knee and tipped it up to watch her. Morgan turned into the consistency of the pudding at his contact. Her eyes closed, she felt herself trembling, and when she opened her eyes back up, Zander's midnight-blue gaze was still waiting for her. She got a grape, although her shaking hand rattled the bowl.

She was hesitant about giving it to him, though. Her

hand moved out a bit, then a little further, before pulling back, and on the third try, he caught at it, had the grape sucked from her fingers, and his lips on her inner wrist before she could jerk it away. Morgan squealed, then quieted as he lapped at her skin, giving her shivers all the way to the centers of her freed breasts. Her eyes flew open at it, and she looked down at herself with no small amount of fear. All of which had Zander laughing delightedly when he dropped her hand.

"Another," he commanded.

"I canna'," she whimpered.

"I want another grape, Morganna, my love, and I want you to feed it to me. Now."

She tipped the bowl sideways with her motion, and couldn't quite get her fingers to work. It took three tries just to get one grape in her fingers. These same fingers that were so sensitive they could feel, aim and perfectly toss a knife, were having trouble with grapes? Morgan looked at her hands in surprise and a slight bit of dismay.

"My grape?" he asked.

"Zander?" She began, looking from her hand to him and back again. "My fingers . . . feel strange. I dinna' ken why."

He laughed again, and caught her wrist before she had a chance to hold it over him. He had the grape sucked free and pushed her sleeve out of his way until he reached the sensitive skin of her inner elbow. Morgan squirmed on the chair, her head back and her mouth open as he tongued little designs into her flesh and then lifted his head.

"Another," he requested.

"I canna'!" she cried. "Dinna' make me! I dinna' ken what is happening. I dinna' think I like it! Oh, Zander, help me!"

He had her plucked from the chair and held to him before she said another word, and his mouth told her everything she was crying out for. Morgan felt his hands shaking, where they were holding her beneath her arms, she felt the bulge of him where he held her atop him, and she felt the insistent demands of his lips as he plied hers open, his tongue grasping, demanding, and seeking.

"Oh, my sweet, my innocent, my love!" He was the one breaking the contact, pulling his head from hers with a furious motion while he glared at her, with eyes so blazing blue, she felt the burn clear to the deepest pit of her where her own body seemed to twinge. Her own eyes widened as she felt it.

"Zander?" she asked.

"Lovely Morganna. My Morganna, mine!"

He had fistfuls of her hair and was inhaling the perfumed oils the ladies had combed through it. And he was shuddering. Morgan felt every bit of it as the hardest part of him changed, softening a little, and she worried. She was still worried when he lifted his head.

"What is it, love?" he asked.

"You dinna' desire me . . . either?" she asked.

He chuckled, and arms wrapped about her, holding her close. "I desire you more than life itself, my love, I just have to gain control of myself. I am na' a young cock, able just to please myself. I want you to experience every bit of pleasure I can give, you ken?"

She shook her head. That seemed to make him even happier, and then he was kissing her again, every bit of her he could reach. Her nose, her throat, her chin, her shoulders where the dress slid.

Morgan was in a whirlwind no rainstorm could approach, then she was back in the chair, the hard wood beneath her contrasting to the warmth she'd just left, and the solid wood arms feeling vacant and cold. Her eyes flew open.

"Zander?"

"I thought I told you to feed me a grape, Morganna," he commanded, his voice lower than she'd ever heard it.

Morgan reached to pluck one, but got two and the stem, and then she held them out to him, watching her own hand shake. She concentrated on controlling it, but then he was sliding a hand up one of her legs, and there was no stopping the tremor. Then, he stopped, and rolled his eyes when he came into contact with the dragon blade.

He didn't move his gaze as he untied the bow and pulled the bundle of knife, binding, and kilt square out. Morgan held her breath, but all Zander did after glancing at it, was wrap the binding cloth about her blade and the gray fabric swath, before putting it atop the table.

" 'Tis unsafe to unwrap you, Morganna, and you feared needlessly. We'll not want to use it tonight," he whispered, and then he winked.

If he'd stopped there, she could have breathed out the gasp. Instead, he grasped her ankle and started up her leg again. Morgan slid on the wood, one foot against his chest while he moved his hand all the way past her knee, until he reached the top of a stocking. Morgan shook with whatever it was. She moaned aloud with it, losing what seemed like her one chance at another breath at the same time. She was melting in place. Her every limb turning into gruel, while he ran fingers back down, taking the stocking with them. And when he had it off, he tongued the arch of her foot, gaining himself screams of frightened rapture.

"Zander? I dinna' . . . I canna' . . . ," Morgan panted. Then she squealed again while he chuckled, breathing hot air on the moistness he'd just left on her ankle.

"You remember showing me balance?" he asked, one hand buried deep up her skirt where it flirted with the top of her other stocking and just barely brushed at her other thigh at the same time.

"Ba—lance?" she asked, gasping out the word.

"Well, this is your first lesson in the world of off-balance," he finished, and rolled her other stocking off.

Morgan had the presence of mind to pull both legs beneath her the moment he finished, and she had both hands out, palms toward him. "Oh no, Zander. Oh no."

"Oh yes, Morganna," he replied. "Oh, yes." Then he grinned, stopping her heart, until she had to gasp to restart it. "I believe I owe you a lesson in sensitivity, too, dinna' I? Let's see . . . how did it go?"

He caught both her palms and proceeded to show her exactly how sensitive they both were, with tongue licks, sucking and nipping every part of them. Morgan was in an agony of sensation, her every part attuned to what he was doing. Then he let both hands go, stunning her into dropping back against the chair as he began unbuttoning his doublet.

"Zander?" she whispered.

He grinned. "Frightened?" he asked.

"Aye, terrified," she answered.

That got her a bigger grin, and then he shoved the doublet off. Morgan couldn't take her eyes off the sight as he lifted the shirt from his torso, rising on his knees to do so, and showing her very definitely that he desired her, and very much. Morgan's eyes were wide, her breathing gaining her less than usual amounts of air and her hands gripping both sides of the chair hard enough to raise her above the seat.

Zander took it all in and grinned harder.

"You ready to see a real man?"

"Nay," she whimpered the word. "Not yet, Zander. Please?"

"Then dinna' open your eyes."

His warning was too late, and Morgan's breathing grew even quicker and more shallow with her panic. She put both hands to her cheeks and tried to hold it in. She had never seen what it looked like gorged and hard, she had never even guessed. Her eyes were as wide as possible as she moved her view up his body to his face. The love and adoration she saw there helped ease the fear, until it settled into a steady throbbing problem in her belly.

"Zander?"

"I love you, Morganna. I will do naught to cause harm or hurt you. I promise, although, faith, it looks large—"

"It will na' fit," she protested, interrupting him, her eyes sparkling with unshed tears. "I'll be ripped apart."

He grinned. "Nay, love. At least, that isna' the usual response I get. Come. Give me your hand."

She shook her head. He responded to that by reaching and plucking her from the chair and into those arms. Morgan shuddered, and then she was on his red sheets, her body tucked in between his legs, and feeling his instrument of torture trying to dig a hole into the small of her back.

"Zander? Please stop," she begged, when he lifted her hair to place his tongue at the back of her neck, just before he started sucking on the skin. That had her arching backward, allowing him to easily unlace every bit of her cording. The gown billowed out when he'd finished.

"Stop? Oh no, my love . . . my Morganna. My life." He was crooning the words, and easing the satin down off her arms and then into a pile of material at her feet, and he was dulling her fear with each low-timbre word. "My love . . . my beauty . . . my woman."

The satin was shoved somewhere between the footboard and the mattress. Morgan only felt it missing by an increased awareness of air and light and heat, and then Zander had her chemise peeled down enough to reach her breast. He bent his head, and at the first touch, Morgan cried aloud, the sound high-pitched, filled with fright and complete shock. Zander trembled with what had to be laughter as he tongued her nipple to what Plato had described, and Morgan's cries turned into whimpers of delight. Then they became moans of absolute pleasure. Morgan was arching for a different reason then, to give him greater access to her. To make certain of it, she held his head where she needed it, all of which got her more chuckles from him.

From somewhere she heard music, and she only thought about deciphering why. Then, he slid out from behind and beneath her to put his entire length against hers, and his hands were finishing the job of removing the last bit of clothing between them, lifting her where it got stuck beneath the swell of her buttocks, trembling as it hung up on the last foot.

Zander was relishing what he saw, and Morgan watched him with wide eyes and fright just below the surface.

"You've a well-conditioned frame, Morganna. I can see why you best me at push-ups." He was running a finger-nail all the way up her leg, the muscles beneath her thighs bunching without her volition, and then he was caressing the lumps in her abdomen. "I like it verra much. A warrior princess for a warrior. What better coupling can there be?"

"You dinna' mind?" she whispered when he reached the sinew and cording of her arms. "Truly?"

"Mind?" he asked, and then he repeated it, surprise flavoring the word. "Mind? Every other female pales in comparison. I think you're a delight to the eye. I'm the envy of every true male, I vow."

Morgan glowed with the praise, and then she lost all thought of being embarrassed by any portion of her body as he fit himself atop her, his chest hair tickling everywhere it touched, his breath billowing across her nose and cheeks and the hardness of him burying itself between her thighs.

"We're going to practice our push-ups, now, Morganna. Remember how 'tis done? I recall a bit of play you attempted when I was in my cups, and too drunk to know I had a female in my arms. Stupid me."

"Push-ups?"

"Something to that effect. You're going to be a very active participant, too. 'Tis more like another exercise. You frightened, still?"

She nodded, her eyes huge.

"I'll try to be gentle. 'Tis not easy. I've been denied a long time, I'm not of a subtle size, and you've a maiden-head to breach. It may pain, but it will pass. I promise on all I hold holy."

He lifted himself, pushing on her shoulders. Morgan reached her own hands up and placed them on his chest.

He looked down her frame, closed his eyes for a fraction and she watched him tremble.

"Zander?"

"You are very special, Morganna. You have the kiss of ecstasy in your thighs, I swear. Release me to pleasure you, before I lose my seed in yon sheets."

She shook her head with little, quick motions.

"Morganna, I have waited and dreamed for this moment. You will experience it, too. Open your legs to me, lass."

She shook her head again. Zander bent his head down, touched his lips to hers, and breathed into her. "Open your legs, darling. Open. Open for me, for your man, your love. Open. Now."

His kiss was different. It was pounding and grasping and compulsory. It was all tautness, it was compelling, and it was forceful. It demanded her surrender, and it would not brook anything less. Morgan's thighs opened as he continued his kiss, sending her entire body spiraling down into their mattress and then back up to the height of the sky, and then he was splitting her with such a painful motion, Morgan stiffened everywhere as he thrust partway into her.

"Zander . . . I canna'! 'Tis too big! You're ripping me!"

"Morganna, hush. Lay quiet. Hush, love, hush." He was whispering his love words and kissing at the moisture on her cheeks, but he wasn't pulling away. " 'Tis only your maidenhead, love. 'Twill only hurt this once. I promise. Hush."

Morgan trembled, and forced her body to accept him. Forced herself to release the stiffness bit by bit. "I thought 'tis pleasure you promised," she finally whispered. "This is na' pleasure, Zander. 'Tis na'. I'd rather taste your fist."

"We have to get through the veil of your virginity first, love. It will na' hurt after that. Dinna' you trust me?"

Morgan looked into dark eyes, that handsome face and nodded. Her body wrenched again as he pushed in further, his eyes darkening with every wince she made.

"You are very fit, Morganna. You can withstand the taste of a blade and the ache of a forced march with your back wrenched. You can withstand this."

Pain was centered all about his entry, it was climbing into her back, and he was telling her she could withstand it? Morgan tried to find the ability to glare at him. She tried, but all that happened was her eyes filled with tears. There wasn't a strong bone left in her.

"Put your legs about me, Morganna. Link your ankles behind my waist. We must get this over with, and I dinna' like it any more than you. In a moment I'm going to force you."

She shook her head. "Nay. I canna'."

"Do it," he commanded.

She tried, and everything shook as she did. Her eyes overflowed with the tears. Zander cursed, lowered his hands to her hips and forced her, just as he said he would. Morgan lay, splayed apart clear to her belly with his entry and tried to accept him.

"Morganna?" he whispered. "Look to me, love."

Zander looked as pained as she felt and Morgan felt a little of her ache ebb as she observed it.

"Forgive me, love. I have na' had many maidens, despite my bragging, and I forget the problems."

"I dinna' know it would hurt so much," she whispered, feeling even more pain ebb as he kept waiting.

"It is better at all?" he asked.

She scrunched up her face. "It does na' feel raw, nor does it burn."

"Thank God," he mumbled. "For if I stay much longer in your honeyed depths, dearest Morganna, I am going to lose all thought of your own pleasure and fill your belly with my own need."

And so saying, he moved.

Morgan cried aloud with the pain. Then, she was writhing with what could be pain, but felt more like something different. She clung to every bit of him, rising and falling with him, and doing push-ups with her entire body. Then, she simply let herself hold on while she experienced what could be rains worse than any storm, lightning worse than any flash, and thunder louder than any blow, that shot through her entire body. It could also be what it felt like to die.

Morgan clung to him, feeling sucked into what he was creating, and heard the thunder, felt the lightning, experienced the rain, for a second time. It was from what seemed a far-off distance she heard him groaning, and then she felt him pulsating and stiffening with every limb she had entwined about him.

His arms trembled, then collapsed, sending his chest onto her. Morgan held her arms about him and waited what seemed a long time.

She was almost numbed by his weight before Zander groaned, rolling to his other side and taking her with him. Then, he laughed, and her frame moved with it. "Although I will never admit it, *that* was worth waiting every moment for, Morganna, my love," he finally said.

"It is that way every time?"

"What way?" He opened one dark blue eye to ask it.

Morgan flushed. "You know . . . the power, the feeling, the . . . ."

"Ecstasy?" he asked.

"Aye. That. Is it?"

"I dinna' hurt you overmuch, then?" he asked.

"You hurt me plenty," she replied.

" 'Twas necessary to breach your maiden wall. 'Twill not happen again."

"With what you possess, Zander FitzHugh, you will hurt me each and every time. I know. I've been around boys all my life."

He laughed again. "Aye, you've been around boys, my love, na' men. I'm not so strange. I promise."

"I will ha' to take your word for it, Zander FitzHugh. That, I will, for I am na' about to check."

"And I will never allow it. You are mine, Morganna, lass. Mine. I will never give you up, either. Never."

She was snuggling atop him, matching every limb's length to his, and fitting her nose into the space below his ear. She almost believed him. "You thinking to sleep?" he asked.

"I . . . was," she answered.

"Not yet, you don't, Morganna lass. We've got more food to eat, and games to play. Up. I fancy another grape."

Chapter 22

Sunlight dappled the crimson fabric she opened one eye to. It was so disconcerting that she opened the other eye. Morgan blinked, and the view didn't change. It still looked suspiciously like morning light coming in through the open window and spreading in a multi-hued prism of rainbow colors against a cut-work embroidered linen. She ran a hand along the meticulously small stitches and wondered what poor creature had the chore of having to put them all in.

The side she was lying on was a bit numb, and she stretched a leg tentatively. She pulled it back quickly as she connected with a much larger, more hairy, and warm one. Her eyes widened at that. She had meant to bed him, that she couldn't deny, and her face flamed as she considered it. She had meant to correct the wrong, banish the demons he'd created in his head for himself, and then she'd meant to find his brother, Phineas, and finish it. She had never meant to stay and sleep with him!

The intimacy was something she'd never felt, and Morgan slid onto her belly, trying not to disturb the growling, grunting, overly- heated male right beside her. *I didn't know he snored*, she thought, and then smiled. It was probably because he was always up before her, getting her to the same state without much warning.

The sheet felt strange against her ribs, her belly, her breasts. Morgan lowered her cheek to the tightly woven linen threads and let herself feel it. It was very nice, a bit like waking with her sleeve or her tartan beneath her face, rather than sod.

Zander's breathing changed, alerting her, and she lifted her head to face those midnight-blue eyes. The look in them nearly undid everything she was using to hold herself together.

"Good morn, Morganna," he whispered, and moved a hand to her cheek.

Morgan jerked back, watched his hand stop, his look grow guarded, and then he lowered his hand back to the space of linen between them.

" 'Tis not a good morn for you, then?" he asked.

"This . . . should na' have happened," she whispered.

He grinned. "Oh aye, it should have. It was a foregone fact that, although it seems nigh impossible, there is a man who is male enough for you, Morganna. And I have the honor of being him. Better yet, I have finally found the woman to equal me, and I dinna mean just at push-ups."

Her face flamed. She knew he wanted it to.

"I want to assure you, too, Morganna lass, that I will prove insatiable when it comes to you. I have a record of five times to meet. I thought it incredible when you set it, but I accept the challenge. Gladly."

He reached over to nip at her shoulder and she moved away. "Zander—" she began.

"Oh very well, I will try for six. Dinna' let me sleep so long next time."

She regarded him silently until his smile faded. "I canna' allow this to happen again," she said.

"Allow?" He snorted the word, and then repeated it. "Allow? Do you think the good Lord knows nothing, Morganna? He knows more than you think. He knows that we were made for each other, even if you dinna'. He knows I canna' keep my hands from you, even now. He knows I grow hard for you just because I am close to you and smell your scent. He knows how it affects you, too." Zander's voice lowered and he raised those eyebrows suggestively. "God made it that way on purpose. He also knows you find me handsome of face, manly in size, and intriguing to look at. Why else would He have made me thus?" His grin was back, along with a certain cockiness.

Morganna swallowed and tried again. "I mean, I will na' allow it to happen again."

He considered her. "You will na'? Did I perform that poorly for you, lass? You must give me another chance, then. I will convince you of it. I will try harder, last longer. I vow it."

He was reaching for her, and *that* she couldn't allow.

"Zander, will you stop it and listen to me! All you think of is play!"

"Well, that is a good thing, since all you find is seriousness and work and horror. One of us has to know how to play."

She made a sound of frustration, and started speaking. "This will na' happen again, Zander FitzHugh, because I dinna' wish it to happen again! I dinna' want it! Any of it! I dinna' want you!"

If she could take back any, or all, of the words that brought the stunned look to his face, and the hurt to those blue eyes, turning them into liquid pools, she would have. Morgan watched him tremble, before he lay flat on his back and looked at the ceiling.

"God, Morganna, why dinna' you just get the dragon blade and use it to carve on me? It would hurt less."

What looked like a tear slipped from the side of his eye. Morgan swallowed before reaching to touch her lips to it. He pulled from her abruptly, and she caught a breath at what rejection felt like.

"I dinna' mean that," she whispered.

"I canna' face you at this moment, Morganna. Perhaps you could give me that much, and turn away?"

Where was the hard-hearted killing machine she had

become? she asked herself. It certainly wasn't there when she needed it, and his hurt was making the ball of pain in her chest tighten and grow until it felt like it might be too heavy to lift. "All I seem to do is hurt others, Zander. I came to you last night to take away hurt, and now I find I give more. There is something wrong with me. There has been for a long time. You dinna' bear the blame."

He turned his head and looked at her. Everything in her entire body pulsed once at the look in his eyes, leaving her light-headed and shaky. Then, she was warm, all-over warm.

"There is nothing in this world that love will not heal, Morganna. Nothing. I want you to know this. I want you to know that it will come to pass, too."

Morgan shut her eyes to make it bearable. "Your sentiments are like those of the minstrel, and they dinna' exist for me. I am a killing machine, Zander, remember? 'Tis all I know. I canna' forget it, because the dead of my clan are at my side with every step I take, and every day that passes without my gaining justice. I am their lone implement for it, too. They canna' get it from their graves, and every moment of time I stray from it, is another I must atone for."

He was still watching her with those midnight-blue eyes of his when she opened hers, and what she saw there made every other thought fly completely out of her body. "I understand you now, Morganna, my love. I canna' say I like your morning-after-love talk, but I understand now. I will allow it this morn. Tomorrow morn, I would like a bit more love talk, and less rejection talk."

She set her lips, "Zander FitzHugh—"

He put a finger on her lips and silenced her more effectively than his entire hand would have. "You canna' allow yourself to open to the love and joy about you until you finish this vow you have made. I accept that. In truth, I would na' want it any other way. So, tell me, how many of the bastards do we need to kill?"

She sucked in air. "How dare you make light of my vow!"

"I am not making light of anything, Morganna. I am deadly serious. I want you for my wife. I will have you at my side, or I will have no one. I will help exorcise your demons, and your vow is now mine. Your clan deserves vengeance. I will help them gain it."

She let the air out slowly, testing how it felt to have someone else know and share. She looked away. "You canna', FitzHugh. 'Tis something I must gain alone. I am not a murderer. I am the arm of justice. I made the vow. I will spill the laird's blood. I will make him pay."

"The laird's?"

"Aye. His alone."

He blew a breath across his brow, lifting stray hairs. "What if he was na' the one at fault?"

"He was," she whispered and met his gaze. Then, a pounding came at the door that made them both jump.

"Zander! Open the door! Zander! Morgan? Come along, you two! Open the door! Zander!"

It was Plato. He wasn't actually yelling, but he was speaking in a very loud fashion. Zander's frown probably matched her own.

"My brother has the subtlety of a dragon. I hope he has a good reason for announcing to all that my door is bolted and we are still abed within."

"Zander! Open the door! Quickly! We have na' much time!"

"Why can't he just spend the time before his wedding in preparation, like everyone else," Zander grumbled before lifting himself over her and striding to the door. Morgan let her eyes roam over every bit of him as he went to the door, lifted the bolt and yanked the door open. Then, she closed her eyes to make the image go away.

"What is it?"

"Thank God." Plato sounded like he was praying. "Now, shut the door. Quickly! Bolt it, too. We have na' much time!"

"Go away, Plato. Your wedding is na' scheduled until evening, and I'm tired."

She heard him yawn at the end of his speech. Morgan opened her eyes on Zander flexing his body in a stretch, while his brother threw his arms in the air. She decided Zander was much more interesting to watch.

"Quick, get your kilt on. Here is hers . . . uh . . . his, too. Get your squire dressed. Now! You have na' much time, and I get tired of repeating it! Zander!"

Plato shoved his brother and Zander scrunched up his face. "That is too much woman to put in a kilt so soon. I'm going to need more time. Come back about midday."

"I see you have cured my brother's blindness, Morgan. You have na' made much dent on his wits. Get up! Get your *feile breacan* on! They have discovered the lie of your romp with Sheila."

"Her romp with whom? Did you bring foodstuffs with you, Plato? I'm starved."

Plato made as exasperated a sound as Morgan had ever heard. She sat up, holding the coverlet about her. The mattress sagged strangely with the weight of her. She put her other hand on it, leaning for support.

"They are calling for your squire, and 'twas only by the grace of God that to Sheila was where they went first. It seems that the lass took Morgan's raiment to her chamber last eve, although she used it to her own ends. I have it on good faith that your squire was seen in Sheila's chambers, and having an excellent time there. Of course, 'tis Sally Bess spreading that tale." He stopped to suck in more breath before continuing. "We're lucky too, that I had the champion kilt and tartan with me. This could have been disastrous. Here, Morgan. Get it on! Quickly! You have to get dressed, and as a lad. Now. Right now. You canna' appear as anything other than what they think you are."

"My squire?" Zander asked.

"Nay. A legend."

Morgan's eyes were wide as she looked over at Zander, and then back at Plato. "Nay," she whispered.

" 'Tis true. Word has spread. The clans are here. They've been arriving all night."

"What clans?" Zander asked, sitting and pulling on his socks.

"What clans?" Plato repeated, rolling his eyes. "All the clans! You should see the sight. 'Twas enough to send the Sassenach packing. Phineas, too. I say good riddance."

"Phineas . . . is gone?" Morgan choked on the question.

"Aye, the English-loving bastard. We're grateful, too. For as much acclaim as you have brought to the FitzHugh name, he has brought naught but embarrassment. He may be our laird by birthright, but he isna' it by choice."

"All of the clans are here? Truly?" Zander asked.

Plato snorted. "Mother should have given me the beauty and you the wits! I've never seen so many. I dinna' know we had so many, that's how it looks. And they are na' here to witness my wedding. Morgan! Get up! Get dressed!"

"I will na' allow my lady to dress with you watching, Plato."

Plato tossed the ceremonial kilt and tartan onto the bed and swiveled around. "Whatever it takes, do it! Do it now! There are clansmen on my heels, and that bolt is not going to hold, and she has to be Squire Morgan a-fore then!"

"Quickly, Morgan. Up. I'll help. The clans are here. I dinna'dare believe it," Zander voice held the reverence. "All I've been trying to accomplish for years, you have done in less than a fortnight. Up, love!"

"Wait until you see it, too! 'Tis quite a sight. Why, when The Bruce saw the extent of Morgan's drawing power, he was out there speaking. He has been all morn. He has been promising the great champion, Squire Morgan, to them. The FitzHugh clan has been sent to do his bidding."

Morgan was shrinking into the midst of the bed, and

felt smaller and smaller. This was nothing like what she wanted.

"I will be at your side, my love. Dinna' doubt it." Zander spoke softly, but she heard it. She met his eyes.

There was a thunderous blow on the door. Their eyes widened for a flicker of time, and then she was flying into her binding, the under-tunic, shirt, and socks. Zander was wrapping the *feile breacan* about her, tossing it over her shoulder, and slapping the belt on her hips. He handed her the dragon blade last.

"I forgot to don the loin-wrap," she whispered.

His eyebrows went up and down several times. "And here I thought you dinna' wish my interest today."

"Will you two cease that and get ready?"

"He is ready, Plato. Can you braid hair?"

Plato swiveled back around, his eyes showing the amazement. "She must be part lad. No female dresses so quickly. And nay, I have na' experience with a braid. My regrets, lad."

"I dinna need help. I have done it myself for years. Where are my dirks? My brooch?"

Plato put the bag on the table, and the clink told her it contained all she needed. Morgan slid the dragon blade into the front of her belt, against her stomach, and then started putting dirks in her socks and the back of her belt, slipped her silver wrists bands on, and pinned her brooch.

There came another blow to the door, and Plato stood behind it. "To spare Argylle the chore of replacing another bolt at your door, I will spring this. Are you prepared?"

Morgan's wide eyes met Zander's again. She was threading hair through her fingers as quickly as she could and Zander was just finishing the hooking of his dragon brooch. Time stood still, and then he smiled.

***

Plato opened the door.

Zander had to carry her. There were too many about the hall, and too many wishing to touch her. When they reached the battlements, Morgan would have fallen if Zander hadn't hoisted her on his shoulder, turning her to face what appeared to be a virtual sea of men in tartans, all yelling, all calling, all cheering.

She was shaking before they reached the fields.

What followed was the strangest day in Morgan's life. She met up with King Robert at the portcullis above the drawbridge. Then, she and Zander were given horses and she was trotted out. The Bruce told her that these weren't all the clans, after all. These were the lowland ones, the ones that were the hardest for him to sway.

Morgan listened and tried to make sense of it. The Highlanders were far North, well away from English influence and used to any hardship. Anything forced upon them by the Sassenach was tossed off until the punishment, and it was usually harsher, too. They lived to fight, and if it weren't a rival clan, it was the English. King Robert preferred that it be the English. Zander fit that mold, she decided.

The lowlanders were harder for Robert to convince. They were like Argylle. They shared the border with England, had wed into English families, used English ways, and since they were closer to English punishments, their obedience was usually swifter. The man who had been crowned king of a country that wasn't even independent, needed the lowlanders if he was to succeed. He needed what was happening, and that meant he needed Morgan.

Zander beamed at her side all through this impassioned speech, and then they reached the first clan. Morgan sat her horse, watched all the faces and shook with fear. Then, some loud-mouthed braggart lifted a walking stick in the air, and challenged her to show why anyone would walk leagues to see a pretty-faced, thin lad in FitzHugh plaid. Before anyone could turn to watch, Morgan had twelve dirks in a row in his stick, and the dragon blade ready for a final toss.

In the shocked quiet immediately following her tosses, Robert the Bruce started speaking. He stood up in his stirrups and addressed all within hearing. He had the same type of great oratorial voice that Zander possessed. It made shivers flow over Morgan's shoulders and down both arms, and that happened no matter how many times she heard the speech he gave.

Morgan and Zander were accompanied by FitzHugh clansmen, and they had the chore of retrieving her dirks and getting them back to her. It became an all-day chore, for each time the King raised his hand to address a clan, she was given the nod to show off first.

It became a competition to see which of the clans could make her miss. Morgan's lips twitched as she watched the young lads take off running the moment she'd finished and The Bruce launched into his speech. The lads were spreading the word, and the targets became smaller and smaller and farther and farther away. One fellow even held up a tankard, open-end facing her, and challenged her to put her dirks in it.

The amusing part was they wouldn't stay, and as each clanged in, it immediately dropped back out, making a warble like a songbird's. The King had to wait for the cheering to die out that time, before he could launch into his speech. Morgan wasn't really listening, though. She was looking into all the eyes that gazed up at her, and her shivers weren't from any speech; they were from some intangible quality of the crowd.

Zander was at her side all day. He was the one handing her the dirks each time. Later, it was a crust of bread, a joint of roast beef from one clan, a dram of whiskey from another. Morgan had never felt so alive. It was better than any bit of skill she'd ever shown, better than bringing down any kill, better than anything she'd known, except loving Zander.

The King was tireless, speaking until he was hoarse, and then continuing in a glorified whisper which Zander orated for him. They reached the castle again. Morgan hadn't realized they'd gone in a complete circle, covering as much acreage as the clans were occupying. There were torches and tents set out as far as the eye could see. The sun was setting, and, as The Bruce announced once they arrived, there was a wedding to witness.

Morgan didn't know if her legs would be able to hold her, but Zander didn't let her drop that far anyway. He eased her from the horse, hoisting her to his shoulder and bearing her to the doors of the chapel before letting her down to the side of him.

"You have done what I have been attempting for years, Morganna," he said. "You have gathered the clans and given our sovereign time to speak with them, and actually made them listen. For the first time in my life, I think Scotland has a chance. If it would na' ruin everything, I would take you in my arms right now, and give you every bit of love I have for you. We might not survive it."

Morgan's eyes were wide from those words, and she'd heard wonderful speeches all day. It was a good thing Zander wasn't using his great orator's voice at the moment, she decided.

The doors of the chapel were opened, and they went from the loud, boisterous noise of the crowd to sanctified, candle-lit reverence in the blink of an eye. Morgan held her breath at the beauty of Argylle's chapel: the stained glass in the windows, the arched beams in the ceiling, the carved wood of the pews, and the swell of music coming from a choir of young boys alongside the altar.

Zander was being directed to the spot of honor at his brother's right side, and Morgan watched him go with the greatest sense of loss in the world. The Bruce had her with him, surrounded by nobles and attendants and humanity, but Morgan felt alone for the first time since she'd awakened. It shocked her, too. She was used to being alone. She was used to having no one, save herself, to rely on, no one to care about, and nobody who cared about her.

She didn't think she liked knowing the lost and lonesome feeling.

Her legs were a little wobbly, too. She stiffened her knees and made herself back to the wall, with the other squires, when the Lady Gwynneth came in. That's when Morgan knew for a certainty, that she had done the right thing, at least by Plato and his bride-to-be. Lady Gwynneth was wearing a bead-encrusted dress, more resembling jeweled water than material, and the train that stretched behind her went the entire length of the chapel.

It seemed everyone was holding their breath, and when the bride's face was uncovered by the shaking hands of her groom, there was an audible sigh at how lovely she was. Morgan knew the difference immediately. Gwynneth was no longer unhappy. She was aglow with joy.

Morgan met Zander's eye and had to look away. She couldn't hold his gaze. She could barely stand to be around such happiness and love and peace permeating the air. It wasn't for her. It never would be. She'd been spawned into hate and death when she was too young to change it, and despite Zander's assurances that love would heal her, she knew the truth. Nothing could change it now. She brought a hand to her breast to touch the KilCreggar square, and for some reason, thought she received the peace she needed.

She still had her face averted when the couple was pronounced wed and led, with wild cheering and ceremony, from the chapel. Morgan had only a moment's hesitation to wonder where Zander was before he was at her side, his hand touching hers as he bent to her ear.

"Plato wishes me to tell you of his thanks. He wants you to have this."

Morgan looked down at the ring Zander pressed into her palm. She had seen it on Plato's hand more than once, and the dark sapphire in its center was an uncomfortable reminder of the shade of a certain FitzHugh's eyes. She curled her palm around it and felt it burn. Not as badly as the instant tears, but badly enough.

She had to blink them away. Now, she truly was being paid.

"I will tell him it brought you to tears, should he ask. Stay close, Morganna lass. We've a celebration to start. I've a plan."

"A plan for what?" she whispered.

His lips pursed. " 'For what?' she asks," he said. "To get you in my bed and at my side. What else?"

"Zander, I—"

She stopped her words as the emotion choked her off. It didn't help that the world stopped making noise, the wedding witnesses all ceased to exist, and dark blue, sapphire-toned eyes grew until she saw nothing else. Morgan gulped.

"I love you, Morganna," he whispered. "Never doubt it. 'Tis all I think of, and all I know. I want all of this for you." He stopped and looked about them, then he returned his gaze to her. She hadn't moved her eyes. "I want you at my side always. I want you as my wife, and I want to be your husband. As God is my witness, it will come to pass, too. You have my promise."

"Zander—"

He put a finger to his lips. "Dinna' argue in a house of the Lord. Wait. I'm being patient, too."

"You are?"

"Aye. I am waiting until we are outside to tell you my plan. That is as patient as I am willing to be."

"Why?" she asked.

"Because I want you in my arms, and I want to be buried in you, and I want to share your breath and your body, and that kilt shows too damned much of your legs, and you wear no loin-wrap, and a slew of other things. What do you mean why?"

Morgan swallowed. "I mean, why do you wait to speak it?"

He frowned. "I dinna' know. Perhaps because what I have planned for you isna' for the ears of the church."

"Oh."

She should have known, she told herself. She was doing exactly what she'd said she wouldn't. She was whoring with a FitzHugh, and receiving payment from his brother. No wonder he didn't wish to speak of it on sanctified ground.

Chapter 23

Zander's plan worked perfectly. Of course, Morgan decided, when she was on the opposite side of his door and doing her best to portray Sally Bess' bulk, it would. The man had a flair for exactly what all the clansmen grouped about everywhere would enjoy, poke each other in the ribs over, and discuss, until her cheeks burned.

Zander had simply said he wanted to see what Sally Bess had to keep young Squire Morgan interested, and everyone had laughed. Morgan, on the other hand, had to loudly proclaim that she was seeking the lass, Sheila's bed. Once there, Sally Bess re-dressed and padded Morgan to the correct width, put a huge cloak over the whole, cautioned Morgan about bending her knees to keep her the proper height, and shoved her out the door.

What she had to listen to, the pinching she had to endure and the fondling of her extra-padded rear, while drunken males tried to steal a kiss and a free fondle, was beyond her experience. She was made her feel every inch the filth of what she'd become.

Then, she was at Zander's door, knocking loudly and swaying her buttocks, and his laughter when he saw her, would have made her toss all her dirks into him, if she still had them.

"Well, well . . . look who's here, lads! 'Tis the wench, Sally Bess. Squire Morgan's Sally Bess. Come in, come in, darling. I've been waiting for you. Lads? I'll not need you tonight." Zander put every bit of that orator's voice into every word, and everyone through every hall could probably hear. "I may not need you tomorrow, either! Come here, my large lovely! Show me what you show young Squire Morgan, and then I'll show you what a real man is!"

Laughter was going through the halls when Morgan shut the door. Then she pulled the dragon blade to slam it into the footstool before she had to vent more anger. Zander looked at it with surprise, then he looked up.

"Dinna' ever do that to me again, FitzHugh!" she cried, tossing off the cloak and spitting the words at him.

"Why Sally Bess, you vixen!" Zander shouted, rising to his feet, and plucking the dragon blade from where it had landed between his legs. "If I dinna' know better, I'd swear you'd never seen the like. Come here, my night-time love. Goodness, Sally Bess! Where did you learn that?"

He put a finger to his lips and listened at the door. She held her breath and heard it, too. Voices. Talking. Chortling.

"My darling, I'd give anything to have this different. To have you at my side, without resorting to such. I love you, Morganna, unto my dying breath." He was whispering in her ear, one hand beneath her chin the other lifting her hair, and Morgan stood mesmerized. "I have searched years for you. I would do anything for you. I will even pretend a passion for a fat, lazy, over-used whore to have you, and listen to insults from my clan over my choice."

"If you could hear what I had to go through, you'd not feel so put-upon. The things I had said to me! The fondling I had to endure!"

Zander's eyes flared and his jaw tightened. "Tell me the man, I'll put a stop to it."

"All of them, Zander. You canna' stop all of them."

Tears sparkled in her eyes, and he kissed the side of one. "Forgive me, my love. I should na' have done this. I should ha' had more restraint. I should not want your body so badly that I will do this to you. Forgive me."

"Why could I not stay as your squire?"

"Because no man bolts the door with his squire inside with him, and I would na' have been able to keep my hands from you, and then a clansman would have seen, and everything The Bruce gained would have been for naught. Come away from the door, darling. I dinna' know how well they hear."

"I should na' be here, Zander."

He sighed, pulling her toward the fire, and undoing her dress as he did so. "Nay, you should na'. You should be at my house, your belly full of a bairn, and your life filled with nothing save how much pleasure I can give you."

She flushed. "I should na' be there, either."

Zander had the dress undone and it fell off as she walked. Then, he started on the first of the four more she had on beneath. That one fell off easily, too, and Zander had his eyebrows rising as he saw the wadded shift that was tied on to make fake breasts to fill the gown. He was trying hard not to smile.

"Oh aye, you should. It will come to pass, too. Scotland's future will be her own, my sons and daughters will be born free, and my life will be complete. Morganna, what is this, now?"

He was looking at the basket that had been tied to her back, to make her waddle sufficiently.

"Dinna' say a word, FitzHugh, or I will take my dragon blade to you and I will na' miss an important part."

"We're going to need that part, though, Morganna. Have na' you been listening to me? I want sons. I want daughters. I want lots of both. I want you to give them to me. You, and only you. I want to start now. Jesu'! How many layers did they strap onto you?"

"We canna' create a life now, Zander."

"Why na'? I'm capable. You're capable. I'm willing. Are you na' willing, too?"

He had too many weapons at his disposal, and none that

didn't pain, clear to the center of her. His breath was a weapon, as he wielded it on her neck, her shoulders, the space between her breasts once he got closer to the chemise she was wearing beneath it all. His touch was another one, as he slid his fingers up her arms, and back down, then along her back as he undid each gown, shoved it to the floor and started anew. His hands were a terrible weapon, too, as he untied the basket, tossed it aside and cradled the real flesh through her final gown, lifting her against him and holding her there.

His eyes were a vicious weapon, too, perhaps his best. Morgan realized it as she looked up, caught that midnight-blue gaze and ceased to think clearly.

"Darling, this Sally Bess act is na' forever. This is only what I can arrange tonight to have you with me, close to me, filled with me. I want to give you a bairn. I would give a year of my life to give you a bairn tonight. I dinna' know why. I only know 'tis important."

"But . . . why?"

"Because I love you. I have never loved another. I will never love another. I loved you when I thought you a lad, I love you now. It grows all about me until I canna' think. I canna' move. I watch how you are with all my countrymen, and I want to worship at your feet. I know I canna' exist unless I know you're at my side, loving me in return. I want to give you my seed. I want to create life with you. I have to. I dinna' bother with the why. I only know that 'tis."

His voice was probably his most vicious weapon, she thought as he continued wielding it, sucking on her ear-lobe as he whispered his continual stream of honeyed words into it.

His kiss was the most fatal weapon of all. Morgan had her arms about his neck when she received it, although he waited until all of Sally Bess's clothing was off her body and kicked aside, leaving her own flimsy chemise. Then, he took her face in his hands, turned her head slightly, and brought her lips upward to his.

Morgan danced about him on her tip-toes, catching all of his groan as he begged her with his lips to open hers. When she did, he only flicked his tongue about before sucking hers into his mouth. Morgan melted, sagging back onto her feet while he released her. Then, he moved a fraction from her and waited for her to open her eyes.

"I love you, Morganna," he whispered.

"Oh, Zander," she replied, and her eyes filled with tears.

"And that is how my lovely Morganna says, 'I love you, too, Zander," he mimicked, before touching his lips to her chin, her neck, to the top of her chemise. Then, he was sucking on her nipples through the weave of her chemise, and pulling away so he could blow on them. That was making her so wild, her cries probably did rival those Sally Bess would have made.

"Are you prepared to see a full grown man, yet?" he teased, when she had lost the ambition necessary to stand up on her own and was lying across the footstool, where he'd placed her.

The way he had posed her had a wantonness to it that she'd never experienced. He'd put her in an arch, her shoulders holding to one side of the furniture piece, while her buttocks had to hold her on the other. And the erotica he'd raised with her breasts was making every breath more tormenting and grasping and needy than the next.

"Zander?" she whispered.

He unhooked his brooch and dropped it on the table, then he flipped the back shawl piece of his tartan to the front, preparing to unwrap it. His hands didn't stop while his eyes devoured her. Morgan's body writhed, with a snake-like motion, and she watched his eyes half-lid while a shudder ran his body.

"Zander?" she whispered again.

The *feile breacan* dropped to the floor. Then, he was

standing at her head, lowering himself to his knees, while his hands moved to her shoulders, cradling her head against his shoulder as he ran both hands over her breasts, her ribcage, the muscles in her abdomen, until he reached the part of her she'd barely discovered existed. Morgan stiffened and then every part of her was crying, starting loud and keening and then ending on a wrenching sob of pleasure. Her head was rocked back onto Zander's shoulder, and she lolled there for a bit, watching the high beams of Argylle's ceiling and thinking of absolutely nothing.

There were no incessant thoughts of clan violence or vengeance, or death. No ghosts, no past . . . she was absolutely free of every part of it, and for the smallest minute of time, she let herself experience joy.

"Morganna?" Zander whispered at her neck.

"I think . . . I might have died," she replied, although it sounded strange with his lips suctioned onto her throat, and teasing the pathway her voice needed.

He chuckled. "Oh no, love. You'll not die. You're going to live. You're going to bring life into the world. You already are. You just dinna' see it."

His fingers were rolling the chemise straps into snakes of ribbon down her arms, and she lifted her hands out of each when he got them down that far. Zander didn't finish it, though, he had his hands cupped over her breasts, using his palms in a rotating fashion until she was screaming at him to either cease it, or finish it.

"But, I'm testing my sensitivity," he replied. "And I do believe my left palm has the most."

She swung a fist up to hit him, but instead wrapped it about his head and forced him to suckle her, and when he did, the footstool became less a hard object and more a slippery slope of warm water, sliding her right off, and into his lap.

Zander lifted his head, his lips seeking for and finding her own, and now it wasn't he that was the aggressor, but she. Morgan sucked the breath from him, and gave her own in return. Her hands found and lifted the hem of her chemise, placing the garment about her middle. Then, she was pushing his shirt and under-tunic up and off his chest, not even waiting for him to get them off the shoulders she pushed them to, before she lowered herself onto him, expecting pain, but receiving only absolute and complete pulses of ecstasy.

The effect on Zander was immediate as his lips escaped hers, and he groaned, curving himself to lay on his back in order to arch more fully into her. Morgan's hands fell to his chest, and she pulled her knees up, that movement making him grunt each time she shoved against him, and she entwined the chest hair about her fingers, before splaying her hands all about the hard flesh beneath.

Zander's heartbeat filled her right palm, equaling her own in stridency, and she rocked upward before coming back down, her eyes wide with the surprise and the anticipation, and a small amount of fear. Then, there was nothing but the pure rivulets of pleasure.

"Oh . . . my! Oh my! Oh . . . *my!*" Morgan's cry was a long, keening sound that hung above her, and she felt the whirlpool that her body was starting to spin into growing, ebbing, spinning, then finally slowing, and every bit of it was accompanied by Zander.

His hands went about her thighs, stroking the muscles there as she rode him, then they were at her hips, making the cadence harden, strengthen. Then, his hands were on her waist, and he was alternately lifting her, bringing her back down, shoving his loins upward every time she descended, and pulling himself away every time she lifted from him.

Moistness grew about them, the feel of mist, a hot steamy mist, and Morgan hung on for dear life as he got faster, harder, stronger and more violent.

"Oh God, Morganna . . . oh love! Oh, God! Oh, Morganna! Oh love! My love! Mine! Oh yea, love! Yea! Oh . . . God!"

Zander's throat was growling the words, filling the gaps in the mist, and she heard each and every one surround her, then she couldn't hear a thing but her own pounding heartbeat and her own scream. Light crashed behind her tightly closed lids and she held onto Zander like a lifeline while shudder after shudder of wonder rolled over her, taking her to a place where nothing but joy and love existed.

Zander was right behind her, and she brought her head down to watch as he grabbed at her waist and held her to him. Morgan filled her eyes with the sight of him, holding her to him, as he bucked beneath her, in a rhythm only he could hear and decipher, his mouth open and sending the lowest, most unearthly groan into existence.

Morgan's eyes were wide as he seemed to pause in time and motion, suspended in place, his every muscle taut, stretched and defined beneath her as his loins pulsed over and over in her. Then, he collapsed, the sheen of sweat filming his body, making it shine as though oiled, and a thing of absolute beauty to see.

Her mouth was open with awe when he opened his eyes, and she had never seen a look so full of love and warmth and surprise.

"Zander?" she whispered.

"Aye?"

"What . . . just happened?"

He chuckled. Her eyes widened at how it felt, and that made him laugh harder. "I'm not a bit certain, myself, love, but I'll tell you one thing."

"What?"

"I canna' move a muscle. There is pudding to every bit of me. I sincerely hope you're satisfied with what you've accomplished."

"Seriously?" she asked.

He grinned, raised his eyebrows and then rolled his eyes before answering. "Aye. Very serious."

"That is interesting."

"You dinna' feel the same?"

She shifted her shoulders. "I dinna' feel weak. I feel warm. Like all my muscles have been given a healing treatment. I dinna' know how to describe it."

"Do you ken how very lucky we are, Morganna?" he whispered.

She shook her head.

"I have had women afore. I will na' lie to you. I thought I knew all there was about love, about this, about my own body. You, Morganna love, have shattered everything I knew and believed. Without a doubt, what we have is the most amazing thing that any of us can hope to ever find. I hope you realize how very hopeless it is for both of us, now."

Her eyes were wide and serious, and she caught her every breath for a fraction of time before letting it out or in. "Hope—less?" she whispered.

"Oh aye. Hopeless. I am completely and totally ruined for any other woman, and you, my love, are the same. There isna' a man you will ever find to replace me."

"I already knew that."

He drilled those dark blue eyes into hers. "Good thing, I would say. Come along, Morganna, and let me up."

"I am na' holding you down."

"Oh yea, you are. You have the weight of a horse and I have the strength of a MacPhee biscuit. At least roll over, so I can crawl from beneath you and over to yonder bed."

"I sleep fine on the floor," she replied.

He huffed out a breath. "Oh very well. If you insist."

He closed his eyes, opened his mouth and within two breaths was snoring. If it wasn't for the slight curve of his lips, Morgan would have thought him sincere. Then, when she jabbed him in the side and got nothing other than a grunt, she found out he was.

Less than two hours later, Zander stroked her awake, his hand running all over her, and stopping every so often when he found a particular ridge he liked, or a like impediment. Morgan tried pushing him away. She tried moving, but the male she was atop only moved more. She tried pouting, but that only gained the feel of fingertips across her lips. So, she opened her eyes.

"You dinna' seem very tired to me," she remarked, when he grinned at her and moved his eyebrows up and down suggestively.

"I canna' create a bairn without your help," he said. "And I did put that assignment to myself. The more times I leave my seed, the more chances I will have. Dinna' look at me that way, 'tis true. I swear! At least, I think 'tis true. I have na' ever tried, so I canna' state for certain, but Ari says—"

Morgan placed a finger on his lips to stop the words, and didn't hear the rest of his mumbled sentence about what Ari said or didn't say. She smiled softly, and looked away. "You canna' create a life with me, Zander. 'Tis not possible."

"I can, and I will! At least, I can and will try. The rest is in your hands . . . or rather, your belly."

"I dinna' have a woman-time, Zander."

He put a finger beneath her chin and turned her to face him. "As much woman as you are, it won't be a problem. Now, are you going to assist me, or no?"

She pursed her mouth and then ran her tongue along the lower lip, drawing his eye, and felt an immediate reaction near her belly. She smiled slightly, but had to look away. "I think, I'll just lie here a little longer, and see what happens," she whispered, and where she put her hand made him go perfectly still.

She looked up at his wide, surprised eyes.

"You can sleep if you like," she whispered.

"I tried sleeping. I even tried sleeping when—" His voice rose a full octave as she molded her hand about him, and then it started up again. "When—when . . . you were sleeping . . . oh, *love!*" He choked on the last word.

"What is so hard about my sleeping?" she asked.

" 'Tis hard to sleep—uh . . . hard . . . uh . . . ."

Morgan giggled, and Zander responded with a groan and further indication that he was not remotely tired.

"Well?" she asked, looking up at him.

"Uh . . . well," he licked his lips. You . . . you purr!"

"I dinna purr. Cats purr."

"Oh yea, you do. Oh, Morganna . . . oh God. Morganna . . . ."

"My purring, Zander?" she prompted.

" 'Tis verra soft, like—like a kitten's purr. It . . . uh . . . it could be snoring. That's it. It's snoring."

"I dinna' snore!" She lifted her hands from him.

"What . . . did I say? What did I . . . do? Jesu' Morganna, why did you stop?"

"You said I snore."

He closed his eyes, trembled a moment, then sucked in on both cheeks and blew out. Then he opened his eyes. Morgan could have swooned, and she didn't even know what that felt like.

"You do snore, my love. You also smile. 'Tis the same smile you had that first morn on that Sally Bess's bed. I very nearly tore the room apart when I saw it."

"I dinna' do anything with her, though."

"I know that, now. Back then, I was a jealous, hulking male, and I dinna' even know why. I only knew if you had that soft smile on your face, and that little purr coming from between your lips, then by God, it was me who owned it. That's what I knew! I dinna' ken why it made me so angry, either. It just did."

"I know why," Morgan whispered.

"You do?"

"Aye. 'Tis because your instincts knew. You were just a little slow, like Plato says." She put her feet on the tops of his to push herself up and connect her mouth to his.

Zander pulled back and glared at her. "You will regret all your teasing now, my fine wench."

"Really?" She giggled. "How?"

Zander growled, rolled to his feet, and hauled her into his arms. She was dough in his arms, and felt it. She wondered if he knew.

"I am going to take you now, Morganna. I am going to show you what it is like. I am going to take my pleasure, and I'm going to make certain you know of it. I'm going to take and take and take."

"What . . . of me?" she panted, her head flopping on his shoulder making the room rotate nicely.

"What of you?" he asked.

Then, he tossed her on his bed, parted her thighs and slammed himself into the part of her most desirous of it. Morgan cried out her delight at his entry, and the sound made a shuddering start deep within her, building with each of his long, slow, savage thrusts, until she could keep it in no longer. Her cries of satiation blended with the beams across the ceiling, until they fell back to her and became panting entreaties.

Then it was repeated, again. Again. The experience nearly driving her insane with anticipation. Through it all Zander kept his thrusting, sometimes with steady, long, slow movements, sometimes frighteningly intense and passionate, then back to slower and milder, bringing her to the brink and holding her, before shoving her over the edge and being there to catch her.

And then he gave her his seed.

Chapter 24

Zander woke her again before daybreak. This time, by blowing gently on her shoulders. Morgan scrunched them and groaned.

"Come along, Morganna. Time to turn back into Sally Bess. Come along, love. These costumes dinna' pass the test of daylight. Come along, love . . . ."

She smacked at him, and his breath came again with a chuckle. Then, he pulled her legs to the bottom of the bed and started putting the bundles of material back on, even to flipping her over and tying her basket-affair back into place.

"Why Sally Bess! You are more woman than I am used to, darling. Why, just let me get my sett straight. Now, stop that!"

He was using his orator's voice, and it was too loud for the space of one room. Morgan opened an eye and glared at him.

"Now, now, night-time love. I will na' let you waste a moment of energy on yon stairs. Why . . . I think I'm up to carrying you. Not that my legs have na' been weakened, you understand."

"What are you doing?" she whispered, as he pulled her to her feet to put the cloak over the entire creation, without having fastened one hook.

"Building my own legend, of course. What other man can heft twenty stone in weight and still run the steps?" He stopped whispering, winked and started yelling again. "Get the door for me, will you, sweet? My hands are occupied with a lot of woman!"

They had an audience the entire way. Zander walked through them at first, and then he did exactly what he'd said he was going to. He ran the stairs, Morgan clinging to his neck the entire time.

"Up, Morgan lad! Time's a-wasting, and we've practicing to do!" Zander booted Sheila's door with a foot that echoed through the hall. "I dinna' know what's gotten into the lad. A little love play, and he thinks to sleep all day."

He bent down and planted a wet kiss on Morgan's cheek through the cloak. Then, he put his head back and hollered her name, with the two-syllable way he had. "Mor! Gan!"

The door opened, and a disheveled Sheila stood there, a FitzHugh tartan wrapped about her nakedness. Zander pushed past her and lowered Morgan onto her feet. The door shut.

"Get dressed quickly. The Bruce has a strict schedule to keep. He wants to be on the march before sunrise."

"The Bruce?"

"Aye. Our king. Scotland's king. He needs you now, Morgan love. Scotland needs you. Hurry." He bent, put a kiss in the vicinity of her nose and started yelling again. "Now lasses! That's no way to treat a lord. Get the lazy squire up and out, or I'll do it—what? I'm not welcome? Well! You dinna' need to push. He's got to the count of ten, then I'm marching him out without his sett on!"

Zander opened the door and backed out, pantomiming being pushed out, and the door slammed in his face.

Morgan was still shaking her head and having a hard time with her smile when Sheila pronounced her ready, her tartan perfect, her silver bands gleaming, all her dirks on her person, and not a hair of her braid out of place. Then, she was marched down to the castle's yard, where legions of people seemed to come out to watch as she tossed knives, shot arrows and flung hand-axes.

Then, everything went still.

The sun was just rising when pipes began to play. Everyone parted to see why, and Morgan's mouth dropped open along with everyone else's. It was the Earl of Argylle, and he wasn't wearing anything frilly or pretentious, or remotely English. He was attired in his red, gold and navy *feile-breacan*, a tam on his shaved head and a claymore at his hip.

"Has no one ever seen a laird attired a-fore?" he yelled when everyone stood about open-mouthed.

"Why, my lord Earl. You look splendid!" Zander's voice was large and loud. The crowd roared approval.

"Earl, no longer, young FitzHugh, but a Duke! My true king and sovereign, Robert the Bruce, has placed a Dukedom upon my shoulders, and I have pledged my clan to freeing Scotland and enjoying my new title. Dinna' stand about with nothing to do! Gather the clan! We march!"

Zander grinned at her. "*Now,* do you see your power?" he whispered to Morgan.

The first campsite wasn't but six leagues from Castle Argylle, and it could still be seen from the right treetop, but the distance felt enormous. The swelling groups about The Bruce numbered in the thousands, and as each clan set up camp, the king seemed to be there to welcome them, Morgan and Zander at his side.

He was tireless—it was exhausting to keep with him—and he was regal. Morgan flew dirks, showed slings, and at one point was given a shaft to show her hand at it. She held the spear for a time, testing the weight, the rigidity, the length, how it flexed, upward and back down, in her hand with any movement. Zander asked her what she was doing. Morgan looked over at him, and smiled. Then, she planted her feet and ripped a hole clean through the center of their target.

Everyone gasped, then cheered. Then, the Bruce started talking, about Scotland's ancestors, her beauty, her strength, her unity, and her freedom.

Zander waited for Morgan to look at him, and she knew it. She slid her gaze to his, and lifted her eyebrows like he always did.

"You are amazing," he whispered.

" 'Tis God's gift, remember?" she replied.

"God has certainly blessed you, I would say, then. I am hopeful our sons are as blessed." At her hard look, he sucked in on his cheeks. "Oh very well, our daughters, too."

Morgan turned her face away to hide her smile. Then, they were up on horseback and traveling to the next clan, telling all of Scotland's glory.

It wasn't until dark was well and officially on the land, that The Bruce called a halt, and within moments had tents erected all about the enclosure. Morgan shied away from even looking at Zander. She was going to share his tent, and it was going to be impossible to resist him. She knew it. He must know it, but it didn't make what they did right or sanctioned by God. It still made her a whore, who just happened to be a talented marksman.

"Come along, Squire Morgan. My tent awaits. You take the floor. Assist me."

He had a candle lit, and was posturing and acting for all interested watchers as he tied their door flap down, spoke ceaselessly about what was happening right in front of their noses, and banged and knocked tankards and dishes about. Then he blew out the candle, and Morgan waited.

She was just to the point of thinking he didn't wish anything of her, when large hands began their caresses. His body fit behind hers while he murmured something about being extra-thankful for kilts, cautioned Morgan about sound traveling with the lightest whisper, and proceeded to show her that a kiss was an excellent way of catching and holding the sound of her cries of ecstasy. And he gave her his seed, again.

The second week of Bruce's tour of the country, they came upon the Mactarvat and Killoren clans, and they weren't worrying over anything about Scotland, or The Bruce or the Sassenach. All they wanted was to do battle with each other. The King's entire mass of warriors, squires and lasses spread out along the crests of the valley the two rival clans were facing off in.

The Bruce rode over to where Morgan sat astride Zander's horse, Morgan. It had been an easy selection, although the horse was huge. The stallion Argylle had gifted to her was too unbroken for her to ride, so Zander had taken it. The one hand-span of difference in size between their mounts made the riders equal in height. It also made them very noticeable.

It had rained all day, but the clouds had broken at midday. The field sparkled with moisture, hatred and blood-lust was in the air, and it seemed that at any moment the clans facing each other below them would charge each other.

"What is the situation?" Their king asked Zander.

"I believe Mactarvat had some whiskey stolen and reacted by stealing a lass. They dinna' know it was the Killoren lass, and they used her. Used her well and soundly. The Mactarvats dinna' like it." Zander explained. " 'Twas the same feud that almost did me in before my squire Morgan came through the mists and saved me. Isna' that right, Squire?"

Morgan lowered her head to hide the smile.

Robert frowned for a moment. "This sounds like an English situation."

Both Zander and Morgan exchanged glances.

"Aye, it does," The Bruce continued. It sounds as though the English are the reason good Scots whiskey has to be stolen, and fine Scots lasses have to be taken in payment. The Sassenach have too many rules against whiskey and the making of it. They also have that right of first consummation which the Killoren lass was snatched up to avoid. The English caused everything."

"I dinna' believe that is what happened," Morgan said quietly.

He grinned. "True enough, but that's what I'm going to convince them happened. A Scotsman fighting another Scotsman is a dead man. I dinna' want dead men. I want warriors, live ones. I need warriors. Live ones. That's why I'm here. Stop their clan skirmish, Squire Morgan."

"Stop them?" she asked, eyes wide. He didn't know what he asked. "How?"

"That's why you're here, Squire Morgan. Why do you ken the good Lord put you with me here, at this moment, with all your expert marksmanship and valor and fame? I'll tell you why. He did it so you could stop these clans from killing each other, so they can live to free Scotland. Now, stop them. You will know how. You always know. I will speak when you have done so."

He rode off and Morgan stared after him, her mouth and throat absolutely dry. "Zander?" she whispered.

"At your side, my love. What will you need?" he asked.

She got down off the horse and looked for a high, stable spot that would be easily seen. There was a boulder wedged out over the field. She nodded toward it. "I'll need arrows. More than a quiver full. I'll need that boulder. Follow me."

She had the quiver in place before she was atop the rock. She had a longbow ready. She had Zander at her side. "What is the emblem on the farthest shield?" she asked.

"Why do you ask it of me? I canna' even see the fellow carrying it!" Zander looked every bit as offended as his words sounded as he stood beside her, squinting.

" 'Tis a bird, I think. A falcon. I may not have enough arrows in my quiver."

"For what?"

"Hush!" It was a far piece away, and she had to concentrate if she wanted this to be surprising enough to interrupt warriors at war. She reached back to get three arrows between her fingers, drew her bow taut and sighted.

A war cry sounded, heralding the charge. Morgan started raining arrows into the clan bearer's shield, outlining the bird, and didn't stop until the bearer threw it to the ground. The entire line stopped and looked. Then, she was letting arrows fly at the others. Since this line was more at an angle, all she could do was plant them into the ground at the bearer's feet, surrounding each with a ring of shafts. Her quiver never emptied. Every time she reached back, there were more.

Both clans stopped and looked up at her. Morgan was standing alone, since Zander was flat-out on the rock beside her. She hadn't even felt him fall. Then, a rainbow broke the clouds, like an omen, lighting from the sky to the field, where the men below her had been planning to die.

"Morgan, drop!"

"What?"

"Drop! Now! Beside me! Now!"

She did. There was such an immediate, deafening quiet, she could hear her own heartbeat. Then, she could hear the king, his voice loud enough to carry.

"Can you crawl backwards?" Zander whispered.

"I can do whatever you can," she replied.

"With one exception, please," he answered, cupping her buttocks as she reached a leg down to the turf.

"Zander!"

"Quick! Before someone gets bright enough to come check. Follow me!"

"My quiver never emptied, Zander. How is such a thing possible?"

"Because I was putting them in as fast as you took them

out, that's why. 'Tis a good thing you have me about every time you wish to show off, isn't it?"

"Zander—"

"No time. Now, move!"

"What about our mounts?"

"You dinna' know how to disappear very well, do you, Squire Morgan? I let them off. They're at camp by now. Now, run! Now!"

He had her hand in his and they were leaping dead-fall, downed trees and rocks, and she held to him the entire way. Her heartbeat was louder, stronger and more rapid than ever, and her lungs felt like they'd run for hours before he slowed, then stopped, bending forward to gasp for breath. Morgan did the same, dropping her hands onto her thighs for support.

Then the gap in the clouds sealed over, and heavy drops pelted them, before becoming a full deluge. Moments later, Morgan's sleeves were soaked through, her kilt was getting heavy with moisture and her hair was helping the rivulets find her eyes.

Zander threw back his head and roared with laughter. "God, I love Scotland!" he shouted, opening his mouth to catch as much rain as he could.

Then, he was hauling her into his arms and holding her against him, and showing her that his heart was just as loud and fast and hard as hers. The rain was stealing what breath Zander let her have as he took her mouth, sealing them together, and Morgan jumped up, opened her legs to straddle his hips, and linked her ankles together at his back.

She felt him move; it would have been impossible not to, in that position, and then they were beneath a large pine, sheltered from the force of the rain, and finding out that kilts were wonderful for that position, too. And he gave her his seed, again.

***

Exactly a month after they left Argylle's castle, they turned north. It was what Morgan had been waiting for. She kept it secret from Zander, though. She had to reach FitzHugh land, and she had to finish it. Then, she could see what life was going to hold for her. It wasn't going to be with Zander, though. What man would want her after she'd taken his brother, his blood, his laird?

She already knew the answer, so she never asked the question of herself. She wasn't going to tell Zander any of it, but she was feeling on edge the longer they stayed in the lowlands, meeting with clan after clan, while the Highlands they seemed to ignore. Her role was shrinking, too. That was fine with her. It seemed to have Zander's approval, too. All that was required of her now was that she make an appearance, show off her talents, get everyone's attention, and then disappear, while rumors of her mysticism grew. No one knew what she and Zander really did all those afternoons when they were out of sight.

It was as special and wonderful as the nights were, and night after night Zander plied her with kisses, love talk and his body, always giving, always making certain of it. Zander had his own plan, and getting her with a bairn was it. He wasn't even subtle about it. He made certain there were at least two times a night and once each day that he gave her his seed. He was starting to look peaked and exhausted some mornings, although he was still the most handsome, virile man anywhere, in any clan.

The Bruce had even commented on it, and told Zander he'd better take an afternoon off, and stay away from the wenches. He advised him to stay in his tent, with his squire at his side to serve him. If the king had looked toward Morgan when he'd said that, he'd have suspicioned the squire was sickening, too, since she was flaming red with a flush.

The followers filtered away bit by bit as they went farther north, and that was expected. It was less costly to find food for them, hunt game for them, and their progress was faster.

It also got colder. More than once, Morgan had to lift her own shawl over her head and over her nose while atop Morgan, the horse.

During the nights, however, she was in Zander's arms, and no place was as warm, or as loving, or starting to feel as desperate.

One such night, when they'd been followers of The Bruce for a full season and a month, Morgan lifted her head on her elbow and asked how close they were to FitzHugh land, and then she waited.

"Why?" Zander replied, rolling onto his back with a grumble of sound she could hear through the chest she was lying atop.

" 'Tis said it's a spacious, beautiful place, with not one, but four lochs. Is that true?"

"Aye. FitzHughs have been atop it for centuries, too. We claim ancestry back to the Norsemen, too."

"Vikings?" Morgan asked, eyes wide.

"Aye. How else do you explain the blue eyes we all have, and Caesar has a full head of the sunniest yellow hair you ever saw."

"Caesar? You have a brother named Caesar?"

"Aye. I'm terribly tired, Morgan. I canna' stay up very late tonight."

"I know. You did very well. I am completely satisfied and very much content with your loving. I won't be requiring your services again before dawn, and you need your rest."

He groaned. "You are insatiable, Morganna."

She giggled. "You just want to make certain to get me with a bairn, although I already told you 'tis not possible. Nor would it be a good idea."

"I just want you to get you with a bairn? What sprite stole your wits? I find you extremely tempting, Morganna, my love. I nearly went crazed over it, remember? I canna' deny I dinna' wish a bairn with you. 'Tis no secret, now is it? But, you are a very desirable woman, too, and I am no *auld* man. I canna' ride my horse without thinking of your supple thighs. I canna' take a step without recollection of your thirsty body devouring mine, and I canna' sleep without making certain you know how loved you are. I must have failed this eve, however."

"You never fail at . . . that, Zander."

"I must have. You're still talking."

She giggled. "So tell me then, and I'll let you sleep. What is your other brother's name?"

"Ari," he replied.

"Is that short for something?"

"Probably was meant to be," he answered, "but that's the entire name." He yawned. "Ari. Second born. Phineas was first, Ari second."

"Who's the other one?"

He started his deep, grunting breathing that was the beginning of snoring. Morgan jabbed him in the ribs. "Zander!"

"What now?"

"Who is the other brother?"

"Oh. Third born is Caesar. I just told you of him."

"And . . . ?"

"There's Plato. Second-youngest. Two years of age on myself. You know. You spent some time in his arms atop his horse, now that I recollect. I am rapidly awakening, Morganna, if that is your game."

"You're not about to be jealous, are you?"

"If you were apart from me, and in another's arms, then aye, I'm damned jealous, among other things. Plato had better watch his back."

Morgan giggled. "I am not interested in Plato, Zander."

He stilled. "It is a very lucky thing for my brother, I would say."

"You are very good at changing the subject, Zander. Very."

"I seek to answer her questions, so she'll leave me to

sleep, and she calls it other than what it is. Changing the subject? What subject are we on?"

"Your brothers."

"Oh. Them. Trust me, Morganna, when I tell you you've latched on to the finest FitzHugh, and losing another moment of sleep over the rest of them is a waste of good sleep."

"Zander FitzHugh!" she whispered, giving it the emphasis it deserved.

"What now?"

"You haven't told me the middle one's name."

"Oh. Cae . . . sar," he said, splitting the name with a yawn.

She poked his rib, receiving a grunt for her trouble. "Morganna, 'tis a lucky thing you are the squire, and I the lord. With the schedule you place on me, I'd not survive your service."

"Zander . . . I'm warning you," she said in a playful rumble of voice.

"Oh very well. I would love to die in your service. What is it you asked of me, again?"

"I already know about Plato, and Ari, and now I know about Caesar. I already met up with the eldest, your laird, Phineas . . . so who is the sixth FitzHugh?" Her voice caught on Phineas's name, but he seemed not to notice.

"Oh. The one between Plato and Caesar is named William."

Morgan's eyes widened, even in the dark of the tent. "You have a brother named William?"

"Aye," he responded, sleepily. "Morganna, we reach Old Aberdeen burgh tomorrow, early. We'll have a long day. We really need our rest."

"Why do you have a brother named William? 'Tis too normal a name for your family. Zander!" She had to nudge him again.

"What?" he replied. "You are a slave driver, Morganna. Did I leave you wanting? Is that it?"

She giggled again. "Nay, never that. You are every inch a man, Zander FitzHugh. Every inch." She ran a fingernail over a thigh and under his kilt and then she was stroking, loving, enjoying. "Every, glorious, hard—"

"All right, love, all right. That's very nice. What is the question again?"

She huffed the sigh out, with an exaggerated sound. "Why do you have a brother named William?"

"William? Well . . . I think my da was home when he was whelped. He had a say in it. My mum was annoyed, she was. She never ceases to harangue him over it, either. Remind me to tell you of it some day."

Morgan couldn't restrain the laughter that time, and had to choke with it.

Chapter 25

Morgan came to the horrid, sickening realization that Zander's plotting had worked the exact moment that she rode her horse, Morgan, into Old Aberdeen's marketplace, Castlegate. The Bruce had been regaling anyone who would listen about how important the burghs of Old and New Aberdeen were to him. They were a blend of new, such as the trading and fishing village on the Dee, known as New Aberdeen, and of old. The home of the Celtic bishopric of Aberdeen, Old Aberdeen had been there for centuries, as had the historic Cathedral of St. Machar. He had also spoke long-windedly about the construction Aberdeen was experiencing. He pointed out the bridge they were building to span the Don, that was going to be named the Brig o' Balgownie. He talked about the residences that were being built to house single families. He talked of the commerce and trade that was available for this booming city in the Highlands.

He was very proud of the city, and he should be. It had more stone-built buildings, more streets, and more people than any settlement they'd yet gone through. There was also a bustling marketplace, known as Castlegate, and he cautioned them to keep their horses in rows no wider than two abreast, in order to keep from upsetting the order of business. Then, he led what looked like hundreds of men on horseback through the streets, causing just about everyone to stop what they were doing and gape.

Morgan and Zander were the seventh pair behind their sovereign and liege, and had just ridden under a large wooden archway, when her belly literally moved. She put both hands to it and waited. When it did it again, she looked down to herself and saw her hands were shaking.

It couldn't be. While it was true her belly had a slight bulge to it, she'd thought that due to lack of exercise. Except for her daily and nightly lovemaking with Zander, she hadn't gotten in any serious push-ups or lunges or squats in weeks. She had also been eating more than she was used to. All of which had combined to make her gain a bit of depth to her, but not enough to mean anything.

Her belly twinged a third time, and her eyes widened in shock, amazement, and horrendous guilt, in all the same moment.

Dear God, I'm carrying a FitzHugh bastard! she thought. She didn't question it, either. She knew. She couldn't afford anyone else to know, however. Especially the man riding at her side and looking at all the wares spread before them, his eyes alert and watchful, and the strangest quirk to his lips as he did so. Morgan moved her hands back to the horse's mane, amazed she still had the reins in them, and that Morgan, the horse, had continued walking with the reins pulled like they had been.

"Morgan?"

Zander sidled his horse closer to hers, until their ankles brushed with each step of either horse.

She tightened her jaw, looked straight ahead and ignored him.

"I know you can hear me. The Bruce is setting up a show tonight that will be talked of for years."

She turned her head slightly, but she refused to look at him. *You've given me a bairn!* She knew her face would be shouting it. *Worse, you made me take it! You've given one of the last KilCreggars on earth a FitzHugh bastard to carry!*

Her hands were still shaking, and she rested them on the front of her saddle to hide it.

"What is it?" Zander spoke again.

"This show . . . it will not be difficult?"

"Difficult? For me, aye. For you . . . nothing is difficult. It will be like play for you. He's using fire."

She glanced over at him then, but couldn't hold his look. It was too immense, too loving, and too inescapable.

Her hands tightened. "Fire?" she asked, because Zander seemed to be waiting.

"More in the way of flaming arrows, dirks with fire-lit fishing twine, that sort of thing."

"I have no dirks like that."

"I know. He ordered them made."

Morgan forced herself to concentrate. "Why would he do such a thing?"

"Because Scotland isna' just a country. It is a thing of immensity, beauty, contradiction, and pride. The Bruce wants to stir their senses, inflame their pride, and fill them with the possibilities of all a Scotsman can and will be. He wants you to set the stage, so he can say the words."

"What is a Scotswoman, then?" she asked.

He took a couple of loud breaths. She heard them. "All that and more, of course. She is the vessel that holds and delivers the future, with each bairn she carries. Look about you, Morgan. Do you see the future?"

She saw the future all right. It was grim. There was a FitzHugh bastard being birthed to a KilCreggar lass, who was portraying the legendary Squire Morgan. The Bruce would be reviled, mocked and vilified all over the face of the British Isles, not just Scotland. She shifted on her saddle. "Aye," she replied finally. "I see it."

"How about the emotion that is here? Do you feel it? I do, and it's right here in this beautiful city. Like a pulse of Scotland, itself. Hard and fast. Strong and virile. Fresh and pure. Canna' you feel any of that, too?"

The emotion? he asked. What did she feel? Dread. Hate. Sadness. Anger. Fear. Shock. Wonder. *Which of those am I supposed to say I feel, Zander FitzHugh?* she wondered. It wasn't the last-born of the FitzHughs that would deal with the mortifying results of their coupling. Nay, he'd be strutting around like a peacock, with his chest puffed out, and with his pride intact. It was going to be the last-born of the KilCreggars who would have to live with the humiliation and shame, which would grow and become more apparent as the baby did.

God, how she hated being a woman! Especially right at the moment. She didn't want anything to do with this bairn. She had a mission to accomplish, and then she was ready for what life held. Carrying a FitzHugh in her belly while she killed another was not part of her plan. She didn't know if she could handle it. She knew it wasn't right that she had to handle it, and it was Zander FitzHugh's fault, damn and blast him, anyway!

"Are you all right?" Zander asked from right beside her.

"Get away from me, FitzHugh!" she snarled, shifting her horse a good yard's distance from his.

Midnight-blue eyes blazed at her for as long as she could hold the gaze, then she moved ahead. He always could see too much with that intense look of his. She wasn't going to let him see this. She was going to deal with this the way she dealt with everything: by herself. She didn't think she would ever speak to Zander FitzHugh again.

The Bruce's camp was already well under way and nearly set up by the time the procession reached it. They were encamped in the valley connecting the two burghs, and as far as the eye could see there were tents, making a huge circle about an epicenter that held a large conical affair. Morgan sat atop the horse, Morgan, and looked at the small hill they were constructing of logs and sod.

"What is that, Zander?" she asked.

He was grinning when she glanced his way. Probably

because her curiosity had forced her to forget her own vow of silence. There was something else in his look, too, and she was afraid to decipher it. It was too loving and gentle.

"Off-hand, I'd say it's your stage. Since I already helped envision and design it, I'd have to say it definitely is your stage. Come. I have a lot to do today."

He led into the camp, wending his way through tents until they reached his. He didn't ask Morgan to follow, either. He just reached over, plucked the reins from her hands and led them. Morgan didn't mind. She was looking over at the scaffolding they had put together, and noting that it was at least three stories from the ground.

"Dinna' worry yourself, Morgan. That there is Scots pine, good Scots damp to the inside, and heavy Scots peat atop the whole. There's na' stronger wood and na' better materials on the earth. It could hold a dozen men if need be, na' just your slight weight." He paused for the briefest moment before continuing, ". . . combined with mine, of course, as it should be."

Morgan jerked her head to his. "What did you just say?" she asked.

"Only that I'll be there with you. Holding to you. Getting the pitch on your arrows lit, handing them to you. I'll be making certain nothing save the arrow shafts catch fire. I'll be there, Morgan, just as always. Are you certain you've not caught an illness?"

She swallowed the instant moisture he always conjured in her mouth. For a moment when he'd mentioned their combined weights, she'd thought he'd guessed about the bairn. She'd go to her grave before admitting it, and it was his fault that now it would have to happen sooner, rather than later.

She sucked in on all the emotion that thought caused her. She was not afraid of dying. She was more afraid of living. At least, she always had been before.

"You look flushed, Squire Morgan. You have a fever? Chills? Sickness to your belly?"

She opened her eyes and glared at him. "I am never ill."

"True. We're here. Come, Squire Morgan. Get your raiment on for the show. You, there!" He hailed a clansman. "Send Scribe Martin to me! Tell him I need a message sent to my brother, Plato."

"Plato? Why send for him? He stays with his winsome Gwynneth in Argylle," Morgan remarked to herself as she entered their tent. "She has a fiefdom to secure for the Argylle clan, and legitimate bairns to create to do so."

Morgan's voice was very soft and bitter when she ended. She could only hope he hadn't heard. She went cross-legged on the floor and flattened out a dirk that had rolled in her sock and was chaffing at her ankle. Then she looked up.

Zander stood at the door, holding the flap on his head and looking at her with such warmth in those eyes, the hand holding to the dirk trembled. "Plato is na' with his bride. He, and FitzHugh clan, ride two days ahead of the king. He always has been. 'Tis he who marks the camp-sites, and 'tis his responsibility to regale all who will listen about the king and the squire who rides at his side."

"He does?" she asked.

"Aye. I am not the only FitzHugh gifted with this big voice you have noticed. Plato has one just as large. He uses it to tell all who will listen of the arrival of Scotland's future, and to watch for it. Have you never wondered at the crowds awaiting us everywhere we go?"

"I thought word of mouth was bringing them." For some reason, she felt even more deflated by this news, if this could be possible. She was delaying her clan's justice for the glory of a unified Scotland, something that had seemed forced on her by the fates, and *now* she finds out it was being orchestrated?

"Word of mouth? True enough. Plato's mouth. It may be larger than mine. That is a surprise, I think."

"Zander—" she began.

He grinned, dropped the door flap and stepped in. "He also has the chore of making certain there are enough foodstuffs ready and enough game downed to feed everyone before we arrive. We haven't time to do all that. We have to speak to the masses."

She lowered her head and lifted her eyebrows.

"Very well, The Bruce has to speak. We have to get their attention."

She set her jaw next.

"All right, stop giving me that look. 'Tis Squire Morgan who has to get their attention, but his lord, Zander FitzHugh, is at his side. A squire canna' be a squire without a master, you know."

Morgan looked at him for another moment, and it was difficult to ignore the wide smile, and teasing glint to his eye. She looked back down. There was nothing teasing or amusing left in the world. There never had been. *Damn Zander FitzHugh and his notions of play!* she thought.

"But he just wed," Morgan whispered.

"Aye, but he had a day and two nights with his bride to put his love into her, and his seed. Unlike me. I am the luckier one, I think."

"Will you cease speaking of that, and get serious?"

He went cross-legged before her, and waited. Morgan had to look. It was what he was waiting for.

"There is too much death and hate and pain and seriousness to the world, Morgan. And, while it canna' be avoided, and has a place, there needs to be equal time given to the joys of life. I am trying to teach you that. I would like to think I have shown a little of it. I would double my efforts, if I dinna' think it might kill me."

She sucked in the breath. "Zander FitzHugh," she said, in what she hoped was her sternest voice.

He sighed hugely, making that chest rise and fall. "Oh very well, Squire Morgan. You are the most humorless

person I know. I am not an ugly man. I am not a weak man.
I am known throughout the Highlands as a very wealthy
man. Any father would want me for a husband to his
daughter. I have been so told. I could have had any number
of lasses begging for a glimmer of my smile, a flirtatious
glance, the chance to match their body against mine, and
receive me. Why, I could have fallen in love with dozens of
lasses who find play as absorbing as I do . . . but no. I had
to search out and pluck the most deadly serious woman
ever birthed. Very well. What is it you wish to know?"

She looked up into those midnight-blue eyes and couldn't
find one iota of thought in her head. Everything fled. Then
he grinned, and the rush of emotion to the top of her head
was so quick and vicious, she very nearly returned his smile,
despite hating him for what he had done to her. Her eyes
widened, and at that moment, the bairn she already was so
mixed-up about, decided to make his presence known again
by the gentlest twinge.

Morgan caught the breath, thanked the heavens for her
already wide eyes, and prayed the shock didn't show.

"Plato knows he will have Gwynneth for the rest of his
life. 'Tis the gift you gave to them. She canna' travel with
us, though. She had too gentle an upbringing, and is too
weak. She'll be awaiting his return. He knows it."

"Wh—what?" Morgan stammered on the word.

"I think you asked of Plato. I think your question was
one of surprise to find out he was ahead of the king, and
na' at Argylle Castle attending to putting a bairn in his
wife's belly. I think you wished to know the why of it."

Her face burned.

"Plato is a Scotsman, Morgan, and while he likes play
as much as the next man, he has a glorious speaking
voice, too. He uses his talents for the same thing we use
ours for . . . creating a new life."

"Wh—what?" she stammered through the simple word
again, and felt the gut-choking reaction at the same time.

He does know! she thought, with what could only be described as complete panic.

"A new life for Scotland, and all her people. Plato would na' let me have all the glory. Besides, he is repaying a debt."

"He owes the king?"

"Nay. 'Tis not that sort of debt. Oh, here is Scribe Martin, now. Look at him, Morgan, rolled scrolls beneath his arms, quills stuffed behind his ears, and ink-stains on most of his fingers. His services are in such demand, and I freed him two moons past to do so. I am impressed, Scribe Martin, but what is this? Turn about. A braid?"

The boy flushed, pivoted and turned back around. Morgan watched him do it. It was true, too. He hadn't long hair, but what he had was twined into a braid and the end tucked beneath his shirt. Morgan met Zander's eyes and when he nodded she looked away.

"They all wish to look just like my squire. They wish to be my squire. I wonder why. I must be a wonderful master."

Morgan snorted her amusement, along with Martin, who went to a knee beside them. He had a scroll unrolled and draped across his knee, a quill poised atop it, and a serious look on his face. This lad had certainly changed since the sling-shot contest at the fair, Morgan told herself as she watched him.

"You wish a message written, Lord Zander?"

"Get a message to Plato. Tell him it is time. Tell him I wish him in two days hence at the Cathedral of St. Machar, and he is to bring all I specified. You have that?"

"Aye." The boy was concentrating and writing. He stuck his tongue out one side of his mouth as he did so. Morgan watched him do it. It was clear he had the talent for stone-throwing, but he looked to be an excellent scribe, too. She was surprised that Zander had known, and seen it accomplished, and wondered why she should be. He always seemed to know.

"You have wax for the seal?" Zander asked.

Martin nodded, stood and went from the tent. Morgan watched him do it. Wax? she wondered. He was back within moments, a thumb-sized blot of dull yellow at the scroll's edge. Zander reached for the dragon brooch he wore on his tartan, removed it, and pressed it into the wax. Morgan watched it all, including the finished result.

"You think a brooch simply for ornamentation, Squire?" Zander teased.

"I dinna' know that purpose. 'Tis grand. That may be why. 'Tis only the nobles who need such."

He frowned at that and lifted the dragon to look at it. "Hand me the dragon blade," he said.

Scribe Martin made a sound of awe as she pulled it out and handed it to Zander. She'd forgotten how impressive the blade was. Zander held it to the light, looked at his brooch and then looked at the blade again. Then, he looked at Martin.

"Can you design another crest, Scribe Martin?"

"Design?" the lad choked.

"Aye," Zander continued. "Not one dragon, but two. Intertwined, like the hilt of this knife. You see how the tails spin together, making a whole? You see?"

The lad nodded.

"Can you transfer that to your paper? Can you design a seal?"

"But you already have a seal, Zander," Morgan pointed out.

He looked across the blade at her, and Morgan's back went ramrod stiff with how it felt. She knew then exactly what he'd been speaking of in Aberdeen earlier. It was hard and fast. It was strong and virile. It was fresh and pure. Her ears roared with it on every heartbeat. He held out her dragon blade. She took it.

"True enough," he replied, and looked back at Martin. "Well? I would like to see the result on the morrow. Now go. You have a design to envision and bring to life. I have a stage to see to, and check. My squire has the task of resting. He needs his rest. His aim must be true and accurate and faultless this eve. For that, he will need some rest. You can do this, Squire Morgan, or will you require me to stay and make certain of it?"

She narrowed her eyes at him. "I dinna' need rest. I am as capable as always."

He grinned, and leveraged himself back to his feet. "Come, Scribe Martin. What the squire is saying is he canna' sleep if we sit on his bed area on the floor. Isna' that what you speak of, Morgan lad?"

"Zander—" she began, using a threatening tone.

"Eagan stands at your tent door, Squire Morgan. He will make certain none disturb you until 'tis time. Seek some sleep. You will need it. This eve's performance will require it. I guarantee it."

He was winking as he left, slapping the door flap back into place, and even though he couldn't see it, she put the dragon blade into the pole in front of him, anyway.

Chapter 26

Morgan stood on the top cross-piece of an entire lattice-work frame and waited. She had been dressed in a different *feile-breacan* this time. The wool strands had been spun thicker, and brushed to a softness she'd never felt the like of, before being woven into the FitzHugh sett. They had woven strands of purest silver through it, too, giving off slashes of light whenever she moved. It was warmer, too. Almost warm enough to stop her shaking.

She had an under-tunic of the softest flax next to her skin, and a shirt that was a masterpiece of embroidery, with silvered threads plied through her short, wide sleeves and over her shoulders, where they turned into two dragons at her back. She had her silver bands at her wrists, her silver belt about her hips, and silver ribbon woven through her braid. The richness of her attire had amazed her when she first dressed, and it still did.

She had her long bow at her side, and they had hammered silver into it, too. She was a FitzHugh squire, and the FitzHughs were very proud of that fact. Every inch of her body was covered to show it, even down to the new, thick leather boots on her feet, and the dark blue socks on her legs. She had very nearly cried when she'd donned it earlier with Zander's help and for once, he wasn't playing, but reverently placing each article of clothing on her body, his eyes never leaving hers.

It was fitting, she supposed. She was the whore of a FitzHugh lord, she was carrying a FitzHugh bastard, and she was bringing glory to the FitzHugh clan beyond what they'd known. She might as well be dressed head-to-toe in FitzHugh color and wealth.

For a KilCreggar intent on vengeance, she was an abject failure, however.

There was a row of thirty-nine dirks placed along the edge of her peat-enclosed cone. They had braided twine attached to each hilt at one end, and at the other, to the top of her stage. The twine hung down to make loops. Each length of twine had been soaked in pitch until it was almost black and made the enclosure reek with it. She still wondered at Zander's optimism with this bit of his plan working.

They had placed a FitzHugh clansman in each of forty trees, too, holding a target, with a bucket of moss at his side. The targets were difficult to see, even for those who knew where they were. Zander had pointed them out. He had also shown her the bit of silver that had been melted, poured, and then flattened into the center of each target, to give her a clear view when the clansman moved it, flickering it for her.

All that was left was lighting the bonfires on all four sides of her stage. There was a raised platform, too. In the largest clearing, directly facing Old Aberdeen burgh, and with a clear view from the mountains, was the stage that The Bruce was going to be waiting on. It was the one she had to hit, with each and every one of her dirks.

"Ready, lads?"

Eagan had too loud a whisper for this type of production, but Zander needed someone to hold a torch high enough he could reach, dip each arrow, and then get it up to her. Morgan looked down at where Zander straddled two cross-beams, taking the brunt of his acrobatic position with his knees. She couldn't believe the chore he'd placed on himself. He was going to swing down, grab up an arrow, then swing back up, to hand it to her. He then had to swing back down, get another arrow, then return. All of forty times.

Then, he had to get the torch up to light the twine. It was as amazing as it was impossible. She smiled. And she'd thought he needed a lesson on balance, she reminded herself.

She looked out. They were lighting the bonfires. All she had to do was await the bagpipers. If she looked, she could still see the acres of people, filling every space of the clearing and every slope of the hills beyond.

Pipes started.

"Now, Eagan!"

The plan went flawlessly. Morgan stepped onto the top of the platform, highlighted easily by the bonfires, and a hush fell as they saw her. Then, there was an arrow in her hand. She planted herself, took aim on the flash in the tree, and sent a flame arcing toward it. The moment she heard it hit wood, there was another arrow in her hand. She took aim, and had the next target. Another arrow, another target. Cheers were starting up by the fourth, and deafening by the tenth, but she didn't hear anything except her own heartbeat.

When the circle about the enclosure was ringed with fire atop the trees, she started planting the dirks. Zander wanted the fire to reach the stage before the treed FitzHughs were to put each target out with their supply of wet moss.

Morgan lifted the blade that was the farthest to the left, and put it at The Bruce's left heel. Then, she methodically put all the others in a ring behind him. Zander was beside her then, on his knees to keep from being seen, in all his huffing, puffing and sweating solidness. He was touching the torch to the pitched parts of the twine, before he was gone again, disappearing to get the torch back to Eagan and out of the cone before anyone saw it.

Morgan watched the fire race down the lines she'd placed, perfectly lighting King Robert, and gaining such momentous applause, the ground seemed to shake with it.

"Time to go, Morgan. Come."

His hand was slick, so she held to his wrist, and he to hers, getting her down the scaffold without incident, and then they were out. Morgan didn't realize the extent of the unearthly realm she'd been a participant of, until he had her in the trees behind the tents, and she sucked in clear, frost-filled air that hadn't a tint of smoke to it.

"Good God, that was glorious!" Zander lifted her and swung her in a complete circle, his voice loud. She didn't stop him, because the noise had yet to die down behind them from the clearing in the midst of the tents.

"Come love, we mustn't tarry. Your evening is just beginning! Hold my hand."

They weren't exactly running, but she had a stitch to her side, before he had her in the midst of some very strangely arranged stones. Zander dropped her hand then, and waited. Morgan looked about. There was mist sneaking through a small circle of pillars that were not carved, but not natural, either. She looked about, watched the moonlight glance off the mist, imbuing it with a translucent quality, and then she looked at him.

"What is this place?" she asked.

"The ancients built it. It is a place of worship. I thought it fitting."

"For what?" she asked again.

He took a step toward her, disturbing the mist with the movement. "For worship," he answered softly.

"We shouldn't be here, I think," she said, moving a step backward as he approached, to keep an arm's span of distance between them.

"Oh yea, we should. I brought you here for a reason, Morganna, and that reason still exists."

"Zander—" she began, only to be interrupted.

"You always prevent me from trying to sway you with words. Why is that, do you ken?"

He took another step. She backed one.

"I dinna' know what you mean," she answered.

"You allow my body to worship yours, but you dinna' allow my heart to. I would like the answer to why."

Another step. A corresponding one backwards.

"You speak ceaseless words of love to me, Zander FitzHugh. I have listened to them nonstop, I think."

"I have spoken them, true. You have na' listened, though."

"I have! I had no choice."

He took another step. She backed into a pillar and her eyes widened with the contact.

"Then, why do you fear me? Why do you back from me now? You know I will na' do anything to harm you."

"Being this close to you harms me, FitzHugh."

He took the step that placed him directly in front of her, and there was no other place she could go.

"The Bruce will na' need us during the winter months. The snows will come. The crowds will na' risk the cold and damp to hear, and he will na' risk it to talk. The winter will be all ours, Morganna. There will be na' unification of the clans, no presentations to make, no showing off, no more tents. You know this to be true. The winter is all ours, Morganna. Yours and mine."

"I dinna' know anything of the sort!"

He reached for her, but she slid around the side of the pillar, out of his reach again. He was right behind her, but an arm's length away again.

"I dinna' know why you fight it so. You know I was made for you. You know you were designed with me in mind. You know it."

Morgan shivered, whether at the chill behind the mist, or at his words. She didn't want to have to find the reason why.

". . . and yet you fight it," he finished.

"I made a vow, FitzHugh. I dinna' take my vows lightly."

"Nor I, mine," he answered, taking a step closer to her.

Morgan backed one again. "Your vows are too lightly given, though. You vowed a change. You vowed to give me a bairn. You vowed to take me to wife, and none other. You vowed your ever-lasting love, and that you would make me find the same for you. You have vowed to change the world. You have vowed that love will change everything. You have vowed to help me end the horror of my dreams. You have vowed one thing or another every day since I came to you of my own free will. Which vow is it you take seriously, FitzHugh? Which?"

He took another step, and she backed into another pillar, startling herself. She'd thought them outside the circular enclosure. He closed the distance, put a hand on either side of her torso, leaned into her and put his nose against hers. "All of them," he answered.

The bairn she was carrying did the answering, as it twinged as strongly as anything her heart could have. She caught her breath at it, and then the solid, soft warmth of Zander's lips were touching hers. Not to demand, not to take, not to seduce, but to worship, just as he'd said.

Morgan sighed, lifting her hands to the chest in front of her, whether to push it away or hold to it, she didn't know.

"Undo my dragon brooch," he whispered against the flesh of her lower lip. "Unpin it, Morganna. Now. Unfasten my brooch. Now. Do it, now."

Her hands were already busy with the catch, and she didn't even notice the minute stick of the pin when she had it gripped in her palm.

"Now drop it. Lower your hand and drop it."

His voice was seductive and low, and brushed against her cheek as he slid his lips toward her ear. She opened her palm and then felt, rather than heard, the brooch land on the ground beside her foot.

"Now my blades. Pull each dirk and drop it blade-down. Then, unfasten my belt. Slowly. Start now, Morganna . . . now."

He had the lobe of her ear in his lips and was darting his tongue all around it, and she curved her neck to allow it. Her mouth was open to pant for air, while what he was doing was making her hands uncooperative with the shivers. She felt his hands undo her silver brooch to drop it, pulling the dragon blade, before letting it fall, blade down.

"My belt, Morganna. Unfasten my belt. Nay! Dinna' look." This because she moved her head a bit as though she would look. ". . . but by feel. Feel the metal clasp. Undo it. Now, Morganna . . . now."

He was doing the same thing with his hands, exactly as he spoke, and he wasn't looking anywhere. He couldn't be. He had his lips sliding down the side of her throat, sucking gently on the skin the entire way, until he got to the juncture of her shoulder, and then he lapped at the skin, the movement pushing her embroidered shirt aside.

"Unwind my *feile-breacan*. Start at the back. Pull the gathers out, feel them give, fall, release. Do it, Morganna . . . now."

His hands were as hypnotic as his voice, and she could feel her own kilt unwinding, caressing the backs of her legs before falling somewhere at her feet.

"Now the blouse. Unfasten my placket. Where I have buttons, yours is laced with silvered ribbon. Very different. Very much the same. Feel my buttons, Morganna. Hard. Slick. Smooth. Slide them from the holes. Do it, Morganna. Do it, now."

Her fingers didn't feel like their own, and seemed clumsy. He didn't have that problem, however, and he had the ribbon out, and was tying his hair back with it before she had his final button out.

She shivered.

" 'Tis chilly, FitzHugh," she whispered.

"Oh no, 'tisn't. You're with me, it canna' be cold. 'Tis very warm . . . heated . . . hot." He opened his mouth wide and exhaled heated breath about her throat. Then he did it again, moving his mouth to the back of her neck, caressing her shoulders with his breath. Then he was at the base of her throat, breathing warmth all over the exposed skin and warming her clear to her heart. "'Tis that way because I am here, Morganna. We are here. We are together. We are one. Forever. I vow that, too."

She made a short cry of denial, but he hushed it with insistent lips on her throat where the sound needed movement in order to be made.

"Now, dinna' move, Morganna, my love. Close your eyes and dinna' move."

She closed her eyes as he'd said, and leaned against the cold stone at her back. There was a whisper of cloth, a sound of movement and then his breath beside her ear again.

"Open them slowly now, Morganna, love. Slowly. Let the moonlight do all the talking. Slowly now. Slowly."

He had his head lowered a fraction, shadowing those blue eyes into black and sending the same shadows to his lips. Morgan sent her eyes over him, where shadows were carving out the cleft in his chin, molding to the mounds of his chest, the thick sinews of his arms and shoulders . . . his hips.

Morganna slit her eyes and looked, and kept looking. Zander was a creature of moonlight and mist, highlighted by one, caressed by the other. She'd known he was handsome. She just didn't know how handsome. He was absolutely beautiful. Her lips opened a bit to pant. Zander didn't have to say a word.

"I was created for you, Morganna. You, and only you. Go ahead, look. 'Tis everything I am, and all that I am, and 'tis all yours . . . now and forever . . . yours."

The cry she gave came from the depths of her soul, and had a wounded sound that couldn't be denied. She knew Zander would hear it, but couldn't stop it. He didn't reply, though. He simply stepped closer, almost touching, but not quite, and he started breathing heated warmth all over her neck, to her nipples, to the depths of her.

"Zander?" she whispered. "'Tis too strange. I dinna' ken—"

He put a finger to her lips and it easily silenced her,

since her knees jerked forward the instant his flesh touched her. Then, he was on his knees before her, lifting the embroidered hem of her shirt and bringing it to his lips.

Morgan had to close her eyes to stop the tears. It took three deep breaths before she had them sufficiently captured. When she opened them again, he was standing, moving the blouse with him, until he had it over her head. She didn't realize that he'd taken the under-tunic, too, until cool night air touched bare flesh everywhere on her. Morgan immediately moved to cover herself, one arm across her bound bosom, the other about her loins, with the most feminine gesture she'd ever used. Zander didn't stop her, but he was beside her again, breathing heat onto her and waiting.

"Oh lovely Morganna. Beautiful, womanly Morganna. Reach out, Morganna love. Touch me. Put your hands on me. Reach out and touch all that I am. Touch me, Morganna. Put your hands on me and touch all of me that you can reach. Touch my belly, my chest, my arms, and mold your fingers to them. Do it now, Morganna . . . now."

His voice was more mesmerizing than before, and then he added to it by holding his mouth close enough to hers that she could actually sense it by the space between their lips. She closed her eyes, shuddered, and then did what he said to do, moving her hands from covering herself, to covering him.

"I am the largest in my family, Morganna," he told her mouth, his breath hotter than ever. She felt her response clear to her toes. "I am the strongest. I am the most handsome. I am the most sought after by women. I dinna' say these things lightly, or as a braggart. I say them because they are all true."

Her hands were smoothing over all the bulges, pits and hard knots of his abdomen, then along the center of him to his chest mounds, then her fingers slid over his shoulders, and down his arms, filling her palms with the sinews and cording of his arms.

"And I say them because I now know why. I was made

this way, so that I could be man enough to deserve to be your mate."

Fresh tears filled her eyes and she had to take breath after breath, and that didn't do much good. Morganna felt the moisture slide from her eyes and down her cheeks, and there wasn't a thing she could do about it.

"You feel all that is unique about me, Morganna? All that is sinew and muscle, flesh and blood, heat and passion, love and pain, sorrow and joy? You feel the life that is within me?

She nodded.

"That is what I feel like to you, and that is what you feel like to me. I touch you and I feel the sameness, Morganna. The warrior heart that beats within you, is the mate to mine. I stand before you not as your lover, Morganna. Not even as a Scotsman. I stand before you, as your God-given mate."

She opened her eyes.

Zander moved back, although he couldn't have seen her reaction. He had his eyes closed, too. His hands moved to her binding, untied it and let it fall where it may. Then, he was attending to the unbraiding of her hair. He wasn't satisfied until he had the length undone, and moved it to cascade over her shoulders, separating the strands with a rubbing motion of his fingers against his thumbs. Morgan watched him, and didn't move one bit of her being the entire time, because she saw the streaks that were on his face, too.

She trembled with the indrawn breath, then let it out. For a heart that was bent on revenge, she had an amazing capacity to feel love, she decided, lifting her hands to cup his face. Zander stopped all motion at the touch, and then she ran her thumbs over his cheeks, wiping them away.

"Come to me," he whispered, and she stepped forward into his arms.

He hadn't spoken lightly when he spoke of his strength, his size, or of being sought after. She knew the truth as he lay them down on the pile of discarded clothing and they joined, her cries and his groans blending with the night mists. He took her with him to a place of warmth and joy, and no room for anything but love.

Chapter 27

"Morgan?"

"Hush!" Morgan's reply sounded more like a brush of wind than the command it was meant to be, as she drew bead on a buck. It was going to be a shot deserving of her talents, for he was hidden behind his doe, while a fawn hovered in the spotted sunlight behind them, making it nearly impossible to see.

The buck was only visible by his rack above the doe's neck, and whenever he reached his head down to pull at the grasses at their hooves. Her shot was going to graze the bottom of the doe's throat with its motion, brush the hair perhaps with a bit of her arrow's feathered shaft, before it would impale the buck exactly where Morgan wanted it to; its eye.

She pulled the bow taut.

"Are you carrying my bairn?"

Zander said it from his indolent position right below her, startling her so the shot went far wide. So far wide, in fact, that both deer raised their heads for a fraction of time, at the sound, and then resumed grazing, not the least bit alerted.

Morgan closed her eyes, stilled the immediate fear and had it under control before she glared down at the FitzHugh at her feet.

"If you canna' stay quiet, FitzHugh, you will na' eat," she answered finally, reaching for another missile.

He chuckled. "They are far enough away, they canna'

hear a thing. Why, I dinna' even see them at first. Aside from which, I have a sow roasting nicely over my spit and no less than sixteen maidens cooking the rest of a nice sup for the great Squire Morgan, and myself. I see no need for splitting that family asunder, do you?"

"That is no family, Zander. That is an animal. One which, I might add, we rely on for food."

She took another aim, hoping he wouldn't spot the slightest tremble of her bow string, and also that it wouldn't affect her accuracy. She'd never had such trouble, and all because Zander FitzHugh wouldn't let her out of his sight, and hadn't since last night at the worship circle.

"So . . . do you? Carry my bairn, that is?"

His whisper was soft, but still it affected her aim. This time, the arrow quivered to a stop right at the nose of her stag, startling the entire grouping into escape. Morgan slid her eyes down to where Zander reclined, his head on a fallen log, one leg bent at the knee, the other prone, while his attention vacillated between a blade of long grass in his fingers, and her.

"Did you miss your prey?" he asked, softly.

"I was na' aiming for it," she lied.

"Truly?" He swiveled his head in time to catch the flicker of white tail and moving brush, that clearly marked her stag's escape. " 'Tis noble of you, Morgan."

She made the best sneer she could. "Noble? When we go hungry? How is that noble?"

"He was a grand stag, full of rut, proud of his doe and of his offspring. He was a thing of beauty, posed for our delectation at what a glorious creature of nature he is. I am glad you let him live."

She shrugged. "He will be taken down by the next hunter, Zander. He is too great a prize not to be. Come. There are fresh tracks of elk. We passed them on our way here. I will try for one of them."

"We have enough game, Morgan," he said softly.

"There is never enough game, FitzHugh. I know this to be true. I have gone hungry. I don't believe you ever have."

He sighed. "That much is probably true. I was spoiled and held, and loved and adored, and my head filled with how wonderful I was, probably from the moment I left my mother's womb. What of it? There is still enough game already taken. We have na' need of more."

"I have a hankering to hunt," she replied.

"Why?" he asked.

She put her bow tip to the ground and leaned a bit on it, and thought about his question. "You have asked this of me a-fore, Zander, and the answer is the same. I dinna' know why I hunt, I only know I need to. Why is it so important to you?"

"Because there is something there, Morgan. Something only you see and feel. I want to ken what it is, so I can understand you."

"Nobody understands me!" She gave the snort every bit of her disgust and turned to check the elk tracks. His hand on her ankle stopped her.

"I am still glad you let him live," he whispered.

"Live? Nay, I let him wander about until the next hunter, with more need, takes him down. I did him no favor."

"You gave him another glorious afternoon with which to enjoy the living. That is what you gave him."

"How did you ever bring down game to feed yourself, FitzHugh, with sentiments such as these?"

"I hunt when necessary, Morgan. For food."

" 'Tis the same as what I do," she replied, "and if you dinna' release me, we'll go without the elk, too."

He blew the sigh out that massive chest of his, and she watched it rise and fall. She had to close her eyes for a moment and force the vibration that went through her at the sight, to a halt, though. It had been bad enough worshipping him in the midst of a field of strangely erected stones, surrounded by mist, and covered with darkness. In the dappled sunlight of their forest glade, it was impossible to cover over, or hide from.

"Do you enjoy the killing, Morgan? Does the thought of stopping a heart from beating thrill you? Is that what hunting does for you?"

Tears glittered in her eyes, but she'd never let him know of it. She shrugged. "What if it is?" she asked.

"I think not. I think 'tis your talent you are flexing."

"My talent is a gift from God! Why do you revile it so?"

Zander looked up at her, and his other hand had her calf, now, holding her in place. "I dinna' revile it, Morgan. I revere it. I worship it. I am in awe of it."

"Then why do you pester me with the why? Isna' it enough that 'tis?"

"I said it wrong. That is strange, for I have a gift of speaking second only to The Bruce. I meant, you have this talent, and I think you have to use it, because you have it."

Morgan shook her head. "It will be dark a-fore we return, Zander FitzHugh, with speech such as you do. Meantime, my elk trots away."

"Let him," Zander replied. "I like that you dinna' wear the loin-wrap, Morgan. 'Tis verra inviting of you. Your lord and master thanks you for such a gift."

He was looking up her kilt, and since he had one leg solidly in his grasp there was nothing she could do but stand and suffer the blush. She knew he wished it so, too.

"You are only lord and master because of the accident of your birth, Zander," she said.

"The accident of my birth? I am fairly certain my parents were overjoyed. Not that they dinna' wish a lass, but I am a bonny sort, you know."

He displayed that physique for her to look at, and Morgan rolled her eyes, instead. "You're a fine male, FitzHugh. You dinna' need me to speak of it, for you already have a swelled head with it."

He pursed his lips. "You are taking an awful long time today to recognize and appreciate it, too."

"You were birthed a male, Zander. 'Tis the males who are lord and master. That is the accident I speak of."

"A woman has all the power, though," he replied.

The sound she made voiced all her disgust, and more. "What power does a woman have?"

"The power to sway males."

"You have shown me I have this power, but 'tis not due to my gender, but my aim. Why, if it became known that I am not a lad, The Bruce would be a target for ridicule and embarrassment."

"It's not that kind of power, Morgan. Would you twist all my words today? You are very difficult to speak with."

"As you are to hunt with. Yonder elk escapes while you delay me with worthless words."

"Worthless. Worthless, she says," he replied. "I have a talent with words, and she calls it worthless. I think I am insulted. With more thought, I realize I am insulted."

Morgan giggled. "You are a fetching male, Zander FitzHugh, and you have a great oratorical voice, which is your gift. Now, if you would unhand me, I will use mine."

"Let the elk go, Morgan. He deserves it. Let him live another afternoon, perhaps another full day."

"Why?"

"If I say, you will anger at me. So, I will na' say."

"Zander FitzHugh!" she exclaimed loudly.

"With a reaction like that, there will na' be game within a league, oh great god-of-the-hunt, Squire Morgan."

His voice was still calm and seductive, and he had moved his fingers to the back of her knee. Morgan had to concentrate on keeping that part of her leg stiff and unbending.

"Have you decided the why of your hunt, yet?" he asked, peeling her sock over her knee and running his fingernail from the back of her calf, to the highest point on her thigh he could reach.

"My hunt?" she replied.

"You are showing off your talent. We dinna' need the meat, although I dinna' mock what you do, any meat you bring would be put to use. It is just you hunt because you can."

"You simplify everything. Nothing is . . . that simple." She was whispering the words at the end, and it was his fault.

It felt like he was sending sparks, straight from his dark blue eyes directly to her heart, and didn't even realize it. The bairn must know, though, for it twinged, stronger this time, and Morgan hadn't the expertise to hide it. She was going to carry and birth a very active babe. That much wasn't in doubt.

She watched him watch her, and he didn't appear to blink. She forced herself to breathe evenly and normally, and very carefully.

"It isna' simple, Morgan, and yet it is, at the same time. You are gifted in targeting, shooting, and hunting. You hunt because of this talent. You may not even like it, but you use it, because you know what a special gift it is."

"You spoil my hunt, and talk nonsense. You are a strange hunting companion, Zander FitzHugh," she replied, surprised she had a voice.

He smiled, and an ocean of sound roared through her ears at the sight of it, and the bairn did antics in her belly again. Morgan caught her breath and begged the babe to cease. She very nearly flicked her gaze to it, since the slightest swell of her kilt betrayed her, and it was in her line of sight to the gorgeous FitzHugh at her feet. If she did such a thing, however, she knew he'd know.

She just didn't know what he'd do.

"God could have given this gift to a hundred . . . nay, a thousand others, but he dinna'. He gave it to you. Therefore, you must use it. Otherwise, it was wasted. So, I think you hunt because you can. Simple."

"And, that must mean you talk because you can. Regardless of whether your words have meaning or sense. You fill the day with words just because you can."

"I am going to feel insulted yet, Morgan. I want you to know this a-forehand."

She giggled.

"There could be another reason to your need to hunt, Morgan. Have you thought of that?"

"I try not to do too much thinking. My lord and master does too much of it for me already," she replied, and grinned.

"You are learning to tease, Morganna. I am proud of you," he replied quietly.

She was going to have to look elsewhere, or she was going to give everything away with the baby's continual twinging, and the effect of the love and pride in his eyes. She also wondered whether if she did look elsewhere, that would give it away. She gulped.

"I have changed my mind, Zander. I dinna' wish to finish this hunt. You have won. Yon elk can live another day. Or another hunter can bag him. Now, release my leg."

"One bit of my teasing about your teasing, and you're ready to run. You are a strange creature, Morganna. I think it's because you will lose control if you allow humor into your world. You are so blasted serious because you canna' allow the slightest crack to your composure. You canna' lose control. If that happens, you'll . . . what? Let something besides your life vow rule your world? Something . . . like love, mayhap?"

She gulped again. She didn't have an answer. She shook her head. He didn't know the extent of her life vow. When he found out, he wouldn't be speaking words of love or losing control or anything else to her, except hate and revenge, himself.

"Maybe you hunt for this reason. Maybe you hunt because it puts perfect order to your world. It puts you in command of it, instead of the other way around. Perhaps this is what hunting is to you."

Her eyes were awash with moisture, and he glimmered through it as a blur of blue and green sett, and long, thick legs and arms. "I already told you the elk could live, Zander. What else would you have of me?" she whispered.

"Do you carry my bairn?" he asked, softly.

Morgan had to look away. She concentrated on a tree, any tree, and she picked a large, stout one, with bark as thick as Zander's head must be. The thought helped as her tears faded.

She looked back down at him. "I already told you, FitzHugh, that I am unable to carry a bairn, whether it is sired by a grand fellow such as yourself, or a mere man. 'Tisn't a fault of yours, if you think to place the blame there. 'Tis mine."

"If you carry no bairn, 'tis na' my fault, nor is it yours, Morgan, love. 'Tis God's will." He shrugged. "I was hopeful you would be by now, though. 'Twas my fondest wish."

"Why?"

She'd give anything not to have asked it. She realized it as he put the entire force of those blue eyes on her. Morgan's eyes widened and she gaped. She actually felt the burning sensation starting at the depth of her and spreading outward, and the bairn felt it, too, if the movement within her was any indication.

"Remember when I spoke of a woman's power, Morganna?" he said.

She nodded. It was the most she was capable of.

"It is in the life she gives. The life she creates for the men about her, it's the realms of valor, gallantry and chivalry that she makes a man strive toward, just so he can be noble enough to deserve to be at her side. And it is the life she grows within her. A man canna' do any of these things. This is the power women have. I ask you again, Morganna, and I beg of you not to lie to me . . . do you carry my bairn?"

She didn't betray herself by so much as a hairsbreadth of motion. "And I asked you why you keep asking," she finally replied, although nothing about her voice sounded normal. She was having a hard time hearing it over the roar of sound in her own ears.

He sighed. "This season? 'Twas wondrous. 'Twas everything I have longed for for Scotland. The Bruce had his countrymen to sway. The need for freedom has gained root, and with every word he spoke, and every crowd he swayed, he has encouraged it and helped it grow. This forced march canna' last, though. The winter months are coming. Snow is already in the air. 'Twas cold last eve, in the circle, was it not?"

"I was na' cold," she whispered.

He smiled, and it had everything warm and loving and pure about it. Morgan heard the ocean in her ears crest in waves of reaction. She felt them to her gut. The baby within her didn't move.

"There will be an end to this season, and then there will be living to do for everyone. You, too."

There wasn't going to be anything for her except Phineas' death, and then, she hoped, her own. Or, she suspected, it would be worse than dying. Zander was going to be lost to her. Forever. Death would probably be more merciful.

The bairn twinged, almost painfully, and her breath caught at it. How could she will herself to die, when she was carrying life within her? Her eyes went huge with the thought. Did Zander suspect that was her plan, and was that why he gave her his baby, on purpose?

". . . and there is the future. This bairn you're carrying, Morganna. It ties us together. It is as much mine as it is yours, you know. You do realize that, dinna' you?"

She forced herself to listen to him, and caught the tail

end of what he was saying. Her heart sank. "Zander, I grow tired of—" She'd found her voice, but before she could start her rebuttal, he was interrupting her.

"I will have no bastards, Morganna. I told you that what seems a lifetime ago, when we first met. You carry my bairn in your belly. I will na' allow you to bring my child into this world without its father. Hear me well, Morganna, for I vow this to you, too."

"I dinna' carry a bairn!" She shouted it. "Now, cease speaking of it!"

Silence descended all about them. Morgan looked at him and waited. He twisted his lips into a semi-smile, raised those eyebrows and very slowly blinked at her. The result was worse than having a bucket of cold water tossed on her. She wondered if he knew.

"If you dinna' carry my bairn, then this talk is but a bit soon, for you will be. I will make certain of it."

"Please . . . don't touch me again," she answered.

"Oh, Morganna, my love. That is the most teasing thing you've yet said," he responded.

"Even if I carried a bairn, Zander, it would na' change anything. I have a vow to fulfill. I have always had this vow. You knew this. You knew this, and still gave me your seed. I will never forgive you for that, I think."

"I had to. The way you see your vow ends in death."

"It always did!"

"I will na' allow death about you, Morganna. Dinna' you ken anything I have said? You are the receptacle of my love, and the bearer of my future. I will na' allow death near you, ever again. Ever. That is another of my vows."

"Zander . . . please?" She was begging. She only hoped it swayed him. His words were doing more damage than any sword.

"You are carrying my bairn, Morganna, and it makes you more beautiful than before. That is how I knew, actually. You deny what is, and yet I already know. I *know*, Morganna. This makes it right and true that we wed. I would have wed with you a thousand times over a-fore this, but I had to have the means to force your hand. You will wed with me, Morgan. You will not be given the choice. I canna' risk it."

"Do you not ken what that would do to me, FitzHugh?"

"I am afraid to ponder it, actually," he answered.

"Would you have me fade into a shadow of myself, because I had no pride? Is that what you wish of me, FitzHugh? To lose every sense of pride I have? I will na' wed with you, and I will na' birth a bairn for you. I will do nothing save what I vowed to do over eight years ago. I will have justice for my clan, and I will na' allow you to sway it. I canna'."

He put her sock back into place on her leg, and sprang to a crouch, and then slowly stood to stand beside her. Then, he reached to lift her chin to make her face him, but she jerked her face away.

"This has been a bad day for a hunt, I think," he said finally.

"You think to finish this by ignoring it. 'Twill na' happen, Zander FitzHugh. You say I am serious, and 'tis true. I had to be. I still have to be. The man that destroyed my family still walks the earth. He still talks, eats and enjoys this life you are always spouting to me about. I will na' allow it. I will na' rest while it is so. I canna' wed with you, or any man, until there is an end to this. I canna'. You dinna' understand!"

"I understand, Morgan. Forgive me."

"You will na' press me?"

"I have pressed you enough for one afternoon, I think. I will ponder the means for my next attack upon your defenses, although I am uncertain as to what it should be. You are immune to talk of love. You are against talk of future and babes. You are prickly with anger at the thought of a warm house and me at your side as your husband. I will have to think of another tactic to sway you."

Her eyes flooded with tears. She gulped and sniffed and held herself stiff, and absolutely nothing worked. She was humiliated that he saw it.

" 'Tis all right, love. Forgive my forceful words. I forget myself with the desire I have. Come. Our sup awaits, and I've a long night planned ahead."

"Zander FitzHugh!"

She said it in response to the hands he was cupping about her buttocks, in order to lift her against him.

"You wear no loin-wrap, flaunt yourself above me, putting all your charms within easy reach and sight, and now say me nay? You are a tease, Morganna, lass. I am surprised I dinna' note that afore."

"And you are insatiable, my lord Zander."

He grinned, and used his thumb to wipe the tears from her face. "If you have complaints, you are to voice them."

"What would happen if I did?" she asked, trying to chuckle through the last of her emotional weeping.

He cocked his head and regarded her until she looked. "I believe I would consider them," he answered. "And try to change to what you need. What say you to that?"

Nothing. That was the only answer she had. She didn't voice it.

Chapter 28

They came for her just before midnight, and without warning. Morgan wasn't asleep, mainly because Zander hadn't arrived back, but when FitzHugh man after FitzHugh man entered the tent, she was on her feet, rubbing at her eyes, and trying not to look as terrified as she felt. There were five of them altogether, Zander bringing up the rear. She recognized Plato, but that was all.

"Morganna?" Zander said, and at his use of her name her eyes widened to their full extent.

"Zander, what have you done?" Morgan whispered the question.

"I have brought my brothers. They wish to meet Morgan, the great marksman, the squire who has brought such fame and recognition to our clan, and who is also the woman, Morganna, whom I love."

Morgan's eyes were huge. She was afraid to breathe.

"This is Ari FitzHugh, second-born. Ari? The maiden, Morganna."

A man, the same height as Morgan and looking a bit like Plato, but with Phineas's light-blue eyes and a slim physique that defied any relation to Zander, went on his knees before her. Morgan watched him do it and took a step back.

"Next born is Caesar. Caesar FitzHugh? The lass, Morganna."

The next FitzHugh male stood to her eyebrows in

height, had hair as blonde as Zander had described, and was as slight in build as Ari. He also went to a knee before her. Morgan's eyes were still wide and now her mouth opened.

"The fourth-born, and the lone one with a strange name, William FitzHugh. William? The lass, Morganna."

This brother had midnight-blue eyes, and receding medium brown hair. He was a bit taller than Caesar, but shorter than Ari. He was more solidly built than the preceding brothers, too. He went on a knee beside the others, and bowed his head.

Morgan looked toward Zander, but he had a taut look to him, and anger in every pore. She looked back at Plato. The apologetic slant of his eyebrows didn't give her a clue, either. Zander hadn't said a word that wasn't true. His brothers were all small, less prepossessing, and not near as handsome. Plato and Ari were the only ones to stand to Morgan's height.

"We've met, my lady," he said, dipping his head. "Plato FitzHugh."

And then Plato went to his knee.

"Zander?" Morgan whispered. "What is this about?"

"I have told my brothers that you are carrying my bairn, Morganna."

His face was as tight as before while he said the damning words. Morgan went white. Then, she had to hold to a tent pole to keep upright. She was shaking, stunned, demoralized, and totally degraded. Tears flooded her eyes and she wiped angrily at them before she pulled away from the tent pole and sent every bit of hate she possessed into the look she gave him.

"You have lied then, FitzHugh, for I dinna' carry anyone's bairn. Yours, or no," she replied, finally.

"Aye, you do, and I have brought my brothers to attend the wedding that I would force on you."

Her mouth wouldn't function, and her knees wobbled. "Zander, I . . ."

Then, she fell, but he caught her and pulled her against him before she could be hurt. His chest was huge, strong and comforting, and she let herself rest against it for the span of a heartbeat. Then she was hitting at him.

"I will na' wed with you, FitzHugh! I will na'!"

He caught her fists and held them, holding her in place while he did so. "You will, Morganna, if I have to force it. And I will force it. Dinna' doubt me."

"Nay," she whispered.

"I will na' do it alone, either. I have brought over a hundred clansman to make certain of it. I will have you to wife. You are na' longer being given the choice."

"But . . . why?"

His jaw was still set and a nerve bulged out the side of it. "You carry my bairn. I will have no bastards to claim. You will wed with me. This night."

"Nay, Zander, nay. I canna'. You dinna' understand." If she wanted him to listen, she was going to have to find a stronger argument than that, accompanied by a hint of tears, she told herself.

"You can, and you will. Dinna' you listen? I will force it."

"Oh God, not this, Zander. Please? Not this! You dinna' understand!" Morgan looked about wildly.

The other four FitzHughs were still on one knee in a line, and acting like they couldn't hear a word. It was horrible. She'd had nightmares about this baby, about facing the eventual size she was bound to become, about birthing a member of the FitzHugh clan, about facing the members of her dead clan when it happened. None of her nightmares matched the one Zander was forcing on her.

"Morganna, you carry my bairn," he repeated softly, more gently than before, but just as implacably. He had his head lowered, pinning that midnight-blue gaze on her from an angle beneath his eyebrows. The hands holding to her were trembling, too.

"Please, not this. I'm begging you. Please?" Morgan felt the tears of self-hate mingling with the same emotion with which she begged him. A KilCreggar was stooping to begging from a FitzHugh. She didn't think she could stand it, but wedding to him would be worse. She knew it.

She couldn't do it. She couldn't vow before God to be his for their entire lives! She couldn't! She couldn't put his name with her own. She couldn't vow allegiance to a clan that Phineas FitzHugh was laird of. She just couldn't! The betrayal to her ancestors would be more than she could bear.

"You are carrying my bairn," he repeated again, in the same calm, controlled, emotionless voice.

"Very well, Zander, aye!" Her voice was low, although she felt like screaming. "I carry your bairn! 'Tis what you wanted, what you schemed for, worked for, and made certain of. You convinced me it was love, when it was nothing of the sort. It was a trap you were setting. Well I will na' wed with you. I will na' vow to a FitzHugh. I canna'. I canna' stop this child you have given me, but I dinna' want it, and I will na' accept it. I will decide what I will do when 'tis birthed, but I will na' wed with you, FitzHugh! I canna!"

Zander was perfectly still, although she could tell he still breathed, because there was the slightest grunt of pain to each one. He was pale beneath his tan, too, and his jaw looked even more set, with his teeth clenched. The hard, reflective, midnight-blue of his eyes was more like the surface of a winter-blocked loch, and just as warm. Morgan looked away. She couldn't keep the gaze. It was killing her. The bairn wasn't reacting well, either, for it seemed to be doing push-ups in her belly.

"Well, you heard her, brothers? She carries my bairn. She is going to wed with me, whether she wishes it, or no. Now, do I have to force you, Morganna, or will you cleave unto me without it?"

"You dinna' understand, Zander! I canna' wed with you. Even if I wished to, I canna'! You dinna' understand!" Tears were running down her face now, and she ignored them.

He sighed hugely. "If you dinna' walk of your own power to the horse, Morgan, mount it and follow me to the cathedral, Morganna, I will bind you, I will gag you, and I will carry you. Now, which is it to be?"

"If you force me into this, FitzHugh, I will hate you. I will never forgive it. I want you to know this."

Nothing. She saw no reaction from her words. Morgan looked down. She looked at the four kneeling FitzHughs, and then she looked at the door. She tightened her thighs to run. If Zander weakened his grip at all, she was ready.

"Dinna' you hear me, love?" Zander whispered. "There are a hundred clansmen outside this tent. You would na' get two steps from me. Now, which is it to be?"

Morgan closed her eyes, tried to send every emotion to where it wouldn't hurt her and opened them. All the weeks of love, all the words of worship, and all the vows he'd made were for this? He'd done it to force her to wed him, when everything that was KilCreggar in her would rather die.

She yanked a hand free and reached for the dragon blade.

Zander was quicker. He had her against his chest, and plucked the blade from her, and then the dirks hidden at her back. Then he was advising Plato to get those from her socks. Morgan fought. She kicked. She twisted. Everything failed. She was forced to cease when they had all thirteen of her weapons, and she had nothing except Zander's arms about her like iron bands.

"Get the ties, Ari," Zander said.

"Wait," she said, stopping everyone. She was defeated, and she knew it. They all knew it. All that further fighting would do was get her trussed up and taken like a fresh kill before the priest, and all that would change is that the church would know, too. They wouldn't stop it, though. There was an unborn bairn to consider, and women had forever been forced. They always would be.

She bowed her head. "I will marry you, Zander FitzHugh," she whispered, and then the tears started.

Morgan wept when the cloak was put on her, covering her from head to foot. She wept when she was put atop the horse, Morgan, and then pulled back into Zander's arms. She wept with every step of the horse and every tear felt as though it carried blood. She wept when they arrived at the cathedral. She wept when they went inside: not just the six of them, but all the FitzHugh clansmen he'd brought with him. She wept when Zander carried her into a small room, just large enough for the two of them, and unwrapped her, and showed her the beautiful dress that was hanging there for her.

She wept hardest when he left her to dress.

Morgan took every bit of FitzHugh-given squire's raiment from her body. Then, she untied her breast binding and looked at the square of fraying cloth that had been her constant companion. She scrunched her eyes shut at the same moment she wrapped a fist about it. She no longer deserved to wear it. She certainly wasn't worthy of owning a piece of it. She opened her eyes, slashed an arm across her ceaseless weeping, and placed her KilCreggar plaid atop the bench by itself. There wasn't any way she was going to allow it to be near FitzHugh colors . . . not now. The only time she'd pick it up again, was when Zander turned his back and gave her time to join her family.

Morgan sighed, wiped at her eyes again, and then she turned her back on the last remnant of her clan. She put the FitzHugh-given dress on almost viciously. There was a chemise. There was a linen sheath over that, and there was an off-white, woven flax dress, with a square neckline and long laced-on sleeves that fell below the wrist.

There was no veil, so Morgan undid her braid, and

combed her fingers through her hair until she had her veil. There was a silvered mirror on the wall, but she ignored it. She couldn't see through her tears, anyway.

There was a faint sound coming from the front altar when she stepped out, and she noted Plato was the FitzHugh standing outside her door to escort her. Morgan looked up the aisle-way of the cathedral and saw the altar. She saw the huge, pointed hat on the bishop, who was to wed them, she saw that every available bit of standing room was taken up with a FitzHugh, and then she started walking.

There were altar boys singing as she grew closer, their voices combining to make heavenly, reverent music. That was strange, when they were doing such a desecration, she thought. Her feet grew heavier the closer to the altar she came, and that was strange, too.

Then, Zander stepped out to the front of the altar, and time stood completely still for the briefest moment of time. Zander FitzHugh was dressed from neck to knee in a *feile-breacan* of her beloved KilCreggar gray-and-black plaid.

Morgan's steps faltered, her breath completely left her body as she felt and heard the reaction of shock, disgust and hatred all around her. Then, she heard, from a long way away, Zander telling Plato to catch her, for God's sake, and then she heard absolutely nothing.

The din was enormous when she opened her eyes, and she was lying in Plato's lap, directly in front of the altar, and Zander was speaking in that great orator's voice of his.

"Listen to me, I say! Nay! I dinna' say it, I command it! Listen! Hush your tongues and listen to me! I am going to wed the last KilCreggar in Scotland, the lass Morganna, and there is na' going to be more clan war about it! There is a story to tell, and every single man amongst you is going to listen. Ewan FitzHugh is going to tell it. Ewan!"

"Ewan FitzHugh is a deaf-mute!" Someone called out derisively.

"Nay!" Zander shouted. "Ewan isna' deaf, nor is he mute, although he would give his soul to be both! Ewan? Step up! Now. Step up and tell your tale."

The little old man who moved to Zander' side looked even older and frailer than he was, simply standing next to the youngest FitzHugh. He also looked very colorful beside the muted grayish sett worn by Zander. Morgan blinked and sat up, and Plato let her, although he put a finger on his lips to silence her.

"Speak loudly, Ewan. This church has great space for sound to seek out and amplify words, but 'tis na' everything. Speak loudly. Tell them the story. Make them hear!"

The little old man opened his mouth, and the fact that he was actually speaking was probably what hushed them more than what he was saying. Morgan watched as man after man stopped clamoring and shaking his fists and started listening.

"What Zander says is truth, my clansmen. I am no deaf-mute, although I have sought that condition for more than fourteen years. Fourteen years when I have aged far beyond my two score!"

The man is forty? Morgan thought and gasped. She wasn't the only one astounded as they all looked at him.

"Listen and know the truth, my friends, my blood, my kin. I am the man you see before you because I carry guilt, great guilt. I was going to my grave with it, until friend Zander here spoke with me two days past. He begged me to right a wrong, and that is what I must do."

There was absolute silence at the end of his words this time, and all waited while he gasped for breath to continue.

"Fourteen years ago, I was na' the *auld* man you see before you now. Nay, I was young, I was virile, I was every inch a FitzHugh warrior, and I was a companion to our laird, Phineas. I tell you that, so you will know. Some of you may even remember."

"I remember!" Someone shouted from the rear. Ewan nodded.

"It is well to remember. It is well that we have that capacity. It is horrible, too. Let me tell you my story. It was a chill morn, not unlike today, when Phineas asked us to accompany him. He took Robert MacIlvray, Leroy Fitz-Hugh and myself."

They were murmuring at mention of the names, but Morgan didn't know why.

"Phineas wanted to teach a certain lass a lesson. He told us he didn't wish to harm her, he just wished to show her the error of her ways. I dinna' know as we approached her house what he meant. He told us he only meant to scare them. We came by way of the loch. We docked our boat silently. We went into the house.

"The old woman was the lone one awake as we crept in, and then Phineas and Robert and Leroy were upon her. They were na' scaring anyone. They were raping, they were punishing, and it was na' even the correct lass. I remember the screaming. I remember the blood. I remember backing out the door and retching my belly out on the soil. I remember Phineas laughing when it was done, and then he was pouring the contents of his sporran all over the woman and the table in order to set fire to it. Dear God, I only hope she was already dead."

Morgan was shaking. It started as small tremors and grew.

"Then, I heard the screaming from the back of the house. It took the flame easily, I recollect thinking. I dinna' know fire swept that fast. Explosions had sent flames shooting up and outside the windows. I heard the screaming and I snuck around to see why."

Morgan's shaking was intensifying, to the point her body was hitting the ridges of carving on the altar's base.

Plato gathered her into his arms and starting rubbing at hers, but it wasn't helping.

"I saw the lass we'd come to torment. She was swelled and huge with child, and she was screaming at a wee one about being a killer and such. I remember wondering why she'd be screaming that at such a little one, and then Phineas saw the woman. The roar he gave was indescribable. I knew then what he was going to do.

"I prayed for the wee one to hide, and miraculously, she did. She dinna' see what Phineas did to Elspeth. I dinna' want to, either, but I was transfixed with the horror as he took her and hit her with both fists. Took her and hit her, took her and hit her, until Robert and Leroy pulled him off and started running for the boat.

"I almost missed them, for they were intent on escaping the evil they'd done, and I was sick with the evil I'd been a party to. Phineas made us swear to secrecy. He was covered with blood, and his face a mass of scratches, and he made us vow never to tell a soul what had happened. He said there was none left to witness. He'd made certain of it.

"I knew the falsehood of that, for I knew the wee one had survived, but I kept my vow. I kept silent. I never said a word about that morn, or about anything. I would have taken the secret to my grave, if not for Zander's words to me two days past."

Morgan's shaking had reached a plateau of sorts, and simply held her there, and Plato responded by continuing to massage her upper arms, his hands gentle and warm. His touch was the only thing she was aware of feeling.

"Tell them the rest, Ewan. Tell them everything," Zander commanded the man at his side.

The old man took a gulp of air and spoke again. "Phineas told all who asked that a she-wolf of the KilCreggars had gotten to him. He explained away the marks on his face, and the blood that would na' wash from his plaid no matter how many dunkings he gave it. He told a wild story of being beset, and none of us contradicted him, but you already know that much.

" 'Twas Leroy that got it first. I dinna' ken how many of you remember it, but Leroy FitzHugh was taken one morn, taken and had his manhood sliced clean off and a claymore buried in his chest, and then he was draped in KilCreggar plaid. That was the start of it. The killing. The feud. And it was no KilCreggar that started it. It was a FitzHugh. Worse yet, it was the new laird of the FitzHugh. It was Phineas FitzHugh."

The crowd was absolutely silent. They might as well have been statues.

"Tell them why now, Ewan." Zander's voice was gentle, probably due to the man's sobbing right beside him. "Tell them. Go on."

Morgan's shaking was subsiding into trembling. Plato held her still, stroking the skin of her upper arms and supporting her back.

"Five years earlier, when Phineas was na' yet the laird, but the heir, he saw a lass not unlike the one Zander has brought tonight to wed with. She was winsome, she was as tall as he was, and she was brave. He courted her, and she laughed in his face. Then, she turned down the rich heir to the Clan FitzHugh, and wed a man with no land and no title, a man named Richard Beams. Phineas never forgot the insult. No matter how many women he took, he said he always saw the black-haired lass who had laughed at his suit and then wed a pauper."

Richard Beams. Morgan remembered that name. Elspeth's husband. Her shaking ceased, easing out of her back and leaving her absolutely calm. Then, Zander started speaking again.

"So, now you know, my clansmen. Now, you know the truth, and I wish you to also know—"

"You arrange such a spectacle, and dinna' invite your sovereign and king? I would have the reason!"

Morgan's eyes widened as The Bruce used every timbre of his large voice from the back of the cathedral. Then he walked steadily and rapidly up the aisle, a retinue of guards at his back.

"My liege." Zander dropped to a knee as The Bruce reached him, and the king placed a hand on his shoulder.

"We have fought so long and hard to unify Scotland and cease feuding, and now you seek to bring an old one back to life? What am I to do with you, young FitzHugh?"

Zander stood, dwarfing everyone. "You are to stay and witness my wedding, Sire," he answered.

"And who is it are you wedding?"

Zander turned and held his hand out to Morgan. "I am wedding the fair Morganna KilCreggar, Your Majesty."

The king looked at her, and she saw the instant recognition.

"Aye, my liege," Zander started orating again, turning to encompass all in the room. "I am wedding the sister of my squire, and I wish all the FitzHugh clan here now to know that my squire is not from 'no clan or no name.' His name is Morgan KilCreggar. He is the twin of my bride. You have already been applauding and accepting a KilCreggar in your midst. Now you know that it has been for just and fair reasons."

There was a wild reaction to this and Zander had to put his hand out for quiet.

"I also wish you to know that I am requesting here and now that the king change my allegiance. I wish to have another name restored to earth. I wish to wed with a KilCreggar, and I wish to be known as Zander KilCreggar-FitzHugh. I wish our bairns to carry the name of KilCreggar-FitzHugh. I wish my wife to be known as Morganna KilCreggar-FitzHugh. It was for that purpose I had this tartan woven. While it is not exact to the KilCreggar plaid, it is just and right that is has blue and green woven within its sett. These are the colors I wish for my new clan, Your Majesty. This is the wedding gift I wish for my bride."

" 'Tis a poor wedding gift, I would say," the king responded.

Morgan gasped. She wasn't the only one.

"Poor?" Zander choked on the word.

"Aye, poor. What clan can do without land, without a title? On your knees, Zander KilCreggar-FitzHugh. On your knees so that I may confer the title of Earl upon you, and bequeath you with half the FitzHugh holdings. This is a fair wedding gift. Morganna?"

The Bruce was holding out his hand for her, and Plato helped her rise and find her legs, although they felt the consistency of very wet peat bog. When she reached them and gave him her hand, he bowed. Then he gave her to the kneeling FitzHugh, at their feet.

Zander held her hand to his forehead. He was shaking more than she had been, she realized, and everyone was watching him do it.

"Will you have me to husband, Morganna KilCreggar? Will you stand at my side and help me found and grow the new clan of KilCreggar-FitzHugh? Will you wed with me now, and cleave unto me, and love and honor me as I would you?"

Midnight-blue eyes looked up at her, and Morgan responded in her very core. "I am not satisfied, my lord," she replied.

"You are . . . na'?" Zander's gaze dropped.

"Nay," she replied. "For I will na' accept your new plaid unless the sett carries equal amounts of FitzHugh blue and green, as KilCreggar black and gray. That is my condition."

He rose slowly, and she knew there was a commotion all about them. She just didn't hear a word of it.

Chapter 29

"Oh, my God!" Zander sat up, groaning, and he was clutching a hand to his forehead. "What have I done?"

Morgan took longer to awaken, and she stretched in the pre-dawn light. "What have you done, love?" she whispered.

I dinna' want to be a laird! I canna' even get structure in my own life. How am I to do it for an entire clan?"

Morgan giggled.

"No wonder my mum was for this plan. She is even now, at my house, restoring order . . . or creating order for the place."

"Dinna worry yourself, my lord, Earl of KilCreggar-FitzHugh," Morgan whispered. "I will help you."

Zander looked over his shoulder at her. "Help? What help you gave me throughout the night leaves me weak-kneed and fit for nothing save plying a needle with the ladies of my clan."

Morgan giggled again. She had been the insatiable one. That much was true. What wasn't true was Zander was weak anywhere, especially the legs. "Let me see," she said, trying to lift their cover.

He held it to him protectively. "I have duties to attend to, my lady. I should probably see to my new clansmen. You would steal my strength from that?"

"I would," she replied.

He grinned. "I also have to set weavers to spinning once again. Do you na' realize what you've done?"

"What is it I have done?" she asked, sliding a hand along the line of his thigh, over his knee and to his ankle, where it was outlined by the sheet.

"You have caused the sett I had designed, ordered woven and made into *feile breacans* to be discarded, while all our sheep will need to be re-shorn, the wool carded and spun, re-dyed, woven again. Why, my new clansmen will be long naked afore we get them their new colors."

"They can wear FitzHugh until then," she remarked, running her fingernail back up. "They dinna' appear to worry last eve."

"I have declared death to the FitzHugh laird," Zander said solemnly. "I will na' have my new clan clothed the same as the man I must kill."

"I vowed to kill Phineas, and I will," Morgan replied, lifting her hand from his hip.

"Oh no, you will na'. You will stay at our home this winter, grow our bairn, and bring it to life. I will na' allow you to kill anyone. I may not even allow you to hunt. That is how much this means to me."

"Zander! I live to hunt!"

"Then, we must find targets that are more life-like for you."

"You are turning into a tyrant, and we've been wed less than a day. I dinna' think I like it."

"We've been wed forever, my love, just a half-day in this lifetime. I will bend. If we have need of meat, you may accompany me on the hunt."

"Accompany you? Why, you over-blown, over-muscled, big-headed, arrogant—"

"Dinna' forget handsome," Zander interrupted.

Morgan's lips twitched, and then she was laughing.

"Ha! The wife laughs at me, her new husband. Dinna' think I will let that go overlooked!"

He was tickling her, making her do all sorts of chortling, and then he sobered. "You realize how little you have laughed since I have known you, Morganna? 'Tis a joyous sound, too."

"There was na' much to smile about, my lord, Zander KilCreggar-FitzHugh."

" 'Tis a mouthful, our new name, my love. You dinna' think it too much? I would ask for KilCreggar to be restored, and take it, if that is your wish."

She wasn't laughing anymore. She was having a hard time keeping the tears at bay. "Oh . . . Zander," she stammered, catching a breath between the words.

"I can bring you to tears, too. 'Tis a good thing for Plato. I thought him the lone one with that gift. Here, love. Dinna' start a storm of weeping. They will think I abused you, rather than the other way about."

She giggled again. "I dinna' abuse . . . you."

"Nay?" He lay back and stretched, making the bedstead creak. "I am well-used, then. I will be worthless to my king until eve. Mayhap not even then."

"What about your clansmen? I mean, our new clansmen? What would you have of them if their new laird lays about all day?"

Zander lifted his head and gave her a level look. "A newly named KilCreggar-FitzHugh man can out-drink any man. Why, they can put down an ocean of whiskey. I believe they proved it last eve. There's na' a one of them desirous of moving until eve. Trust me."

"Zander?" she asked.

"Aye?"

"Those men who came to you last eve and swore fealty? They are all coming with us? What of the FitzHugh clan?"

"Those men were already my men, Morganna. They fought at my side and have been with me since we reached manhood. 'Twas not a one of them that would na' follow me. Were I to swear allegiance to the devil, they would follow. I would ha' been insulted had they but tried to keep from following me."

"You have followers, too?"

He lifted his eyebrows. "I am a KilCreggar-FitzHugh, you ken? I have a great orator's voice. I give speeches. I have followers."

"I dinna' mean to insult," she whispered.

"You?" He snorted. "Insult? Why, if I remember a-right, you called me small enough to rival walnuts at one point. Insult?"

She giggled again. "I have since changed my opinion, sir."

Zander grinned. "I can learn to love that laugh sound you make, my love. I truly can."

He was holding her in place with his chin at her shoulder blade and rolling it about. His hands were everywhere, too. Morgan clucked her tongue as she caught at him beneath the sheets, time and again.

"But, what of FitzHugh, Zander?" she asked.

He lifted his head and sighed. "You will na' rest until Phineas is no longer of this world, will you? Very well. I will don my new colors, and I will go and do battle with him. Then, I will return. You had best prepare yourself for it, too. When I return I'll not accept meek submission from you. I will expect to be attacked again. Like last night, only longer. Can you grant me that, when I return?"

"I am serious, Zander," she replied.

He sighed again. "You have not been working on your next-morning love-talk, Morganna, for it has not improved. My brother, Ari, has sworn to bring Phineas to justice. I have sworn the same. I will na' accept Ari's idea of justice, unless it matches my own. *Now*, can we go back to being a newly wedded man and wife?"

"I meant . . . will the FitzHugh clan seek the land back from us?"

"Why would they? These are my brothers you speak of, Morganna. They are as penitent as I am over the demise of the KilCreggar clan. Why, there was not one amongst us that was na' at the last battle. We fought. We killed. We celebrated. I dinna' seek to cause you grief, I only wish you to know of the deep sorrow, remorse, and guilt we feel. We dinna' know we should have been on our knees begging for forgiveness. We are, now."

Morgan's heart twinged, the bairn in her belly moved and her eyes swam. Then, she blinked the moisture away. She didn't want to spend another moment with regret. She wanted a future, and for once, it was in sight.

"You are much too serious, Zander KilCreggar-FitzHugh. I hope you dinna' intend to speak this way all day," she replied.

His eyebrows rose. Then, he grinned. "Why do you ask of it, then?"

"I only ask if there might be a problem with your brothers over it. The king ceded half of FitzHugh land to us. Surely that is enough to start a clan war, isna' it?"

"You need a lesson in the man you have married. That is it. You have little regard for him. I dinna' know what I must do to change it. That, I dinna'."

"Is this going to be another 'I am the most handsome, biggest, glorious, well-endowed, strongest' speech again?" Morgan teased.

"It is a good thing I am all of that, too. Your lack of regard would shred a lesser man. I pity the poor fool that tries to best my wife."

"Zander—" she said, in a threatening tone.

"Oh, very well. I will answer your question. The FitzHugh clan will na' worry over my possession of the land. 'Twas my skills that won us most of it, wife. In fact, my sword arm was what brought most of North Pitt Vale into FitzHugh hands. So, in truth, I already owned it."

"You already owned it. How?"

"I dinna' do battle simply for blood-lust, love. I did it for spoils. I took land. I took gold. I took maidens."

Her eyes narrowed. "You had better be teasing me, Zander KilCreggar-FitzHugh."

"By the time you say my name, I've an excuse dreamt up, and aye, I was telling a story. Not a large story, but a story. I dinna' take any maidens. They came willingly."

She hit him square in his rippled abdomen. He responded by curling into a sit-up and pantomiming an injury worthy of a sword. Morgan sat up, cross-legged, and watched him.

The king had spirited them away from the cathedral with a stealth worthy of Zander's showmanship. It wasn't but a half-league to this stone house, belonging to a mayor or like official. It was warm, had a myriad of servant lasses to giggle, slap each other and promise healthy portions of food and mead delivered when it was requested, and complete privacy. That was another of The Bruce's gifts to the new laird of the KilCreggar-FitzHugh clan. It was a wondrous gift, too.

"They truly will na' wish us harm?" she asked.

"My mum is already at my home. Were you na' listening to me, earlier? The lady of FitzHugh rules the castle. She has already decreed what I received as just and fair. Aside from that fact, I must tell you that some of my land used to be KilCreggar land."

"Oh."

"Dinna' say it like that. I dinna' know when I received it that it was betrayal and murder of the worst kind. My mother has deserted the FitzHugh Castle as long as Phineas is laird. She will na' return until he is na' longer there. She wishes you to know this."

"She . . . will abide Phineas' death?"

"Phineas is her first-born, true. He is also a murderer and defiler of innocents. She will abide clan law. You heard Ari last night. He will be laird. Phineas will be no more. And you heard me, true?"

"You said so much, Zander. I canna' recall all of it."

He tilted his head at her and raised those eyebrows again. "Phineas is mine, Morganna. He isna' going anywhere, except to Hell, and I will put him there. I vowed to gain KilCreggar justice. I vowed it."

"But, what of my vow?"

Zander sat, crossed his legs, and held out his hands. Morgan faced him, and put her hands in his. She didn't move her eyes from his.

"When your vow was made, Morganna KilCreggar, you were but a girl-child. There was na' a man left in your clan. There was a grave injustice done, and na' one to see it rectified. You vowed to see it done. You vowed to kill the laird. All true?"

She nodded.

"There is a laird of the KilCreggar clan now, Morganna. There is a man to do this justice. There is a man who has taken your vow and will see it done. Your vow has become his. Your hand will be his. Your aim will be his. You understand?"

She squinted her eyes. "I am trying to," she answered.

"You are a woman, Morganna. A woman. You canna' change your birth and I, for one, would not see it changed. You are also carrying the future of the KilCreggar-FitzHugh clan. You are bringing life into the world, not death. You carry a bairn in your womb, and this bairn was conceived in love, will be birthed into love, and will know love. All of this he will learn from his mother. His mother, Morganna. There will be time to learn death and hate, but from the moment of his birth, my son will learn love. He will not learn love from a killer. He will learn love from a woman. His mother. You."

She couldn't even see him through her tears.

"Phineas FitzHugh is mine. I will see justice done. Your vow will come to pass, and then I will return to the same love as my son receives. From you. Dinna' you understand now?"

She nodded.

"I dinna' vow lightly, either, Morganna, although you

have accused me of such. All I vowed to you before, I have done, have I not?"

She nodded again.

"Now I have vowed to see the KilCreggars avenged. I will do so. You trust me enough for that?"

She blinked, letting tears slip down her cheeks. She nodded again. She didn't trust her voice.

"You will not be idle, Morganna. There is so much you need to learn, for I need certain things of you, my love. I need you to learn more about play, and less about death. I need you to help me gain structure in my life. I need you to help Scribe Martin design a dragon emblem for our clan. He canna' put to parchment what I see in my head. I see two dragons . . . intertwined, each forever an extension of the other. Do you see it, too?"

She nodded, yet again.

"I also need you to assist with this kilt design you announced to all. Is it four broad bands of color, all of an exact width? Is it two broad bands with small lines, followed by the other two colors in broad bands with small lines? Is it one background color, with three other colors all of a like width? You dinna' know the havoc you continually create for me, do you?"

She giggled, cried and snorted at the same time. It sounded as strange as it felt.

"I need these things from you, Morganna, my love."

"Oh, Zander," she whispered.

"I also need some other things, Morganna."

"More?" she asked.

"I also need you to tell me of your love. You have never said it. I wait, and I hope, and you have never said that you love me. I would like to hear it. Now."

"Oh, Zander," she whispered, and for some reason she blushed. Morgan couldn't believe it. Sunlight was coming through the window, and she was sitting in a large conjugal bed that had seen immense passion through most of the previous night. She was facing the naked beauty of her husband, while in the same state of undress, and was she blushing? Morgan had to swallow.

"I do love you, Zander," she whispered. "I have loved you since . . . I dinna' know for certain. I think I have loved you forever."

He grinned, and the light in his eyes made them look exactly like the sapphire Plato had given her.

"When did you love me?" she asked.

"If I'd had my wits about me and guessed your true gender, I'd have to say it was the moment I came from the water and you asked how you had missed my vital part. The look on your face held such awe, Morganna! I nearly strutted about with it. Or perhaps it was when I saw your face when you fell atop me at the MacPhee croft. That could have been it. I dinna' know for certain."

She rolled her eyes, and wiped at them before looking back at him. "You dinna' ever think of anything else," she said.

"I do. I think of my bairn. It makes me feel warm, right here." He pulled one set of their joined hands to his chest. "When I first realized you carried him, I canna' tell you how it felt. I wanted to dance, sing and shout with it. I'm truly amazed that I did nothing."

"When did you know?" she asked.

"The moment we reached Castlegate. You had the oddest expression to your face one moment, and the next you reached for your belly. I nearly fell off my horse with joy."

"That is the same moment I knew."

"How did you know? What made you so certain?"

"He moves. Oft."

"Our bairn? He moves already?"

"Aye, but I dinna' think that rare. 'Tis been almost four months, Zander."

"The night in the chamber? Sally Bess night?" he asked,

and he wasn't feigning surprise. It was written on every bit of him.

She shrugged. "I dinna' know for certain, Zander, but I think it was that night."

" 'Tis what I asked and prayed for. I should na' be surprised, but I am."

"You canna' be surprised. You planned it. You meant it to happen. You tell me so oft how manly you are, how virile, how strong, how much the ladies seek you over your brothers."

"You make it sound as if I've a swelled head."

She raised her eyebrows, but said nothing. She watched him flush. It was very becoming on him. He cleared his throat. "Besides, that does na' mean we can create a bairn every time, Morganna. 'Twas what I'd prayed for, and what I needed, but that does na' guarantee it."

"It was what you'd planned for and set about gaining, Zander. You canna' fool me. You told me such. You even told me how Ari told you it was done. You knew what you were doing, Zander. You were entrapping me."

His snort carried every bit of his disgust. "I was getting you into my marriage bed the only way I knew how. Dinna' you ken how difficult it was for a FitzHugh to coax a member of the KilCreggar clan to the altar? Do you ken it was easy?"

"You should have told me earlier that you knew who I was."

He smiled gently. "I knew that back when you told me your story at Argylle. I just dinna' want to believe it."

"You did believe it, though?"

"Morganna, you carry a small square of plaid with you. I've seen it many times, from our first night. I recognized it and then I knew. It started a sickness in my veins and a heat in my heart. I knew you spoke truth, Morganna. I even recalled the scratches and the blood Phineas had on him. I also knew my clan would need proof of it. I remembered

Ewan. I got proof. I had to have time to get the sett woven. I needed time to convince Ewan he had to speak. I had to ask Plato to arrange everything, because I had other things occupying me. Things like loving my woman, and creating my bairn. It has been a very busy time for me, Morganna. I have na' just been lazing at your side as your consort."

"I am properly impressed, then," she answered.

He lowered his head, to look at her through his eyebrows. "And am I forgiven?"

"For what?"

"Entrapping you. Getting you with my bairn. Forcing you to the marriage altar."

"You wish forgiveness for such?"

"Aye. I do. Now, please."

"I love you, Zander. I forgave everything the moment I saw KilCreggar plaid. I think I swooned."

"That you did, which was very womanly of you. Plato caught you. It was very impressive, too. Got my clan's minds off of killing me long enough for me to speak to them. I am grateful for that. I am also grateful for Plato for his excellent hands. He has paid off his debt. He can go back to the lady Gwynneth now."

"What debt?"

"You gave him back his love so they could wed. He is eternally grateful. That's why he gave you his ring. It had not left his finger until he gifted it to you. I understand. I would rather die than see you wed to another. He dinna' hurt you with his catch, did he?"

"Plato kept me from harm, Zander."

"I would rather it had been me, though."

"You had speaking to do. You did it well. I only hope our bairn has such a gift."

"I'd rather he had his mother's sight and her talent with weapons. Scotland will need such."

"Scotland will need both, Zander."

He nodded. "True enough. Come here." It wasn't a request,

it was a command. Zander made certain of it too, by picking her up and twisting her until she sat atop his legs with her back against his chest.

"Why?" she asked.

"So I can touch this place where my son is." He had both her hands again, and was cupping the bulge of her belly. Morgan felt the shudders of his breath over her shoulder as he held to her. The baby was reacting, too. She wondered if Zander felt it.

"Have you settled on a name for our bairn, Morganna?" he whispered, finally. She shook her head. "You must spend some time thinking on it. Dinna' let my mother sway you, either. She has strange ideas."

Morgan giggled. The babe twinged.

"You should hear what she helped Ari's wife name my nephews," he said.

"What if 'tis a girl, Zander?"

"FitzHughs dinna' have girl bairns. KilCreggar-FitzHughs might, though. If 'tis a girl-child you carry, then I will have done what my sire and brothers are unable to. That has merit, Morganna. Dinna' let my mother name her, either. She has been looking for an Aphro-something for her entire life. I dinna' wish my daughter to have a name none can say."

Morganna giggled again. "We can name her for her sire. Zandria. We can also name her for an uncle. How about Caesara?"

He groaned, and lay back, pulling her with him, until she was stretched out atop him. "We had best design a large dowry, then," he answered.

Chapter 30

Morgan and Zander got two blessed days in the official's house before it ended. It was a wondrous learning experience, when everything was said once and then again, when Morgan let Zander know, verbally and physically, of her love, and he left her in no doubt of his.

It had to end, though. Nothing lasts forever, despite Zander's words. It was Robert the Bruce who ended it. He was requesting the laird and lady of KilCreggar-FitzHugh in the great room, and amid a great deal of giggling and play, they went to greet their sovereign.

"I see wedded life agrees with you, KilCreggar-FitzHugh!" He announced, his voice overly loud in the room.

"Aye," Zander replied, and bowed.

"And you, my lady. A more lovely and contented lady I've yet to see. You enjoyed your reprieve?"

"Reprieve?" she echoed.

"Aye. 'Tis all I can do to keep order in the camps, with the FitzHugh tent empty and no sign of the squire. I'm afraid it's time."

"I am ready."

Morgan checked for her dirks, her dragon blade, and touched the silver bands together at her wrists. Zander had helped dress her, so she knew everything was in place.

"You misunderstand, my lady."

Robert the Bruce took one of her hands and then went

down on his knee before her. Morgan's eyes widened and she looked to Zander for a cue. He lifted his eyebrows and shrugged.

The king stood. "It is time for Morgan, the squire, to return to the mists from whence he came. Squire Morgan is a legend. He is in the heart, sword arm, and aim of every Scotsman in Scotland. He will live on there. He canna' survive as the twin brother of the wife of one of my lairds. Dinna' you understand?"

She shook her head.

"My vassal, Laird KilCreggar-FitzHugh is a wealthy man. He is a stunning man, well attuned to leading a crowd, albeit he says differently. He is noticeable. His wife will be the same. It will na' escape notice how closely related she is to Squire Morgan, especially if Squire Morgan is rarely seen."

"I never thought—I wouldn't have . . . . I'm sorry, my liege."

"It isna' anyone's fault, Morganna. It simply is. Scotland needed unification. We needed a champion who could best the English. We needed a rallying force to get the clans together so I could speak to them. You were all that. I canna' ever repay what you have given me, although I have high hopes for these."

He pulled a small leather wallet from his waistband and held it out to her. Morgan's hands were shaking as she took it and unfolded it to reveal a dozen dirks in separate sewn compartments, all with jewel-encrusted, silver handles. Her eyes went wider.

"I canna' accept such a gift." Her voice shook.

"Test the balance." He smiled. "Laird KilCreggar-FitzHugh tells me of its importance to your aim. I had the best smithy in Scotland design and smelt these for you. Test them."

Morgan slid one from its embroidered sheath. She closed her eyes and held it, tipping her hand this way and that. It was amazing. The handle was the same weight as the blade. She opened her eyes.

" 'Tis perfect," she whispered.

"Very good. I'll tell him of your pleasure. Creating blades for the legendary Squire Morgan has increased his value a hundred-fold."

Morgan smiled. "My thanks," she answered.

"Good. Now, as to your plan, FitzHugh?"

"KilCreggar-FitzHugh," Zander corrected.

Robert smiled and shook his head. "That is a mouthful, Lord Zander."

"I . . . truly have to disappear?" Morgan asked.

" 'Tis best for Scotland," the king replied.

"But, will the crowds still come?"

"What you have put into motion has na' chance of stopping, my lady. I will forever be in your debt. And rest assured, if there is need of Squire Morgan, I will send for him. I will get a message through to my loyal subject and nobleman, the earl of KilCreggar-FitzHugh, and his lovely wife. My subjects will know this. Squire Morgan comes when he is needed."

"Squire Morgan will be disappearing, Morganna," Zander said. "Not the Lady KilCreggar-FitzHugh. You will be reappearing as my wife at our home. My only regret is that we will be separated for the small span of time it takes to finish with Aberdeen."

She must have looked as confused as she felt.

"If Squire Morgan's master disappears, too, then you will be besieged at your own castle gates. They will know where to find you. Zander must stay at my side. I told him of it, already."

"For how long?" Morgan asked, swallowing before anyone guessed that she was on the brink of tears. For a woman of few emotions, used to having only herself for company, she was learning the feeling of loneliness again.

She didn't realize how bereft she felt, and she and Zander weren't even apart, yet.

"Now, here is my plan . . . ."

Morgan listened to Zander, but didn't pay attention. She couldn't. Her entire being felt like it was aching with grief, and she didn't know why.

Zander's plan worked perfectly, which wasn't surprising. He seemed to have a knack for creating and executing plans. Morgan stood atop her conical stage, shrouded by torchlight through the mist, and put dirk after dirk at Zander's and King Robert's feet. They depleted her entire stock, all her old ones, and the new jeweled ones. She felt rather naked with just the dragon blade left, but Zander had promised her the blades would be returned, and he always kept his promises. That much, she knew.

Then, she was sliding over the cross-pieces and crawling out the bottom, fading into the forest away from the sound of Zander's voice. She heard all about how the Squire Morgan had come upon him. How he had been mortally wounded, with an English sword through his belly, and had nothing left to do in this world than watch his lifeblood spill, while all about him, Scotsmen were perishing at the hands of the Sassenach. Then, she heard how, through the mist, a youth had come to rescue him. Squire Morgan had pulled the sword from his belly, sealing the wound, and then he had turned on the enemy, and routed all.

Morgan's ears were burning from the story. Her entire body felt aflame with the blush, and then the four FitzHugh brothers; Ari, Caesar, William, and Plato, stepped from the trees.

"Our bairn brother would na' trust you to anyone less," Plato whispered, as he approached, and her eyes widened as she saw what he was giving her. He was holding up a fur-trimmed, black wool cloak. Morgan couldn't say a word. Her throat felt choked with them.

She didn't know who assisted her atop a horse, smaller than Morgan, the horse, but just as stable, nor did she know who lifted the reins to lead her. She knew it was Ari at the rear, however. Plato spoke of it after they left the last of The Bruce's camp well behind them.

"Ari rides behind. As guard. We dinna' want our worse sword arm at your back, my lady," he whispered.

"Sword arm?" Morgan asked.

He flashed her a quick grin from the length of tartan he had wrapped about his head and shoulders. "Ari is well-known for his skills. Phineas won't even challenge him at it."

"Sword arm?" she asked again.

He sighed loudly. "Very well. Claymore. Ari is the best at wielding one. Is that what you wish to hear?"

"You know what I wish to know, Plato."

"Actually, if I said words about swords and skill, it was untrue. We decided at the last moment who would ride beside you, who would lead. Ari wanted the rear. Skill has nothing to do with it. My mistake."

"Dinna' take me for a fool, Plato FitzHugh. Why have we need of such?"

"I was making talk. To ease the ride. Ari is very skilled at weapons, especially the claymore. He used to be the best. He isna' anymore, but you know that. Squire Morgan has that title. We were all trained on such skills, though. We learned well. With one exception, of course."

"Who would that be?" Morgan asked. "You?"

"Me? You flay me with your words, Morganna lass."

"Then who? Caesar? That would explain his position at my other side, while William has the lead. That is William, is it not?"

"'Tis Caesar at your other side, true. It was an easy choice. He has no sense of direction. Were he leading us, we'd falter."

"So, which one of you is the exception? Who has the worse sword arm? Well? Speak, Plato. You have my curiosity now."

"You dinna' guess?" He snorted. " 'Tis your lord, Zander."

"You tease me. Zander is good. He beat you."

"Is he as good as you?" he asked.

"Well . . . I think he would make up for my speed and accuracy with his strength. If he could keep his sword, he'd probably best me. I dinna' know. We've never fought with such."

"Only because I stepped in to stop you."

"Plato!"

"Dinna' speak too loudly. There's others about."

"I know. I can see them."

"Na' my brothers. My clan. The FitzHugh clan is large. It's powerful. It's steeped in tradition. We number in the thousands. There's many that have heard the tale and agreed with the justice. There's probably just as many hearing it and still cleaving unto their laird, because that's the way it's always been. There's many still to be told. Dinna' worry. They'll all hear and sway, given time."

"We may still be beset by FitzHugh? Is that what you're saying?" Morgan's voice easily mirrored her dismay. She'd just started to feel feminine and soft, and to trust again in the promise of each day. To have it changed back to a state of constant alertness didn't seem real.

"I dinna' say anything of the sort. You've a quick tongue. I dinna' think I like it. I'm well rid of you to Zander. He's always in need of a tongue-lashing. Do it daily, to soften his hard head."

Morgan couldn't help it. She giggled.

"Remind me not to argue with you. 'Tis an earful of words one gets for such. That is the mark of a woman, you know."

"Do tell," Morgan replied in a sarcastic tone.

"Well, at first when women talk, men listen. Why, at

first, when women talk, even children listen. But something happens after that. Women talk and talk and talk. Soon, nobody listens. Everybody has tired of listening. Women still talk. Find me an *auld* woman, she'll still be talking. Find me an *auld* man, he'll be deaf. You see?"

"The lady Gwynneth has my condolences, I think," Morgan replied.

Another grin. "You may wish to seek some sleep. 'Tis a long ride ahead for us."

"Zander told me it was five leagues. We'll be there midmorn."

"Not with the hiding we have to do. We have to keep to the trees. We'll be making our own path, too. Can't risk it."

Morgan eyes went huge. "You weren't teasing me?" she whispered.

He swore almost too softly to be heard. "It was well-planned, Morganna. Dinna' worry. We have FitzHugh clansmen and the newly named KilCreggar-FitzHugh men about the woods and paths, diverting attention with their presence and their noise. Dinna' you listen to a word I said?"

"Which ones? You FitzHughs speak more of them than any *auld* woman possibly could."

"I dinna' know why I bother. I try to set your fears to rest, and you turn my words on me. I'll speak them again. Listen this time. It is a long ride to your new home, nothing more. Your seat and legs will pain you with the time spent atop your horse. You'll need a swift dram of whiskey and a quick slap to revive yourself once we arrive. The trees offer more shelter from the sun. That's why we ride amongst them."

"What sun?" she asked, interrupting him.

He ignored her question and continued. "We're also trying to keep your presence a secret. It's for self-preservation. Once we reveal your beauty, we'll have even more crowds than your fame created. That's all I said. That's all I meant."

Morgan giggled again. Then, she sobered. "Is it dangerous?"

"No more dangerous than riding my wife. Oh. Forgive me. I forgot you are a woman now."

Morgan swatted at him.

"Hush!" William turned to hiss it.

Plato gave his brother a nod. Morgan watched him.

Near morn, they called a halt. Rain was threatening; Morgan could smell it in the air. William dismounted first, and then Caesar. The blond FitzHugh unstrapped a large bundle from his saddle and brought it over to her.

" 'Tis raiment for the Lady KilCreggar-FitzHugh, my lady. Zander had it prepared. We'll wait for you to change."

"Why canna' I stay as I am?" she asked.

It was Ari who answered. " 'Tis too risky. The FitzHugh squire is well-known. 'Tis also known now that he is a KilCreggar. Sentiment runs deep here in the Highlands, my lady, almost as deep as the bottomless lochs. I canna' change that. None of us can."

"What Ari is trying to say is, we've tired of looking at each other, and being in the company of lads. A lovely lass will make the journey more pleasant, and the leagues pass quicker."

"Plato," Morgan said, using a warning tone.

"What?" he replied, innocently.

Ari answered. "Plato makes light of what isna'. You know the reason. We've four leagues left to travel. With a lass, we'll stand a better chance of arriving safely. I know my clan. I know the depth of their hatred. I know the risk. We all do. Zander, especially. That's one of the reasons he prepared this bundle for you."

Moisture was making Ari glitter as she looked across at him. She nodded.

"There is another reason, Morganna," Plato said at her side.

"Is this another tease?" she asked, looking across at him.

"Nay, although I stand accused of that oft, this time what I speak is truth. My brother wishes all to know you are his lady wife. You are being clothed for that position. You dinna' understand. Zander is the wealthiest FitzHugh. 'Twas not fated that way. He was birthed with a mercenary streak we must lack. He has challenged and conquered and competed, and excelled at everything. The spoils in his house will amaze you. Truly. I dinna' tease you. Not this time, anyway."

"He bargains well, too," William piped up. "If you fancy anything he has, he makes you pay dearly for it. Even his brothers. Especially his brothers."

" 's Twill be morn soon," Ari spoke again. "There won't be a better time to change. Go. We'll await you."

Tears were threatening worse than rain as Morgan slid from her horse, took her bundle, and walked into the trees with it. The emotion wasn't at their words. It wasn't at the luxurious clothing she knew Zander had given her. It was at how she was going to feel. Morgan unfastened her silver wrist bands, caressing the clasps of each one, and watched them blur with moisture. It felt like she was leaving it behind forever. She'd never again don a *feile-breacan*, toss dirks against a challenger, or best an opponent. She sighed, crossed her arms over her eyes to blot at them, and then set her shoulders. She was being ridiculous. Scotland wasn't free yet, and Squire Morgan would be needed still. She was stupid to feel so maudlin about a change of clothing.

As she unwound the FitzHugh champion's sett and folded it reverently, the feeling grew into certainty. Squire Morgan was disappearing and the Lady Morganna was going to replace him. It wasn't a guess anymore. It was truth. It had been since she was born. She was a woman. She would always be a woman and she knew she wasn't going back. Zander, and the bairn, had changed her too much.

She unfastened the breast binding and peeled her KilCreggar square from it. Daily wear had taken its toll on the little piece of material, and all sides were fraying and losing strands of wool. It didn't matter. It was just as beloved. Morgan brought it to her lips reverently before replacing it onto the binding.

Then, she bent to pull on the tightly woven stockings he'd given her. The dragon blade wasn't going to stay safely in such a feminine item. As a skean dhu, the knife should have been worn tucked into a sock the entire time she'd owned it. She'd known its purpose, but she also knew its power. The dragon blade had too much to stay tucked into a sock. She tied her skean to her right thigh with her breast band, directly over the mesh-like stocking Zander had given her. It made her womanly curves look dangerous. She wondered what he'd think as he unwrapped her.

The shiver that ran through her body wasn't brought on by the damp, or the night, or even the chill. It was at the thought of Zander seeing what she was. She sighed heavily. She wasn't Squire Morgan, after all.

The satin chemise and accompanying slip had pink-toned ribbons laced through them to gather to her body. Morgan's hands trembled as she tied the ribbons into a little bow below her breasts. She was having a bit of trouble with her breasts, too . . . such a feeling! No wonder women wore ribbons and satins and bows, she thought. It felt delicious, free—and it felt wicked.

Zander had given her an ecru under-dress, woven of flax. It flowed to her ankles. That probably required a special order, she thought, running her hands along the material where it caressed her waist, before she held both hands to her hips and swayed slightly. The flax slid around her limbs like it was poured over her. That was a strange feeling, but entirely too pleasant for her to want it ended, she decided.

There was a bit of pre-dawn light threading through the forest mist all about her. She was grateful for that bit of illumination as she lifted her dress.

Zander had gifted her with a velvet bliant, so dark blue it might as well have been black. Morgan knew it would be close to the shade of his eyes. She didn't doubt it for a moment. She caught her breath as she unfolded it and shook it out. The same cut-work embroidery had been put to use on the edges of the velvet. She knew, even before she donned it, what it was going to look like.

She wasn't disappointed.

The velvet had a trellis design along the hem, following the line of her bodice and down the outer edge of each sleeve. Ecru flax, from her under-dress, filled the gaps. Morgan finished tying her sleeves on before picking up a silver filigree girdle for her waist, that would cinch the dress against her form. Little free-form flowers jointed her belt together, giving it flexibility as it wrapped. Zander had included a silver mirror, and a comb. Morgan's hands were shaking so badly that she had a difficult time fastening her girdle and undoing her braid. She had her hair combed out and rippling over her shoulders before she picked up the mirror.

Zander had called her the loveliest lass he'd ever seen. It just might be true. Morgan narrowed her eyes. They were gray, all right. They were also set off with black brows and lush lashes. She'd always thought Mother and Elspeth had been beautiful women. It was an absolute pleasure to realize she was, too.

Zander had gifted her with women's slippers, too. Made of soft leather, and sewn with the stitching along the inside to keep moisture out, they looked as fragile and insubstantial as they felt. She almost put on her boots over them, but stopped herself. Squire Morgan's boots belonged on a male. The new leather slippers belonged on the lady KilCreggar-FitzHugh. She sighed and stood in her new footwear, knowing she would feel each and every stone beneath her feet, and probably each blade of heather, too.

The last thing Zander had included was a lacy ring-stole, named because it was so finely woven it would fit through a wedding ring even when scrunched. Morgan shook it out and covered her head with it.

She had everything neatly tied back into the bundle when she approached where the FitzHughs sat, astride their horses, breathing mist into the morning air about them.

"Yon lady approaches. Finally. Plato lied about your swiftness, I fear," Caesar teased.

"Not so," Morgan replied. "I was simply making certain everything was on correctly. I'm a novice, you know. So . . . is everything on correctly?"

The man at the front made a choking sound.

"What is it, Will?" Ari spoke up.

Morgan looked up and caught the amazement on William's features. Despite the fact he was her brother-by-law, she blushed.

"I do believe you've made our brother speechless, Lady Morganna. That does na' happen oft' to a FitzHugh. Trust me."

"I'm na' without speech. I'm deciding the words to use."

Plato smacked his forehead. "You'd best don your cloak, my lady. I fear my brother needs the rest."

"From what?" Morgan asked.

"From the beauty of your presence. I dinna' lie, earlier. You're a vision to make any journey that much quicker."

Morgan colored more. She handed her bundle back to Caesar and approached her horse.

"Here. Allow me to assist you. My brothers have lost their tongues, and their wits, at the change in your appearance. I canna' say I find it anything less than astounding, myself.

'Twill make our journey easier, although we may be accosted for another reason, now that I think on it."

It was Ari putting his hands about her waist and lifting her. Morgan hadn't even heard him move.

"If you dinna' halt this . . . all of you, I'll put my *feile-breacan* back on. I'm warning you," Morgan said.

"Not possible. I'm in possession of it," Caesar pointed out.

"I'm going to make him pay for this, I think," William muttered.

"What?" someone asked.

Morgan was sitting astride her horse, and she moved to place her skirts as close to her ankles as she could. She was wearing more than she had been, but it felt different. She didn't dare look at any of them when she had finished and kept her eyes steadily on her hands.

"Well, my brother Will is for wishing he'd seen you first, and he was a sight bigger," Plato replied. "I can vouch for it, lass. Come. We've some distance still to go, it's threatening rain, and my brother has become a half-wit at sight of your beauty."

"I am na' a half-wit," William replied.

The brothers chuckled and Morganna blushed worse.

Chapter 31

The attack came as they entered a small glade just large enough for all five horses.

Morgan had begun to doze when the horse beneath her startled, sending her sliding off one side before she could react. Then she knew the slippers were useless for anything other than standing about in a carpeted room. Rocks and lumps of ground scraped at her insoles as she lowered to a crouch and moved her hand beneath her skirt for her blade.

Morgan wasn't the only one on the ground. The four FitzHughs were all either lying, standing, or in the process of getting there in order to check the body that had been dropped into their midst. Morgan had time to see it was covered in KilCreggar plaid, and to catch her breath in horror, before blue-and-green, tartan-covered forms started raining from the bowers above. If they made sound, it wasn't heard over what mist was covering the ground, and the ringing in her own ears. Morgan watched as Zander's brothers were swarmed, overpowered and then captured, without one cry coming from anyone.

It was over as silently and quickly as it had started, and aside from a small trickle of blood from beneath Caesar's scalp, the ambush had been without incident. The FitzHugh brothers were trussed and suspended by their hands and feet, from long poles. Morgan ignored them to kneel beside the body they'd used as a projectile.

Everything about her numbed. She forced it to. Even the

bairn within her quieted, as she forced herself to hear little, see less and feel absolutely nothing. There was only one KilCreggar plaid in existence that she knew of. He'd worn it to his own wedding not a fortnight since. She knew it. The brothers must know it, too, for there wasn't a movement aside from her own as she peeled back the tartan.

It was a straw-filled dummy.

Relief came as tears, and Morgan shoved them as far back as she could, ignoring the ripples of emotion that flowed over her time and again. Her hands were visibly shaking as she lowered the sett back into place, covering the form.

"It isna' him?"

Morgan suspected it was Ari asking it. She didn't look. She was still showing too much emotion. She shook her head.

"Thank God."

"Nay. Thank your host, Robert MacIlvray. That's who you must be for thankin'."

The name shuddered through her consciousness as much as the slick tone of the words did. Morgan had it already decided who would receive her dragon blade first as he continued speaking.

"The holder of that sett would like to be seein' the lass. I was sent for the invite. Powerful easy it was, too, I might add."

Morgan slanted her head until she could see the owner of the voice. It wasn't a comforting sight. Robb MacIlvray was as large as Zander, meat-covered and possessed a flaming beard to match his hair. Her mother hadn't stood a chance, she realized.

"I canna' speak with my blood to my head. Unbind us." It was Ari speaking again.

The large, flame-haired man laughed. "I've KilCreggar blood on my hands when I get to Hell, Aristotle FitzHugh. I'd as lief not add FitzHugh to it."

Aristotle? Morgan wondered.

"Call me by name, Robb, and cease this. You're delaying an escort."

"I know what name you were blessed with. I like my version better. You're in no position to argue it, now are you? This the squire?"

Morgan let her hand lie slack, atop the bulge from her blade as the man swiveled and looked down at her.

"Unhand us, Robb. 'Tis nothing save an escort party."

He laughed again. "And I'm Father Time. She's the squire. She's a beauty, too. Looks just like her sister. Like she used to, anyhow. Fancy that."

Morgan patted the entwined dragon hilt before standing. She watched him as he was watching her before she reached her full height. She didn't like the look in his eye at all.

"So . . . this is the FitzHugh squire."

"I am his sister," she replied.

"Oh. I don't think so. I know exactly who you are, and I know what you are. Phineas knew, too. He knew the moment he saw you."

Morgan raised her chin.

"I've also heard you're carrying a bairn. Is this true?"

"Untie me, Robb, or by thunder—!"

MacIlvray lifted a hand and Ari's words were cut off. Morgan didn't shift her eyes to see why. She was still sizing up her opponent.

"Well? Is it?" he asked in the silence that followed.

She nodded.

"Excellent. I can't think of better tidings to take to the laird. Come, lads. Hoist the FitzHughs into Reaver Cave. Let them perish or free themselves. Either way, I've a prize to take to the laird. He's awaiting it."

"If you touch a hair on her—!"

The voice was Plato that time. Robb MacIlvray's motion was the same, with the same result. Morgan gulped the extra moisture from her mouth and hoped the motion couldn't be spotted.

"If yon FitzHughs wish to try shouting their way to freedom, they'd best start by holding their tongues. There's two more to gag or leave free. Your choice, lads."

He was speaking to Caesar and William, but his eyes didn't move from her.

"Besides, why would I wish to harm her? She's much more valuable alive. Especially heavy with a bairn."

"Why?" Morgan whispered the word.

"You dinna' guess?" He guffawed. It wasn't for pleasure, but effect. "Laird Phineas is an outcast here in the Highlands now. That does na' sit well with a powerful laird. You made it so, but it will na' always be. He's no outcast in England. Why . . . down there, 'tis a good guess he'll be lauded and feted and even set upon a pedestal." He paused. Nobody said a word. "Especially if he brings what the Sassenach king most desires."

"What do you mean?" Morgan already knew the answer.

"Why, Phineas is going to have The Bruce's champion with him. We'll stage a demonstration of his—I mean, her talents. We all know what will happen then, don't we?"

Morgan's heart missed a beat as she realized what he meant to do. He was going to ruin everything Zander and Scotland's king had gained, and worse. "If . . . I refuse?" she asked quietly.

"Then the blood from the owner of that tartan is on your hands, not mine."

He gestured to the dummy at her feet.

"If you harm a hair on Zander's head, it will be—!"

The threat by William was cut off, too. Morgan watched it as dispassionately as she could.

"I guess they dinna' wish the use of their voices to free themselves. Silly lot, would na' you say?"

She stared at him for a long moment, and then looked aside.

"Put her back on a mount. Any mount. I've a notion good horseflesh won't be turned away by Phineas, especially as it looks like it came from a FitzHugh stable." He chuckled at his own joke.

"Ungag them," Morgan said.

"You don't give the orders, lassie. I do."

"And I have a terrible aim of a sudden," she responded. "Perhaps 'tis the bairn. My skill comes and it goes. It's a pity, really."

He looked her over with a level look. She gave it right back.

"There's na' much else I'll need to find a berth in Hell, lassie. Killing a few disloyal FitzHughs would na' make it worse, you ken?"

"You know, I've felt sickly lately, too," Morgan replied. "I may not be able to hold a weapon without dropping it."

"Blasted woman!"

"Ungag them, and then untie them," Morgan replied evenly, to his rising agitation.

"If I do that, I might as well free them!"

Morgan waited, watching him without blinking.

"I'll not do it, lass. They're FitzHughs on FitzHugh land!"

"You already have me. You already have Zander. Untie the others and let them go."

"I dinna' bargain with a lass. I rarely spend this much time with one in speech." He swiveled and started barking orders. "Get the FitzHughs to the cave. Aye, untie them! Take as many men to guard them as you need. I can handle the woman. I can handle any woman."

Morgan felt the minute sag between her shoulders as he did what she asked. She hadn't truly believed he would. She waited until the brothers, and all but two of the clansmen, left the clearing.

"Now, fetch me that KilCreggar tartan you have used in such an ill fashion."

"I dinna' take orders from a lass, either."

"I'll not mount and ride docilely for you without it."

"I'm about ready to take a fist to your noggin', that's what I'm about to do."

"And risk harming my aim?" she asked sweetly. "What king would waste his time looking over a plain, unskilled Scottish lass, especially one heavy with child, such as you intend to present to him?"

"Phineas is going to rue this morn, I fear. I don't think he knew that when he sent me. Taking orders from a lass? I'll na' live it down. I'd na' have believed it, were I not here."

He was stripping the dummy of it's *feile-breacan* as he spoke, tossing it this way and that as he unwrapped the gray-and-black plaid from it. He was still muttering about his sanity when he wadded the material into a large, unwieldy bundle and slung it at her. Morgan caught it deftly, wrapped her arms about it, and brought it to her nose to breathe deeply of what scent she could.

All she smelled was damp wool.

What had started out a trip of five leagues, became a day-long ride through unforgiving country. Morgan held to her horse's mane with one hand, and held the bundle of plaid with the other. Rain had started up before noon and she welcomed it every time the red-haired Robert MacIlvray cursed it.

She heard him cursing the weather, the mud, the slick hillsides, the lunacy that had him leaving the FitzHugh brothers untied and most of all, he railed at her. Morgan was hard-put to hide her smile, if she chanced to look her way after a particularly vicious spate of words left his lips.

She knew where he was taking her. The only place

Phineas would still be safe. She was being taken to the FitzHugh stronghold, the black castle, itself. Castle FitzHugh had been the seat of the FitzHugh lairds since anyone could remember. She had seen it as a child. She had memorized it. She had prayed for the chance to be going exactly where she was, and she was actually being escorted there. If it wouldn't have spoiled everything, she'd have thanked Robb MacIlvray for it, too.

Zander had tried to change her. He had almost succeeded.

Every part of her hurt when she thought of him. Morgan squelched every place it pained, one by one, until nothing remained except the burn just below her heart. Zander may have lost his KilCreggar plaid. It didn't necessarily mean Phineas had him. Phineas could have had one made, too. He could have stolen this one. There could be a hundred ways he had managed to get a KilCreggar plaid in his possession, other than that he had Zander, too.

In fact, Zander could still be at the king's side, blissfully unaware that a plan of his had finally gone awry. The longer they rode, and the further they progressed, the more certain of that she became. The hurt eased from her and she knew why.

Something about the sett in her arms had unsettled her from the moment she received it. Something wasn't right. Morgan finally realized what it was, and was dismayed that it had taken so long.

It wasn't Zander's plaid at all. It couldn't be. The weave beneath her fingers was too rough. It wasn't the same quality she had come to expect from a FitzHugh loom, although she'd never have admitted it before. If Morgan had her wits about her sooner, she'd have checked with her sight what she was suspecting with her touch. It hadn't looked to contain any hint of blue and green. Morgan knew Zander had his woven with such a distinction.

It wasn't Zander's *feile-breacan*. Phineas didn't have his youngest brother, at all. He'd been courting death, if he had

Zander. He'd gained certain death with the lapse. Morgan knew the dragon blade still rested against her thigh, she felt its power, its purpose, and knew finally why she'd been given it.

She really was going to kill Phineas with it.

The storm hadn't eased when they reached Castle FitzHugh's gate. Morgan lifted her head and looked up at it through the blur of rain. She lifted her hands to hold the sodden cloak out from her head, shielding her eyes to see. All about her black rock rose from the bedrock it seemed to have been birthed from. The ground was sodden, and rain was bouncing when it landed, making a droplet-imbued mist at the horses' hooves. She listened to each step, and then the horses were crossing the drawbridge, their hooves echoing in the silence.

There wasn't a soul in sight.

Castle FitzHugh looked to be a three-story affair, with crenellations, guard towers, and curved archways at every sanctum they entered. They passed through a stable yard. It was the size of Argylle's, although it was difficult to tell. The elements, the night and the bedrock all blended together. It could actually be larger, she decided.

They went through more gates. At each, a portcullis came up, and then dropped, lifted and put back into place by invisible hands. Morgan halted her own shivering.

The keep was a formidable structure, seated behind the fortress walls. It looked to be three stories high and stood by itself in the inner bailey. It was made of black rock, although there had been an effort to make it more hospitable with wooden shutters mounted on the sides of long, narrow windows, and a banner hanging above the double-wide oaken doors. The horses came to a stop in front of those doors. Morgan waited. Robb MacIlvray dismounted with more of his cursing. Then he approached her. He didn't ask if she needed assistance, he just reached up and plucked her off.

She was still swathed in the black wool, holding to her

bundle of plaid, and her legs probably wouldn't have held her upright at first, but his touch was abhorrent and unnerving. As was the deserted quality of the courtyard. It probably rivaled an Argylle courtyard in size, she surmised, but without a servant in sight, it looked bigger.

He set her on her feet at the entry steps and stepped away. He didn't move far. Morgan looked up at the recessed oaken doors, and shivered again. She told herself it was nothing, and meant less. The rain-soaked cloak wasn't conducive to warmth, that was all. She tipped her head and looked up, untied the fur-lined cloak and let it fall to her feet. Robb MacIlvray didn't stop her. All he did was watch her. She unfurled the KilCreggar sett without looking down and wrapped it about herself, warming the moment she did. She ignored the man at her side, no longer caring that he watched. She was a KilCreggar. She was wrapped in KilCreggar gray and black, and she was at the enemy's own doorstep, ready to lay open his heart. She was fulfilling her purpose. It was a strengthening thought.

The banner above them had one dragon on it. Morgan looked it over for another moment before looking back down. The door opened inward, and not just one half of it, but both sides at once. She had the impression of space, lots of space, and then she was escorted up the steps and into the great room. Her elbow was gripped by MacIlvray, and he walked her up the steps and into the room.

Morgan noticed there was a servant woman holding to each side of the door, although both looked tired, dirty, worn and wouldn't look up. Morgan kept her face forward. The room was enormous. There were two long banqueting tables intersecting it, with benches on both sides. There were torch sconces made from animal antlers all along the walls, each holding an unlit torch. There were huge chairs at the ends of each table, looking like thrones, with a head-piece of deer antler. There was a roaring fire on the opposite wall, making it too humid and hot next to the damp chill they'd just come from.

Morgan watched the steam rise from her own damp clothing and tried to see the figures in the furthest chairs. Then, she knew who it was as Phineas FitzHugh stood slowly to face her, and at his side he had her sister, the hag, Elspeth.

Morgan sucked in on the shock, then let it go. Elspeth looked sickly, but she'd always looked sickly. She had a paler tint to her skin than usual, and it looked like she'd lost the last bit of black in the mass of matted, gray hair she had. It was hanging to her waist, and it looked like she might have made an effort at combing it. She looked as skeletal as usual, too. Elspeth was still looking vacant-eyed and haunted, and something else. She actually looked a little frightened. Morgan felt a nerve twinge in her cheek.

"Hello, Morganna," Phineas said finally.

"Get her out of here." Morgan spat the words.

"Now why would I go and do such an inhospitable thing?"

"Get her out of here, or we have no bargaining to do. You understand?"

"Mor . . . ganna?"

Elspeth's voice trembled on the name, making it a strange sound. Perhaps it was only seemed that way since she hadn't heard it from the hag's lips in so long. Morgan's lips set and then she sneered.

"We have nothing to say to each other, hag. Less. Get out."

"You are Morganna, aren't you?"

Morgan stiffened. "You kept this sett. You kept our father's ceremonial *feile-breacan*, didn't you? All these years you had it. You hid it. You kept it from me. You let me raid the dead for a sett to wear when all the time you had this one."

Elspeth nodded vigorously. "It was a secret. From Da.

He promised me . . . I canna' recall what he promised. He'll return for it, though. He told me so."

"And you let this monster have it?" Morgan's voice rose, despite the control she was putting on it. She narrowed her eyes. It was to hide any further hint of emotion.

"Monster? Nay, Morganna. He gives me things. See?" Elspeth held up her arm where a silver bracelet dangled. It looked incongruous on her bony arm, and next to the frayed sleeve.

"You're mad." Morgan said it without a bit of inflection.

"Am I?" Elspeth's voice trembled, then stilled. Morganna didn't move.

"Sisters, sisters . . . please." Phineas clucked his tongue to make a chastising sound. If Morgan could have stiffened beyond what she was already, she would have. "I didn't invite you here for a family reunion, although it will prove entertaining, once I do allow it. We've a journey to prepare for. We haven't much time."

"We've less than you think," Robb MacIlvray spoke up from beside Morgan.

"What does that mean?" Phineas asked.

"She was under escort by your brothers."

"Which ones?" Phineas's voice was sharp as he asked it.

"All of them."

"All?"

"Save Zander. He resides still at The Bruce's camp."

"My brothers have no loyalty." He sighed. "You know the feeling now, surely?" He addressed the question to no one in particular. Morgan flexed the nerve in her cheek again.

"I had your brothers untied when I left them."

"What? Why?"

"They're guarded."

"My brothers are a force singly. United, they'll be almost unstoppable. I want no FitzHugh blood spilled. None. You knew the rule."

"Aye."

"Then, why did you disobey?"

"She's a very persuasive lass, my lord. Very."

Phineas eyed her with that cold blue stare of his. Morgan returned it. "She must be," he replied, finally.

Chapter 32

"Get fresh horses saddled, Robb. See it done. *Now.* If you had any lead on my brothers, you lost it traveling here with a lass."

"She's na' just any lass, my lord, and if I lost time, 'twas due to weather. Your brothers will have the same."

Phineas continued to eye her. "Na' true, Rob. She's a lass. A gifted one, but just a lass. You'll see. She's weak . . . and she's dense."

Morgan lifted her eyebrows, but said nothing.

" 'Tis true, you know," he continued. "A strong lass would na' be here. She would ha' died rather than accept bondage. As for dense? Why, a smart lass would na' have left The Bruce's encampment with a guard of but four men. You're on FitzHugh land, you're a FitzHugh enemy, and I'm the FitzHugh laird. I still command FitzHugh strength and loyalty. I repeat myself so you make no mistake. You're weak, and you've na' much in wits. It appears to be a family trait."

Morgan didn't say a word. She let her silence answer for her. He snarled at her, then looked over her shoulder.

"Go saddle horses, Robb. Prepare foodstuffs. Get my loyal clansmen gathered from the rooms they've hidden in. We leave the moment we can. We've a gift to get to the Sassenach king . . . as much as I detest the bastard."

Morgan refused to give him the satisfaction of an answer

as MacIlvray left the room, going back the way they'd come.

"You thought I kneeled to the bastard because he deserves it, didna' you? Well, join the ranks of the disloyal FitzHugh with their talk and their guessing. I know which side has the power and the might. Every man knows. They know the penalty, too. Death. It isna' pretty. It isna' civil. I've seen it firsthand, and I made my choice." He lifted a shoulder, and then let it drop. "I choose English rule for one reason. I dinna' want to die. I choose life over death."

"Then, why would you take me?" Morgan asked softly. She could have bitten her tongue for that much, however, as it seemed the glacial blue of his eyes warmed for the smallest moment. She knew why. She'd been goaded into an answer.

"You're the ticket to my freedom, lass . . . my pass out of this country and back into power. I may have a price on my head, but what Highlander would harm me when I've got Squire Morgan of the Clan FitzHugh? And what king would turn me away when I possess the means to ridicule and ruin his enemy, The Bruce?"

Morgan answered him with silence again. He smiled shallowly.

"We waste words, when we should be preparing. Drink. Eat. You won't have much time for such, you know." He gestured to a side table, dim against a wall. Morgan didn't move her eyes. "It's in your best interest, lass, for you will na' like me once I force you."

"I dinna' like you now," she replied.

He laughed at that. "No matter that. We've a long journey ahead, you've a bairn to protect and birth, and we've a king to impress with your skills at the end of it." He rubbed his hands together.

"Let the hag go," Morgan replied.

The hand movement halted, but he kept them clasped at

his belly. "Now why would I go and do a fool thing like that?"

"I have a bad aim sometimes. It comes and goes."

"And your sister has a lot of flesh to lose should you attempt it."

Morgan didn't move. Elspeth did. Her head started back and she stared, almost unseeingly, at Morgan.

Morgan shrugged, almost imperceptibly. "You have me. That's all you need. Let her go."

"I think I like her better right where she is."

"Why? So you can rape her again?" Morgan saw Elspeth's frown from the corner of her eye, but she didn't dare move her gaze that direction.

"Ah, lass, you're confusing her. She charges for her favors now, she does. Has na' to do with rape."

"You took her? Again?" Elspeth's frown was changing as Morgan continued speaking with a low-toned, non-emotional voice. "Was na' beating, killing and raping the one time enough for you, FitzHugh? You dinna' get your satisfaction, then?"

"Dinna' place words in my mouth, lass. I dinna' like it."

"Then, let the hag go. You don't need her."

"I dinna' say that, either," he replied.

"So you do need her?"

"Na' for the meaning you put to it. I need her to control you. I should think that much easily seen. And, despite your words, I know the truth. She speaks of little else save her bairn. That would be you, no doubt. And I dinna' touch your sister. I dinna' like another man's leavings that well. The lass sells herself now. I'd catch the pox."

"Let her go, then."

"She does na' have much to go back to."

Elspeth wasn't just pale at those words, she was ashen. Morgan tried to ignore her, but the wide-eyed look of shock on the woman right beside Phineas was reaching clear to her breastbone.

"What have you done to her croft, Phineas? 'Twas not much, but all she had. Dinna' tell me you razed it . . . too." Morgan clucked her tongue after she finished, and waited for the pause she'd been so deliberate about, to sink in. She knew it had as tears slipped from Elspeth's unblinking eyes and ran down both cheeks.

"There was a fire," Elspeth whispered brokenly.

"You burned her croft, dinna' you?" Morgan asked.

"She dinna' give up anything willingly. We had to tear the sett you're wearing from her arms after she ran back into that hovel after it. Stupid lass, risking her life over a bit of plaid. That appears to be another KilCreggar trait, does na' it?"

Morgan swallowed, but it felt as dry as ash would as it scraped all the way down her throat. Elspeth had gone back into a fire-eaten croft after the gray-and-black *feile- breacan*? She very nearly turned her eyes to her sister, but knew she couldn't bear the suffering she was avoiding looking at.

"You'd best wish your horses brought soon, Phineas," she whispered.

"Why would that be, lass?" he answered in the same type of whisper.

"Because you're about to reap what you have sown. Elspeth?"

"Bastard!"

Elspeth reacted on cue. Her screech and movement to pummel at Phineas gave Morgan all the time she needed. She dropped to a knee and started fumbling for her blade.

It didn't help to curse women's clothing, or the impulse that had made her swathe herself in KilCreggar plaid, but she did anyway. She was losing precious time getting to her skean, and it was her own fault. She had but another moment or two before Phineas would be overpowering her sister, and she wasn't going to waste them. Then, it was moot as a booming sound came, so loud, so abrupt, and so intense, the antlers in their sconces rattled.

There was a moment of shocked silence. Then, Elspeth started up her screeching again. A second boom came.

"They've broken through the bailey!"

Robert MacIlvray yelled it as he ran in, dropping a tree-sized bolt across the double-door behind him.

"Why was it na' guarded, like I ordered?"

"It was! They did na' come that way, as we expected, but the rear! I dinna' have enough men for that!"

"The sneak-thieves!"

Phineas' cursing gave way to more of Elspeth's screams, and Morgan had her blade. She was almost to her feet again, when another boom came, this one harder and louder, and making the floor tremble so much that she was safer at a crouch. She went back down.

They were ramming the castle. From the sound of it, they were already at the large, oaken doors of the keep, too. Morgan eyed Phineas from her position near the floor. She'd freed her blade, but it had taken too long. Phineas had her sister in front of him.

"Get her, Robb!" he shouted from behind the shield of her sister. His words were full of frustration and anger, and they blended with Elspeth's wild screeching, making the walls echo. "We'll need the squire! They'll bargain for her!"

He made a choking noise at the end of his speech. Another hit came, bringing roof and floor material raining down on everything. Morgan wiped at her eyes with the backs of her hands, blinking at the dust and debris. Robb MacIlvray's arms were just as hard as they'd looked, as he wrapped about her from behind, lifting her easily from her crouch.

"Good! You've got her! Hold her! Hold!"

Elspeth wasn't screeching, anymore. She was clawing and slapping at Phineas. Morgan couldn't help. She was above the floor, and MacIlvray's arms weren't giving any space, even for breathing. She sliced blindly, curving the blade into his arm. Then, she was dropped.

Phineas hadn't been lying about his status after all, and

Morgan's eyes widened at the outpouring of armed clansmen into the room from every orifice the chamber seemed to have.

"You can't fight them, you fools! There's too many! Get the squire! Get her! They'll stop if we have her!"

Phineas was having trouble speaking. It had something to do with Elspeth's fury in his arms. Morgan spun from the sight. She dodged chairs and stools and men. Then she was running, slamming into the first man she reached, and using that motion to push a way out of the room at exactly the same moment the door gave. She didn't gain it easily, and lost the KilCreggar *feile-breacan* as someone tried to use it for a hand-hold. Behind her, she heard oak splintering, and the sounds of battle as claymores hit shields and more. Morgan didn't hesitate. She couldn't. She wasn't going to be the bargaining wedge Phineas used to escape justice.

Doors opened for her, beckoning her one way, and then another, and they slammed behind her as soon as she passed through. She caught more than one glimpse of a servant woman as it happened. Hadn't Zander told her once that Phineas mistreated his servants? She twisted her lips grimly as she ran. His servants appeared to be repaying the treatment.

"Here!"

Another hissed whisper, another opened door, and Morgan waited while it was bolted behind her before moving again. She had gained distance and time, and a pain in her side from her flight. Unfortunately, she may have lost every sense of direction, too.

She spun. The woman who had helped her was just disappearing behind a tapestry. A body hit the door, bowing the bolt as she watched.

Morgan gasped a breath and started running again. The castle was a maze of halls, caverns and interconnecting rooms. One room led to another, and from there to a third. Nothing looked the same. Morgan's heartbeat was loud in her ears. She stopped, sucking in breath. There wasn't a hint of a pursuit.

"Where is she, Phineas?"

The muffled yell was Zander, and it was coming from somewhere above her. She found a door, gained a hall, and debated which way.

"If you have harmed a hair on my wife's head . . . a hair—!"

"Oh . . . you're here . . . to kill . . . me anyway. What does . . . it matter what I did to her . . . or how much . . . she enjoyed it?"

Phineas was huffing between the words, but they were still brutal. The resulting roar from Zander had pain at its core. It also had Morgan's feet flying. She didn't care whether she was going the right way; she only knew she had to get out and let Zander see her.

"Where is she, Phineas?" Zander yelled again.

Morgan had to twist the door knob with both hands and then she was out in wind-whipped rain. Her eyes found them easily. They were on a battlement between towers, two stories above the ground, and climbing higher with each lunge and thrust of their swords. Morgan was directly below them, but apart. She moved to the rock wall, looked up the black rock sides and into groundless mist. There was nothing she could use—no access, no steps, no ladder. There didn't look to be any way from her position to theirs without flying there.

Her fingers massaged the dragon blade she still carried, drawing on the strange power that it possessed as she looked back up. The combatants had moved from her sight. She had to stumble backwards until her angle was right again. She couldn't hear how the battle was going, didn't know where any other clansman was; all she saw was Zander and Phineas.

Her breath caught, then came again as she watched. Zander was a warrior. Phineas was not. It looked like the outcome was already decided as Zander backed Phineas against a battlement, slamming his claymore over and over, putting dents in Phineas's shield deep enough that it was concave. Still, he wasn't satisfied.

Morgan watched as time and again Zander pummeled Phineas, using his left arm to inflict the most punishment. With one blow, he appeared to have him, and then the laird was dancing away, rolling himself along the crenellations to escape further punishment.

Then, Morgan saw the red-haired Robb MacIlvray. He was in a tower above Phineas and Zander and directly in her line of vision. He had his bow already pulled, and he wasn't aiming for Phineas. Morgan set her feet, and let fly the dragon blade straight for Robb's eye.

She didn't know what gave her away, or why Zander pivoted, but her eyes widened with horror as he caught her blade in his shield at the same moment his eyes met hers.

"Zander! Nay!"

She was screaming it as Robb MacIlvray's bow twanged, sending an arrow behind the stone wall, where she couldn't see. Phineas and Zander disappeared, and there wasn't any sign of Robb anymore, either. Morgan panicked. Her heart caught in her throat with fear, and her breath came in great gulping gasps that hurt.

Then, she was running. She had to find the way to them, and the passages weren't any help. Morgan flew along them, scraping the soles of her feet in the women's slippers, and slamming full-length against each oaken door she came to, before taking the knob in both hands to twist it, and opening the door so she could shove through it. She was lost. No faceless servant women were guiding her, no unseen hands were opening and closing doors. Tears were fogging her eyes, burning at her lungs, and making her nose a mass of clogged tissue. Still, she ran.

She came to a double-door, the match to the entry one. That was ridiculous. Her mind disavowed it even as her eyes ran over it. She was not in the great room with the banqueting tables, nor was she outside on the stoop. FitzHugh Castle had another door, identical to the front door. She grabbed a handle and pulled. Nothing.

The door swung out, Morgan with it, and then Zander was there, grabbing her to him before the force he'd yanked the door open with, sent her to her knees.

"Morganna!"

His orator's voice hadn't lost a note of stridency, but she didn't care. She was up in his arms, against his chest, her legs about his waist, as her hands ran all along his shoulders and back to check for the arrow shaft, and she was raining kisses on his face the entire time.

"Oh Zander . . . oh love! Zander!"

She didn't get another joy-filled note out, as he had her mouth. Her laughter was at odds with the tears streaming down her face as she checked him over and found nothing. He wasn't letting her get far enough from him to see and verify it, though. He had her arms linked around his, his hands at the back of her head, and was making certain she lived with every movement of his lips on hers.

"I hate to intrude, but it is devilish weather outside, and you are blocking the door, Lord Zander KilCreggar-FitzHugh. Oh. Pardon the intrusion. I see it's your lady. We'll just stand in the elements and wait. Won't we, lads?"

Robert The Bruce is here? she wondered. Morgan giggled, and the motion halted the vacuum of Zander's lips to hers.

He raised his head. Midnight-blue eyes searched for and found what he was looking for. He started shuddering, and then he was burying his face in her neck, and he was barely keeping from sobbing. Morgan held to him, crooned to him, and waited.

"Dear God, Morganna . . . I feared I would na' be in time."

"You were in time," she whispered back.

"Phineas . . . he is a devil. He takes—! And after all I

promised you! After the horror that was your childhood. I have never felt such fear as when my brothers came back without you. Never."

"I was na' harmed, Zander."

He sucked in breath, and sniffed loudly with it. He wasn't shuddering anymore, but he was trembling. He lifted his head. Morgan waited for him.

"Truth?" he asked.

"Truth." She tipped her head to one side.

"Thank God." He had her to him again, and it was impossible to see anything except the skin of his neck, then his ear.

"You are na' hurt, either?" she asked.

He shook his head. His light brown hair brushed her face with the motion.

"Then, how? Who? I saw the arrow fly—" she began, but she was interrupted.

" 'Twas Squire Morgan you saw, my lady! Squire Morgan gained justice for the FitzHugh clan! We all saw it! Dinna' we, men?" The king was the one interrupting her, using every timbre of his booming voice on the crowd behind him.

Zander pivoted at the same time that Morgan lifted her head from his shoulder. There was a sea of FitzHugh men on the walkway beyond the door, and all patiently awaiting entry since she and Zander had been blocking it. Morgan grinned and put her face back into Zander's shoulder as the cheers grew.

"Aye! 'Twas a great shot, too! From yon tower! Our Squire Morgan stopped the *auld*, Sassenach-loving FitzHugh laird in his track, an arrow straight through his neck. I have na' seen the like! Isna' that so, lads?"

There was a correct response to this, although the bellow of cheers made it an indeterminate sound one way or the other. The king gestured with his arm.

"Then there is the MacIlvray man! We all heard of his guilt, too, did we not? 'Twas just and fair that Squire Morgan got him, too! Why, he still lies face-down in the courtyard below us. That was a great shot, too. Who else, save Squire Morgan, could have made such a toss? Why, Clansman MacIlvray has a blade with a hilt made of two dragons, deep in his own chest, and all know who carries that blade! Squire Morgan! You see? He has not left us, my fellow countrymen! He comes when needed. He will always come when needed!"

Morgan's eyes sought Zander's. " 'Twas you who tossed the knife? You?" she repeated.

"You are ever in doubt of your husband. I am a fair marksman. I toss. Your dragon blade used to be mine, remember? Besides, I tossed left-handed . . . under-handed." He raised his eyebrows up and down several times. "I've been practicing."

"Lead us to the great-room, KilCreggar-FitzHugh. I fancy a sampling of the new laird's mead! Better yet, get me Ari FitzHugh!"

"Ari?" Morgan whispered.

"Aye," Zander replied. "All of them. They wasted little time, save getting back to us. " 'Twas a good thing, too. They could na' have taken the castle by themselves. It took a score of men to hoist the ram used on the gates."

"Step forward and pledge yourself to your king and sovereign! I am blessed to have you at the head of the mighty FitzHugh clan! I accept your allegiance to Scotland's side, too. Where is the man?"

Ari was being shuttled through the crowd nearest the balcony. He was puffing with exertion when he strode through the door and went to one knee at The Bruce's feet.

"As the new laird of the mighty FitzHugh clan, I pledge my loyalty, and that of my clan, to my just and true king," he said solemnly. Then he stood, and turned to the crowd. "May it be written that Sassenach-loving FitzHughs are no more. A FitzHugh clansman is a true Scotsman. Now, and forever!" There was another wild cheer at the end of his speech.

"Come then, FitzHugh, show us your hospitality. Serve

us your mead, until we drain your supply. Roast us a sup! 'Twas a wild ride here, and no time for foodstuffs. My men thirst! They hunger!"

The king put his arm around Ari's shoulders, and they started the procession through the halls. Zander didn't follow, however. He stood against the wall, held Morgan to him, and before many men had passed by, there was a semi-circle of his brothers, Caesar, Plato and William, in front of them, shielding their embrace.

Morgan didn't even notice.

Epilogue

A.D. 1323

"Tell us the story of Squire Morgan again, Da. Please?"

"I told it once this sennight already. Ask your mum."

"But ma does na' have a voice like yours. She does na' tell it right, either. If she tells it, Squire Morgan is a *girl*." The disgust in their second-born, Robert KilCreggar-FitzHugh's voice was obvious.

Morgan had to bite her lip to still the giggle.

"And what would be wrong with that?" the beautiful, tall, black-haired lass asked, lifting her skirts with a graceful motion as she walked over to the fireplace. "Women can toss a blade as well as any man. Why, I'll wager mum can out-toss any man, even Da."

Zander raised his hands in defeat. "No contest there, Aphrodite, my love. Your mother always could best me. She has better hands."

"She's still a girl," Robert complained

"True enough, and I'm very grateful for that." Zander stopped and cleared his throat. "Have I ever told you the tale of how Squire Morgan helped me save your mum from the evil, English-loving laird of the FitzHughs? Sit. I'll tell you that one."

"I'd rather hear about the Killoren-Mactarvat skirmish, where Squire Morgan pegged arrows in every one of the warrior's shields!"

Zander rolled his eyes and Morgan giggled. Then, she stilled as those midnight-blue eyes caught and held hers.

"Oh no," Robert complained. "There they go again. We'll never get our story."

"Hush!" The lass nudged her brother. "They're in love. I may find such a love, some day."

Zander shook himself and turned back to his eldest, and Morgan watched his face soften. "Oh, you have my word, there's a man out there for you, love. He's been fashioned just for you, too. Trust me. I know these things."

"He'll have to be very tall," Robert snickered.

"True enough," Zander replied. "He'll have to be tall and strong and righteous. He'll have to be a Scotsman, too."

"Dinna' forget handsome," Morgan inserted.

"He's going to have to be extra handsome, too, if he wants to catch my beauteous Aphrodite's hand. That much is certain, too."

Morgan watched their eldest blush at her father's words. It made the girl even more lovely. She was nearly thirteen, willow-thin, and as tall as her mother. She also had perfect stitches in every one of her tapestries, a talent for paints, and an excellent hand when it came to the running of the KilCreggar-FitzHugh household.

"You're not telling us about Squire Morgan," Robert complained.

"I swear, Robert, you grow more like your mother when I first met her, with every passing day. Why, there was once a time when she never smiled. Not once. She was always serious, always thinking of one thing, and one thing only. She was impossible to sway . . . well, almost."

"What was it?" Their second son, Garrick, spoke up, lifting his head from his ledgers.

"Me, of course," Zander replied.

"Zander . . . ," Morgan said, in a semi-threatening tone.

"Oh, very well. She was bent on clan war. She hadn't a bone of softness in her. Why, she hadn't even any notion that she'd met the man made just for her, either. I had to show her. She was very stubborn about it, too. Very."

Robert sighed loudly. "When are we going to hear about Squire Morgan?" he asked.

Zander laughed and cleared his throat. Morgan watched him, and couldn't prevent her smile. The one thing he loved was talking with that great orator's voice of his. She bent back to the parchment she was sanding, prior to sending it off.

She twirled the large ring which hung from a chain about her neck. She tipped her candle and poured a little wax. Then, she blew until it was the right consistency to hold the intertwined dragon symbol into it. She would call for a messenger later. They had news. The baby she carried wasn't going to wait another fortnight to be born, and Zander's mother wouldn't wish to miss it.

That woman had Morgan's promise that she would get to name all the lasses. Morgan shook her head. Zander's mother always seemed to get her way, and it wasn't by anything more than a sweet smile, a constant stream of soft words, and a loving embrace.

"Gather round, children. I've a story to tell, and it's one of blood, pain, war and victory. It's one they'll be telling for all time. It's the story of Squire Morgan."

Garrick put down his quill, Robert leaned forward in his chair, Aphrodite picked up her sewing hoop and sat beside her father, and even the baby, Rory, started crawling toward them. Morgan watched Zander scoop the tot up and put him on his lap before regaining his seat. He was in his element.

"It was a mist-filled night, back before any of you were born. Back afore Scotland was even its own country. We were under the English, then. It was a time of darkness. A time of suffering. Why, there wasn't a clansman on the earth who hadn't been toiling for years under the yoke of the Sassenach tyranny."

"What's tyranny?" Garrick asked.

"Hush!" Robert replied.

"English laws and rules. Why, they dinna' even allow us to carry a weapon. I know why, too," Zander said.

"Why?" Garrick asked again.

"They were afraid of us. A good Scotsman with a bow is worth ten Englishmen. A Scotsmen with a dirk is worth six with a sword. They knew it, so they kept us without. They kept us poor. They even had laws against the wearing of our colors. They had us pay taxes to support them. They took our lasses. They put us under an English king's rule. It was more than any good Scotsman should have to bear."

"So, what happened on the misty night?' Robert asked.

Zander blew the sigh, and Morgan smiled again. Robert was very like her in temperament, although he looked exactly like his father probably had at that age. He was also deadly with whatever weapon they put in his hands. He always had been. Better yet, he had already matched his sister in height, and was going to meet, or exceed, Zander's. It was enough to make any mother's heart proud.

Morgan thought hers might burst with it.

"That lad has as much patience as a rutting elk." Elspeth spoke up from her position in a rocking chair. She had a shawl about her thin shoulders and was nursing the cup of broth in her hands. Morgan smiled across at her. Elspeth wasn't up to moving much anymore, but she had a bit of age on her, and that was expected. "He's been spoiled."

"And who might be the party responsible for that, I ask?" Zander asked from amid the children.

Elspeth's lips twitched. Morgan had to look aside. All knew the lad had his aunt's adoration. It had been that way since he was birthed. Elspeth doted on each of them in turn, however, and told Morgan she couldn't wait for another bairn to hold.

"I 'fess up, Zander. I spoiled him. I held him when he

cried, and I held him when he slept. I'd do it now if he was na' so large. You dinna' understand how healing it is."

"Aye, we do, Elspeth. We do."

Elspeth and Morgan smiled at each other, and it was 'n complete communion and acceptance.

Zander cleared his throat. "Now . . . where was I?"

"The misty night, the battle, the wound!" Robert replied.

"Yes, well . . . I had taken a sword blow, and had nothing left to do in this life but watch my blood stain the soil, when out of the mist strolled a lad, as bold as you can be, and as strong. He pulled the sword from me, stopping the bleeding, and then he turned on the English with the most horrid yell. He had a dragon blade in his other hand, the mate to the one your mother has mounted up on the wall, beside her square of KilCreggar plaid, over yon."

They all looked to where Zander pointed. He waited for the effect. Morgan's lips twitched again. When it came to telling a story, Zander had no equal.

"Then, Squire Morgan took his blade, and he turned on the Sassenach, and he routed them. All of them. I never saw the like."

"Zander." Morgan interrupted, and everyone looked over at her, except Rory. He was already nodding off in his father's arms.

"The king tells the same story," he replied, defensively. "Dinna' embroider it too much."

He smiled, and although she lamented the gray streaked in his hair, and the lines about those midnight-blue eyes, her heart swelled the same as always. Zander KilCreggar-FitzHugh was still a very handsome man. He always would be.

"There is nothing I can say that would do so, love."

Morgan's gaze was caught and held. She recognized the sensation, and she was blushing worse than her daughter had, before Robert complained again with the same tone of disgust.

"There they go again," he said.

Embrace the Romance of
Shannon Drake